————————— Praise for *Tributary* —————————

"You'll love resolute Clair Martin, the equal of any man —or religion. Clair's strength and survival are the heritage of western women." —Sandra Dallas, author of *True Sisters*

"Seldom does a novel come along that is as beautifully written and emotionally honest as *Tributary*. Barbara K. Richardson captures the grandeur and harshness of the Old West in a young woman's struggle to find a home and a family without losing herself. A lyrical and haunting story not to be missed." —Margaret Coel, author of *Buffalo Bill's Dead Now*

"*Tributary* is a novel whose characters and time are so well inhabited, whose landscapes are so lovingly evoked, we wonder if Richardson is not speaking to us directly from the late 19th century, from a high bench above the Great Salt Lake. The language and writing are surefooted and fresh and often startling the way the best poetry can be startling. Richardson is a new American voice worth listening to."
—Peter Heller, author of *The Dog Stars*

"Just when *Tributary* seemed like a story rich enough for an entire novel—an account of a feisty young Mormon woman in the 1860s—it turned into a story set in the South, and then another in the West. In the end, Barbara Richardson's deceptively simple book is nothing less than an epic."
—Jesse Kornbluth/Headbutler

"Tributary is a remarkable odyssey of the American West, told in one of the most clear-sighted, unjudging, and original voices I've come across in years."
— Molly Gloss, author of *The Hearts of Horses*

"This is a gorgeous novel.... *Tributary* takes the incomplete history and mythos of the West to task, and instead shows us some of the far more interesting and unexplored stories of American West—Mormonism, racism, women who don't need marriage or men. Beautifully written and engaging, this is a story of one woman and her refusal to cave into societal norms in order to seek her own difficult and inspired path."
—Laura Pritchett, author of *Sky Bridge*

"From polygamist Mormon desert settlements to the yellow fever-plagued Gulf to an Idaho sheep ranch, Richardson evokes the 19th Century West and the human heart in all their complexity." —Barbara Wright, author of *Plain Language*

"I've been hungering for a book like this since I finished *Lonesome Dove*—a tale of the Old West big enough to crawl into completely, full of magnetic characters, unspeakable dangers, and beautiful language.... *Tributary* is the story of a ragtag group of frontier survivors. There is an exiled Mormon prophet who lives in a cave and a truth-telling black man married to a Shoshone medicine woman. They are constellated around Clair, whose disappeared parents and independent heart lead her from a joyless Mormon childhood to New Orleans and back to Utah's sheepherding outback.... It's a big hot fudge sundae of a book—you wolf it down, and then you regret it's gone. I loved it." —Lisa Jones, author of *Broken: A Love Story*

TRIBUTARY

Barbara K. Richardson

Torrey House Press, LLC
Utah

First Torrey House Press Edition, September 2012
Copyright © 2012 by Barbara K. Richardson

Published by Torrey House Press, LLC
P.O. Box 750196
Torrey, Utah 84775 U.S.A.
http://torreyhouse.com

International Standard Book Number: 978-1-937226-04-6
Library of Congress Control Number: 2012938793

Cover photographs: pioneer woman by www.recollections.biz;
     desert landscape by amygdala_imagery/iStockphoto.com
Map by T. Ellwood Zell, 1873, provided by Barry Lawrence Ruderman
     Antique Maps Inc., www.raremaps.com
Cover and book design by Jeff Fuller, Crescent Moon Communications

for Jeff
who holds fast

Let nothing come between you and your heart.

— Red Hawk

TRIBUTARY

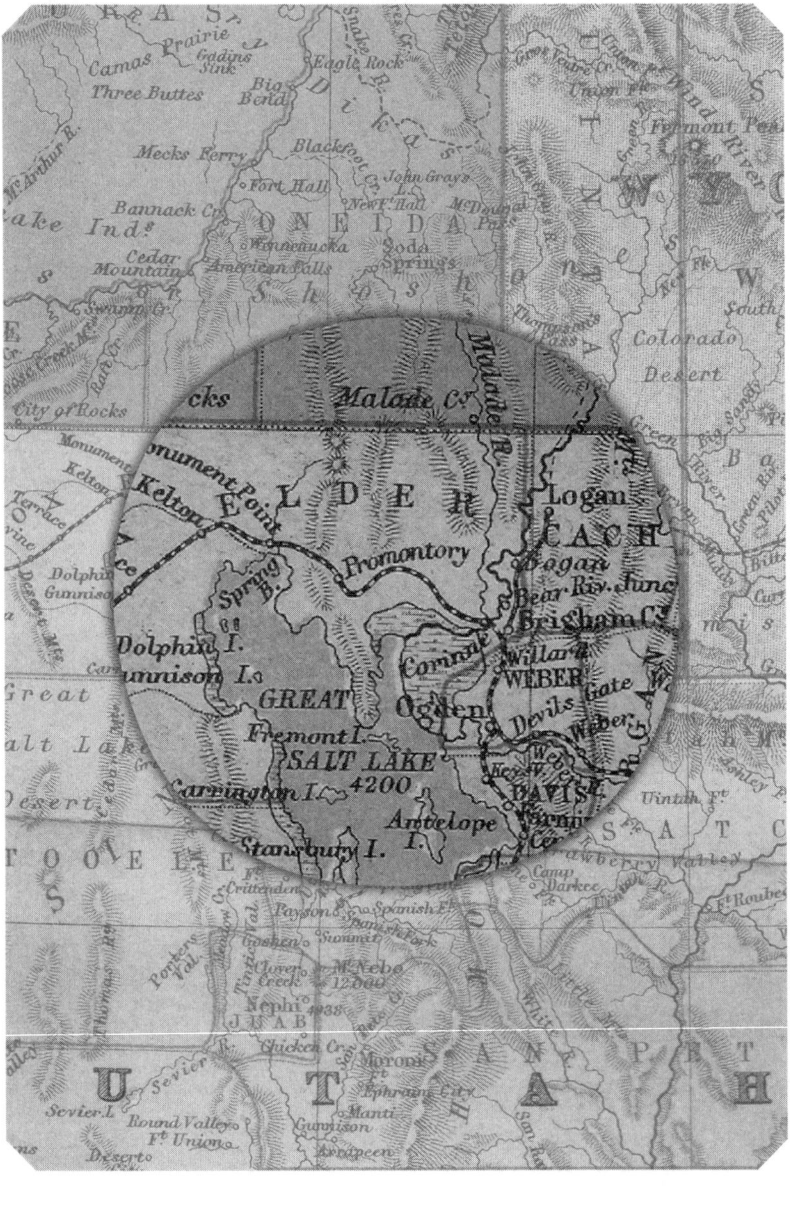

Camas Prairie
Gadins Sink
Three Buttes
Eagle Rock
Big Bend
Mecks Ferry
Blackfoot Cr.
Fort Hall
John Grays
New Ft. Hall
Bannack Cr.
ONEIDA
Winnemucka
Soda Springs
Cedar Mountain
American Falls
City of Rocks
Colorado Desert
Malade Cr.
Malade R.
Monument Point
Kelton
ELDER
Logan
CACHE
Promontory
Spring B.
Bear Riv. Junc.
Brigham C.
Dolphin I.
Gunnison I.
Corinne
Willard
WEBER
Ogden
Devils Gate
GREAT
Fremont I.
SALT LAKE
4200
Carrington I.
DAVIS
Antelope I.
Stansbury I.
Great
Salt Lake
Desert
TOOELE
Uintah Ft.
Camp Darkee
Payson
Spanish Fk.
Goshen
Summit
Mt. Nebo
Nephi
JUAB
Chicken Cr.
Moroni
UTAH
Sevier L.
Round Valley
Ft. Union
Ephraim City
Manti
Gunnison

CONTENTS

Desert

Brigham City, The Utah Territory: 1859-1871

CHAPTER I

My childhood among the Saints was no such thing. In a land built on belonging, I did not. I arrived in Brigham City in 1859. Some Brother who hauled freight had found me in Honeyville, a six-year-old girl living among Gentiles and miners, all of them men. The good Brother couldn't conscience it. He hauled me from the dusty boardinghouse yard up into his wagon, and the view from such a height—that lordly prospect over my life, the very ground I'd been at home on—struck my heart to tatters. I rode, eyes closed, thirteen miles south, all the way from Honeyville to Brigham City.

It took the Elders less than a week to find me my new home. Marked, shy, motherless, I must have seemed a pitiable creature. But pity never blinded the Widow Anderson to her own good fortune. She was as quick to set me hauling kindling as she was to slap a fly.

Daytimes, I did the work the widow had no zeal for, while she boiled up a fury in the kitchen, cats kneading her skirts, the window glass running with steam—turnips or peaches or tripe. Every evening, we crocheted, and the parlor filled with the spoilt milk smell of the Sister's breath. "A marked girl needs home skills, above and beyond!" It passed her purse-fold lips like the refrain of a favorite hymn. How I longed to run the crochet hook through the back of my own throat and end my misery.

I scrubbed and chopped and endured her nightly sermons until the day the widow died. I was fourteen. Then the Elders found me my new calling: to scrub and chop and endure the likes of Lars Larsen, a widower who kept the smithy out at the edge of the Barrens. Brother Larsen was Danish, older than time and hard as a passed-over turnip. His house and livery lay out west of town, facing the broad mud flats of the Great Salt Lake. Never mind the beauty of the Wasatch Range to the east, with the green city fleshing itself along the banks of Box Elder Creek. Lars preferred the quiet. He preferred salt waste to green trees. Just like me among the Mormons, Lars' life was set apart.

Morning one, Brother Larsen did not flinch at the sight of the purple-red stain that covers my left cheek and flutes down my neck like I've been scalded. Lars crossed the kitchen without even looking over—like I was one and the same wife been standing there for years, ready to serve—and demanded ebelskievers for breakfast. "Able-whats?" I asked, not meaning to be intractable. And two years later, my skievers remained disabled. Lars never complained, as long as they were more round than flat, as long as I kept his clothes clean and pressed, even his work shirts for the smithy, canned his preserves with honey, and took his dinner to him, rain, shine, smithy or fields.

I got food, as I could harvest and prepare it, and a bed in the tack room off the stable. No adornment money. No burden on the Ward. The Prophet Brigham Young would surely have been proud the way the Priesthood had handled it, my life.

I spent summers tending Lars' half acre in the Big Field. Brother Pratt paraded by us on his sweaty horse as the Sisters planted and weeded their plots, bent over in the high heat in calico bonnets. I planted the expected rows of corn and squash, but my kitchen garden took a daring turn, the shapely curved plantings all bordered with marigolds and nasturtiums. I told Brother Pratt it was to draw off pests. He saw no beauty in things.

I secretly lived for beauty. During luncheon breaks, I would climb the foothills in search of wildflowers. Sego, paintbrush, lupine, wild blue flax. Theirs was a calming company. When I had a private evening, I arranged and glued pressed wildflowers onto paper with lace and ribbons that were castoffs from Florrie Gradon. Florrie was my best friend. My only friend. She would have said, my champion. Florrie chose to see more than orphan, servant, the liveryman's girl. "Sisters in the Gospel, if not the flesh," Florrie said, swinging hands with me as we walked down Forest Street to school together. She kept the boys from taunting me in public, and silenced gossip among the girls.

Her ma seen a barn burn down.

Her ma stood too next a fire while encumbered.

Her ma had cravings, she craved and ate strawberries till her baby inside broke out stained.

Nah, the way I heard, her ma seen Indians and the fright crawled right up her own baby's neck.

Those were the schoolgirls' reasons for my facial marking, but they were just tales. I knew the origin was not fear or fire or craving. The origin was sin.

I'd opened Brother Lars' *Book of Mormon*, once, seeking solace for my loneliness. The myriad *And it came to pass*es, the *Thus saith*s and the columns and columns of men's names made me blench. Men killed and men died. I couldn't pronounce their names, much less fathom their workings for or against God's

will on this continent. Nothing for me, nothing at all. Dread
swelled my heart, until I reached the page where God cursed
Nephi's wicked brother with dark skin. Then the scriptures
spoke right to me. Then the passages came clear. God cursed
the idolatrous Laman with dark skin to keep his kind separate
from holy Nephi and his seed. The Lord declared He would
mark everyone who mingled his seed with the Lamanites', that
they would be cursed also. And lastly, God promised Nephi to
"set a mark upon him that fighteth against thee and thy seed."

I was so marked. My private fights against the chosen,
battles of jealousy and willfulness, never quite believing myself
a Saint—these were why the Spirit had never spoken within,
why every prayer in memory only echoed in my skull.

I wept at my forsakenness. I mourned through the night
until a strange, strong peace offered itself. Failure is a soft bed
once striving dies, a rest from all care. God clearly despised me.
I'd earned all of the unfairness of my life. The most sacred book
on earth showed me my place. It also told me why I dared desire
a Lamanite. A Bannock Indian, the first man I ever loved.

I met him in the mountains while picking wildflowers.
Looked up from a stream bank covered in blue flax and saw a
horse grazing. On the horse, a man. Black eyes, broad mouth,
black hair down to his waist. He carried a rifle on his back.

Words could have passed between us, we stood so close.

The Bannock never moved, never shifted his eyes from
me. The jagged hair along the crown of his head told me he was
Bannock. Braids twisted with buckskin hung from temple to
chin. A green feather rose from his hair. I thought to touch it. I
would have drowned in that hair willingly, died gladly without
protest or reproach.

He did not flinch at the sight of my skin.

I managed to break his gaze—the handsomest human

face I had been blessed to see—and look out over the valley, the gray mud flats, the uncoiled rope of the Promontory Mountains ghosted in the waters of the Great Salt Lake. I took it all in. Then, when I knew my legs would carry me, I climbed the bank and ran, skidding downhill toward town.

I did not go for help or call the Brethren to make chase. I marked that place as sacred, the man sacred, memorizing my route back to it, to him.

I never once felt fear.

The Sisters working in the Big Field already thought me indolent or crazy, trekking through the scrub in the heat all summer long to gather weeds. If they only knew what I really sought.

Didn't his hair fill the darkness of the rafters in my room, almost familiar there? Couldn't a smile have rested behind that stern, generous mouth? He'd shown no fear at the sight of me. Cursed as he was with dark skin, perhaps my face hadn't mattered. It made us kin. I dreamed that I would win him, convert him to the truth and claim God's mercy. We would sit side by side at Sacrament Meeting, holding hands, both our skins scrubbed to whiteness from repentance.

These were the waking dreams.

At night, my dreams grew searing bright, the green of a private grove far from contentions, where the Bannock sang to me, his black hair loose, shade and branches overhead glistening. Oh, the keenness to elope with God's forsaken! Being as young as I was foolish, I prayed fervently that my Father in Heaven would end the dreams for me. I begged Him to remove their sting, since I had no power to. And for the first time in my life, a prayer was answered. The sacred grove, my joy, my kin—erased.

I stumbled through the next few days bewildered, lonelier

than I had ever been. I searched the foothills noon and evening, without result. I baked plain vinegar pies, and cut them in small slices. From the cemetery to the flour mill, I placed a piece in every gully, hoping the Bannock would find one while watering his horse and know the taste of my distress.

The summer passed. The curse stood firm. I would stay separate. Who could ever bridge a gulf designed by God?

CHAPTER 2

Florrie Gradon never guessed my sins. She wouldn't stand for any differences between us. She had a mother and a father sealed in marriage for time and eternity, seven happy siblings and a green two-story house amid the poplars on Forest Street. Florrie taught me to play piano so we could perform duets, but I wouldn't play a note outside her house. She swooned over my "pressed flower cards," and made the Sisters behind the Co-op counter display them and sell them for scrip. She dragged me to church socials, asking this boy or that to dance with me. They tolerated it in good humor, to get closer to Florrie, until one evening at a harvest dance, Tom Dean refused.

Florrie said, "Don't be log-headed, Tom."

"I ain't log-headed," he said. "And sure as salvation, I ain't gonna dance with no girl has a face like a brush fire."

It cut me like a felling axe.

Florrie trembled. Her voice raised up. "Our Heavenly Father does not stop at the skin. He sees us inside out."

"Well, if God was here, He could dance with her," Tom said, rocking back on his heels. The pack of girls nearby lit up at the blasphemy. Tom grinned. "He could, I would not stop Him."

I stood there, dry and wooden about the eyes, suffering their laughter, waiting for the next blow to fall, when a stranger stepped in, asking Florrie to dance. He was tall and lean, serious beyond our years, with pomade in his red hair.

Florrie composed herself and silenced Tom with a stare. She smiled at me. Then she took her suitor's hand like she'd found gold amidst the dross. Everyone parted to let them pass.

I stepped outside the Wardhouse. The air in the poplars had a fine substance, a powdery slow drift. The cut alfalfa smelled like it trailed to Heaven, but Heaven gave no comfort. Not when the Lord tolerated boys who crowed with stiff-necked, bandy-legged cruelty. It rubbed me to distraction how they did it, how they brutalized and brutalized and never felt a hitch! The stars overhead swelled to white pools. I started toward the side yard to cry in private, but voices from the dark there stopped me.

"I don't know what my pa would say." It was a woman's voice, young and frightened. "He ain't—"

"He abides by the Celestial Law. Would he keep a daughter of his from the reap of such benefits?" A man spoke, blunt-voiced and sour.

"Well, Pa needs me at home, to tend the children while Mother works the Co-op counter."

"Your daddy needs a twenty-year-old mouth to feed? God in Heaven knows he don't."

The young woman pushed down sobs.

"Fussing only proves it. You need a husband to work you, Sofie, need a hungry child to suck the poison out of your vain heart. You got no suitors, young nor old. Huh. You'd get a room and strong children as my fifth, never want for food. It'd give your tired daddy one less mouth at his table. I seen his crops. He'll bless your going."

Sofie answered him with silence.

"Don't you seek for eternal glory?" He said it with force. "Don't you know you can't refuse the Everlasting Covenant once it has been opened unto you? You'll be damned, sure as the Prophet Joseph spake it, damned to Hell and the buffetings of Satan. That what your folks deserve? Their board burdened with your hungry mouth and their souls burdened with your shame?"

Her voice had shrunk to pearl-size. "No."

He yanked her a few steps toward the light. I gasped at the sight of Erastus Pratt, stout bellied, shaven clean, with the lines of his mouth drawn unnaturally into a smile. "That's a good girl," he said, breathing down into her face. His fingers stroked outward, alongside of her breast. "I'm one to enjoy my privileges, like the Prophet says." He kissed her as hard as a hand's slap, then turned and walked toward the dance.

As manager of the Big Field, Erastus Pratt worked us all—men, women, and children—like tools, without the least affection. But to see him bully in love—his chosen one without defenses, and him sharpening the words of God to blade points. He'd bloodied God's words, and he'd won.

"Courtship's over, Sofie," he called back. "I'll tell your pa when I see him in the field."

I stayed in the shadow of the church steps. Sofie kept to the side yard, out of sight. The music rang, and the feet upon the boards, but under the noise of the assembled I heard a sobbing, low and steady, that brought bile into my throat.

I rode home that night in Lester Madsen's fringe-topped buggy. Florrie sat in the middle smiling at him, her suitor, her penny-haired man. A slant moon had risen. The usual chorus of frogs gave welcome, but all I could hear all the way home was Sofie's weeping.

Mormons do not marry for this life alone. They marry

for time and all eternity. A man and his wives and all of his children are bound together forever, and guaranteed a place in the Celestial Kingdom, where they will dwell with God. Other believers might inherit a lesser glory as angels, as "ministering servants," but without being wed in the Endowment House you can never gain the highest realm: the eternal presence of God. That is the Mormon goal—to dwell with our Father in Heaven. Just where our Mother dwells, no one mentions. No one even feels the need to know. In a decade's worth of sermons, I had never heard one Saint inquire.

Brother Pratt took Sofie to the Endowment House that November. Florrie and Lester Madsen followed. When Florrie moved to Logan at Christmas to be his bride, I lost my only friend.

February held greater losses. I rang the supper bell one chill night, and waited at table for Brother Lars until the hull corn cooled. I slopped it back on to heat and looked outside, thinking it odd the smithy fire still smoked at the chimney.

The horses waiting to be stabled and fed whinnied as I skirted the corral.

I found him dead in the smithy, crumpled on the floor with an arm flung out and his work tongs out of reach. *I'll get them for you*, was my first thought. Dour and indifferent, he was the closest I'd had to a father. I sat in the dirt and cried for him and his.

I knew a few short days of freedom, then. Freedom of the darkest kind, waiting for the Elders to declare the next place I'd be let to fill. Rumor was, at seventeen years of age, I was sure to be made some man's third or fourth. Erastus Pratt had five wives. I prayed he'd never want a sixth.

I read the only book Lars kept in the barn, listening to the sounds of my household through the night. I studied the thrift of planting living fences, in his almanac. Horses bumped their stalls. Ringdoves purred in the loft. I closed my eyes and gently stroked my right cheek with the back of my hand, then stroked the left. Barely any difference, in the dark—

My teeth ground together. My eyes wrung salt. *I'd rather kiss a pig. I'd rather die than be a wife!* Motherhood appalled me. Childbearing sickened me to think on, close as it was to the ground of my own misery: my mother, my mark. A sweep of red hair was my only memory of Mother. She'd left me at the boardinghouse without a word, no gift, no way to trace her going. An orphan at four years. Had it been my mark, my temper or my foolishness that had driven her off? Whatever the cause, Mother had left me of her own free will. I never knew my father. No memories there to find. I worked that misery like a field, every day, just to keep a path beaten through.

I prayed to God, that night. I prayed mightily to Jesus Christ to let me have some other calling, any call but a woman's call. I was not cut for it. My prayer spun like a wheel, like grief come to life. I prayed till there were no more words inside, no want, no request of God at all, just anguish, hard as whitened bone. Anguish and the answering dark.

Walking to town the next morning, I stopped to watch the run-off ponds glitter in the February sun. The two ponds were the endpoint for all of the waters that flowed from the Wasatch Mountains down through the town. Ice circles. They looked like kin, still and cold as my godless heart.

A woman at the Co-operative Mercantile Store caught me unwinding the soaked wool muffler from my cheeks. She was short and blunt and dressed like a range hand, with a head of brown hair that must have been too much for any bun to contain. It lay on her shoulders, wiry and thick. She gestured to a stool near the pot stove. "Don't mind me. Settle yourself."

And so I had to undo and unclasp.

"Ada Nuttall," she said. Her voice slapped words like tacks. "I take it you're the floral artist. I saddle the right horse?"

"Sister Clair Martin, and yes, ma'am, I dabble with flowers."

"Dabble, do you? Don't play modest with me, honey dear. You could sell them pressed flower cards in San Francisco by the packing crate and clamber the heights of Nob Hill. But that would be the Gentile way, now wouldn't it? You are paid, aren't you, by the good Co-operative, for your labors?"

Nob Hill, Mob Hill? I hadn't heard tell of either.

"Honey, do they pay you?"

"With scrip enough to buy the glue and paper. And twenty cents a week for me."

"Dog in a deer's eye."

"Ma'am?"

A Sister backed toward us, dragging a bag of grain from behind the counter. Her hips wigwagged like a horse's down a chasm. "Sorry for the wait, Aunt Ada. Barley was under the wheat flour."

"Don't pop your gussets for me, though if it gave you ease, I'd bless it." Ada grinned. Then she winked at me and hefted that fifty-pound bag of barley like it was a day-old child and took her leave.

When I asked whose aunt she was, the Sister only sucked her teeth. "Oh, she ain't anybody's aunt. Then again, she ain't no Sister. We only call her kin. Lord bless her, she'll need it come the final trump. That woman," she breathed, "has a liquor still. She stews our barley up in a shed behind her mansion. No God-fearing Brother would help her. She pays a Lamanite to chop wood and tend the works. In cash! That filthy redskin. That old buck, Pocatello Jim."

I knew Pocatello Jim, as well as any Mormon could. He

had lived in Brigham City since I could remember. He was the only Indian who'd stayed on after the treaty was signed, when I was ten. The one and only adult who had ever lightened my days. I knew sharp pleasure, felt keen little bursts of revenge seeing the normal folk reflected in his gait, his gestures, his elastic face. Bishop Olsen. Widow Andersen. Erastus Pratt. He aped them, proud and pinched and crafty—until they sensed they'd gained a shadow self. By the time they'd wheeled around, Jim would be leaning back, arms crossed on his chest, admiring the courthouse steeple. The men cursed him. The women looked wounded to the core. Their hatred only deepened as Jim's laughter closed the game. That loose-hinged laugh was, to me, a tonic.

I didn't cower from Jim, as the other girls did, or let him trip me up at the heels. I looked him right in the eyes whenever I passed him. His leathery skin, his mashed nose and razor-lipped smile didn't frighten me. Jim was the only grown-up who had ever required my attention. I paid it to him, in full, and he always paid me back. Now I knew Jim's other calling—brewing liquor for an apostate in the foothills above town.

That apostate, Aunt Ada Nuttall, occupied the one and only house east of Box Elder Creek. Ada's pink granite mansion nearly matched the slopes of the Wasatch Range that rose steep and free behind it. Scrub oak and sage were her only neighbors. That suited everyone fine.

The Sister at the Co-op said Ada made a fortune selling liquor by the wagonload in Corinne, the wicked railroad town thirteen miles west of Brigham. *Corinne, Corinne, the City of Sin.* All of the Gentiles asked for "Nuttall's Leopard Sweat" by name. And they paid cash money for her labors. Ada paid her tithe in U.S. dollars—the only Latter-Day Saint who did.

She was the only woman who dared live alone, and the Elders could not touch her. They needed Ada's money just as much as they did the irrigating waters of Box Elder Creek. Cash flowed around Ada like a waterwheel, and the Brethren stood just close enough to prosper from the turning.

Three days had passed since Lars' death when I met Ada Nuttall. I'd barely slept, fearing what the Brethren would choose for me: servitude, or marriage and madness. The night of his funeral, a Tuesday, I dreamt of a cabin, the old herd cabin that stands on a knoll above the cemetery south of town. I had sheltered in its lee at Lars' funeral for awhile. First the Brethren gathered at graveside, and then all of the city vanished in the light-filled cloud of snow that spun up from Lars' grave. That drift begat my vision: a solitary place where I could live and work alone.

I pled with Bishop Olsen, the following day, to let me make use of the cabin, to work and do for myself, burdening no one's stores. The plan had enough frugality in it to catch him off his guard. As steward of the First Ward, he would consider it, he said, he'd take it up with the Elders. Though a girl alone in a cabin in the hills—

I reminded him the Tingeys' orchards bordered the cemetery, and their house lay just beyond. Homer and his wife and daughters, they would be my neighbors, my helpmates, in times of need.

Then the Bishop cleaned his glasses on his vest and warned me I would have to gain permission from the fearsome woman who owned the cabin. She'd been one of Brigham City's first settlers and the wife of its first Bishop. A headstrong and intractable apostate. Fallen from the straight and narrow way. He blessed me with his doughy white hands and I hiked up to Ada's.

I sat in her parlor in a wingback chair looking out over the city. The poplars on Forest Street stood like bound brooms heaped with old snow. They marched from Main Street out to the edge of the Barrens, past the icy run-off ponds and Lars' livery, in a stark promenade, two by two. Even the trees in Brigham were coupled. What could a girl alone do?

Sister Nuttall served tea in china cups. I kept my hands to myself. Tea broke the Word of Wisdom, as surely as liquor. I waited for her to speak.

She added cream and drifts of sugar to her cup. She stirred. She downed a steaming gulp. Then she looked at me. "Due to a recent death, you have been left without a home. Is that the case?"

"Yes, ma'am."

"And you aim to occupy the herd house, which is by legal title mine."

"Yes, ma'am. If the Brethren allow me to, I would bring it no harm."

She leaned forward. The sleeves of her dress tensed at the seams, her shoulders too ample for the cut. "You are how old?"

"Seventeen. Or, eighteen this month. I can't be sure exactly. But February, that's my birth month. I'll be eighteen." All of the courage I'd shown in front of Bishop Olsen had deserted me. Here was a greater obstacle, housed in luxury, wearing taffeta and black lace. I smoothed my worn calico skirt into straighter lines and waited.

Ada squinted and crossed her legs. A bright beaded moccasin angled out from under her skirt. "Let's crimp the formalities, what say? I never did take to the dignified." She drank her tea down. "Now, in payment for the leasing of my cabin, one-half of your earnings in Corinne will be mine. In cash—"

"But—"

"But what? You think that's a steep cut, Sister? You don't like my terms?"

"No, I wouldn't know, ma'am, I'm sure. But I have no earnings in Corinne, in cash or any other way."

"You will have. Pack up those cards of yours in half dozens. We'll get a quarter per pack." Ada Nuttall didn't blink. Her eyes were almond-shaped, a dull green like the underbelly of a fish. They stayed dead level, though she spoke of fantastical things.

I pressed my feet to the floor to keep from toppling.

"Unless you'd rather take Erastus Pratt to your bosom or some other good God-fearing Elder, in which case I won't see a profit from your gain, and the good Lord does indeed work in mysterious ways."

I shook my head *no*.

"I empathize. Now, hold out your hand."

She slipped a pistol into my palm. It was small and silver and warm from her pocket.

"Comes with the cabin. Renter's insurance."

Refusal was doomed. I doubted this woman had ever been refused anything, so I put the pistol in my pocket and thanked her, saying we would have to see what the Elders thought of our plan.

Ada snorted and said, "It's done."

I said, "But the Elders—"

"Mean well, Lord love 'em, though it comes to their advantage, you can bet on it."

"'Let the Priesthood handle it.' That's what Bishop Olsen said when I asked him about my future."

"Let a horsefly drive the team?" Ada laughed. "Not while my arms can take a rein!" She stood up. "Now, there's one last nosy bit. I've been in this town since the dawning, and I don't recall the name Martin. Where are your own folks from, if you don't mind my asking?"

I swallowed a knot of pure pain. "Martin is my father's name. I did not know him ever. My mother worked a board-inghouse in Honeyville. I was four when she left, six when they brought me here. I can't say if she abandoned me, or came to harm, or harmed herself. No one ever told." I looked up from the floor. "If that's all your terms, Sister Nuttall, I could make it home by dark."

"There is another thing, just one," she said. "No more 'Sister'ing. You call me Ada."

We shook hands on it, like men do, and Ada fetched the bullets for my gun.

CHAPTER 3

The Saints made such a fuss about their city: pride in the railroad, the telegraph line, the courthouse, and now the stone foundation for a Tabernacle laid right here in the northernmost outpost of the Prophet Brigham Young's empire. He'd led his people West, from affliction and torment among Gentiles—we'd heard those terrifying tales— to a hard peace in salt desert so sere no one wanted it. No dispute over the Mormon claim to the Utah Territory at all but for the Shoshone, the Bannock, the Ute, the Paiute and the Goshute, Ada said, who'd all tried coexisting, then fighting for their homes. Brigham said, "feed them, don't fight them," which lasted a short while. In the end, sheer numbers settled their differences. The Mormons multiplied and replenished and subdued the desert, and the Saints had their promised land. The Great Salt Lake shimmered in its midst. The Wasatch Mountains flanked it to the east—a granite battlement which kept Gentiles out and Mormons in. Not that any of the faithful wished to escape. My mother had. By what means, I cannot say.

I hope her faith sustained her.

My own peculiar faith, which I dared not repeat, decreed that a cluster of houses, one knee-high church foundation, a set of shiny tracks and a telegraph wire did not mean much in the grander scheme. To me, these civilizing feats just hunched, small-shouldered, at the base of the Wasatch Mountains. The Wasatch gave us our life, man and animal, temporal and spiritual. They were the source. All the rest came late and after.

Ada and I were pounding a tiny indent in the shine of Brigham's shield. Only Ada's pink mansion and my one-room hut stood above the town of Brigham on a long, sage-covered ledge we called the Bench. It ran the length of the foothills, north to south, marking the sudden ascent of the mountains from the desert floor. All of the houses in Brigham lined the gridwork streets, facing nothing but each other and a cardinal direction. Ada's house perched on the North Bench at a southwesterly angle, taking in the sunsets and the compass of the town. My cabin, to the south, looked out over the cemetery, the checkered gardens of the Big Field and, beyond, the Promontory Mountains rising from the waters of the Great Salt Lake. Box Elder Creek ran below the cabin, cutting a line between the bare incline of the Bench and the rooftops of Brigham City, separating the settled from the wild.

On the day I moved from Lars' stable at the Barrens up into Ada's cabin on the Bench, I gauged my happiness by this sight: dusted with snow, the Wasatch Mountains seemed to cup the valley like a bread-maker's palms. I would live on the fleshy pad of their thumb.

I moved my few possessions in and stood a long while in silence. I set the books Ada had loaned me in the window sill. Then I scrubbed the river rock walls until they gleamed. I would press flowers at the window right of the door, place one crate there. Hang clothes on a cord strung in the back corner. Firewood to the left of the hearth, washtub and kitchen supplies to the right. I hoped to find a large table to place in the center of the room. I had no bed and the door needed mending. Leather strips would do for hinges.

That night, I watched the lamps on Main get lit, one and two. The copper-faced creek angled north, toward Ada's windows, which were bright. And a hymn came, with words that filled my breast:

> *Oh, Zion! dear Zion! land of the free,*
> *Now my own mountain home, unto thee I have come—*
> *All my fond hopes are centered in thee.*

My move across town released me from Bishop Olsen's so-called care. I now resided within the confines of the Second Ward, and under the eye of a new Bishop. Daniel Dees was tall and strappy, and he presided over the Sunday meetings with mannish ease. I believed I might enjoy this change, until he took me aside that first Sunday and told me my new calling— to sew holy garments for a living, the sacred long johns worn by couples after they'd married in the Endowment House. I objected, panting inwardly *Me in close quarters with the holy underwear?* But he silenced my concerns with a generous smile, saying married Sisters would attach the holy symbols, marking breast and knee. As if that made it better. As if that made it right.

His smile lingered in my mind for days. *What would it mean to move through life with such assurance? How would it feel to know something, anything at all, beyond a shadow of a doubt?* I asked myself, until the questions became riddles I knew I'd never solve.

Bishop Dees also called for a house-making, that first Sunday. He asked the Ward members to open their bounty to the newest householder, to share whatever they could. All week long, items arrived at the top of the hill. A tin tub and bent ladle, hempen bed cord, tatted couch covers, crockery, three and a half bars of Sister Karen's oatmeal soap, a bread can, yeast starter, an axe, flour, molasses, an old Dutch oven with two legs, one kerosene lamp and a flax broom.

Homer Tingey hiked up late that first week. He greeted me with a smile so large, his jaw begged rest.

I said, "Brother Tingey, I do not need another thing. I am beyond thankfulness."

Homer blushed. "Bishop said, 'Guard and deliver.'" He called down to the boys in his wagon. They shoved a tarp back, and my heart leapt in recognition.

Brother Larsen's cast iron tub.

It was the only claw foot tub in Brigham. Lars had ordered it by mail. Some said he'd ordered it for Sister Larsen just before she died. A quiet Brother, but his heart was true. He may have meant it for his ailing wife but Lars didn't blink an eye, changing its purpose. That tub, brimming with water, lay to the belly in muck outside his own black geldings' stall—the best horse trough in Zion.

Four boys muscled the claw-foot tub to the top of the hill. I knocked snow and dried manure off its sides while Homer's boys and two of Bishop Olsen's sons threw off their coats. They tipped the tub and squirmed in the doorway. Four steps, they turned it right and touched it down.

"Don't take your ease, boys," Homer said, stepping in. "Sister Martin may not want the tub set there."

Inger Olsen ran his hands along his sleeves, grimacing. "We ain't slaves," he said, "and she sure ain't no queen."

But when I looked in—the long white tub aligned with the door, a dumpling set square center of the room—I thanked them, Homer and his sons and the Bishop's boys. "It's where I'd have it. It is just right."

I would find three planks to lay across it for my table, by day. By night, its purpose was clear. Never had I felt so safe or slept so sound, enclosed on all sides by cast iron.

And so it started. I sewed for the Saints and hiked the hills. I read all the books I could borrow. I cooked whatever I wanted. I watched every sunset bury itself in the waters of the Great Salt Lake. I loved my life.

One afternoon, late in March, I hiked to the mouth of Box Elder Creek on a whim. The path ran through a maze of scrub oak trees. Cottonwoods marked where the river emerged from the canyon. The sharp odor of pine led me upstream. I walked boulder to boulder, avoiding the gravel of the bank to spare my boots their leather. The clear water tumbled, forward and down. Grasping a willow branch, I bent for a drink, and leaning there, felt the pull of the fast-moving current. *Let me take you under* slid from eye to throat to navel like apple cider running through a muslin bag. Oh, to surrender! To relinquish all cares! My wet transit to Heaven would no doubt puzzle the devout, who would find me when the water slowed and banked at Reeder's Grove. It was not death, it was a joining, the inevitable slide of crosscurrents. I vowed my life would be like that. I would find my own track to follow. Or I would carve it out as this creek did, with the rhythms of work and rest.

About my work, Ada Nuttall had been right. The pressed flower cards sold in Corinne faster than we could ship them. This took me to her house each Monday to renew supplies and transact business. We held court in the kitchen, while Ada cut biscuits from a double batch of dough.

"Tea breaks the Word of Wisdom," I said, when she offered me another cup of greasy amber tea. It seemed the only way to meet someone so strong, stroke for stroke.

"So I don't guess you'd like to come out back and see my liquor still?"

Trouble was, Ada could outstroke a drowning dog.

"Do you know, Clair, how I came to take up distilling? The tithing office in Saint George. They took in hundreds of barrels of grapes in tithing each year, and what was they to do with them? Let 'em rot in the heat? No, the Brethren made the best of what God gave them. They stomped those grapes into wine, and used it for feasts and occasions when the Prophet came. Brigham loves a good party. Then they sold all the surplus to the Gentiles passing through."

This was my first lesson in Mormon history, my introduction to the larger scheme. Ada Nuttall held the jaws of the Church open for me to see, the powerful thing I had grown up with, ward of its care, telling myself *that feeds on dew and pollen, that feeds on air*. Well, once I'd seen the indent of its teeth, she made me stop to reconsider its maw.

I asked her where her husband was.

"I lost him to plurality."

"He was Brigham City's first Bishop?"

"Willie? Yes, he was, indeed. For two years. I threw him out in 'fifty-four."

"But weren't you sealed for time and eternity?"

"Oh, we're still married, honey dear. It's just that William lives in Ogden, thirty miles south, with his mild-tempered, moon-faced, second-choice wife." Ada stopped to scrape the dough from her little finger onto her front teeth. "I threatened to wring the neck of any child born to him outside my womb. So he set up house with the Forsgren girl in Ogden and crept home, weekends, to help raise our son Stephen. Willie slept out in the tool shed. A patriarch of shovels!" Ada grinned. "Sheepish toward me, but that was how we'd sliced the pie."

"So he became Bishop in Ogden?"

"No. Seems Willie had not shown the proper zeal for the new Principle of Plurality. The Brethren said he'd been overled by a headstrong wife. No, they voted against disfellowship, but they took away my husband's calling. And Erastus Pratt, willing servant of the Lord—who by then had bedded himself three wives—well, Pratt became Brigham City's second Bishop."

"Couldn't your William have said no? Some Brethren don't choose polygamy, Ada. Florrie Gradon's father hasn't."

Ada cinched her apron and looked right at me. "Brother Gradon is the Stake choirmaster. And that's all he'll ever be. Polygamy ain't demanded of every man, honey. Only those who hope to rise and rule. Willie always was a ruler."

"And what happened to your son?"

"Stephen?" She flushed with pleasure. "He rides herd north and east of here, but the boy ain't ever too busy not to visit his mother at Christmastime."

"He's your only?"

"He's all a mother could want."

I walked home dazed, vibrating in my boots with Ada's version of Celestial Marriage. *A patriarch of shovels!* Like most of her translations of the gospel, it struck me as just right. I had no idea where Ada's view of history would take me, but it felt like a creek of promise, like the tumbling Box Elder that banks at Reeder's Grove. I confess it, I thrilled at the going.

CHAPTER 4

I bellowed out hymns, ironing my way through my laundry. I had taken to ironing all my clothes—the smell of sizzling cotton pacified me. At each light tug, the folds of my underwear lay open, stiffening at the touch of the iron. Four pair. I searched my bucket for the fifth. I scanned the floor and around the room, and stepped out back to the clothesline I had strung from the eaves to a stake in the ground. Gray snow ringed the sagebrush. Nothing white on the line or in the scrub.

I looked up at a sky so piercing blue it made me wince. Then it rushed in on me: *someone has gleaned a token of me.* Lord bless it and vinegar pies. The Bannock had returned.

That Sunday after Sacrament Meeting, Bishop Dees asked to speak with me in private. His were the eyes of a well-fed creature, open wide to things. Green flecked with gold. I kept my gaze below them. The points of his moustache moved like spears when he spoke. "Sister Martin, word of your industry has preceded you here. Brother Gradon tells me he has trained you personally at the keyboard. I am calling you to be Ward organist while Sister Burt is in her confinement."

A guttering snort hit the back of my throat. I had played the organ in Florrie's front room half a dozen times. "But Bishop—" Deep humiliation would carve its way into this call. My stain would fascinate and repulse the congregation. The boys would howl at me up on the stand.

Bishop Dees employed no force, used no persuasive words. He only smiled. His smile did battle with my fear. I wanted to be left to myself. I also wanted to be good. I said, "But Bishop, must I sit on the stand all during service?"

"Well, yes. Staying awake, that is the greater challenge, Sister. But you'll sit at the organ, so you've only to keep the one eye open."

I looked up at the stand. I would sit right side to the congregation. Only the right side of my face would show. Gratitude flooded in. I must have smiled, and that smile been taken as a *yes*, because Bishop Dees bowed and then I curtsied—curtsied!—and he took his leave.

The organ is not a celestial instrument. Not in my hands. Not with my feet. I played it, poundingly, to march thoughts heavenward:

> *Oh ye mountains high, where the clear blue sky*
> *Arches over the vales of the free,*
> *Where the pure breezes blow and the clear streamlets flow . . .*

I hadn't realized how poundingly until, at hymn's end, the chorister grabbed the handrail, composed his face, and turned to me. "Sister Martin, you're sure to help the musically infirm to keep the beat."

And then, an odd sensation. The congregation laughed, lovingly, as if I were one of them. As if we all were worthy of God's grace. It softened me greatly for the blow that followed.

In the opening announcements, Bishop Dees said that three Bannocks had been killed in a herder's camp near Malad. No lives or cattle lost, as the Brethren were armed and ready. "But the lesson is a grave one. Stand ready. Vengeance raids are likely. Our prayers go out to the people of Malad."

A piteous wheeze rose from my throat. *Bannocks?* I covered my mouth, but the keening rose in pitch and force. My body shook. Hot tears ran down my hands as a memory emerged, one I had lost for years, of the raid I'd heard of near Bear Lake: a Bannock raid that left a five-year-old girl with her eyes gouged out, scalp taken, and ears and legs cut off. The pieces of the child's body had been scattered among the bodies of the other Saints.

Bishop Dees placed his hand on my shoulder. The crying slowed. My throat relaxed, just enough for my breathing to settle.

"We should all of us feel as deeply for the welfare of our Brothers and Sisters up north as Sister Martin does. Let your concern make you ready.

"Now, the second announcement seems to have taken care of itself. Two sheepherders up to Mantua have a dog can't herd anymore, lost the sight in one eye and too old to run the edges. They asked if any of our members needed protecting. Seems to me Sister Martin could use shoring up in her sense of safety there on the Bench, so if none of you Elders sustains any objection, I'd like to give that dog to Sister Martin, a 'thank you' for the weeks she'll be Ward organist here."

The Bishop gazed out over the congregation and turned to his Counselors on the stand. No objection came. "Well, then. I hereby set apart Cotton Thomas' dog as guardian for Sister Martin. The Brothers will bring him to town soon. May our Heavenly Father further and bless him in his calling."

I awoke that evening to the crackle of fire outside my cabin. I threw a quilt around my shoulders and found a broom to swat the flames. In the doorway, I paused to watch the grass and sage send ash spiraling off into the darkness. Then I ran outside, barefoot. Hands caught my breasts. They wrenched me back. Snow blurred with flame as fingers raked my nipples.

I swung hard, hit bone.

"Sow!" He tore the broom away. "You goddamned breeder—" He pinned me to his body with the broom, tightening the handle till I could not breathe. Then he hit my left leg hard with his groin, arching into it, smoothing up and up, concussive blasts of "Ah!" in my hair, smelling of hate and licorice.

"Made for the—made for the man!" He ground against my body again and again until—cursing God—his body stiffened, shuddering upward. He arched in a savage swoon till I thought we'd both fall back. Then the arch reversed, and I fell to my knees. He bit the small of my back through the nightdress, cutting in, working his jaw on it, gorging and gouging with his hands on my hips until I sobbed into my hair for mercy.

Then he slung me to the ground. Salt and dirt in my mouth. Snow under my hips. I watched him jump the flames he'd set and run down home. Little hips, spindly arms, his whole figure back-lit by fire. Inger Olsen, the Bishop's oldest son.

I knew a chill darker than fever, then. Body cold, crotch hot, I slapped my hips and buttocks, beat at them until I could feel nothing, scratching and slapping, spilling snow in a shower around my feet.

When I stood, I said, "I have survived it," but the whisper seemed a lie. Snow fell, and I was little as those words.

Inger had delivered the cast iron tub. He, not the Bannock, had stolen my clothes from the line. He'd robbed me even of that.

I doused the fire, weeping. A page of newspaper trembled in the scrub. The broom lay where he'd hurled it. I would not touch them, his kindling or his weapon.

It snowed six inches that night. I barred the doors, wedged firewood across the windows, stoked the fire—nothing gave comfort. A hundred times I suffered his attack. A hundred times I asked myself, *Am I still virgin?* All the talk of it they passed at church, all the importance the Elders laid on it—a woman's purity. At any and all costs she must preserve her virtue, even to the taking of her life.

But what exactly had a woman to protect? Copulation was sacred, not secret, the Elders said, but they never told the particulars, those particulars which tormented me so now to hear. I didn't know if I was ruined by him, or damned because I hadn't killed myself. Had Inger had his way? He'd never kissed me. We had not lain down. He'd never touched my body under the nightdress. But he'd bitten me, he had profaned, I had not struggled to the death . . . nothing I knew answered the question, was I still virgin?

And struck to silence as I was, nothing would.

I could tell no one. It would have ended my days of freedom on the Bench. And whom would they have believed—Bishop Olsen's son or a girl living alone in a cabin, her so high and mighty, putting on airs, making her way without husband or hope? I did not even go to Ada. She might have told the Brethren, demanding justice. Or taken my cabin. Or lost her fondness for me, in disgust.

That Sunday, when the Sacrament was blessed and passed, I watched Bishop Dees take the bread with his clean hands, and knew that I could not. The Deacon with the plate of torn bread stopped before me. I shook my head. He didn't pass. I looked him in the eyes and scowled. His ears turned red above the loose stalk of his father's starched collar. I scowled again, and he retreated at last. In the silence that followed, everything I saw reversed into a photographic negative. The walls of the Wardhouse were burnt black. Small comfort, to refuse blessed bread. I was only doing what the damned must.

Bishop Dees requested a second private meeting, this time at his house. I walked into his parlor that afternoon as God's forsaken, with every intention of playing my part full on. But he called me a good girl, a "radiant example to us all of industry and unflagging resolve." I never expected kindness. It drove into my heart, as did the green of his eyes. "You have taken what little your life offered and multiplied it to greatness. Sister, do you know the parable of the talents?"

I nodded, my face hot.

"Christ rewarded the man who used his talents. Christ praised and loved him. Set him as our example down through time." The Bishop's breathing was measured. I heard it mark the pause. Then he asked how I could bypass the Sacrament, a girl gifted and blessed as myself.

I said nothing.

"Have you sinned, Sister Martin? I would guess the Lord has already forgiven you. The important question is, will you forgive yourself?"

So sweet, and so unfair. I shook my head. "I am unsuited."

He considered this. "For what? Can you say it?"

The bristle on his horsehair sofa made my legs crawl. "For a woman's calling." I closed my eyes, caught my bitterness up and stuffed it into the space between us. I would not confess, or seek his comfort. I looked right into Bishop Dees' eyes. "I am marked out different. No man will have me. It is God's own curse no forgiving will erase."

"You think your marking means damnation?"

"They've told it from the pulpit since I was six—'the white and delightsome' are the chosen of the Lord! The evil are marked to stay separate. That and the narrow gate of a woman's call."

"It is the truth, what's been told. It is truth—but not the whole truth. Motherhood is sacred, a divine calling, Clair. And there are other calls. I suggest you stop doubting the Lord and listen for yours. Have faith and let the Lord do the worrying. Will you think on these things?"

He took my hand, his skin as smooth as sand-scoured pine. "The marking on your face may be a test and not a curse, Sister, both for you and those around you. There may yet be a man wants to take you for his wife."

I felt something pass into me, a strange power, piercing, deep, unpleasant. I put my hand in my pocket and tried to quiet my breathing.

"Don't toss that pearl before the swine, as yet. None of us know God's whole truth. None could withstand it," he said. "I will pray for you." And that intimacy unsettled me more than all the rest, the thought of Bishop Dees holding me within the circle of his private prayers.

CHAPTER 5

On April 3rd, my dog arrived. I found him tied to the outhouse with a short length of wire, bawling like lost souls and outer darkness, maybe some inner darkness, too.

I smeared a pan with chicken grease and broken corn bread and eased it forward with a stick. He licked it with his blunt pink tongue until the pan spun off into the brush. Then he smiled at me—no other way to say it—and rolled his back in the dirt. I longed to pat him, longed to invite him in and scratch his belly, but my grizzled, half-blind herd dog reeked of campfire and sheep dung.

I cut his hair back to the skin with sewing scissors. He chased the clumps and rolled in them, jumped up and rolled again. I gave him his day to exult. Then I heated a tubful of water and plunged him into the suds. I braced one arm to keep the astounded dog in place, and scoured his back with oatmeal soap.

Once he had suffered immersion at my hands, there was no question who the dog answered to, who he waited for, who he loved. He placed the delicate bodies of chewed rodents at my doorstep. He leaned against my legs, watching the sunsets, till we almost toppled. Dark of night, I heard his sides puff in and out, chasing some good dream at the foot of my bed. I was glad knowing someone slept, knowing someone still could dream.

Swede's hair grew in, reddish-brown mottled with gray. Swede the Lionhearted. I brushed him daily, as I had seen Lars do his beloved black horse, Loquacious.

"You still have room in your life for an old acquaintance?" Ada Nuttall filled the doorway. A strip of sky the color of peach flesh showed beyond.

"I'm fixing fritters," I said. "Pull the rocker over for the sunset. I always do."

Swede bounded in. Ada raked her fingers down his back and rubbed his ears. "Nice home you got."

I didn't trust my face, with Ada. Didn't know how much it might reveal. I added flour and a dose of salt and said, "You've walked its halls. You are patting my life's companion."

"He won't go plural on you," Ada shot back. "Size and simplicity do not alter the fact: you got a home."

I turned and thanked her.

She laughed. I smiled. And the month since we had been together melted off.

"I got news, Clair. News of your parents, if you'd like to hear. Your ma, especially. I remember her, now. I remember I seen her."

The blade in my throat wouldn't tolerate a breath.

"I did some scouting through the records, the emigration logs, the Ward ledgers and such." Ada took the spoon from my hand and sat me in the rocker. Strands of red lined the shore of the Great Salt Lake.

"Your mother's name was Marie Claire LeBlanc. She

was Louisiana French. Your father, Tucker Martin, worked the Mississippi River. A river man. He converted to the Church while delivering the John Forsgren party of Saints up to Winter Quarters, the first Scandinavian group ever to emigrate West. He was baptized in March of 1853. Died three months later, from the cholera, along with two hundred other Saints making their way upriver by steam.

"You was likely born in New Orleans. Church records indicate a Marie LeBlanc Martin and child joined the Hans Peter Olsen Company in May of 'fifty-four. The group started West in late June, arrived in Salt Lake 5 October, and here in Brigham City on 11 October.

"That's where my memory of your mother comes in, the autumn of 1854. Our burg was barely two years old, and a new party of Saints had just arrived. I paid them little mind. It seemed the end of things, for me—my husband gone, my boy to raise and our fort running over with bedbugs and vermin. What little we settlers had must be divided up with the new-comers, so my future felt half again as safe.

"News of the Principle had preceded your mother's arrival by months. Erastus Pratt brung it with him and a second wife from Salt Lake City. Said the Prophet Brigham Young had given her to him to 'build up the Kingdom,' and the rest of the Brethren should follow his lead or be damned.

"We was wrestling with it, each couple in their own way. But where we'd heard rumors of plurality for a decade and more, the newcomers had had no warning. Still the fervor was strong and our spirits high as we sat together in the split wil-low bower to welcome them and bear testimony. Whatever we lacked, whatever our trials under the Principle, we had escaped the oppression and mob violence of the Gentiles and found a home in Zion. We sat together with one mind, prayed and sang together with one voice—half-starved, ill-clothed, uneducated—the chosen of the Lord!

"Saint after Saint bore witness at that testimony meeting, until a young red-haired girl stood up, weaving a little on her feet. She was a slight thing with ringlet curls and white skin, clutching a baby to her. 'You people,' was all she said. 'You people!' A plea or a curse, I could not tell, but it was testimony, and it pierced my heart. Some Brother near her sat her down. The meeting carried on. Days later, when I thought to inquire, I learned your mother was gone."

I kept my eyes on Ada. As long as she kept talking I had a history, I had a past.

"Where did she go, Ada?"

"I don't know, honey. There wasn't anyplace to go. Brigham City was the northernmost Mormon settlement."

"Well they found me in Honeyville, she worked in a boardinghouse in Honeyville."

"A way station for any Gentiles fool enough to think Brigham Young wouldn't own this place. Men en route to the mines in Montana, or on their way back broke or crippled up. There's a hot springs there the Shoshone used, to pass the winters in comfort. I suppose your momma could have found some work in the midst of the miners, washing or cooking or—" Ada didn't complete her thought.

"Why was she so serious, Ada? Why do you think?"

"Well that ain't hard to figure. She'd lost her husband. Left her home and all her kin. Had a little baby girl." Ada's cheeks went slack. "A girl child who was different. She must have grieved for your health, your future. And the Olsen Company, they was swallowed up by cholera—stomach cramps and agony, till vomit or diarrhea or both brought on collapse. One third died. It must have been a terrible migration.

"It seems to me a widowed mother, young and pretty and in need, arriving at last in the land of Zion to lay her burdens down, just when the Principle had took hold . . ."

My mother's history became my own. "You think—?"

"Well, like as not, some man would've asked."

Pratt, or Olsen? Which of the Elders had dared? My mother had trekked eighteen hundred miles only to find herself among lechers and lunatics. I grew ravenous and chilled. I coughed up a sob as Ada said, "That's all I know, honey dear. Short of a trip to New Orleans, it's all I could find out."

"It's more than I have ever known!" A furious gratitude made me shake. "They won't. They'll never. They will not parcel me out!" Ada embraced me. My sobs worked against her dress, raising the smell of starched cotton. She did not rock, just held on as if her body had been built on the spot. I leaned in, leaned and borrowed her strength, and gradually breathed clear.

When I looked up, Ada's lashes were wet.

"Child," she said, and kissed my mouth. Her fingers gripped my ribs. Without a thought, I kissed her back, drowning in warm breath and shivers.

I am Louisiana French. I was not born in Zion, not anywhere in its bounds! Born in New Orleans—

Joy shook me and Ada held on. She held on and rocked us side to side, and it felt like singing.

Ada cooked the fritters. I washed dishes, for the first time in my life as my mother's daughter. Glad to be, then as now, a single bead on a long chain.

CHAPTER 6

Since I'd arrived, age six, I had never left the bounds of Brigham City. I had only ever known the communal thrift of the United Order, where every householder contributed his all to the Church stores and received in turn just what he needed to sustain his own. This ensured the survival of the town and gave the Church supremacy. It kept us humble and bound us to our place. Some men were called to farming, to husbandry or carpentry, according to their talents and their means. Bishop Dees was a weaver, the best in town. He'd brought his looms with him from England. I had been called to sew the holy long johns, which I much preferred to wearing them.

My friend Ada didn't rail against this holy Mormon communism. She simply said I ought to see the fruits of capitalism firsthand. I asked if their fruits were different than the peaches and apples Homer Tingey grew. She laughed and insisted that we travel to Corinne.

We left one mid-morning in June, when the valley trembled with heat. Ada's wagon followed the raised railroad tracks west. I asked her why the Union Pacific had chosen Corinne as their transcontinental link, when Mormon men had laid the rails with their own hands.

"A snub," she said. "A snub to the Prophet. They used our labor and they paid Brigham Young handsomely for it. That was all the linking up they cared to do. So Corinne grew up on the banks of Bear River, the Gentile capital of the territory." She eased her elbow into my side and said, in mock solemnity, "If Brigham Young moved the Wasatch Mountains forty feet west, the Gentiles would erect a monument to continental drift."

I swooned as we drove over the bridge that spanned the Bear, the broadest river I'd ever seen. More a table than a river, it held little boats and flocks of birds and cloud patterns on its top. The marvels of Corinne only started there. Red awnings marked the several hotels downtown. Tiny dogs pranced on leashes among the strolling Corinthians. Ada drove right past the dock leading out to an enormous paddlewheel steamer, whose flags shook in the wind. This excursion boat hauled lumber for the railroad and Gentiles for pleasure, up and down the length of the Great Salt Lake.

Wonders promptly ceased when Ada turned off the main street and parked by the Methodist Church. We'd been warned about the apostate church in Corinne. I kept still, expecting scythes to drop or nets to fall. But the plain clapboard building produced only a small man in shirtsleeves, who carried a fishing pole.

Ada said, "That's Pastor McCabe."

"He's the apostate leader? The ruler of the Gentiles? That little man?"

She grinned. "It's a slow trade, shopping for souls in Corinne."

Ada wished the Pastor a good day and we headed to town. Ladies smiled as they passed. A businessman made way for us. A little girl on tiptoes pressed her nose into the blossoms of an apple tree. The entire street was lined with saplings in bloom.

"Well, I see nothing to pity here, Ada, and no one to scorn."

"In truth, you might, if we toured the portion of town given to gambling and soiled doves," Ada said with a frown. The white streaked rafters in Lars' barn, the cooing and the acid scent, the rustle of wings settling—but my soiled dove-musings were interrupted by a gentleman calling to Ada.

She took my arm and squeezed it.

Her face bloomed into gladness as he crossed the street, and that was the rarest sight I'd seen. She introduced me to her friend William Godbe, who took my hand and asked if I was a daughter that Ada had kept from him. Ada laughed and said, "Lord help any would-be daughter of mine. This is Clair Martin, an artist friend."

We lunched with William Godbe and his two friends at a Gentile farmhouse outside of town. They served white oyster soup and store-bought bread, tearing off pieces and dunking them in their coffees. Ada laughed out loud, a bachelor among bachelors, swearing oaths and talking business. After lunch, in the parlor, she sat next to William Godbe and listened to him exposit and held his hand. The three men sobered to their subjects: polygamy and revelation and free will. They dissected each, as if they had a right to, and called the Prophet Brigham Young to task. No statement went undebated, until Godbe claimed that the highest principle of the coming age was the equality of women with men, and his friends roared their assent.

"Therein," Godbe said, rising to his feet, "therein lies the downfall, the inevitable end of the Law of Celestial Marriage. The disparity of the sexes essential to it forever deprives woman of all but a portion of male society, while men possess a corresponding excess of female society."

"Together with excess of power, excess of say-so, excess of glory." Ada almost grinned. "Together with those."

"Precisely! Woman should be man's equal in marriage. Equity is the basis of perfect law. But we are left with our dilemma: how do we end this sorry system, this imperfect one-sided order of social life which we endure? It has been weighed in the balance, and found wanting, sadly wanting, in the chief essential of human happiness to both sexes."

Males and females equal, and happiness for both? I sat wondering at this notion until Ada said, "I chose to marry and I ended that marriage by choice when polygamy came. Each should answer for themselves."

"But my dear Ada, how many Sisters are as strong as you? Most are bound to their homes by dependence, fearing poverty. Some are bound by the ungodly duty of keeping face. Still more vexing are those wives bound by affection and unselfish love to their extended family, though threat of eternal destruction has wrung their hearts sorely." William Godbe paced to the window and back. "In the end—in the end, no ties but those of affection and their own free will should continue to unite women to their husbands. Love and free will!" He fixed me with shining eyes. "What, Miss Martin, do you say to that?"

I sucked in breath and stilled my feet. I'd veered from anger to concern to hope, to a dazed sort of anxiety for the welfare of the children while listening, my mind a thimble and his talk a stream. "I believe . . . well, I'd say, Mr. Godbe, that as long as you go about *will*-ing, you aren't like to be free."

It stunned them silent. It stunned me too, unsure I followed my own meaning.

Ada laughed until the ceiling shook. "Ain't she a pistol?" All of them joined in, and the little knot they'd formed in the room loosened. William opened the parlor door. The breeze smelled of reeds and cattle. I looked out into the tall shade cast by cottonwoods. I stepped outside. And there was Zion.

The peaks of the Wasatch Range looked cut from paper. The mighty Bear River was a strand of green amid miles of uncultivated sage and salt. The land was not a fortress, here. It spread out like a cloak, an opened fan. For the first time in my life, the power of distance came clear to me: the magnitude of distance and its attendant freedom. Freedom being both empty and full. Radiant all. And that was that.

I didn't want to shake my fist at life like a spoiled child, day in day out, asserting my will or God's will or anyone else's. That shaking fist explained most all of the people I'd known. I closed my eyes to absorb the Gentile view of freedom. Not abandonment to evil as I'd been warned. Not a frivolous freedom, either. No one to pity here, no one to scorn, myself included. The warm cloak of afternoon pulled in around me.

That night, visitors came to call. Swede coughed out a string of epithets as two men knocked and identified themselves as Visiting Teachers. I aimed Ada's pistol at the latch and said if they needed to visit, they'd best do it where they stood. Come hell or the Prophet Joseph in a cloud of glory, I would open my door to no one after dark.

A hand smacked the door, turning Swede all fangs and frenzy. "You will not let us in?"

"I doubt I could contain my dog, Brethren."

Then their questions started, close as the door frame, and I wondered who was teaching whom.

"Did you travel to Corinne, today, with a Mrs. Ada Nuttall?"

Bear's ass. A gun couldn't save me from this.

"And didn't you and Sister Nuttall take company in the persons of several men?"

"And weren't those men," the second voice shrilled, "Godbeites? Weren't they, out east of town?"

"Godbeites?" I disliked the relation to William's surname. "What I know, Corinne has just one church, the Methodist. And I'll admit, Ada insisted we drive out to visit that poor lone cleric Pastor McCabe and his pretty white house and all the cows you'd ever care to look at—"

"You and Sister Nuttall socialized with a Protestant minister, all afternoon?"

"I wish I'd known you were in Corinne today, Brethren, you could have joined us. The pastor makes a fine oyster soup. I assured him that the very next Sunday no worshippers attend his church, he is welcome to come join us at the Second Ward. We would make him feel at home on the Sabbath."

"You asked—"

"Course, he declined, saying the inside of a Wardhouse put him in mind of a chicken coop, and he would rather clean his vestryments and go fishing."

A silence followed this, then a voice pressed the door. "You contend and assure us that you and Ada Nuttall did not meet with any Godbeites this very afternoon, out east of Corinne?"

"If there's a Godbeite minister who needs consoling in Corinne, I would be glad to give him my best welcome. Would you pass that on to Bishop Dees, Brethren? I'd be willing, if I should ever go back. He has my word on it," I said.

Then I let Swede rush the latch and the Visiting Teachers stopped visiting.

Ada blenched. She smoothed her hair back with both hands and tightened her apron. She seemed smaller when her face wasn't set to lead the charge. In fact, she stood no taller than me.

"You was questioned?"

"I lied for you. And I want to know, was it worth my lie?"

Ada leaned against her kitchen table, pale as a bowl of lumpy dick.

"Who is William Godbe, that you would take us into harm's way to visit him? What are Godbeites, and why do the Elders care if we met with them? Why were we spied on? And, just for verity's sake, does the Methodist pastor live in a pretty white house out east of town?" I smiled.

"Let's us sit down," Ada said.

A trace of steam rose from the Ironstone tea pot. I took down a cup and poured Ada some tea.

"If I am damned," she said, "it'll be for endangering others. When did they come?"

"Dark of the night. Two Visiting Teachers, though they never did get around to teaching." I smiled again, Ada the one who usually got to be wry.

But Ada only trembled. "And you told them . . ."

I spun my tale for her, then said, "Hell's breakfast, Ada, did you take us to some apostate church?"

"No, honey dear, worse. Apostate church, political rebellion and literary gadflies—all three in one. You genuinely think you're better off knowing all of this?"

"I am nine-tenths ears."

Ada sipped her tea. "Well, some folk, much as they love the Church, cannot sit by and be dictated to, dominated like they was children. William—that man has traveled the world, has a business mind to rival any, educated and forward looking. Well, he'd lost several fortunes following the Church lock step for twenty-odd years, and then it settled on him, knelt on his chest like a fiend: he could go on casting his fate to the steerage of others, or he could stop and speak for himself.

"So William did speak, in respectful tones, but he spoke what he believed, his very own views on doctrine and labor and wages. That was the *Utah Magazine*. William loves a free press. The Prophet, you may know, feels otherwise. William Godbe was excommunicated. And he lost his fortune, yet again."

"How so?"

"When a man is cut off from the Church, Clair, his earthly goods are up for the taking, fair gain for any Brethren who can get their hands on them."

Spiritual death involved a physical death, too. It chilled my bones. "But he survived it. What happened to his two friends?"

"Excommunicated. For refusing to believe God Almighty intended the Priesthood do their thinking for them. Brigham and the Brethren had a heyday at that council meeting, feasting on three carcasses at once."

"You haven't made mention of their church."

"Well, William talked with angels. For three nights, he asked them questions and garnered guidance. Providence, he was given to know, would demolish the worst of the Prophet's work so that the best might be preserved. And that was the start of Godbeism."

"It sounds like blasphemy, I have to say, Ada, friends of yours or no."

"Only shows how far this Church has shifted on its basestone. Hardly find the man any more has visitations, or the grandmother blessed with second sight. That was the early fire fueled this people: personal communion with Heaven, angels and spirits among us in the Latter Days."

"I can't believe William Godbe talked with angels."

"We all did. And still do."

She appeared not to be joking. Which raised in me a protective concern. "So, tell, are you in danger, that the Brethren watch your moves?"

"They suspicion me of every evil. Catching me at a Godbeite gathering would have locked up me and my future. I've brought you in too close. Forgive me, Clair."

"The Elders took my story. For the while, I think you're safe."

Ada pulled a small sage bundle from a basket near the door. She lit it and waved the pungent smoke all over us. "Shoshone custom. Sage clears the pain from the pure. May we be blessed." Then she rapped the table and offered to fix a meal. She sifted flour into a pile on the board and cracked eggs in a bowl, humming in her loose-cocked way.

"You fond of William Godbe, Ada? He surely had a shine for you."

She whipped the contents of the bowl till her hair flew into a trot. "He's married. Two times over."

"He's a polygamist!"

"Must trouble him, nights, him and his drive for equality—those duplicate wives."

"And you claim no interest of your own?"

She let the spoon float free and gave me all her attention. "I admire his mind, I'll confess it. I believe he approves of my strength and daring. You seem awful attentive, Clair dear, to the winds of court and spark."

"You were the one held hands with William Godbe in the parlor. I only marked the holding. Did you hear, Ada, that Bishop Olsen's taking himself another bride?" I couldn't help but tell it. The news made me feel mean. "It's Jensine Waylet. We sat school together. Jensine and me were baptized the same day. You know who did it, who dunked us? The Bishop, only he wasn't Bishop then, he was Elder Olsen. He baptized her and now he'll marry her. Must be thirty years her elder. Tom Dean'll be pleased—he's only been courting Jensine since Florrie left."

Ada flipped the cakes on the griddle. "I guess Sister Olsen will be as well satisfied with one sixth of a husband as with one fifth."

I shoved the bench back. "How is that fair? Tell me how that is right. Taking young girls off to do your pleasure while the young boys have no chance, not an earthly claim to offer in compare."

"You think it's pleasure, pleasure they're after? God in Heaven, honey dear, Mormon men aren't lechers. Most don't have the imagination!"

I saw Inger, that white head, that lank body standing to one side watching his new mother Jensine with a look wouldn't be found out, as quiet as a beast blended in with its surroundings—hungry heavy beasts parading as men. "Tell Jensine Waylet that in Bishop Olsen's house!"

Ada shook me as the tears spilled out, then shook me again when I would not speak. "What is it?" she said. "Tell it, Clair! You tell me what has poisoned your heart. Tell me who, and tell me when."

I pulled the old scab off. It bled.

"Well you was raped, sure enough, by that sneaking pusillanimous pup, but not in full, not according to the letter of the law. Did you know his rod? His penis-bone, honey, I'm sorry to be so blunt. Was it naked in you? In between your legs? You'd a known it."

Inger had raked my bosom, he'd pinned me to him with the broom, he'd banged on me and bit down on my skin, but never was he once between my legs, never once, I felt quite certain.

I told her I thought no.

"The sniveling runt. He'd better sing low and keep out of my path."

"So, Ada, I'm still virgin?"

"Honey, yes."

This cruelty carved deeper, that I had suffered so from an unfounded fear. The Saints did not give comfort or help to a daughter in need. They offered haughty self-delinquent mothering tyranny!

"How did you stand it, Ada? Stand the nights when you lived with your husband?"

"You mean the loving, the mating up? Every sweet has its bitter. You got the bitter alone."

"What sweet? I saw Florrie Gradon, last week, on her first trip home. She took my arm—my dear married friend—and whispered, 'It is a mean thing. Quick and mean. *Consummation* it is called, and they consume you!' Her words gripped like spoiled food in my belly. Inger hurt me once. That ache, that brutality, now it's Florrie's daily bread."

"You've had a bad introduction, a poor start into the pleasures of things, that's all. I could have told you Lester Madsen had a kink in his bridle. My guess is his daddy set the crimp. As for Inger—" She covered my hand with hers. We smelled cakes burning. "Someday, Clair, someday when you're at hand's grips with love, he'll just be a memory, like offal, like smoke."

"You sure there's a sweet as well as bitter?" I asked, though I knew it for myself. Sweet sat on Ada's mantel in the parlor. Every time I stole a glance at the photograph of her son Stephen on that massive horse, my heart burst open like a rangy sunflower. Jensine had chosen age and the comforts of the fold over untested youth. I wished her well. I doubted, when it came to love, that I would be so tractable.

CHAPTER 7

S trange to be smitten by a thing so small: the little gold frame all by itself on the mantel above Ada's fireplace. I felt I knew Stephen—her only begotten, her darling son—though I'd only seen this one picture of him sitting on a mountain of a horse. Cowboy on a black beast, smiling. A steed so big none of Utah showed behind it. Stephen Nuttall clearly loved that horse. You could see it in the set of his chin.

Ada relished telling tales about her son. How he'd bumped a saddle up the front porch steps, age three, all by himself. How he'd banged on his mother's pots with a spoon during Brigham City's first Sabbath meetings, held inside her cabin. However was Ada to know the Brethren didn't cater to their children's musical talents, or that the Sisters never played catch-as-can with their sons on their swept dirt floors? Ada caught hell, as usual, and her husband was chastened by the Stake Council for having lax influence over his wife. Two years later, he'd married wife two and gone.

Stephen loved his father, and longed for him to come. Ada said the weekend visits lasted until the boy was eight. Then William Nuttall laid his hands on Stephen to baptize and bless him and, having fixed the boy firmly in the Lord's great plan,

Brother Nuttall walked out on him and Ada for good.

This set an echo in me, this loss of a parent when you had no say. I asked Ada how Stephen took it. Not a second to think on it, she said, "Stephen stepped up and took his father's place." Which awed me. He'd raised his mother's livestock, kept the horses groomed and fed. At twelve, he rode herd for the First Ward, and by fourteen, he owned his own mount. Then Stephen hired on with sheepherders out of Malad—roaming and earning his way. My admiration became pure envy, hearing this. He'd slipped the reins of the Church as easy as a wet dog shakes off a river. Stephen had seen Idaho and Montana and the near corner of Wyoming. He came and he went as he pleased. Every Christmas, he would ride home to visit his mother, cut her a tree up Box Elder Canyon, light the candles on the high branches. He sang her "Silent Night."

I called Ada's photograph "Love at Home" after the Mormon hymn. How splendid that a mother and son could be so close. I never told Ada, but I hoped that I might meet him one day. Felt that we might share some things. At very least, a love for Ada. I never told her. I never did.

Late one summer day, Brother Stocks came to my cabin. His body blocked the doorway. He stood looking in at me with his good arm cradling his bad. His chest was immense, his body full of power but for the little twisted hand within his rolled up cuff.

"Brother Stocks," I said.

He weaved a little on his feet.

I gripped the broom I held. It was day, but daylight offered no protection. My screams for help would reach no one.

"You sew them garments?" he asked.

"Yes I do. For the Co-op. Bishop Dees called me to it."

He turned away. Greasy cowlicks covered his head. He swiped his nose at his shoulder and looked back. "I need me some."

"They carry sizes at the Co-op—"

"None of them sizes fit." He jerked his hand away, letting the short arm swing free. The flash of anger told me how often his crippled right hand had failed him, how, day after day, it had beggared hard work and the religion of success.

I eased the broom behind me, out of his reach.

Brother Stocks inhaled. Then he heaved all his breath out. "Ain't no one could fit this accursed body—" In two strides, he quit the door.

"Brother Stocks," I called. He turned in the yard. "If you would step inside, it'll just take a measurement or two."

I moved around him, measuring chest and shoulders and both arms, though I had only to measure the shorter one where the child-sized hand bent sharply in, blush pink. The narrow fingers fit together like the claws of a bird. I gazed at the hand, at its absolute softness. I thought to touch it—the hand that never ripped a plank or drove a nail.

I promised to deliver three pairs of custom garments to the Co-op wrapped in brown paper. The Brother left as quickly as he'd come. For days, I thought about his hand, the one without a claim to worldly successes. I doubted Brother Stocks loved it. He had cradled it, but not tenderly. Perhaps at night, when its inconvenience faded, and he let go the looks of others, let go his bitterness at being made differ-ent, maybe then the hand became an ally, a dear friend, sign of the freedom of the heart to wonder, only to wonder, *stay gentle, stay small.*

The Prophet Brigham Young decided to extend his Central Line north from Brigham City to Fort Hall, Idaho. His new Utah and Northern Rail would connect Zion to the sheep and cattle lands of Idaho, and eventually reach up to the rich mines in Montana. Mormon goods and Mormon crops could flow out to those settlements, and Gentile cash could flow back down. In time, the Prophet hoped, a watery flood.

Ada asked to take me to the ground breaking ceremony. I tried to tell her how little love I had for human wonders, but Ada said I could bring a rock for company. A heavy one, the size of my addled head.

The night of August 26th, 1871, was clear, with a three-quarter moon, when I met her at the cemetery road for a ride down to the Barrens. Pocatello Jim hummed a tuneless tune in back. I climbed up, and he stood and did a little dance in the wagon. His legs pumped under him, his feet scattering hay, but no sign of life showed in his torso or his arms. The legs cavorted, then ran wild as Jim's eyes widened in mock terror: *Captive,* they said, *we are captive to the will of our lesser half!* I didn't know Shoshone, but Ada had taught me a little hand talk. I signed *attention-getter*, striking my open left hand with a few fingers from my right and waggling them at him. Jim shook his braids and covered his mouth, the cries of a three-year-old coming from behind his palm. I looked to Ada to interpret.

"Surprise," she said. "He's as surprised as you are, at the dancing feet."

I signed *good*, to give Jim leave to end the game. He slid into a pile and leaned back against the wagon, panting. His right hand lay flat on top of his left, chest-high, which was obvious: *I am just exhausted.*

"He's a silly cuss," I said, laughing, as Ada started the team.

"Point of pride, to his people. Shoshone don't reprimand with blows. It's humor keeps the tribe in line. A good dose of ridicule can strike deep."

"They don't visit like they used to when I was little. I remember the encampments out west of town. Singing and games, though the Widow Anderson never would let me get close enough to really see. Where have the Shoshone gone?" I looked at her closely. "Ada, where are Jim's kin? Why is he all alone here, working for you? I don't suppose we sent them out of this valley with 'a good dose of ridicule.'"

"It ain't safe anymore, Clair. White settlers hate 'em. Ranchers hate 'em. Even the Mormons lost patience with a people so wild. They've got a reservation, now. Most of Jim's people prefer to keep to their kind."

"That was the treaty they signed?"

"The treaty of Box Elder sealed it up tight, yes."

I gave Jim a drink of cider from Ada's old jug. You could not tell from his stern countenance if he ever felt lonely. Ada was indeed a powerful force, but could she replace a whole tribe?

We drove west through town. The Lombardy poplars shone like torches down Forest Street, silver with moonlight. At the bridge, the surface of the runoff ponds lay milky with stars.

Ada pulled off into the chaparral amid shouted directions. Wagons left and right, people everywhere. We stopped the team some distance from the rest and Jim hobbled the horses. "We'll meet you back here, Poker, after," Ada said. She and I merged into the crowd.

A bower had been built to frame the stage. A dozen choristers stood assembled. Brass instruments flashed with the light from passing lanterns. Brother Gradon, Florrie's father, sat at a small pump organ. The crowd was easily a thousand strong.

We lay a blanket in back and settled in as the horns blew their first notes, a high winding curve that seemed to be mapping loneliness. The channels of loneliness. The deep loneliness of Christ. In church, they said his death betided comfort, but I only ever felt sorrow. How he could stand to die misunderstood, one such as him. Where was the deep and abiding comfort in that?

The horns sharpened. The crowd stood to roar its greeting as two men mounted the stage, one thin, the other broad as a grist wheel, whose presence had been kept secret from us. Apostle Lorenzo Snow and the Prophet Brigham Young stood grinning at the crowd, happy as little boys holding striped lizards.

The shock of recognition, the burst of pleasure from the assembly more than gratified the Prophet—it deified him. He looked out, waved his fist and the brass horns played their last.

The Apostle offered the opening prayer. Then Brother Gradon struck the first notes from his organ for the opening hymn. It sounded like no hymn had, ever. The chords reared up a wall of sound, as if the wood encasing the pipes must burst— but the wall was not to stay and the notes came down, friable as sandstone, as soft shale. Out of that grumble of dashed chords came the cry of two sopranos. *Alleluia! Alleluia, Praise and Glory to our God, for His judgments are true and just.*

The horns made answer, draping low, and the male choristers entered the song. *His judgments are true and just.* They stair-stepped up and down, taunting the women to try and stop them. Now Brother Gradon stood in front, conducting, while the horns mourned all of the world's dull unforgiving work, and the altos fled before them, lost, cold birds. *Glory to our God, Praise and Glory.* Brother Gradon flung himself, arms wide, down the length of song and the music, in answer, held him up. It held the crowd up, held us safe against gales of trouble and doubt. I wept at our good fortune, our sure inclusion, until I looked at them, at the blank faces, the babies lost to sleep gripping their mother's bosoms, and the plait of concern on the Apostle's brow as he watched Brigham Young lean heavily on an elbow, eyes scanning the heavens, his big boot tapping out its own time.

I watched that slow black boot until a different time-keeping caught my notice. Near the platform, Poker Jim moved to the music. He held his arms aloft like Brother Gradon, his hips crashing in arrhythmic waves. The children nearby hopped from leg to leg, clapping at Jim's crass enjoyment. I closed my eyes on all their silliness and their indifference. I left everything but the sound of the music, which soon ended as it had begun, with Brother Gradon at the organ, playing the chords down, gently down, like a mother singing, beautifully, to naught.

The crowd sat utterly silent. Ada took my shoulders. I leaned back and let her have my weight, heart open, eyes closed, while Brother Gradon and his players took their seats.

The Prophet walked to the lip of the stage. He stroked his beard with his great head cocked to one side. "You all of you know how much I love this city." His voice, soft as lambswool, soon rose in pitch and vigor discussing the Utah and Northern, his great Northern Rail. Labor and wagons, graders and gravel, none had escaped his concern. The Prophet laid it out for us, laid it plain as if the rails already rang before us with the heat of an oncoming train, and Brigham City stood enriched, the shops busy and all the tables fully laden.

I saw the Prophet's scene in my mind's eye, but something imminent scotched the vision. Below the platform, clutching a watch chain that did not hang from a vest he did not wear, Poker Jim stood, the spit image of the Prophet. When Brigham leaned, Jim leaned. When Brigham cocked one foot over the other, Poker beat him to it. And when the Prophet grew spirited—waving his arms, challenging the assembly to accept God's call as the architects and the builders of Zion— Jim slid in a paroxysm to and fro, his mouth about to retch, working around big, unsavory *O*'s.

I gripped Ada's hand, even before the Elders grabbed Jim and hauled him out of sight.

"Ada?"

No word from her, just a nod.

"Can't we go to him?"

Ada tightened her grip.

The Prophet stood with both arms raised. His massive hands could have stopped a flood or wrung a hundred necks as easily as given shelter. "In the name of the Lord Jesus Christ, I promise you, I guarantee it: any family willing to take up this great task and give labor and wares to the completion of the Utah and Northern Rail, I say all of those families will rise up whole in the Last Days and be greeted by the Prophet Joseph Smith himself. There will be feasting. Yea, you will feast with our first and beloved Prophet Joseph in the flesh, in the presence of the Lord our God, eternally."

I strained to hear what might be happening to Jim. I wished myself beside him. I wished I had my gun.

Brigham palmed a slab of hair off his forehead, and pointed into the crowd. "Those of you who lack faith, I say if you lack faith of your own, take mine. Take mine!" He smiled and his mane shook as he slapped his silk jacquard vest. "I am all the God and all the scripture you will ever need."

I nodded full agreement. I'd had enough of all four—

faith, God, Brigham and scripture. Ada grabbed my skirts and yanked me down as I leapt up to find Jim.

Apostle Snow came to Brigham's side, face of triumph, face of relief. "A plow and scraper with oxen await the Prophet's signal to begin. Let us proceed to the site behind us and watch the earth be moved!" Crack of guns, Brigham threw an arm around the Apostle, and he waved the Saints to their feet.

The audience broke in two streams, right and left of the stage. I cut a quick line through the body of the crowd, careful to dodge the picks and shovels, then cut back behind the stage. No sign of Jim, no sign of the men who'd taken him. Just streams of happy, ambling folk.

I shoved a tarp up and called his name.

Ada stopped me, all terse common sense. "Remember? Remember what I told him?"

I could not.

"Meet us at the wagon. Short of death, I'd say Jim's there."

We covered the distance in darkness. So many wagons had pulled in, I would have searched all night, but Ada led us right to it, the horses still hobbled and no one about.

Cannon fire launched me against the spokes of the front wheel. Wood tore my hands as the team lurched forward. Then bells filled the air, cow bells and dinner bells, and the school bell, a fractured ringing, far off and wild to mark the first strike of the shovels.

Ada called, "He's here."

A body lay in the shadows of the wagon bed. Ada asked could he move into the light. Grunting, Jim obliged. The blood from his mouth trailed down to his belt in a streak as wide as his face. One of his hands lay crooked and his legs seemed dead. He scooted on an elbow like an insect minus limbs. Though the sight of blood had always caved me in, I crawled into the back without a thought and placed my legs under, to support Jim's head.

Ada wiped his mouth. "Jaw's broke." Several teeth were missing wholesale, and his lips had swollen up. "Now Jim, what's the matter with your legs?"

He answered in Shoshone.

"They kicked you?"

"Ose."

"Tell it, how?"

He spoke so low, I worried for his life.

Ada said, "Punched him in the face, twisted his wrist in a knot. To finish, they kicked his buttocks till he could not walk nor stand."

I smoothed the hair from off his cheek.

His eyes turned up to me. "Namitse."

"Will he live?" I asked, frantic.

"He says, 'Sister.' Jim called you sister."

And I cried because at last it sounded right.

"You stay in back, keep his body from rolling. I'll drive us home and doctor him what I can."

Jim coughed. "Niyokottsi."

Ada bent down over him, her voice flat tired. "I know you was playing. Some folk cannot be played with."

He spoke again, coughing harder, resting his bent hand on my knee.

"'They do not laugh, the dead.' That's what Jim says. What the Shoshone say."

"He's going to die?" I was bawling.

"Jim'll live. He was talking about the dead who walk and preach."

CHAPTER 8

"Once in a while, and sometimes twice in a while, I think I'll leave." Ada stood at the window. She spread the curtains, and sunlight took the room. "But, honey dear, most times I feel like a spike well struck. Twenty years here, my boy grown in this house, my labor in those fields and my money so tied up in the streets and buildings of this town they verily call my name, though you'll never see a Nuttall Street or a Nuttall Square or a Park, not in a hundred years, that I know well and good. History falls to those who press their suits—and I don't mean wives with flat-irons."

I sipped some tea, the taste pleasing, bitter as cast iron. "But they almost killed Jim! The Prophet Brigham and the Elders regale us with pretty tales from the pulpit—but look behind the scenes and it's blood and broken bones."

"Poker knew the horse a danger, and couldn't resist the ride."

"Why do you call him Poker, Ada? He good at cards?"

"Jim pokes fun. And you know how good he is at that."

"The grand master."

"Well, Clair, most Saints don't have your appreciation of Jim's gift. Specially not when helped to laugh at themselves. So,

Jim's a poker, a red hot poker."

I could still feel the slack weight of Jim's legs dangling in my arms as Ada hauled him into the house over her shoulder. How many years had I felt as useless as those legs? "How is he?"

"More than some swole up today, but sleeping sound." Ada sat on the bed, exhausted. She had spent the night doctoring Jim, and still found the strength to fix me breakfast and bring it to me in bed. French toast and jam. Hot tea. A feather mattress and lace pillows. Storybook comforts, yet I had not slept and my mind held no dreaminess. The hope of justice kept me up all night, kept me wondering if it was ghost or real.

Men on earth delivered justice, and meted out punishment. Based on exactly what authority I longed to know, their inscrutable Father in Heaven? Who sent crippled hands and rapists and Indian raids to bless the chosen—

"Do you believe, Ada, that God is a man in the flesh like we are told? That we are made in His image, bone for bone?" It was a bedrock Mormon tenet.

Ada opened her eyes. "You mean is God a male, or is God flesh, which?"

"Both."

Ada blinked back a yawn. "What's your experience say?"

"My experience, men and flesh make a woeful combination."

Ada grinned and struck the quilt. "God is too big for a title, honey, much less a body, manly, fleshly, or of whatever sort."

"But last night Brigham Young said we could picnic with God. He said we would have a sit-down meal with the Lord and the Prophet Joseph Smith in the flesh."

"You quoting me the old Empire Builder?"

"The Prophet Brigham?"

"Oh, honey. Sure as there ever was one. Calls for a communal order here in Zion, but won't pay in himself. Says he'll throw his gains into the communal pot when he's met the man can manage his holdings better than himself. Calls polygamous marriage holy so he can take on fifty-some wives. Inspired the Brethren here in Brigham to grade and lay track for the Union Pacific, then the Central Line, now the Utah & Northern—every man hour and felled log and ox team given for free, in loving faith—while Brigham pockets the income from the Gentiles. Acquire and acquire and acquire, for the Lord! I stopped counting once he'd earned a million dollars. That was two years back. And you just watch how long it halts the completion of the Tabernacle. There won't be a man or a sledgehammer to spare in Brigham City for four years. Maybe five. You seen him, Clair. That man has the spiritual reach of a bent axle—and thinks God was made in his image." Ada sniffed and smoothed her skirt. "Bully and a businessman, those are Brigham's strengths."

She lifted her hair back off of her shoulder. She squinted, then pursed her lips. "You ever seen the layer of sheet ice forms over a puddle, blinding to look at if the sun strikes just right, and torn apart in a second at a child's footstep or a day's spring thaw?"

I thought I followed. "Yes, ma'am."

"Reflects the whole sky and crumbles at a touch? God is like that. Divinity is. It's everywhere. Question is, do we bother to see it or don't we?"

"So then . . ." I ventured, not sure if that meant man or flesh.

"My God comes and goes."

"Like sheet ice?"

"Try to round it up or snatch it for your own, it's gone."
She gave my mind awhile to move around in this. "All the
talk the Church has passed of 'white and delightsome' like
unto the Lord?" Ada snorted, leaning out over the edge of the
bed. "We are not white or delightsome, Clair. Not you or me.
We're speckled, like trout. Like spotted ponies. Herd dogs that
turn and circle the herd but know that they ain't sheep." She
laughed into her hand, wiped her mouth dry. "You think God
don't require all of creation? You think God picks and chooses?
Herd dog, pinto pony, trout or Indian or Saint, the Shoshone
worship God in all of 'em. Jim does. I do too."

Ada looked almost pretty sitting there, utterly still, bal-
anced on her high thoughts.

"But what'll Poker Jim do now, Ada? He won't be welcome
here in town."

"Once he can sit a horse, he aims to join Chief Pocatello's
band. A few ride down from the Fort Hall Reservation to trade
skins every autumn. Shoshone keep their horses at a camp on
Bear River. Jim can find them, if they come. It's a sorry rem-
nant of their wide-wandering life. Used to catch small game
here in Brigham in spring, then harvest summer camas root in
Idaho, meet up with all their friends to play games and knock
down pinyon nuts in the autumn over north and west of the
Raft River Range, enough to feed the entire tribe. Then Jim's
own band would circle back north of us here, to Honeyville—
yes, where you was found as a girl child—camp at the hot
springs, rest and play awhile before they headed off to winter
in Montana where game's aplenty, whitetail deer and grouse
and sage hens. Sleep in their buffalo robes. It raised a stripe of
envy in me, the way Jim told about it."

"You make it sound rich."

"It was rich. The Shoshone lived a thousand-mile round."

"But I heard the Indians eat locusts. That's what I heard, them digging up larvas from the dirt."

"Them and John the Baptist," Ada shot back. "You're talking Goshutes, not Shoshone, honey. The Goshutes live south of the Lake, south and west, in the desert. In a drought summer, if the jackrabbit and antelope and pocket gophers fail them, if they no longer can gather pinyon from the hills and cast seed at the mouths of the rivers, like the rich mouth of this river here we live at—"

"They'll eat grubs."

"Yes, ma'am. We ate a few thousand ourselves, years one and two in this valley. The Goshute women showed us how to make 'em palatable by slow roasting over a fire. And the similarities don't stop there. The Goshute elders heal by a laying on of hands, just like our Elders do, and gain powers by visionary dreams. The best of their hunters even take on plural wives! Joe Smith and the Goshutes." Ada chuckled. "Course they're nomads, where we like to settle. Biggest difference I account, their ways to ours, is that their women own the seed harvest. Flat ownership of what sustains the tribe."

I pulled my knees up within her borrowed nightdress. The neck lay open and unlaced. After the night's trouble, I hadn't wanted to be bound, not even by silk strings. Seeing me stir, Ada invited me to stay on for dinner.

"I have to get on home to Swede, Ada, he'll be pacing. Those men who beat on Poker last night. Will you try to get justice?"

Ada sagged forward. "Jim's leaving. No one would step forward. Like as always, the entire mess would be laid to me."

"Can that be Ada, the fearsome Ada Nuttall talking?"

"That's preservation talking. My way of thinking, you couldn't have better neighbors than the Saints to keep a town sleepy and green. But as rulers of the roost, as patriarchs? Lord preserve us, they're a worrisome lot."

I slid my feet from the covers to the floor. "I'll say good-bye to Jim, my way out."

"Don't take fright," Ada said without turning. "Both his eyes are swollen shut."

Since my arrival in the Second Ward, Homer Tingey had been kind enough to give me a ride to church with his family on Sundays. I walked downhill to their place every Sabbath, and shared the back of his wagon morning and evening with his six children, and shared their bench in church. The Sunday morning after Jim's ordeal, I went to the Tingeys' one hour late to leave a note saying that I was ill and wouldn't be attending evening service. I needed a break from righteousness. I could not stomach the thought of hearing a single word of praise for the Prophet. Let them sing without the organ. Let them walk blindfolded through the brute force of their own survival.

Homer's middle daughter, Lavina Tingey, saw me through the curtains. Red hair in a tumble and her nightgown on, she stepped out on the porch and read my note. "I am not going either," she said, smiling. She could hardly have been happier. Lavina was fourteen and freckled, sweet as the cooked meat of a pumpkin. Homer called her Angel Bright. I believed he'd hit the truth.

"You know Brother Wrighton, who teaches my Sunday School class," she said. I nodded, having survived a year of Wrighton's unsmiling sermons. "Brother Wrighton laid a trail of breath last week telling us about God's holy body. Well, I just had to ask, 'If God has a body of flesh, how come we can't see Him?'"

"Lavina, you didn't—"

"He colored some, saying if I prayed for the spirit of submission, understanding would come clear as a photograph that God has a body. 'Well then, if our Father has a body,' I said, 'seems like our Mother would, too. Is she pretty?'" And Brother Wrighton just slung open the door and howled, 'Leave us, leave this minute! Mother in Heaven can't be named and you ought not even to think on her, it's a sacrilege. Leave and don't come back until you have more faith.'" Lavina stepped off the porch barefooted. She plucked and twirled a morning glory bloom into her hair. "Faith can't be asked for, Clair. It has to be gained. I aim to spend my Sabbath in the garden, taking the Lord at His best. I feel closest to God in the garden."

She was so earnest, so silly sweet, I could only ask, "What does your pa say about it, Lavina?"

"Pa says, 'Hold to the wheel! Hold to the wheel, young lady, and you will be up half the time—'" She gripped the lowest limb of the cherry tree shading their walk, crossed her eyes and stuck out her tongue. "Do you really think, Clair, do you think that half the time's enough?"

"Lavina," I said, "I've held to that wheel all my life and only ever ate mud."

"Well, is there a Mother in Heaven, you think?"

My breath stopped. I'd waited eighteen years to hear that question. I'd sat beside Lavina in countless Sacrament Meetings and never once suspected she felt the same as me. I quieted my heart. "If there's a Father, there must be a Mother—"

"She wears maroon laces. And has powder white hair. And she has twelve lovely daughters!"

"Twelve daughters," I said, caught in Lavina's talespinning. "Each with a virtue all her own." We named them: Confidence. Love. Endurance. Intelligence. Curiosity. Ability. Wisdom. Truth.

"One daughter creates beauty," I said, "and sends it off for all to see. She is strong, so strong she never has to prove it."

"That's so, Clair. You see it deep. One daughter tends the earth," she said, wriggling her feet in the brown dirt. "She loves and tends to it like it was her child."

"There's a daughter of justice," I said. "And one who sees far. She sees the dead and tells their stories for them, and we listen and do right."

"That twelve?" she asked.

"Can't be. We didn't say joyous or funny."

"That's daughter thirteen!" she shouted, as she slipped an arm around my waist, walking me out to the plank across their irrigation ditch. When we reached the road, I said, "I have enjoyed our Sunday sermon, Sister."

Lavina answered, in all seriousness, "But there's one thing more. Would our Heavenly Mother's daughters ever marry?"

I took her hands. I shook them hard like the reins to an obstreperous horse. "If so, their husbands live in lean-to shacks, eat boardinghouse food, break rocks and wait on their dear wives' visits like a field awaits a freshening rain."

Lavina nodded and smiled. "Our Mother makes sure they don't ill-treat each other. You know how men can be, waiting on a good thing."

CHAPTER 9

Pocatello Jim rode out of our lives as if he'd never existed. No court, no trial, no justice. Only Ada and I grieved the loss. But justice had its chance to shine in Brigham City two weeks later. I overheard the Sisters at the Co-op tell it, how Lavina Tingey had been attacked in her orchard the previous night. Her father heard her cry and shot at the molester. Blood stained the cherry tree where Lavina had sat, dangling her legs, singing at the evening star.

At the trial, they blamed a young Gentile named Ron Carom, a hungry, bony boy been pushed to the side all of his life. His mother was a prostitute in Corinne. The Elder in charge of his defense couldn't get more than a whine out of him—the low unearthly whine that comes from a cornered animal.

His only defender was a girl of fifteen. She stood to testify in a woman's faded dress. The sleeves were torn. Her nipples poked like snouts at the cloth. "It ain't the truth, what's got told! Ron niver. Niver went out nights. I know him and his place. You none of you knows him." Her voice was thin as a fish knife. She looked at the accused, barked out her love. "He niver left home, niver been here, niver rode no wagon, how he's gonna get to Brigham and back home, acre miles of dark? That's the damn joke," her laugh came out spittle. She turned to Homer Tingey. "I seen you wants and needs it, Mister, your girl so fine, but Ron boy, Ronnie Carom ain't your kickin' stool."

One of the judges asked if she was related to Ron Carom. She said she was his "neighbor like," his half-sister. A voice rose from the Brethren. "Boy is trash. Born and lives with trash. Been tried in Corinne for thievery and mischief." It seemed to win the crowd, like the court had finally stumbled on what mattered.

Only one man saw it different. Daniel Dees' line of logic said a boy who lived thirteen miles distant with a history of petty thievery might not have been their culprit. This was a case of female molestation. And no bloody wound, to cinch it. Whose blood had stained that tree?

Homer Tingey kicked an empty chair. "Chickens, cherry trees or women! It's all the same. It is a crime, a crime against me and mine," he blared at Daniel.

The three judges prayed and conferred and found Ron Carom guilty. They had it on God's authority that this boy dared to attempt to drag a daughter of the Lord into darkness and foul sin. They had their man. And Homer Tingey had his justice.

But standing in the crowd of Elders after the verdict was read, Inger Olsen cradled a bandaged hand. When the Brethren started down the center aisle, talking of crop blight and the quick thrift that came from the planting of living fences, Inger slipped from their ranks and headed for the side aisle to take his leave. I never had borne my testimony. Never stood to say what I knew beyond a shadow of a doubt. I stood then. I moved to meet him. Mouth to navel like a slow boil of molasses and my bowels set against gale winds, I took that aisle.

Inger walked toward me with a look that said I never had existed on God's green earth, and never would.

"Cut it off," I said.

He made to keep right on.

"Your right hand knows what your left hand did, cut it off!"

Evil flashed in his snap-shut sunny countenance. He dipped a shoulder, to pass by. Though it cost me, touching him, I slapped his bound hand twice. Once for Lavina and once for me. Half a grunt, he pulled it in close, loping down the aisle and out the double doors, as free as his taste for sinning.

I faced the empty judging table, my body filling with rage. Always the warning that men were beasts, always the words, passed off as truth, that a man had "inborn" animal needs and he would have them filled, women and children take care. Yet these same men were our protectors, men who admitted they were beasts, men ruling over, trying other men for crimes they all expected—who worshipped a God of flesh and claimed His power, then slept satisfied at night, having given fair warning.

I stayed until the courtroom had emptied and the sun lost its heat. Three Elders had prayed and taken God's counsel and found the wrong boy guilty. How many mistakes had been sanctified by prayer and passed on as holy Gospel? I gazed straight into the image of this God—cruel, selfish, blind—a Lord who hated Gentiles more than falsehood, and held His daughters in even less regard.

I never entered a Wardhouse again.

Bishop Dees wasn't long in noting my absence. One of his boys came up to deliver the message on Monday. "Seven o'clock would suit." And so I was called back to his parlor, this time, I knew, for a Bishop's Court. Chastisement and disfellowship were certain, that or excommunication, my express trip to the damned.

I showed up on his doorstep at sunset, a sour apology of a woman. Sour and unwashed from wood-splitting, and just starting to feel mean. His first wife, Evelyn, came to the door.

She paled at sight of me.

She opened the screen door wide and winced at its creaking. "Father says he'll fix that hinge one day. It's a good thing we have the Hereafter." Her dress was the orange of a summer dusk when the air had been still for days. She'd fastened teardrop lace at the neckline, and thin lace borders at the sleeves.

I stepped inside.

A tall, angular woman stood in the foyer. She was someone's wife, someone's mother, but the thread of recognition wouldn't quite pull out and through.

"Vere, have you met Sister Martin? Clair, this is Vere Dees." Daniel's second wife took sharp stock of me—my old work dress unbelted, no apron or sash, the day's sweat wetting my hair to the scalp—and grinned, thin as a razor strop, her mouth that long and sloping taut.

"You must have worked beyond your strength, today," Evelyn said. "Would you like to freshen at the basin?"

"Oh, yes—" I said. Anything, to leave that hallway.

She offered me a daughter's room. A small room with a narrow child's bed, neatly tucked. A row of identical cloth dolls lined the window sill. Knots for eyes. Collars of lace. I could have cried the way their arms dangled down—the hands, the empty hands.

When I entered the parlor—cool air where the water ran down under my breasts and clung—the family rose, Bishop Dees, with his moustache oiled to blade points, and a wife on either side. I couldn't believe that my gape-empty soul would be exposed, my faults read out in front of them. I thought to bolt, but Daniel held out the remaining chair for me.

The table was set with cake and checkers and tumblers of cider. Strange as truth, I could not guess their next move.

"End of a workday. Company picks," the Bishop said.

Two checkers lay in his open hand. I could only stare, red or black, quite lost, till Evelyn Dees spoke up. "Daniel, she may not know the game. Clair and I will play team, to make a start."

I managed to sit still as the game progressed. With my fearful thoughts and my hot arms to keep pressed close, it only came clear, middle of game three, that this was the full intent and import of the night, this checkers playing and sipping at drinks, the little jokes slipped quietly in by Daniel Dees or one of his two wives.

I could see the Sisters had swallowed the pill of sharing him long since, and ridden out its attendant fevers. Still, I sensed great cost. Neither dared to claim her husband for her own more than a moment, in talk, in service to him, or in passing glances. Any other girl, visiting their home, would have admired the domestic ease which played out among the three, best faces forward, through the waning night. I could not. It seemed a house of tight elaborate moves, all propriety and polish. Though I'd never had a family, I didn't long for this. I longed for what was rough, still partly hewn. I had never shared my heart, but when I did was there a parlor wild enough?

Daniel's wives stood and excused themselves to round the children up for bedtime. He smiled. "Shall you be red, or would you like to see if black checks raise your luck?"

I did not share his ease. I said, "I dare not take the hill full darkness, Bishop. I will also say good night. And thank you."

"Wait," he said, pushing up from the table.

A match struck in my throat—the eyes of the Bishop,

green flecked with gold, dark golden-brown, and his lashes
short and thick—it startled me, then fell and lit my thighs: his
eyes, his chest, the length of his arms. Burning for him there in
his own front room, I wanted to run my wretched self—

But Daniel had come back. He carried folds of hand-
woven wool over his arm, a beautiful blue plaid Tartan cloth.
"This is from Evelyn and Vere, a gift. Now, if you'd like, I'll
walk you home."

I felt that I might suffocate. I felt my indrawn breath
might never let go.

We walked the dry-packed road together, side by side, my
heart starting up at every lighted house we passed. We did not
talk, not once, which made the night seem closer, blacker. The
shock of the Bishop's hands almost drowned me, his hands on
my face at my cabin door. And the question—only he never
framed it into such, but only said, "Think on it. My wives
would welcome you."

"Your wives!" Seed cones. Burst milkweed spreading on
celestial winds. It was a woman's final glory in Heaven, to
spread the seed of God. Daniel kissed my forehead. I leaned
into him, dangerously.

"You said to wait, another call—"

He shuddered, kissing my hair. "None is as high as this,"
and it seemed terrible and true until his hands released me.

"What if I'll not marry?" I said, thrusting the cloth toward
him.

"Then you have the makings of a new dress, Sister," he
said, turning to go. "You of all women deserve it."

The Prophet Joseph Smith claimed that our Father in
Heaven was human, once, a human male who'd learned his lessons. And every male who joined the Mormon Church could

be a God and people his own world. But the peopling required a woman. These God-men needed their wives. Their faceless, nameless wives who did no deeds, acted no acts: the brood mares of eternity! I would not stay in a church which spoke for the exaltation of its men, but did not speak for women. I couldn't lend myself to such oblivion.

I told all this to Ada when she tried to blow any spark of chance that I might stay into a fire. I said I had no place in Zion.

She begged me to keep on at her cabin, rent-free.

"I won't attend their meetings, won't sew their silly garments. How long you think I would be let to stay?"

"I could set you up in Corinne, selling flower cards and playing organ at the Methodist church."

I frowned and said I'd consider it.

Ada smoothed her hands up her sleeves. She looked away. "And though he's asked for your hand, you will not have the Bishop? Do you love him? Do you love Dan Dees?"

"I endure a pain in my nether parts whenever I think on him. Is that love?"

Ada laughed a bit. She heaved a breath. "You're as ignorant as a scrub jay when it comes to love." Her eyes softened and her smile went slack. "Well, I can give you one choice more, Clair. Live with me here. Be mine. Eighteen years since Will and me made our home together. Eighteen years the heart longs, and meets with love. You'd come, well, frost my cake . . . "

I glanced at her well-appointed living room and blushed with shame. Six months hadn't dimmed the memory of Ada's kiss, the kiss that spilled me and my life like dirt from a barrow. "Are you asking—are you asking me to bring my flesh into this house? Are you? That what you're asking?"

Ada's face grew round, big with amazement. "I'd like to see you cross my threshold without it—now there'd be a wonder and a miracle! I am offering you my life, Clair, and the sharing of it, which includes my flesh if you need to particularize, to vulgarize it."

Ada loved me. This smart, affluent woman who could worship God in a mud puddle. I knew it and also knew that I would have to deny her. The force of Ada Nuttall's will would have pulled my life behind it like a box on a string. Every form of love I'd known seemed to call for oblivion.

Ada tossed her hair back and said, "You got a choice to make. Artist and a misfit—I guessed you wasn't long for this place. I saved against it. Twenty-three dollars and coins you've paid in rent for that dustbin cabin of mine. It's right here when you need it. It is yours."

The patterned wool rugs and Indian beadwork, the glossy carved tables I'd always admired, they could be mine. I looked at Ada, looked at her body—the body of a Mormon Saint, fat with successes—and hated her for it.

She took my hands in hers, blistered, hard, alike.

I could only say, "I'll go on home, think about it."

"There's one thing more you got to consider. Stay or go, Clair, you're the only one knows which boy is guilty. Guilty twice. You think Inger Olsen'll stop his lights, with a poke in the arm from a woman?"

I squirmed as Ada cleared her throat.

"Tell whoever, whosoever you think will listen, but tell somebody, honey. Only you can stop Inger's plundering greed, and save some other Sisters untold grief. You keep it to yourself, it's just a different kind of greed."

I sat on my trunk at the Brigham City station, watching yellow poplar leaves carry off like sparks from a fire onto the tracks. The young trees stood erect, for all their inner wavering. Their two by two march faltered at the station, where the trees spread out to form a simple line. No couples, just sentries for the oncoming trains.

A phrase of Ada's had surfaced and resurfaced in my mind, that only "a trip to New Orleans" could reveal more than she had learned about my parents. My mother had trekked eighteen hundred miles west to Brigham City to find a spiritual home. I would go south to New Orleans. To find my family, my real kin.

I had Ada's cash money in my pocket. Swede had a bed in her kitchen. My body still felt flush with the heat of Daniel Dees, his even eyes, his even, even ways. So that was the kindly touch of a man.

Still, Daniel Dees had his answer:

October 7, 1871

Dear Bishop,

Inger Olsen is the boy you want, the one who tried for Lavina. I know it. He tried for me. If you cannot believe me, examine the wound on his left hand.

I will not be marrying, nor staying.

Yours truly, Miss Clair Martin

Gulf

Mississippi Delta: 1871-1877

CHAPTER 10

A t first sight, New Orleans had all the charm of a rattlesnake—a snake flattened by a carriage and then smacked on the head with a shovel. I'd spent seven long days on a hot train tormented by a blue wool dress and passengers who escorted their sniggering children quickly by me. My face or my dress or both kept all but one female passenger from offering a moment's kindness. She stopped to ask politely where I was traveling to and from. As soon as the word "Utah" exited my lips her face contorted in disgust. She thought the Mormons horned or scaled, or devils in the flesh, and told me so with malice. After that, I kept my eyes turned to the windows, longing to see the familiar sights of home.

People of every shade swarmed the levee in the blinding October heat. The river stench stayed my hunger. The wide arms of the live oak tree I stood under quieted my nerves. The hot mayhem of the Mississippi River, loud with the curses of dockworkers and boat whistles, white bread frying and fish on display—if I had poked a hornet's nest, I could not have seen more activity. I felt no inner *yes* at having been born here. The sprawling softness frightened me, lush plants, thick air, old buildings, dirty streets. There were no contours, not a mountain or a hill to guide me, nothing but a sluggish bend of hazel brown river and oak trees the size of tabernacles. I told myself it may only have been a stopping spot for my parents, not a home. I had to hope they had stopped long enough to leave tracks.

A barge flowed up the Mississippi without ripples, its progress was that slow. My father's profession, and my only clue. Courage I did not have in a city so large its bounds defied the human gaze! I leaned into that oak tree, praying to nothing and no one for my survival. Then, crushed by the midday heat, I grabbed my bags, descended the levee, and entered the human stream.

Determination propelled me through a few hours' timid exploration downtown. I made inquiries at a hotel and two lodging houses. The prices seemed staggering. I ate a small bun, while tucked in the shade of an alleyway. This helped arrange my thoughts. As the businessmen ambled by, pleasantly occupied with their lives, I thought, *they are right: earnings before expenditures.* I would search for employment, first. I could sew. I could tally numbers. I could tend children if I had to, though I doubted they'd welcome me such as I was.

And therein lay the problem. That and forty pounds of luggage in a hundred degree heat. I left the grandeur of Canal Street, stopping at corners to shift my valise and satchel. The first shop I dared enter, a small dim sliver of a place, the dressmaker only glared and pulled her lapwork closer when I asked for work. It raised my ire. I told myself hers was the loss, not mine, as I entered the next shop. The manager of this children's mercantile stopped me with a "no" before I'd uttered one word. Whatever I wanted, he would have none of it. I fled the store, slamming into the wiry frame of a gentleman bent on passing.

He seemed intent to keep right on until he caught sight of my face. Then his skinny neck lengthened, his eyes snapped open and he smiled.

No one had ever responded to my face with spontaneous pleasure.

"Audwin Fife," he said, offering his hand, which seemed all ligament and bone. His mop of yellow curls looked like the dolls in the store I had just exited, their frames moved by strings, their features painted delicately in. But first impressions belie us. If there ever was a man who moved independently, it was Audwin Fife.

"Clair Martin," I said, introducing myself.

"Staff microscopist at Baruch Place," he said. "At your service."

"I've heard of Baptists and Methodists, sir, but never My Crosscopists."

This pleased Audwin Fife more than my face had. He doubled over in a laugh. Baruch Place Hospital, he said, served the sick and the indigent. He studied their sicknesses under a lens. "What of you? By your dress I'd say you've seen the far side of Nebraska."

"Utah—" Too late, I let it slip.

"Ah, you've done some settling, some homesteading? Putting this 'fragile female' lie to rest?"

The easy flow of his words disarmed me, like hail pounding a new crop down. I told him I had just arrived. He looked at my face intently down his long nose. "On the train," I said, to fill the gap. Still he said nothing, gazing at my cheek with rapt attention. Twice my age, with a frayed jacket and dirty lapels, I saw that "gentleman" overstated his circumstance. Still, being hot and tired and soundly defeated, I wondered if I might trust him to suggest a night's lodging place. I weighed the wisdom of asking this of a stranger, when Audwin Fife said, "Come to Baruch Place!" with such force, I believed for a moment he'd read my mind. "When you have the time. If you do, it's the old gray fortress off Esplanade Avenue." Then he warned me, in friendly tones, that I should keep my wits about me and my belongings close—neither the Faubourg Marigny nor the levee were safe for a woman alone, though the French Quarter in daytime would be. He wished me well and strode off.

The power of one act of kindness to offset a hundred slights! The microscopist's interest gave me hope. Perhaps the Mormons and every one I'd ever met were wrong. *Kindness rules this world* flowed through my body like a pulse, as I my made way up Esplanade Avenue to the gray stone face of Baruch Place.

Baruch Place Hospital had more doors than any building I had ever seen. More doors and fewer windows. The frightening clang of the matron's long keys in the latch. "You are a Christian, miss?" she asked at our interview that afternoon.

"I always have been," I said. And it was true. In the past, I had been Christian.

"You sew und iron?"

"Yes."

Her eyes moved, fast, black and unreadable in her enormous face. "The marking of your cheek, you have had it since birth?"

I stilled my heart. I hoped this would not ruin my chances. "Yes, ma'am."

She laid a hand on my face, turning it side to side as if inspecting fruit for spoilage, tracking the edges of my stain from the base of my left ear out across my cheekbone, curving around my mouth and down my jaw onto my neck. Then Frau

Schnell pressed her palm to my forehead and drew it back, satisfied.

She sat, and the chair beneath her yelped in protest. "You are of virtue? A virtuous girl?"

I blushed. It was enough for her.

"Und nikgers?" Frau Schnell asked.

She could paw my face, but my underclothes were none of her business.

"Nikgers, the dark ones, black of skins. You will wash for them?"

I'd seen throngs of them in Jackson Square. I'd passed them on my way to the hospital, tending goats in the weedy strip up Esplanade Avenue, vending cooked meats. Without staring, I tried to understand the colorings of their skin. Black to brown to robust tan. The women bound their hair from sight with wrapping cloths. None of them paid me the slightest attention. I passed invisibly through their world, which seemed to me preferable to the slights and insults from my own kind.

"Yes, ma'am, if they won't mind me."

"Unh, girly. Curious child." The matron shook her head in disbelief. "Robert will fetch your trunk from the station, now come to see your rooms und start the day."

We climbed the central staircase, all four flights. The nikger ward was housed in the attic along with the killing October heat. The supine bodies and the roving hot bodies of dark children—I didn't see how any of them could breathe much less heal and recover. Loading a pile of soiled sheets on my hip, I followed Frau Schnell out. I felt pure gratitude descending the stairs, stairs that never knew sunlight, stairs that trapped the smell of blood and cleanser and decay.

It was several degrees cooler in the first floor laundry. Two vats, a stool, a coal iron and plank table stood waiting for me.

The room was no bigger than a root cellar, piled with stained bandages and bedding in various shades of gray. I worked alone, as my laundry was *Niemals! Never!* to be mixed with the laundry of white patients. I washed and ironed the pile down by one third and sorted the rest for soaking.

I spoke to no one, that first day, gained only a few sharp glances, until at last I opened the door to my bedroom, which lay under the diagonal of the central stairs.

A man stood over my trunk. Black, tall, lean of leg, intensely muscular, he turned and rose to his full height at sight of my face. His gaze intensified and he puffed out a breath. I felt every inch accused, struck silent and without defenses.

"The erysep," he whispered.

I thought to back out of the room but his eyes locked my body in place. Then, strangest of all in this strange city, he extended his arm and touched a fingertip to my cheek. To my forehead. I suppose I should have fainted from terror or shouted down the hall for Frau Schnell to rescue me. But the man said, quietly, "Ain't warm," and I saw the relief in his penetrating eyes. "Ain't the erysep."

With that, he left the room and climbed the central stairs.

I had to wonder at my frozen will. I'd stood like a sacrificial lamb before one who might have come to slaughter. Or to steal from me. Or Heaven knew what.

I checked my trunk. All was present. I heard his footsteps turn and turn again up each of the four landings above me. That ended my first day at Baruch Place. My night was a tangle of dreams.

The stroke of a woman's finger on my cheek drew me out of sleep. It was tender as a mother's touch and thereby stranger than a slap. A second stroke across my temple drew my eyes open to the glitter of pins in fur, and breathing. I screamed and threw off my sheet. It jerked and rippled on the floor as three rats fled beneath it. When I clanged my cup on the night stand, the rats belly-crawled under the door. Holding the cool cup in the dark room under the central stairs at Baruch Place Hospital, I crouched on my cot until bells somewhere in the city tolled morning, and I rose to dress myself.

I tied rolled bandages under my chemise to soothe the raw flesh where my plaid traveling dress had chafed those seven long days on the train. I joined the staff for breakfast: white gravy on a biscuit as big as two fists. When I passed the central table, Frau Schnell gripped my arm. Shock sent my breakfast to the floor as she pulled herself upright. "This girl!" she called out, her fingers tightening on me, "she is not a fever case." Her voice silenced the nurses and laundresses. "Not erysipelas. No blisters here, no fever," she said.

Even the cooks stopped serving.

The man who had fled my room the previous night knelt with a pail at my feet, pushing gravy and broken bread into the pliant strands of his mop. Nausea swept my eyes outward, over the twenty and more faces caught up at sight of me.

"Not contagious!" the matron said as if to finish it once for all. She lowered herself to her place. "Have another plate, Miss Martin. Keeping healthy und strong."

I retraced my steps to the serving line as told, though the hatred of a lifetime reared up in me: hate for all who'd ever stared at me, more for those who'd shamed me publicly, hate for being ashamed, for being marked out different, for belonging nowhere on the earth—not where the "white and delightsome" prevailed.

Staring at the grain of the low table, I could not touch my food. How could stone digest stone? How could I become still more immovable, unmoved until my heart flared at nothing, not even hate, became brittle as fired clay, empty as a darkened lamp?

"Napkin, Missy." A strong hand placed a cloth on the table and tapped it. "You'll might needs it." The steward's eyes caught mine. No expression there. No warmth. He simply nodded and turned, lifting his bucket and mop.

As steward of the colored ward, Robert Durham saw to all our needs. My first need was educating. "Nikger" was far too heavy a word for me to carry, so he suggested I use "colored" instead.

Now, I had never worked a day in a hospital. I had no cause to wonder at Robert's techniques. When the steward held his patients in his arms while I stripped sheets, it only seemed natural. I came to call this above-bed journey the laying on of hands, though it was different than the Mormons ever did it. Very tall, very steady, Robert cradled his patients in his arms and sang to them. Like full-grown babies. And the singing that came from him in bursts and slides, *Oh, the way to Heaven is a good old way*! His deep voice smoothed our way through the troubles of the day. The attic ward had the feel of an encampment, imperiled but sound, under Robert's care.

When the staff physicians came to do their rounds, they razed all pleasure. I kept the left side of my face toward the wall and kept my movements simple, hoping the two young doctors had ills enough to see to in the ward.

"Blood of bitches, steward, what have you done with Number Eight?"

Robert stopped singing.

"Well?" The little doctor's mouth crimped.

"Jule Ravenel?" Robert said. "He give leg bond, sir."

"He what?"

Robert shifted the patient higher on his chest, saying in the same even tone, "Jule up and elope, Doctor Hackett, sir."

Hackett frowned, then tore the chart he held down the middle and let it flutter to the floor. "One less nigger to waste our combined attentions on," he said to his colleague. "What do you make of Fourteen?"

"Botched suicide. Tried to choke himself with a handkerchief last night. Son of a bitch lost his personals in a bar fight."

"The mind of a child, the crotch of a eunuch and the body of a twelve point buck!" Hackett laughed.

I whispered when I had to speak—*Finished now* or *Bed ten next*—wishing myself sightless and mindless and all of the Baruch Place patients already recovered or dead. I managed to endure the doctors' bitter progress until a wrenching wail from under one of the windows turned me full around.

"They's mine! Every one! I's free and they's mine." Anchored in bed by a leg cast, a small boy could only strike out with his hands as the physicians swept the leaves he was hoarding onto the floor. His fist caught Hackett on the ear.

"You insolent moke!" The doctor slapped him. "Litter and insolence! Sit still or expect the strap."

The patient did sit still, but howling all the while, as the doctor twisted his leg right and left at the ankle, right and left till I thought I would scream. Robert loomed behind them, just to one side where the boy could see him, with his hands cocked at his back. I fancied he could take both doctors out with one fist.

"Who set this splint?" Hackett asked.

"I've never seen the little shit—"

"I sets the colored splints," Robert said.

Hackett tilted his head, as if listening for mice in the rafters. He stepped away. "It is excellent. Sweep the floor at once. And get this charcoal nigger up and pushing a mop before bedsores start to form."

The boy's cries renewed as the doctors descended the stairs.

"You know better, better'n to cross them doctor men," Robert said, his voice white-hot.

"They's mine!" The boy wailed, his cast the only stationary object on the cot. "I is free, and I don't take no foolishment off white folks, just like you say, Robear."

Robert stepped toward him. At the sound of crushed leaves underfoot, sobs racked the child again. "It ain't fair!"

"I'll brings you more magnolia leaves," Robert said, but it brought the boy no comfort. "I see'd a cassia bush just coming to blossom. Yellow like the stripes on a bee. Yellower'n Old Buck's tail at sunset. Yellow of a new squash blossom. I'll brings you some."

The boy flung an arm over his face. "It ain't fair! It ain't!" His raging did not stop. Robert shook his head and went to get the broom. Still, the child wrangled out his woes to the inner reaches of that elbow. The insults didn't slacken or the crying cease.

I walked to the head of his cot, where he couldn't see the stain up my left cheek. I watched a moment. "Is your leg bothering you?"

The nodding of the elbow said it was.

"Well, let's see if we can't change that." I put my hands on the boy's shoulders and spoke into his ear. "I want you to get comfortable, now. Find a better position for that cast."

He blinked, his short lashes crimped fan-like over the lids. A thread of mucous, nose to lip, glistened against his dark skin. And though he hadn't moved his leg a bit, I said, "Now, that looks fine, are you sure it's better?"

His eyes closed, concentrating.

"Yes. I think that might be just right." And before I'd lifted my hands, the boy was asleep.

I tiptoed up to the colored ward that night to see for myself if the boy felt better after his tangle with the doctors. I'd never been to the attic after dark. Robert read aloud from a newspaper. The boy lay propped on his elbows, taking in Robert's every word. I couldn't tell from the stairwell if he was smiling. When I stepped in to see, two arms fastened themselves around my calf with the force of a gale.

A child laid her face against my knee. "Mina."

I tried to step back.

"Mina, mina, mina, min," she sang, louder.

I shook my leg, but the fierce little toddler had both feet on my shoe and rode the shaking.

"Why, it look like Delia got herself a pony," Robert said, not overloud. "You like to ride her on in, Missy?"

I had no choice. I clomped the child past cots and sleeping patients, my heart pounding, past bedpans covered with rags, clomped up to the group gathered near the window and stopped.

My passenger did not relent. She sang a few more *mina mins*. Robert gave his chair to us, saying, "Let her ride a spell," and he sat on the boy's cot.

The two men playing dominoes stared.

The boy pointed at me with a seesaw laugh. "She splint-legged, like I is! Only my cast, it'll be come off soon."

Robert guffawed, once and deep, and the rest of them joined in. The child had sucked a wet spot through my dress at the knee, the fabric balled in her fists. "Hold on, child," I said, then crossed one leg over the other and rocked her, bobbing my foot.

"This here's Bug and Dilly, at the bones." One of them

nodded, a domino in his hand. "You got Delia at your knee, and I believes you and the boy done met."

"I never," he said with sass. "My name's Tierre. Tierre Durham. I'm nine years goin' on ten, and that's a'most a man."

"Is that so, Pierre?" I said. He was so skinny, I doubted manhood might ever find him.

"Pee-air? Pee-air! I ain't no Pee-air. This girl got a brain, you think?"

"Don't be smart-alecky with Miz Martin, T," Robert said, "she'll hide the snake in your new-launderied pants."

Tierre's eyes flickered with alarm. "She never would." Then he grinned, sinking me with the weight of ready charm in his eyes.

That night, I tried but could not tell it in my letter to Ada, how I'd been blessed. In a world of so little love, and less belonging, I had found T.

CHAPTER 11

At supper two weeks later, sitting alone as I always did, I looked up into the hands and plate and the rust plaid vest of Audwin Fife. "Yes, then. How does the evening find you, Miss Martine?" He dropped himself across the table from me.

I could not find my voice. Doctors ate in the dining hall, with china and old lace.

"Hellish stew they've fed you girls, tonight. Some species of yam mash?" He bent over my bowl and a wicked smell, the smell of oil left too long to sear in a hot pan, came with him. Smell of a bachelor. "Eegods. Have some of my drum—" He shoved a portion of gray fish toward me, with gray rice clinging to its sides. "No, perhaps not. Swill is swill, from the doctor's table or the drudge's."

Audwin smiled, immune to the whispering from the other tables. "It is all right, my joining you, Miss Martine. I am a eunuch's eunuch to all of them." He stuffed a large bean into his mouth.

Uneasy at the stares of the others, I fixed my eyes on his face.

"You've taken employment here?" he asked.

I nodded *yes*. The thought pleased him, as did the bean, minus a fibrous string he drew from between his lips. Audwin wiped his hand on his lapel, darkened from use. "And how do you find our fair city?"

Frightful wouldn't be kind, to the city or my parents. I stuck to facts instead. "I shop the French Market, Sundays. And I watch boats on the levee—"

His fork stopped, the tines pointed at my chin. An accusation was coming, so I said rather loudly, "I have a pass, a Sunday pass, and I don't much take to preaching."

But Audwin Fife cared nothing for churchgoing. "Pox and feathers, woman, the levee? Haven't I warned you?"

I explained that my one hope of finding kin, my only method thus far, was studying the faces of every boatman and dockhand to find a likeness to my father, Tucker Martin. Not that I knew his face. So I watched for any likeness to my own.

"Martin, you say, not Martine?"

I nodded gratefully.

"And you go to the levee to watch the crews of the flatboats and the steamers?"

I nodded.

"On your own?"

"I do."

"On the levee—"

"Yes."

Air moved in and out his long nose. "To find kin?"

I nodded again.

"And you don't like preaching on Sunday."

My voice dropped. "Sunday or any day."

"Bordellos, drunks and thieves!" he said, narrowing his eyes. I waited, my stew cooling under a thick oil scum. The stares of the others made my skin creep. Surely they couldn't believe I fancied the man, spindly as a walking stick and nearly twenty years my elder.

"Well, we can improve your odds in the family hunt," he said. "I have an idea or two."

"Really, Doctor Fife. Could you help me?" I said, as this particularly kind walking stick became my ally.

"It's Audwin," he said, eyes alight. "Please, call me Aud."

Odd he was, but I wouldn't have liked to say it.

"And I'll be escorting you to the levee, Sundays. From now on."

Audwin Fife devoted part of his Sundays to the task of ferrying me through the crowds at the levee searching for kin, though the futility of it was instantly apparent. He joked about a good many passersby, saying they had my moustache, my extreme overbite, my splayed feet and coal black skin. Drinking chicory coffee and laughing, he put my levee watch to shame. Giving focus to a far better search, Audwin sat me down with coffee and beignets, noted all the details I could muster about my family, wrote them in a tidy list, and at the bottom listed as well the agencies where I might trace my family's tree: the assessor's office, the courthouse, and the public library.

The thought of entering the doors of the tax assessor's or the county courthouse to make inquiries struck such a fear in me I drank two cups of coffee and did not sleep that night. The library seemed the better start. Libraries had books. I loved books. As it turns out, I did not also love librarians nor they me. If you are ignorant or appear so, if you are poor, if you smell of lye soap and your dress sags strangely from a hundred washings, educated people may not take to you. They may, in fact, scorn your approach, turn from your questions and whisper to the other staff members to flee the information desk, haughtily.

I stood in that hushed hall with street sounds echoing at the windows. A little flame of unfairness moved me from one set of aisles to the next, books indexed to the ceilings, patrons lost in page-turning thought, and Clair Martin as important as a dust mote. A brass sign near the door, as I exited, said *Patrons Only, Inquire About Fees.*

I cried in a short dry burst, walked out into the late sun drenching the corner of Iberville and Bourbon Streets, and bought my first beer from a street vendor. The beer was warm and exploded through my nose, streaking the one clean portion of my work dress. Merciful alleyways. I actually laughed into the insult, and formed an unswerving plan.

I would use that library. I would learn to drink warm beer.

Each work day, I took my basket of cleaned bandages up to the attic, to wind them with sunlight and company. The boy had a face worth gazing at. Being stuck in that leg cast, T was always there. On this late November day, with flies buzzing in slow loops near the windows, I thought to find out about Tierre's past.

"Where are you from, Tierre?"

"Tallest tree in God's orchard," he said, "I fell from off'n that."

"And you are Robert's son."

"Son a Robear? No, ma'am."

"His nephew? Your last name's Durham."

"Robear let me borrow it."

I smiled and chose to ask Robert later, about the loan of his surname. "Have you known Robert long?"

"Robear?" He stroked his pointed chin. "Since always, since he come back from the War."

"Oh? Which war was that?"

Tierre stopped scratching inside his cast. "You for real, lady girl? Robear kilt fourteen Yanks barehanded."

I thought on this, said, "He did?"

Tierre sniffed, then wrinkled his nose. "You never heared of Robear Durham in the War a'twixt the States?"

"Well, no. But I come from out West."

"Y'all ain't heared of the Civil War out there?"

I heated up at his chagrin. "I heard of it. I heard of the Civil War. It's just that it was all type and hearsay to us, being so far away. We heard that the nation would surely suffer and the States go down, drowning in bloodshed, and the country would be torn asunder." I trembled at the memory of Joseph Smith's prophetic curse—an entire country laid to waste for its persecution of the Mormon Saints.

Tierre nodded, solemnly. Church bells had been tolling steadily since morning, outside the streaked windows. Tierre asked, "Who you think done died today?"

"Well, I don't know."

"Old body butcher, he be glad," T whispered. "He cut off its arms to make for legs, and ears stitched on for mouths. He be swiping out its liver for a midnight meal—"

"Tierre!" I began to question all he'd said, his Rebs and Yanks and bloody wars. "What a nasty thing to—"

"Body butcher, he keep watch, night times, who be the next a'neath his blade. Who'll gets to it next?" T's fingers encircled my wrist. "Not me!" He yanked my hand. "Not me in that bukra butcher's hands!" My bandages spilled across the floor.

One stopped at Robert's shoe.

"But we ain't scared, heh. Me and Robear ain't scared of no puny bukra doc," Tierre said, grinning at his strong friend.

Robert stood there openhanded. He didn't stoop for the bandage, didn't answer T back. With a look in his eyes like water on fire, he said, "Lieutenant-governor Oscar Dunn, he dead."

Tierre slapped his bed as the tears spilled down his cheeks.

We had read all about Oscar Dunn in the newspaper, a colored politician, a fearless and powerful man. And a truthful one. He was second-in-command to the governor of the state. He fought for women's suffrage and colored civil rights, a gifted public speaker. So gifted, some said Dunn would become Vice President of the United States.

"Word is," Robert said, "them lily-white Democrats poisoned him. Lord save us. Our own Black Pericles . . . he dead."

Doctor Fife found me in the laundry the next day, and insisted I go with him to the funeral procession. When I protested, he said, "Didn't I say I'd show you the city?"

"You said the levee, on Sundays!" I poked at the clothes in the vat and drew up a sopping fistful to check for stains. He did not leave. "I didn't know Mr. Dunn, Doctor Fife, and I don't have leave to go out afternoons."

Audwin laughed. "Good God, haven't you rinsed enough mucous for the day? For the week, for all the coming years? We won't be missed, Clair. I know a back way out."

He led me down the street at a near trot. My skirts swung against my knees as I worked to keep up with him. A goat bleated and yanked at its short tether as its owner cuffed it on the head. Sun drenched the beleaguered trees on Esplanade. I took a deep breath. The confines of the world of my dim laundry room began to fade.

"This day, my dear, is a day not to be missed," the doctor said, and turned abruptly south. He talked as fast as he strode. "You have come to New Orleans, the death capitol of our newly-United States. Yellow Jack fever and cholera fill whole cemeteries at a stretch. But Oscar Dunn is the first colored man to hold executive office in the country. Even here, Dunn's is a death apart."

He dodged a sagging porch roof, swinging me out into the street. There were no yards here, side or front, and all of the buildings leaned off square. Truly, New Orleans seemed built on the proverbial sand. I thought I might show Audwin the Fisk Lending Library, to see what he made of the fee and my chances of ever finding kin there, but the good doctor turned west at Bienville, heading away from the river and Jackson Square.

"Where are we going?"

"I thought we'd have a better view—" he said as he rounded a final corner. "Oh, damn! They've beat us to it."

Hoop skirts and dress jackets, top hats, work jeans and shawls, babies in swaddling—even the third story porches swelled with people. I stopped in wonder.

"Damnation." Audwin sank into the crowd using his elbows and slight frame, pulling me along behind. The chase went on for blocks, grazing a hip here, a black bustle there, looming over children wedged between their parents, stepping around boots new and patched and held together with baling twine. I knocked into Audwin as he stood upright. The smell of rancid oil engulfed me.

"Excellent," he said, oblivious to his aroma and my blocked view. All I could see was the jacquard of a bald man's greatcoat. I made to lay my forehead against the middle of his broad back. Audwin grinned and burrowed back to a wall. He lifted me up onto a window ledge. The bricks were ragged, but my dress withstood his heaving. I looked out and could only gasp. "There must be thousands!"

"Fifty thousand, I'd guess. And Canal Street dressed for a king!"

Though immense, the crowd was solemn. The couple standing next to us wept openly, given over to their grief. The wife, whose skin was the color of Ada's strong-brewed tea, had her chin tilted up so the tears ran down her neck. The son sat astride his father's shoulders, his black arms dangling like the loose straps of a helmet. I had seen a dozen parades in Utah, when church officials came to town, all with the same purpose and tone: devoted uplift. I had never seen devotion set free.

"Oh, my. Oh, Doctor Fife, I've never—"

"How old are you?" He joined me on the ledge.

"I'm eighteen."

"Well, I am thirty-four. It's no good calling me doctor."

"Mister?" I squirmed. "I will not call you Odd."

"Audwin, then."

The crowd began to sing about a chariot swinging down low, as the wagon bearing the coffin approached.

"Look how the horses are draped in black, Audwin."

"Legions of horses, legions of men!"

As the wagon drew by, a wailing started up. It came from everyone. It loosed the nails in my own coffin—I wasn't only embedded in the grain of Mormon wood, I belonged to human history. And there is a time to mourn.

CHAPTER 12

I joined them in the colored ward most evenings for the reading of the *New Orleans Tribune*. Robert never skipped the advertisements:

Reward. Thomas Wharton took from this city, as his slaves, our daughter, Polly, and son, Geo. Washington, in the year 1854, and when last heard of they were in Pontotoc, Mississippi. We will give $100 each to any person who will assist them, or either one of them, to get to Lafayette, or get word to us of their whereabouts, if they are alive. Ben. & Annie Dove

Reward. Adam Smart wishes to know the whereabouts of his wife, Laura Smart, sold by Col. Geo. Smart before the War, and now presumed dead. Laura, I have your two letters. I keep them always in my pocket. If you are married I don't want to see you again. Respectfully yours, Adam Smart, Opelousas.

None of us had ever heard of any of the folk, those inquiring or those to be found. But the longing in their letters made it seem we had. I asked, with a pounding heart, if any of these people ever did find their kin.

"Some does," Dilly said, "though the meeting up can be troublous."

"Old Jordan," Bug intoned.

Kneading the cloth at his knees, Robert told us of a slave named Jordan Barber, who'd been sold to the Durham plantation, ten miles down the road from his home. Jordan was a married man, but the new master gave him a woman, made him live in a cabin with her like his wife.

"But that's polygamy!" I said. "I thought that only the Mormons—"

"You can calls it poligrammy, calls it what you may, the master been hungry to get hisself more slaves. Jordan done cry and his new wife cry—"

"And they weren't even married?"

Robert's lips bunched. "Oh, yes, Missy, they was married. Master Durham, he say: 'That yo' wife, that yo' husband, I's yo' Master, she yo' missus, y'all married.' And then they jump the broomstick."

"Who jump the furthest?" Tierre asked him.

"Nah, boy, that ain't the point," Robert said. "Point a fact is, jumpin' that broomstick same as a couple sayin' 'I do.' But Jordan, he hardly jump at all, only to keep hisself the far side of the overseer's knuckleduster."

"Don't mean a thing less you say, 'What God done jined, no man cain't put asunder,'" Bug said.

"They never did say such like that. Just say, 'Now y'all married.'"

"Then what? What Jordan done?" Tierre asked with the heat of a dare.

"Like I was saying, Jordan he cry and the new woman cry. And me? I could read and write, so I wrote him up a pass to go see his Millie, ten mile distant. He went and seen her the one

Saturday, but jealousy grip him like a strangle all the week till he run off 'thout a pass."

"Oh, Jordan," Tierre said, shaking his head.

"Paterollers caught him hiding up the chimney in his own house, strip him front of his wife and childrens, give him thirty-nine strokes, her hollering louder than Jordan hisself did."

"Jordan low," the boy groaned.

"He gonna get lower," Bug warned.

"Nah, it cain't be."

Robert shook out his jeans, both hands. "Yessir." He looked into Tierre's wide eyes. "Master Durham he sold Jordan off some hundred mile north. After the 'Mancipation, when Jordan Barber gots hisself free and all and come to claim his wife, she cry, 'No sir.' Cry, 'No sir,' at the door and wouldn't be led nor bullied out, a little yellow skin child in hair ribbons at her side, some flowery color rug 'neath of her feets.

"Jordan take up work nearby, work to win Millie back and his children, but all they is is chopping cotton for the boss. Jordan been going nowheres fast, when this reporter—"

"What's that?" T asked.

"Newspaper writer, from up the North. Well, he happen to ask some old house slave, one of them petted niggers, how he been treated by his master 'fore the War, and that slave he say, 'Kindly.' Jordan shoves in, say, 'Kindly! Kindly? The master give me corn enough, and yes, he give me pork enough to live, but he sold me from the wife of my bosom! Take away the pork, I say, take away the corn, I can raise those for myself, but where's my wife? Who the father of that yellow skin child she cling to? Where in God's name is my children?'" Robert dragged a hand over his face.

"I told you he been lower," Bug said.

Tierre sighed. "Cain't no man put asunder . . ."

"May anyone run an advertisement to find their kin?" The force in my voice startled even me. The story had been moving. "All of the ones we read are written by Negroes."

"Prefer if you'd to say 'colored,' Miz Clair, 'colored folk' or 'freedmen,'" Robert said.

I blushed, "Why, of course, 'colored' people, but why do they seem to write all of the—"

"I be a monkey's red ass shining at the moon!" Tierre howled. "She don't know," he laughed, "she don't even know nothing." He gasped for breath. "She read, she write, she got white skin. Who say the white folks is smarter?" He made to drop off the edge of his cot—low drama as much to his liking as high—just when a clucking started up at the door, cluck of a chicken on the verge of alarm.

Frau Schnell's face was as ruddy as the end of her nose, blood red in the light from the candles. "Miss Martin?"

"Yes, it's me, Frau Schnell," I said, as Tierre regained his balance.

The matron rang her handbell at our faces, then clapped it to her hip. "You haven't to work past lights out!" she said, her voice a mix of triumph and disgust.

I smoothed the newspaper on my lap. "I've finished my duties. I am here by choice."

For this, there was simply no answer. Frau Schnell dropped the bell into an apron pocket and swung herself noisily down the attic stairs.

"She like to cook my goose," Tierre tittered.

"Mouth like yours, it'll cook itself," Robert said, scowling. "The *Tribune* a colored paper for colored folk, Miz Clair," he said. "They's white folks' papers, too."

"Yes, ma'am," Tierre looked up, the smile of a sweet boy

angel at the gate, "and you could aduh-tise for yourself a new brain there."

I thanked him for his concern on my behalf and swatted his behind.

Two things increased December's darkness. The Fisk Library tossed Audwin out on his "arse." He said even if he'd had the money, they would not have let him touch their books. The smile on Audwin's face as he told me this said he paid little heed to "no." He held to a scientific outlook. *No* was the rocky bit that made rivers sing. "All in good time," he said, leaning into his hands, resolved to make the tax assessor's office yield its bounty to our search for my real kin.

Christmas week, a package arrived from Ada. I admired the fine leather gloves by candlelight. I held them to my cheek. I inhaled. I stroked them, ivory white and soft as suds, with lace netting set into the cut-away back, pearl buttons at the wrists. Gloves so fine I hardly dared to try them on, my hands cracked from laundering until the flesh was hardened shell. Ada's note said, "Come home, Clair. Stephen cut us a noble little tree."

Her words exploded into loss. I had no home, no Stephen, no tree, noble or otherwise. My chances fof ever finding kin were threadbare. If I had no one, forever, and only this dark place—

I lay the gloves against my neck, then onto my breast, then curling in a knot on my sour mattress, I pressed Ada's present over my mouth and wept.

Audwin tried cheering me. All I could see from three months' hard work and paltry pay was a future here gray as wash water. I was failing, and failure dragged at my spirit. He took me to the levee on New Year's Eve to watch the lights across the Mississippi shatter into chaos as the flatboats passed both ways. We heard opera, sharing an alley door, then watched the gowns and shining black suits pour out the front. We ate okra stew and fritters at a sit-down kitchen, and barbecue pig from a vendor in Jackson Square. Audwin bought me beer, and watched my eyes water as my lungs contracted and white foam spewed out my nose. He laughed until his knees gave out. I had to prop him up most of the walk home, wobble-kneed, wheezing with laughter.

One night, when I said I was too tired for adventures, he took me to a church nearby. I balked at sight of the tall granite cross, but Audwin mounted the stairs by twos. A small wooden gallery jutted above the chapel. Music rose from a dozen men in shapeless dresses, their faces sunk in hoods, bodies in cloth, the bulk of the chapel lost in shadows. Audwin took my hand and I felt glad for Ada's gloves. The voices blended together like snowmelt, damp and cool and ever underway.

"It isn't English—"

"No," he whispered back, and I closed my eyes, kept my attention on the sparkling, slow musical thaw and the bony pressure of Audwin's hand.

We walked from the old stone chapel to a miniature city of crypts and crosses. Whole avenues of vaults rose out of the grass. The dead rested above ground here. I tore a lily from a wreath. I inhaled, and on the power of that sweetness, finally dared ask Audwin why he was being kind to me.

He stopped on the shell-covered path. "Why are you kind to me, Clair?"

"You don't have a hideous face! Tell me, the truth." I felt ridiculous as I said it. Audwin always spoke the truth.

He smiled and said, "That's easy. Your face is what drew me. Mark of any scientist, as soon as I saw it I had to know more." His answer was so simple it produced a heady trust, in him and in his scientific interest.

Science, unlike religion, loves what it does not know.

Audwin asked questions that night about my marking, and I answered him freely. The red mark came from birth, it had not grown, it did not hurt, my mother seemed in my memory to have had no mark. I believed this was the scope of Audwin Fife's scientific inquiry, this asking of increasingly pointed questions, until a night late in January when he took me to his room and the picture came quite clear. It had been raining so we couldn't go walking. He led me to a door in the hospital that I both knew and feared.

Light from an oil lamp rippled as he opened the door. The ceiling rocked. The smell of disinfectant mixed with a roasted burning made my stomach roll.

"Coffee?" Audwin asked, kneeling at a little stove. Its flame was smaller than a candle's. Steam poured out the canister set precariously on top.

"I—"

"Clair, the door. The draft."

I closed the door behind me, and the rocking flickering stopped. This was the room I had entered, once, looking for linens. I had found them—draped over a woman's corpse.

"Ah." He inhaled, lifting the canister with a pair of tongs. The boiling stopped. "Cups—" He nodded at a shelf.

I brought two, one with a missing handle, the other with a mud-brown ring. I cleaned it with my coat.

Audwin poured black soup into my cup. When I hesitated, he said, "The grounds add character!" He grinned. His blond moustache dripped. "But we're still standing."

He gave me the low couch and perched on a work stool nearby. Under the velour spread, I felt the ribs of a sleeping cot. Shirt-sleeves dangled from a cabinet drawer.

"Audwin—you sleep here!"

"Is that an accusation?"

"This is your home? Why, it's a laboratory. Where do you wash?"

He grinned and pointed to a bowl behind him.

"How do you—who scrubs your clothes?"

"None other."

I looked at him, appalled.

"I'm capable of putting soap to water, Clair."

"Why don't you have a proper apartment? Why don't you pay someone to clean your things?"

"With whose salary? Hackett's?"

"But you're a doctor—"

"Nearly a doctor."

"—so they must pay you something for your training and your services." I looked around the room. The tables lay empty, cloaked in canvas. I remembered the still gray body. I knew it was a woman, as her shoes and dress lay in a bundle on the floor. "What," I asked him with faint heart, "are your services, exactly?"

"Staff microscopist. Pathological chemist. Curator of the Pathological Cabinet for Baruch Place. That last even merits an annual stipend. Of twelve dollars—one per month—though it's hotly contested at every meeting of the board."

One dollar per month! I had made six times that selling flower cards in Corinne. Here was a full-grown man with medical training, living in dirt and darkness. Audwin explained that for the *canaille*, the vulgar class, hopes for employment were slim. Doctors came from affluent backgrounds. Baruch Place gave him food and shelter and the chance to increase his knowledge. He kept on for love of the work.

"Would you like to see it, my work?" He gestured to a tall glass case.

Standing with him before his rows of jars, I felt the same tight panic I had in school. How might I fail? How mispronounce? How misconstrue instructions?

I waited for Audwin to speak.

"The lungs are new, and the liver as well. This uterus is especially fine," he said, tapping at the glass about eye-level. "I've cross-sectioned it."

I gazed at my own face, reflected there. Flat brow, dainty nose, the lower lip just bent to sorrow. The eye, patient, lashes a wisp, nothing more. Then I saw the contents inside the jar.

"What is this?" I asked of the intricate dollop of clay inside a circle.

"A three month foetus. An infant, Clair, an unborn child."

"Human? But—this is a womb?"

"The mother died of erysipelas. It wracked the lying-in ward some years back. They couldn't have saved the child."

"But where—?" My fingers ran down the cabinet glass. "Bukra butcher," I whispered. "Audwin, did you cut this child out of some woman's womb? Did you?"

"What the living cannot tell us, the dead can and will."

"And this is what you do? Carve up the bodies of the dead?"

"To save the living, yes!" He moved to a table, kicked a stool up and put his eye to a long black instrument. He stabbed his finger with a lancet, spread his blood on a glass plate, covered it, slid it into the instrument and clipped it in place. Then he pulled me onto the seat and set his face next to mine, adjusting the viewer and the nearby lamp.

A pattern of discs, pale, round, elongated, scattered over my field of view. "This is your blood?" I asked.

"That is the leveler," he said, "that is the truth. Plantation owners and derelicts both come down to that." His eyes shone. "We all do!"

Hanging over a whole new world, I smiled in spite of myself. "It's so beautiful. It's—and my own blood?"

"Would look identical."

"T's?"

"Yes, Tierre's, too."

"You are teasing me." But Audwin was not.

We laughed. Here was the world I'd longed for, where T and I and everyone could live as equals. And if it could be seen, it could be lived. Or so it seemed, as long as I beheld it. "Oscar Dunn would be so proud of you!" I crowed into the room.

For this miracle of human equality, this earth-shaking scientific truth, Baruch Place Hospital paid Audwin Fife twelve dollars per year. They kept him poor, smelly and driven. I could help combat one of those fates. I told Audwin I would launder his shirts—four shirts per week, washed and pressed—if he would only let me stay on at the lens.

Early one January evening, Tierre and I explored a new world together, a world we'd heard existed but had never found before. Robert stood with a little girl on each hip, dipping and righting them like ducks on a pond. They laughed and gurgled and hiccoughed.

Delia shouted, "Giddyap!"

Tierre, whose cast had just come off, demanded to have his turn.

"Nah, son, you too big."

"I ain't. I'm light as Delia." Tierre hopped on one foot. "Lighter!"

Robert refused, but T kept begging, hopping, skittering

around the three. He only wanted to belong. Wanted it so dearly that he had taken Robert's surname for his own. T yanked Delia's leg in spite. She kicked him. The kick clearly struck Tierre's pride harder than his ribs. T yelled right in her face, "It ain't fair!" A boy of ten, using vigor and anger to claim his rights, Tierre demanded a spin in Robert's arms.

The words arose from nowhere. I heard myself say, "Tierre, you're shivery as a fish. I'll bet you can't hold still ten seconds, much less to a count of sixty."

He cut me a look, said I could die standing.

"I knew you couldn't," I said.

The bait dangled. Any moment he could resume his old war cry, *it ain't fair.*

"What you bet?" he asked, bouncing on his heels, full of the devil.

"I'll bet a walk to the river and a praline candy."

His body clenched, brow furrowed. "Start to counting."

"No, sir. I can't tell if you're shivering." I opened my arms and pointed. "Right here."

The top of his head came to my chin. It smelled of sweet talc. I crossed one arm and then the other over his body and held him close. "All the way to sixty," I said.

He tensed in place.

"One, two, three," I counted, dreamy and slow, "four, five, six . . ." By fifteen, Tierre had cradled in, never moving, just relaxing into me until I could have been holding myself. I counted on, T never minding the men at the bones table or Robert letting the girls down one by one. All warmth, all stillness. And the minute of grace didn't end at sixty, the slip of a boy didn't break away, triumphant to demand his prize. We stood watching the domino game, of a piece, like mother and son. And when we parted, it was in a daze of peaceful abiding.

Audwin did keep up his search for my kin, though know-ing T eased my need for family. I had plowed my way through eighteen years of accursedness, and learned in sixty seconds that your curse can be your blessing. It was wonderful—a mystery hidden in plain sight. Motherless, I became mother. Lonely child, my very loneliness granted T permission to come close.

Of course, motherhood cannot be considered the easiest of callings when you tally the blinding fear, threats from with-out, chafing want and uncontrollable messes. Not to mention the whole born world saying your son is a worthless moke.

My ties to society loosened and fell to the ground, right then. Whatever they did, whatever they said, I chose T.

CHAPTER 13

February brought a test of our so-called blessings at Baruch Place. The hospital facility seemed to run on dogged persistence alone. Funding never kept up with need. Still, once each year, a feast of thanks interrupted the workday. The nursing staff and laundresses were allowed into the doctors' dining hall for supper, king cake and inspiration. We did appear to need inspiring. We'd risen two hours early to make time for the meal. No one had dressed up, as their everyday clothes were their only clothes, except Mrs. Hoppe, the superintendent's wife, whose pleated taffeta bodice rustled with every breath. When our shining benefactress rose to speak, her abdomen clipped the table making our water glasses toss in place.

Frau Schnell placed her fork and knife forcibly down, signaling without words that we should follow. Only the very youngest of the laundresses required an elbow in her ribs to stop her eating the first fresh-killed drum fish she had ever tasted in her life. "Aw!" she said, clutching fork and knife on her lap, stopped by circumstance but ready at a second to resume.

Mrs. Hoppe did not quite meet our gazes. She arranged the fur collar at her neck and a smile on her lips.

"It is a scientific truth, my dears. In nine of ten cases, sickness comes from making a god of animal appetite. Disease strikes those addicted to bad habits. Insanity arises from constant indulgence in base passion. Even the idiot, though blameless, bears the consequence of Adam's fall and the millennia of subsequent sin."

Somewhere, gravy was burning. Mrs. Hoppe sniffed and firmed her eyebrows and pressed on. "How much more precious is the soul to save, than the body which rusts and corrupts!"

Frau Schnell belched. We did not, this time, follow her lead.

"While you dress your patients' wounds, empty their bedpans, administer enemas and baths, do you note traces of spirits or tobacco on their persons, or traces of ingratitude for service given, and expend no energies at correction? Do you allow indecent language to pass freely in the wards?"

Apparently our faces answered *yes*. Mrs. Hoppe rose up on her toes and cried out, "Put away rum! Make men correct in their ways, fully grateful and industrious—you could as well shut the doors of Baruch Place and all the hospitals in New Orleans. The doctors would have nothing to do."

We clapped as she sat down, wondering what we would do without Baruch Place employment.

Frau Schnell did not clap. She made her own sort of speech, once Mrs. Hoppe had settled. Not an official speech. She did not rise. Her fork, pointed straight up and gripped like a sword, shook with every question. What about the lack of bedding? The dwindling muslin for bandages? The locked privies on the third and fourth floors which no longer served? She mentioned each grievance under her breath, and the superintendent's wife, rearranging but not eating her meal, responded in turn. Devoted nurses could obtain donations from merchants—muslin, blue check, blankets and bed ticking. They could make the mattresses themselves and diminish such costs to the hospital, releasing funds for better maintenance of the facility.

Frau Schnell planted her massive forearms on the table. "My nurses toil fourteen hours per day und their wages have not risen since Union Occupation. Ten years, und the wages do not change?"

Just then the king cake arrived. The superintendent's wife sliced her piece of cake from end to end. No crown, no baby, no bean inside. The fur at her neck trembled. "You are richly repaid in gratitude! If that doesn't suffice, repay yourselves with thankfulness for opportunities to serve rather than burden the good graces of the decent, generous, God-fearing people of this city!"

She ate no cake.

Audwin listened to my version of Mrs. Hoppe's lecture, but he would have none of it. "Sin? Sin! She could as well have claimed disease comes from the moonbeams, insanity from the mockingbirds. God keep such bigots and pietists from me!"

"Nine of ten times, she said, sickness comes from sin."

"Plagues cause nine of ten deaths in New Orleans, Clair. Do they only take the sinful? In a family of twelve, does the plague select and kill just the foul sinners of the bunch? My God, the scientists are no better! They attribute plagues to miasmata, effluvia rising from swamps and putrefying bodies—invisible emanations assumed to be densest and most harmful in hospitals, like ours. Most particularly within its morgues and its laundry rooms." He smiled a wicked smile. He pulled me in. "Encountered any miasma, lately?"

I slipped my hands farther up my sleeves.

"Or any other invisible agents of death? Sin and miasmata are convenient solutions for sore consciences. It is easy to have answers, Clair, harder by an infinite degree to prove their efficacy, their benefit in the face of suffering."

"There are no miasms, then?"

"I never said that. There may well be, it's just that no one has proven it yet, proved the theory consistent or truly helpful." He shook his curls and, rising to his full height, released his grip on my arm. "Did I tell you about the time Mrs. Hoppe visited the first floor ward with the intent to save the inmates' souls?"

"No." I laughed in advance.

"That woman strode up to one veteran's bedside, decrying the evils of drink and dance, and pushed a pamphlet into his hands. He never said a thing to her, never a word, just yanked the blanket back and let his missing legs tell her just how he hankered after dancing."

However slight a hold Mrs. Hoppe had on science, and human kindness, I adopted her plan for improving our lot. Tierre needed new clothes and clean bedsheets, and the ward would benefit from anything nicer than its current tattered state of gloom. I took her council. I placed an ad in the *Tribune* asking for charitable contributions. I stepped inside the office full of educated Negroes and filled out and submitted the form. It was a sort of practice for the day, very soon, when I would dare to enter the glistening double doors of the *New Orleans Picayune* to place an ad for my kin. A test, too, of the response. I wondered if a single woman's voice in this busy city could be heard. I half believed the ad would call forth no response at all.

Blankets, linens, curtains and clothes rained into the colored ward the following week. Frau Schnell grumbled about the noise of Robert's cart as it mounted and descended the four flights of stairs—loaded on the way up, light as a paper boat skidding before him the way down. The matron climbed to the attic herself at week's end to examine the supplies, the linens and clothes which, folded and stacked on shelves, filled an entire wall of Robert's room. She only managed to say, with the force of a sneeze, "Hoppe!" before she returned to her work below.

"Good hearts can change bad fortune," I told her. "See how colored folk take care of their own?" But when I joined them in the attic ward that weekend, Delia wore the same soiled dress, Tierre the old pants made from sacking. Curtains did hang at the windows, but the rest of the ward looked, to a coverlet, just as it had before—tired and worn to death.

I did not hesitate at Robert's door. I held up trousers and dresses and shirtwaists until I found what seemed to be the children's sizes. I selected ribbons as well, for Delia's hair. I found a pair of socks to match, when Robert entered.

"No, ma'am!" Robert stomped his foot.

I laughed. "For Delia and T—"

"No, ma'am." He lowered his shoulders, as if to charge.

I trembled and clutched the children's clothes. Robert had never crossed me, had never shown a moment's anger. Stepping toward the door, I said, "Let me pass please, Robert."

"This my ward!" he said, his eyes never leaving the goods. He swiped at the clothes, but I backed toward the wall.

"The children need clothing!"

"Don't makes me to stop you." Robert breathed, locking his arms across his broad chest.

I took a step forward.

"Hey!" Tierre piped at the doorway. "You give me the slip, Robear."

"T? Come here—" I said.

He stepped to my side, his pant leg still torn to the crotch to accommodate a cast. He'd been free of the cast for weeks. "These are for you and Delia. Take these out to her, please."

He shrugged. "I cain't."

"Tierre!" I sickened as he gave the clothing into Robert's hands.

T bumped his friend's muscled arm. "Come on, 'Bear. You seen my stove wood? I's done, and better than Bug ever stacked it."

Robert held the clothes, looking calmer but still grave. "You like to tell Missy why you cain't do like she asked you to, cain't put on no new clothes?"

Tierre *tch*-ed as if anybody who had ears must already have heard. "Well colored is 'llowed to stay here at Baruch if they ain't got no clothes. They be clothed and healed, they gets sent on. That good enough, Robear? I swear, she a baby girl in a full-growed body."

"That fine. Now get fresh water in the washbowl stand."

"Aw—"

"Scramble, son," he growled, and Tierre set off.

Sorrow bent me down as Robert returned every item to the shelves. "They cannot wear their new clothes?"

"Not the growed ones nor the childrens, not if they well."

The colors of the fabric ran, the shelves ran together, and Robert's back shrank to brown on gray. All of the goodness in the world seemed lost, forever inaccessible.

He stood by as I wept.

"Nah, Missy. You done good." Robert patted my head. I cried harder at his tenderness. *It ain't fair. It ain't fair!* a boy's voice cried, *it ain't!* I reached for Tierre's voice, those days, those fallen leaves and mourned for all our losses.

"Nah," Robert said. "They get their fine clothes when they be leaving us, heal up like new or dead."

Poverty protected them, a torn scrap of blessing. And as surely that same poverty kept us all from rising out of want and oblivion. Whether I wrestled with the entrapment or held quite still, it extended in all directions like a Mississippi Delta fog.

CHAPTER 14

Mardi Gras in New Orleans lets loose the primitive within. It is a sort of Christian party, two weeks of parades and merrymaking without rules. The costumes of the revelers rival the fireworks exploding over the Mississippi River—shocking flowers of light, but briefer than real flowers. Brief as hope. Audwin seemed particularly glum the night we joined the throng. His hand at my arm guided us through the tilting masks, shouts and music clashing, smell of urine, candy crushed underfoot, sulphur and frying fat, beads and hats, and gigantic feathers keeping slow time over the procession. We'd chosen this night to celebrate my birthday, but the fireworks only strained on Audwin. The festival brought no joy. He said little and smiled less.

I myself was still reeling from the news, delivered by him two nights since, that a stripped coupling created all the human beings on earth. Ada Nuttall, Daniel Dees, Frau Schnell, Doctor Hackett—they all came from it. No wonder the Brethren had stopped at telling the particulars of procreation. Eternal helpmates? Queens of Heaven spreading their husbands' seeds throughout the cosmos? Now I understood the planting, it didn't feel one bit queenly.

I had walked downriver to escape the confines of the hospital that night. Gaslight stained a half-dozen porches. A man with a plumed hat leaned in at a gate, touching a young colored woman's hair. He moved to the porch and ran his hand over the thigh of a larger woman who straddled the porch rail. She heaved herself up and followed him inside. I kept to the middle of the street. The young woman at the gate opened her dress to me, her breast a mound, the nipple high and purple black. She licked her thumb and circled it. "Ten cent," she said.

Someone on the porch called, "Sweet black cunt. Ten cent!"

I broke into a run at their laughter. I ran all the way back to Baruch Place and plunged down the darkened hall. I burst in on Audwin, begging him to tell me what set men prowling, grunting and grabbing. "Why are there children, girl children beckoning to strangers on the street in the Faubourg Marigny?" Tears came. "She was only thirteen! Same as in Brigham— same with the Brethren there. What do they want? What is it men are lacking?"

Audwin took my shoulder, sat me down, and tried to end my misery. "A scientific apology I can fit words around," he said. He'd made it seem a matter of fact. Audwin told the male parts. He showed them in a book, the stiffening and the rubbing and the sperm liquid placed inside—his words had left me stunned. Wary. Focused. Clair Martin against the whole born world.

So I was grateful for the relative peace of the alleyway, glad for someplace empty and unmoving after the current of revelers, the bursts of fire overhead, the fingers of ash marking their bright descent over the Mississippi. I sat on a back porch stoop in the light of the half moon. Prowling the alley, Audwin cast a shadow skinny as beggar's pike. He downed liquor from a quart bottle abandoned on a step, tossed it and as glass burst over the cobbles, the words came.

He told me of his own journey to New Orleans. Why he had come. Why he stayed. His father had mined for coal in the Lackawanna mines of Pennsylvania, raising his children with curses and absence. Audwin's mother had died in childbirth at age thirty-two. Audwin took charge, as well as a fourteen-year-old boy could. Once the baby, Gracie, had married at fifteen, he'd tramped his way to New Orleans and put himself through medical school with money he'd saved carving wooden trinkets for the children of the rich. He spoke of his past with scorn, though I admired his fight. Nothing was handed to Audwin. He made his way to Louisiana like me, in search of something better. He'd heard that New Orleans, after the War, made room for talent and spirit, room for a man to rise.

His hair in the moonlight looked white as the seed head of a dandelion.

"Halo," I said, reaching with affection to touch the top of it, "you have a halo, Audwin." I hadn't said or done anything more when he cursed and sagged onto the step beside me.

"Halo!" he said. "I wish it were. You may as well know it, Clair. Your search for kin is fruitless. I have been to the tax assessor's. I have been to the courthouse in search of your parents. LeBlancs are more numerous than Smiths, in New Orleans. Marie LeBlancs too numerous to trace. I'm sorry. Christ. I'm sorry to say Tucker Martins there were none."

This news didn't land as harshly as Audwin feared it would. I assured him that if my parents had left no trace in New Orleans, I could cast a wider net. I would place an advertisement in the *Picayune* with some of my savings. I would send word to the state of Louisiana: Clair Martin seeks kin.

He relaxed a little at my composure. We toasted this

new search of mine with imaginary glasses. Of course, March moved in with a heat wave, and no one answered my ad but a merchant selling sunburn cream. No matter, I would renew the ad for April. Surely a couple named Martin who joined their futures to the Mormon exodus West would be the exception, not the rule, here in Dixie. If not, then hope—as beautiful and brief as Mardi Gras flowers—would expire for the while.

12 March, 1872

Dear Ada,

I have seen the Mardi Gras. The Christians here take jubilation seriously. The fireworks you'd have crowed to see exploding over the Mississippi River.

Tierre is out of the leg cast jumpy as a bug. He asks about the West, but I can't make words to describe it. It stays too deep inside me. That boy wants a horse!

Are you keeping busy, Ada? Busy and safe at home? Pat Swede for me and scratch his belly.

Yours truly, Clair Martin

Tierre tapped at the laundry door. "Hey, Clara. Doctor Fife say to come on." I'd promised T this outing long since, a walk on the levee and a praline candy. Freedom, to him, was a day gallivanting out of doors. Now that his cast was off and his leg as good as new, I couldn't begrudge him the walk or the fantasy. I wrung out the last of the towels, lay them side by side and followed him out.

The April wind coming off the Mississippi River was swampy and brisk, promising rain. Tierre dragged us happily forward, chattering. He skipped on ahead, a little boy rich with time and pralines in his pockets. His drawers flapped, there was so little body inside to fill them, as he jumped at birds amid the bushes on the levee.

Audwin walked nearest the river, to break the wind's force. He loomed pleasantly above me, with a puzzled look on his face. I had just mentioned Ada's latest letter. The one containing news of Florrie Gradon who had gathered a quorum of Saints and sealed me into Outer Darkness for my defection, for my assumed sins. This seemed a strange twist—she who suffered the daily blows of a cruel husband found my life of service unclean.

Audwin asked me about Outer Darkness. I said it was the place God never goes.

"Yet you say this Florrie was your closest friend?"

"She was, yes."

"You've been cast into eternal darkness by your closest friend for riding the Great Northern Rail to New Orleans?"

"I did not hold to the wheel."

"And yet Florrie, with her shoulder to God's holy wheel, continues to taste the sweet milk and honey from His comb?"

His sarcasm gripped me. "She once knew God's sweetness, but her married life is bitter as gall. Bitter as gall and yet she will go on with it, she's bound herself to Lester Madsen till death and beyond, will bear his children and live eternally with him, raised up to a god. No matter that he treats her cruelly—"

"The man will be a god?" Audwin stopped, taking my wrist.

I nodded.

"Because he's cruel?"

"Because they've married in the Ordinance House. It is guaranteed to all the faithful." I described how Lester would get his own planet to populate and rule, with multiple wives to spread his seed.

"The lucky bastards copulate in Heaven?" Audwin balled his fists. My heart dropped at his enthusiasm. A man is a man is a man. "And how many wives does your prophet claim, eternally?" he asked.

"Brigham Young? Fifty or so. No, it must be higher by now. In the Beehive House or the Lion House—" I kicked at a chandler's crate.

"And he is the man who started it all? The founder of this happy den or hive or whatever it is, this Mr. Young?"

"No." I smoothed my hands down my dress as the old pall descended. I knew the tale by heart. "No, it was Joseph Smith. He was the first prophet. All of the churches in his county fought and disagreed, and as a boy he didn't know which to follow. So he kneeled down in a grove, a sacred grove, and—" I watched a steamer crew cast off its lines, the large bow wrinkling the Mississippi. "And I don't believe a word of it."

"Is it any wonder?" Audwin grinned, impish and steely. Wind shook his hair. He hadn't shaved in days.

"But Audwin, you—"

"I appreciate a good yarn, Clair. God knows, every man dreams of unhindered rutting with willing, tender females. But this Smith fellow, he's laid on eternity. Domination and godhood to boot. Grand dreams!" Audwin looked downriver, the smell of fish and woodsmoke on the breeze. T had found a heel of bread on the levee. He crushed it underfoot to toss at a sluggish flock of pigeons. "No, they are never willing, in my case. Mental potency counts for . . ." When he turned to me, his eyes had never been tenderer. "We are ciphers, Clair. Lots, to be added or subtracted. Place holders, paltry sums."

It sounded right. I waited a moment, in respect for Audwin, and then smiled. "Did you really want those wives so badly? How about thirteen! We'll give you thirteen wives, all industrious, all—"

"Give me three harlots and the salary to keep them. Keep them elsewhere, not in the laboratory! Work first. Work always comes first." He signaled Tierre with a wave, and we started back. "That would be my grand religion. Care to join?"

I looked him in the eyes. Hazel eyes, like the river water, only clear and sharp with their usual wit. "As a harlot, your salary, or the urine sample under the lens?"

Audwin winced. "Create your own Heaven, then."

"I wouldn't be a harlot, or even a queen."

"What, then?"

I didn't answer, picking my way down the embankment. When we crossed to the French Market, I ventured, "Desert. A dog. Good work. And sunsets."

"So spare? You can have anything, anyone. It's your religion."

"Oh," I said, stopping to touch a stack of pears, recalling the firmness and symmetry of my days in Utah, "it was plenty. It was enough."

"What of the boy? Where does Tierre fit in your scheme?"

At the sound of his name, T sprinted over and showed us the rocks and two coins he'd found. I held his treasures in my hands. The pralines were gone, but his pockets would go home full. I had no answer for Audwin, unused to belonging, used to dreaming for only myself.

The heat and steam and bloody groaning of hell found us in May. Tierre handed his basket of dirty laundry to me, planted both feet and asked, "That skinny bone man the bukra butcher?" Audwin had told me to stand ready, to scrub every piece of cotton and roll every bandage, in case a fever struck. I would not be distracted. We weren't half through our tasks. "Did you fetch all the bandages from the ward like I asked?" It was doubtful. Tierre's basket wasn't half full.

"Yes, ma'am. That shaggy yellow headed man—?"

"Who bought you candy and went walking with us? Audwin Fife. He's the doctor studies disease and such under the lens."

"He the one carved Affy into fourteen pieces and pickled her head in a jar?"

I made note not to check Audwin's shelves. "Tierre, why is this basket mostly empty?"

T smiled. His eyes widened. His young teeth were fine and white. "Not much changing, Clara, when Robear wraps so good. What else you need done?"

I touched his chin, glad he was mine. Not that he ever called me "Momma" or ever stopped giving me sass. "Go play now, near the cistern. I'll call when I need you again." T shot off down the hall, the only boy I'd ever known who could lie bald-faced and make you feel good about it. I emptied the basket, set it on my hip, and started the long climb to the attic.

The May exodus had occurred as we were told. The superintendent and his wife and all the house physicians had said their good-byes, and rattled off toward the river and the steamboats leaving for the breezy Mississippi Gulf Coast, left the staff waving, sun in our faces, dark moons under our arms. By the middle of May, only Doctor Hackett remained, Hackett the sole bearer of the short straw. Most of the Baruch Place patients kept their symptoms to themselves, after that, preferring the body's imperiousness to Doctor Hackett's. He scolded everyone, slept through rounds, and smoked cigars endlessly in the reception room.

I took advantage of the absence of hospital staff to help myself to reading materials abandoned in the doctors' lounge. I helped myself, too, to the reading lamp nights when it was too hot to actually sleep. I hadn't held a book in months. I rode out on the sentences and didn't ride back in till dawn.

For the colored ward, this change of command also meant relief. We shared a sort of communal health under Robert's care. Fear seldom intruded. Kindness ruled. Still, the sun burned day to night as through a lens, and the old edifice warmed ferociously. By the time I'd reached the attic, I had to stop to open the top button of my blouse. Robert stood near a window, bent over his cart.

"I ironed your aprons," I said.

He nodded, bracing himself with both arms. Sweat covered his face. When I came to him he said, "No, Missy, keep on back."

His eyes were bloodshot. His arms shook.

He turned and vomited on the floor.

Only Audwin could get Robert to admit he needed to lie down. We removed his clothes and sponged his neck and face. At sight of his muscled legs, the word *beautiful* accompanied the sheet that I pulled lightly over him. I'd never seen Robert in repose—he was always working, always helping someone. How dear the human form is, how lovely at rest.

Dilly came to help us, with his own brand of medicine. He lit a candle at the small shrine near Robert's bed—Jesus and a few saints, and a little black doll with a straw hat and cane. He touched Robert's hand to a small clay skull and stirred a bowl of cornmeal flour with bent fingers.

Bug agreed to take the night watch, keep Robert still regardless of what he said he aimed to do. Bug dragged his cot over to watch Audwin finish the bathing. When Robert finally slept, Audwin said to me, "High fever, slow pulse. It's Yellow Jack. I'm certain."

"What can we do?"

"Nothing, nothing but keep him rested. And boil his clothes in the morning." Audwin pressed his palms to his eyes.

"Will the cases mount to epidemic?"

"We'll know soon enough. Not everyone who contracts it dies, Clair. Those who do go quickly, in three or four days."

"Will there be blood?"

His eyes scanned my face. "Cauldrons of it."

CHAPTER 15

Tierre slept with me while the colored ward had the yellow fever. I could not let him see Robert in distress. When you are only ten years old, busy and ignorant surely beats worried and frightened. Delighted to be free of the confines of the attic, T actually stuck with me through the mastering of the pile of dirty sheets. I taught him the ABCs at night. I broke the day work into small tasks, letting him run for this and check on that, in and out the courtyard door until one of the white laundresses smacked his bottom for cutting ahead of her, making her spill her wet things in the yard. His head reared back, a torrent of anger in his eyes, but the wet laundry on the stairway needed inspecting. T picked up every piece— just like the hard-wrung lumps of the colored ward's laundry— and turned them over, placing them back in her basket. "This the only one need rinsing. I am sorry for the one," he said and walked inside.

The woman didn't know what to say.

I did. I praised him, for getting the better of his mood, for picking up all of what he'd caused to be spilled, and for apologizing. I embraced him, then stepped back to let Tierre savor the feel of self-mastery and fair play. What I felt was the imprint of a boy no heavier than a scrub board. He was a fountain of pleasure to me. He was a source of deep joy.

On the fifth day of Robert's fever, I entered his room with a smile and the newspaper. Yellow fever, Audwin warned, often took a two-day rest after raging. Then it would let the patient go or sink its teeth.

Dilly shot up and out the door. Robert made a swipe after his friend, then laughed a little. "Take a fool to enter the lion den."

"How are you, Robert?" I settled myself on the cot.

"Like as you doesn't know?"

I opened the *Tribune*. "Local or national?"

"Let's us go join the boys, maybe they like to hear you read."

I paged through. "Or the advertisements, first?"

"Shah, Miz Clair, I strong as oxes. How about the folk needs tending?"

"Three cases in our ward, the women are bathing them down. Open the curtain a little for me, please."

He shoved the fabric aside. "Any word of the Jack in there?"

It startled me, the notion of a wider world. "Other hospitals may be in trouble, too?"

"Jack hit the city every couple three years. Like as not, they's all 'flicted."

"Then you've lived through a plague before?"

"Yes, ma'am. I nurse Tierre's momma till she die."

My heart raced. "Of yellow fever?"

"The same. It struck so bad they quarantine, shut the 'flicted up together, black and white. Most the patients out of they mind, blood everywheres, and my arms all they got for succor. Weren't a white doctor go near that ward."

"And where was T?"

"Tierre? I pull him out when his momma too confuse to know the difference."

My throat constricted. "He stayed in there? He saw the sickness?"

"Yes'm."

Tears scalded my eyes. "Robert, do you think you will get better?"

"I is tough. Jack take a taste and pass on by, set his mouth for some other. Look here, I gots protections—"

The gifts on Robert's shrine overflowed onto the floor. Bug and Dilly and everyone had piled on offerings. Robert's god appeared to love candy. Even Delia left a piece, wrapped in her favorite yellow handkerchief. That much she'd gained from the donations, a yellow kerchief embroidered with dainty leaves. And she'd promptly given it away.

I smiled. "Tierre says you're a hero, and the fever would not dare."

Robert's brows drew together. "A hero? Hero of what?"

"Why, the War. 'Death cain't touch Robear Durham, not while he kilt them Yanks or after.'"

"That child. How many he say I kill?"

"Fourteen." I tugged at my sleeve. "I believe it was that many."

"Lord in Heaven. All I kilt was the mud on the master's boots, and the wrinkle in his pants. Shine his shoes and scrub the wool. When he been shot, they let me wrap the wounds. I heared his last words. I brang the body back on the flatboat. That child. All I ever kilt was two and some years!" He turned to the wall, butting an arm under his head. "Read me them aduh-tisements first. The rest of the damn fool nation can wait."

Ada's package came wrapped in muslin without a note—the photograph of Stephen on the sturdy work horse. In the midst of a plague I never even mentioned, Ada somehow knew my needs.

Tierre gazed at the black horse and asked a hundred questions. He thought only a king could afford such a beautiful beast—who was this little king? He demanded stories about life out West, and I offered a few featuring Ada, moral tales of strength and daring. I lulled T toward sleep, trotting my fingers around him like a horse on the hills and plains of sheets—"ga-gallop, ga-gallop, ga-gallop." Cowboy on a black beast, smiling. "Time doth softly sweetly glide, when there's love at home"—I sang the Mormon hymn aloud as Tierre fell asleep.

That photograph became my shrine. Through the endless piles of laundry, through the gloom and stench and heat, I kept it as a talisman. A stroke of happiness and home. The young cowboy's beauty grew inside me—a stream, a rambler-rose the width of Heaven. No words, all heart. Stephen Nuttall, for better or worse.

Robert's fever did not return after breaking. When I knocked at Audwin's door to bring him the glad news and heard nothing, I called out, pushing the door open wide. I will never forget the sight of Audwin standing over his wash table, the basin brown, brown water running down his arms. His hair was shorn to ragged points. His eyes glistened. He'd been fighting for his life without me. "Audwin!"

He wavered, pressing a hand to the table to steady himself.

"Who cut your hair?" I took his arm. "Lie down! Come rest." When we reached his bed, the reek stopped me and I heaved onto the floor, then hung over my skirts panting and weeping.

He stroked my hand.

"Sit awhile," I said, folding my skirts together, wiping my mouth onto my sleeve. "Sit, and I'll fetch clean things for you." I had to leave that terrible room. I ran to tell Doctor Hackett, who already knew that Audwin had the Jack. Four of the twenty patients in the white ward looked at me with yellow faces, vacant sweaty faces that rested on their pillows like old fish struggling to breathe dry air. That's when the panic took me. I wanted to run until the state of Louisiana, with its murdered leaders and hate-filled gentry and fevers caused by nothing you could name, ceased to exist. I wanted the safety and comfort and stodgy, boring industry of Utah. I wanted Ada. I wanted Tierre free from all harm.

I saw blood draining from the nearest patient's ears. I closed my eyes, staring the panic down, and asked what I could do.

"Cleanliness is next to godliness," Hackett said with a sneer. "Then death takes all."

I fetched a stack of clean linens and paused a moment in the hall to send all my strength to Audwin, then returned to his room. He leaned into the wall, spare as a scythe, while I remade his bed. I pulled his sheets onto the floor, folded a dozen new ones and layered them on the cot. I emptied his bedpan and the jars filled with water-thin vomit, then set them in the hall. Then I helped him into bed.

He smiled. "I've made a mess of things."

I opened the window, tucked a clean sheet around him and sat down. I took his hand. "You can laugh at even this?"

"Laugh or you'll go under," he said, shivering beneath the sheet. "Who's making my rounds?"

"Frau Schnell, and rather badly to hear Hackett tell it."

"Ah, Hackett." When Audwin closed his eyes, his face lost all its lights. "Not a fair shake, poor fodge."

"Was it Hackett cut your halo off?"

He laughed noiselessly. "Couldn't stand the smell. But that was early on."

I felt such a stab of bitterness at my absence, which made me say the more gently, "Early on." I hoped Audwin understood my regret. I put a hand to his head. "You don't seem fevered—"

"Calm before the storm. No, don't," he said, as I started to remove it. I stroked his damp hair, let my fingers rest on his cheek. "Yes," he said.

I talked all night with Audwin. I tried to keep a tether on his mind. At first, he gave an answer here and there. An hour later, delirium came, and I did all the talking. A sharp banging on the door late that night roused me to anger. Outside in the hall, bouncing on his heels, T stood straight-armed. "Clara? Come on to bed."

"What time is it?"

"T's waited hours!"

"Audwin needs tending, Tierre," I whispered, closing the laboratory door behind me. "You light the candle like I showed you. You can have the whole bed tonight." He scowled. "You can tuck that horse and rider in with you, alright? They will ride you into some very good dreams. They'll have the whole bed as their pasture."

I held Audwin's hands against the violent shaking, pulling the covers back up to his chin. He lay unconscious and the sweat poured down. I talked and I worried. Though I wove tales of Brigham City and Swede and those everlasting sunsets on the Great Salt Lake, Audwin hadn't wakened in hours, he hadn't relieved himself all through the night. Near dawn, he wrenched upright as blood erupted from his mouth, black blood spilling down his chest, smelling of wet earth. I eased his head back to the pillow, mopped the darkness with a sheet, folded it under. Crying took hold of me with quiet force, shaking me till my throat ached from sorrow. The unfairness if death took him! All he ever did was seek the cause of suffering.

I must have slept. I may have dreamed, until the timid knock as of a bird, a brown creeper in a stand of cottonwood trees, woke me. I rose from sleep in an instant. I wove through the tables to the door.

T had not slept a bit.

"T and Sugar—"

The blood stains on my apron sent his eyes to his feet. I took the apron off and tried to smile, as if it were of no concern. When I raised my hand to knead my aching neck, T grabbed it. "Come on to bed and tell me stories!" He pulled hard. Deep exhaustion fell by. I scooped him up under an arm and trotted him down the hall. T's body flapped like laundry. I nearly dropped him, but he tautened, flinging his arms out, playing the currents, croaking like a startled heron just as we reached our door.

I shut it behind us and we froze. "*Shhh*, you're going to wake Frau Schnell—"

"Miz Snell never heared!" he breathed.

"Miz Snell, Miz Shell, Miz Smell, Miz Spell—" I drew the covers back. Tierre hopped in. I covered him over.

"Nah," he kicked the sheet off. "It too damn hot."

"Tierre!" My hands were on my hips as soon as he'd spoken.

"That be how colored folk talk," he said with his lip pushed out.

"Well, fine and good for colored folk. But you? You are not colored, you are black as a lucky domino." I kissed his nose.

He grinned, wiping the wetness off.

"I'll light the candle for you."

"Clara?" he said, when I made to leave. I bent down over the bed.

He blinked. "Nothing," he said.

I kissed him again, touched his forehead to check if he was feverish, and said good night. At the door, I turned. "T?"

A ponderous blink.

I wanted to say *I love you*. It seemed the biggest thing. A big old barge on the Mississippi. Coming at us, however slow. "You weren't afraid of me, afraid of my face the first time that you saw it."

He licked his lips. Sleep was very near. "You ever seen Bug's back, or Affy's bosoms?"

"No."

His eyes closed on the last sight of a long day. "We grown accustom."

The first to come was Hackett. Mid-morning, he opened the door, and drew himself up short of Audwin's cot at sight of me. The bloodied sheets around us, the red rimming Audwin's eyes and mouth, the dried blood in his moustache ending in smeared rivulets under his chin—all said the same thing. Even his ears were bleeding. Hackett took Audwin's wrist up for a pulse. The buttons on his coat sleeve were gold, gold on green, held fast with dark green knots.

"Should he be eating, drinking?"

"If he will," Hackett answered.

"He has not used the bedpan. He doesn't, won't—"

"The eliminatory functions close down." Hackett turned.

He scanned the room and shuddered. "Come to breakfast."

I turned back to Audwin. Hackett left.

A tapping came later, then a loud knock. Tierre put his face in. "Clara? Doctor sent me with a meal."

I would not let him come in. "Leave it there. Thank you."

"Clara?"

"Yes, T."

"The laundry room gots a pile growing up. Big pile of laundry."

"Can you put the stained linens to soak?"

"Yes, ma'am. I done it already."

"You are such a good boy," I said, looking into Audwin's yellow eyes. *Yellow like the stripes on a bee. Yellower'n Old Buck's tail at sunset. Yellow of a new squash blossom.* Robert had given T succor for those crushed magnolia leaves. What succor could I give Audwin for this?

I awoke in the darkness, with Audwin holding me. Came to again, Audwin knotted against my side. When I touched his hair, he sprang up—voice without timbre, breath on sand—"Get out!" He tucked his chin and bled onto my breast.

The sun was aslant when next T came. "I brang the doctor, Clara. You wake? I brang the newspaper. I brang fresh biscuits."

A hand took my wrist.

Light like vinegar in my eyes.

Floury biscuit and a sip of tea.

Hand of somebody.

Button flints.

Audwin's body fought the fever a few hours more. I read the *Picayune* to him, though it burned my eyes, lit by the same lamp Audwin had used with the microscope hour on hour. Doctor Psalter's Soothing Bunion Cream. The train schedules. An opera review. I read him the advertisement for my kin. Audwin had by then stopped moving. His face had lost its lines and seams. He lay there yellow and pacific as Nebraska.

"He will not rise from this," I said.

"No," Hackett said, his arms folded together at his back.

"His notebooks, and his instruments?"

"They will be left for the next man." Hackett's words were clipped. "I have a letter for you, Miss Martin. And though I've tried to keep her off, Frau Schnell cannot be made to wait much longer. The nigger ward lacks laundry."

I took the letter. "Ada," I said, half-smiling.

Hackett had reached the door before I stopped him. "Doctor?"

"Yes." He turned, his impatience to be free of me and Audwin and the deathly room no longer masked. But Audwin's room had a legacy for the living.

"There are no niggers under a microscope."

A snarl cut the surprise from Hackett's face. "We do not live under a microscope," he said. He snatched the door handle. "And thank God for it."

Tierre sat on the floor in the hallway outside Audwin's door. He looked up at me, sad and worried. I knelt down at his side. He said, "It done?" I put my cheek next to his, right against his cheek. We were both too tired to cry.

"Thank you for your good care," I said. "Thank you for mothering me. Shall we take you home now, see Delia and Bug and Robear? You could take a little nap while Robert sings."

I walked T up to the colored ward, to return him to his hot, cramped, dreary, beloved home. Robert saw my despair, right through. He had helped Bug through the fever, and watched his dear friend Dilly die. But Robert didn't take to agonizing.

He tucked T in, then steered me into his room, closed the door and propped me against his bed. Wrapped me in a blanket. Lit every candle on his shrine. He stirred the cornmeal, sprinkled liquor on the dusty floor, cut open a dried fig and made me eat it while he shuffled the sacred images, settling them, singing under his breath.

"Bitter an' sweet," he said, and we each took a gulp of coffee.

"Where is the good route through?" Robert sang out to Papa Legbe, the black straw-hatted doll. He sang and sprinkled more rum and danced barefoot in the room. His dark feet on the floor slowly opened my understanding, erasing the strength that had kept me at Audwin's side throughout his terrible death. Robert's humility became mine. His tenderness became mine. His bravery amid harrowing circumstances did not.

"I need to leave, Robert," I said, awash in fear. "I need to go! I know it. Audwin told me before he died. And not only Audwin—" I gave him Ada's letter. He read her plea: *Leave, honey. Go. I cannot bear to lose you twice.* He placed it on his shrine. He dribbled rum on it, tears and rum, small shining beads. There was no safety here. Even Ada, who feared nothing, feared the maws of Yellow Jack.

Robert said, stopping his dance, "You is free to leave, Miz Clair."

"I've never felt so unfree in my life!" Voice shaking, tears streaming down my face, I said, "I can't go! I cannot stand to lose Tierre. I can't leave him here in this fever hole—"

Robert held my gaze.

"—and I can't protect him if I stay!" The anger brought gasps of air. I'd lost Audwin, lost my parents. I saw and knew and resisted the trapped life I would live at Baruch Place.

Robert huffed a breath. He said quietly, "We all of us lives sixteen times. Eight times a man, eight times a woman 'fore God take us on home. They is all kinds a time to get it right."

"Right? What is right? I am not his mother, I have no rights!"

"He ain't got a mother." Robert paused here, to let my selfishness sink in. "You beats nothin' by a mudslide. You does."

I sobbed, completely unprepared.

"All the peoples I done help to die here at Baruch? they been a gracious crowd. I never once done combat death, Missy. Never. That ain't the battle. I combats struggle and fear. Fear of death don't make no earthly sense. Fear of change, neither. God ain't afeared. Only thing holdin' you back is you—"

Right there I started wailing. He pulled my face into his hands, the cornmeal on his fingers soft and smooth. "Does you feel like it would kill you to leave Tierre Durham behind you when you goes?"

"Yes!"

"Don't be kilt. Take him, Legbe say. Wherever it is you's goin'."

"Take him? But how can I protect him?" I yowled.

Robert smiled, with the army of tranquil dead folks in his eyes.

It could be said I never found kin in New Orleans. It would be a lie. There's the family you're born to and the family you choose. I went downtown to *The Picayune* office the next day to post my reply to an advertisement for a hotel laundress, the hotel as far from New Orleans as the railroad would take me. Ninety miles east, in Ocean Springs, the small resort town on the Mississippi Gulf Coast where the doctors summered— the very end of the plague-free line.

I bought a wooden horse for Tierre at the French Market. We would have one future or two, and I would let Tierre decide—but I wanted to make his choice as irresistible as it was difficult. The horse had a saddle and small rider. I painted the rider black, with a brush made for painting on tinctures. I sat in Audwin's laboratory while the paint dried, looking at his jars and microscopes. I rested awhile. With eyes closed, blurring my gaze to take in Audwin's whole life at one glance, I did not see disaster. I saw love. His every act pursued his calling. Though I hadn't found my birth family in New Orleans, I'd helped a young man through an untimely death. A young man like my father. Both men clung to causes they believed in, one to science, one to religion. In the end, Audwin clung to me. I would take his spirit forward with me, as surely as a parent's imprint.

The Hotel Garriques wrote their acceptance.

I marshaled my courage and went to find T.

When I stood in the sweltering attic, saying my plans to leave, Tierre clasped my wrist. He inhaled. A long starving rattle filled his throat. He tried to talk, but the rattle breath wouldn't release him. It seemed so sudden, this threat of separation. I saw it through his eyes. I watched with dull alarm as T's hand firmed its grip on me. Iron grip and wheezing.

"Did you want to come?" I asked. "Come on with me to Mississippi? You are invited."

Tears and iron, and mucous inhaled.

"I have no right to take you from your home. No right at all."

His eyes flicked open and open, race of a frightened pulse.

"I could try being your mother—"

He kept his grip.

"Or your sister, like," I said. "A big sister you have to mind and be good."

"I will," Tierre said, wiping the wet inside his arm. "And mind."

"Starting when?" I asked.

"Now, Clara."

I took the horse out of my apron pocket. He snatched it from me with his free hand. He adored it, clearly. "Then go and play, let Delia have a turn with your new horse."

T trembled, and showed no sign at all of releasing me.

"Go on, son," Robert said with a wave. "Go on, take Delia to the cistern to play. It like to be your last chance."

Tierre eyed us both for signs of a double-cross.

"Don't make me to ask you twice," I said, stern as any mother.

Tierre laughed, and called to Delia to *come on*.

I reached for Robert's hand. Beautiful strong hand. He tapped his long fingers in mine.

CHAPTER 16

From the Ocean Springs Depot to the grounds of the Hotel Garriques, T and I never once stepped in sunlight. A corridor of piney woods dulled the June day's bladed heat, wrapped the storefronts, dappled the quaint streets. Dogwood trees opened their arms in the shade. A breeze stirred them. People moved at a reasonable pace. One live oak tree dripped enough Spanish moss to stuff a hundred bed ticks. T guessed we'd died and risen into grace.

I walked the half-mile toward the hotel at a strong clip, gripping T's hand. This seeming show of courage covered a hundred pangs of doubt. When we arrived, the cursive *H G* on the closed black iron gate made my palms sweat.

T pushed it open and we entered.

Mockingbirds draped the driveway in flight. The wooded grounds echoed with their raucous singing. A white two-story house lay at the end of our view, ocean water glinting through the trees beyond. Tierre thanked the Lord and laughed out loud. For me, grace would always be the desert, but I squeezed his hand and did a little jig.

The hotel owners, Chick and Peck Fontenot, paled at sight of us. They were expecting a colored woman, not a purplecheeked white girl with a ten-year-old colored waif. I assured them they got two for one and wouldn't regret it. They didn't need much convincing—June was the heart of their summer season. Every room was let, and every bed needed linens.

I took up the laundering work—work that came through me like grass through dirt. I thought of Brother Lars at the livery, brushing his own horse down in the same way he'd read his *Book of Mormon*: once daily, with a stiff back and no apparent pleasure, though I knew he loved that horse. That was the Mormon way, small stabs of the world's great store of joy, whereas in Ocean Springs, Chick and Peck never let pleasure rest. Their merrymaking allowed me a clear path through my workday in the hotel with few jarring encounters, few blunt stares at my face. I changed sheets while the men were off hunting and the ladies were gathered in the parlor for needlepoint and tea. Chick Fontenot wore her red hair piled up, pretty and fair, gracious as a painted fan. I tried to see my mother in that sweep of hair and in Chick's womanly graces. Peck's face and demeanor were brash as his silk cravats.

T did not mourn the loss of his life in New Orleans. For a boy raised in a hellish box of fevers, the Hotel Garriques offered Tierre exquisite freedom. He kept the shell paths raked and the undergrowth cleared. Any time, he might startle a rabbit or uncover a snake. Once he knelt on the porch with his hands closed around a baby armadillo while the patrons searched its face, stroking its pink snout. On the hottest afternoons, Peck Fontenot packed up and took T with him for the hunt—crabbing or fishing or inland for pintail ducks—and then the light rose to Tierre's face and the life to his limbs.

Peck's fondness for T was palpable. Tierre preened under the big man's care. He honed his hunting and tracking skills and, sure enough, the summering gentlemen would ask T to accompany them on outings when the hotelier was occupied with business. He hauled their guns and bullets. He placed them in game's way.

My happiness for his successes was mixed with rue. How quickly T had become indispensable, doing what he loved! But I rebuked myself for petty envy. One Yellow Jack plague had been enough to drive me from New Orleans. T had survived two—and lost his mother before he turned five. Any happiness life could give him, it should.

We became fixtures, in no time, Tierre the lively helper and Clair the reliable drudge. We had our own cabin, a fine improvement from Baruch Place, but within a month at Garriques I'd developed a static downheartedness that I dared show no one. Certainly not Tierre. Whenever I felt trapped and utterly tired of life, about as important as an old bed pan, I took the short walk through live oaks and the wild azalea hedge to the coast. Miles of amber water stretched out to low islands in the Gulf. Close in, the waters were stained the color of the plants and the land. I would stand at the edge of those shining marshes, under giant clouds and flat-topped pines, and think *This is your religion.* The relief and calm I felt there delivered me over to faith. Whereas T fell into the hands of the Baptists, the loud songs and the long tall tales. I looked in at his church one Sunday. *Praise Jesus!* appeared to be the gist of their message. And boisterously delivered. I did not intervene.

When the heat of summer gave way to the six-month autumn—the slow "winter" season when guests were scarce—I kept busy at a loom the Fontenots had. Tierre grew an inch and found religion, while I bloomed to warp and weft. My first rugs were small rudimentary things. Perfect for the servant cabins. When Chick saw the determination with which I wove, she hired a weaver to give me lessons. With tireless patience and stale breath, this wisp of a man opened the world of patterns to me. Large color stripes gave way to primitive plaids and geometrics, by winter's end. I spent hours contemplating the pages of his pattern book, thinking about tie-ups, imagining the beauty within a field of warp yarns taut and ready for the shuttle.

Weaving gives you time to think. Time to feel things in your hands. Time to see patterns everywhere and sense the patterns behind every thing. It was now clear in that Utah my curse had been a blessing. It kept me separate. My facial mark protected me from joining with the throng. However much it wounded me at the time, being different had blessed me with freedom, ensured freedom, which led me to New Orleans, which led us here. This came to me in the midst of weaving my first summer-and-winter coverlet. Summer-and-winter style weaving makes a sturdy double-faced cloth. On one side, your diamond is blue, on the other side it's white—the same diamond. I began to see and trust the goodness at the back side of things.

That spring, Ada sent yet another letter asking me to come home. *Honey dear, Swede misses you. Honey, come make sense of things. You could sell your woven coverlets at the best stores in Salt Lake City. I swear I'd get you a loom and a price.* My response was that I had no home, except where Tierre was. Ada welcomed T as well, said any friend of mine was also hers. I did not share these letters with him. I feared what he might do. He might decide to trade his southern paradise for a look at a swayback farm horse. Tierre was not easily dissuaded. And then where would I be?

I asked Ada to send us books for Tierre's education. I insisted on one hour of study every night after the evening meal. Whether a Baptist Bible or a bill of sale, the boy would need to be able read, to make his own way some day, make his own decisions. He studied because I asked him to. And Ada sent us marvelous tales.

I trekked the woods for wildflowers to press. They gave familiar ease. Life plodded on, adorned with a few good things: the tumult of mossy limbs and bird song at Bayou Beauzage, walks with pelicans on the beach, a few passages of Tennyson that I cherished, and the learning games I devised for Tierre's studies. One thorn pricked my conscience—what was T's real future here? I'd overhead Peck call him a "house nigger" to one guest wary of Tierre's familiarity with the Fontenots, a "petted nigger," a favorite. The ugly appellation made me ask myself how welcome Tierre would be when he was twenty. That day was far distant, but the Civil War hadn't moved the South an inch from its roots. Still sunk in white privilege. Still disdaining T's race. How long would Tierre be happy in this lopsided regime? Were beasts of burden happy or simply used and fed?

Our second autumn at the hotel, my weaving skills increased. Chick hired another laundress to ease my duties and increase my time at the loom. Mittie came to us fresh from her mother's house. She liked the shared arrangement. She could do as much or as little laundry as she pleased and blame the shortfalls on me. She was young and white and pretty. Peck discovered this. Chick discovered Peck, and Mittie was gone. A line of colored laundresses followed, each one homelier than the last. My own position remained steadfast. Peck carried no flame for me, though Chick often told me how pretty I was. "Pretty on the right side. Pretty in profile." It seemed there was room in her world for half a pretty woman on staff.

Especially a half-pretty woman with skills. I wove a coverlet for her four-poster bed, a raspberry red and white overshot weave, which took most of the winter. I had to sew three panels together to make the width. The luxury only set Chick's heart on more. She planned a coverlet for every guest room, selecting all my colors and themes. When she requested a table runner for the foyer, I took a break from weaving. I tried instead the fancy crewel work I'd seen the Sisters use in Brigham. I let my imagination wander through the bayous, my design reflecting the details of the place: the irises and saw palmettos and interlocking ferns. Guests exclaimed when they entered the hotel, pleading to buy it, but Chick would not hear of letting my ornate runner go. It was a signature of the place, she said. With that, I became more artisan than laundress. Two years passed, and I bought pattern books and yarn dyes. I practiced spinning both cotton and linen. I wove in my dreams.

The trust between Peck and Tierre, during these years, brought a rifle into T's hands, Peck's oldest Springfield musket rifle which had done battle in the Civil War. Tierre shot the venerable gun out behind our cabin. Clouds of white smoke and shouts of *Hurrah!* accompanied the death of unlucky pinecones, corncobs and a few swamp rabbits. Peck locked the gun away each night. Going on fourteen, Tierre looked more like a man each day.

The August of our fourth year at the hotel, Chick announced that she was carrying a "special cargo." At this news, all our usual routines stopped. Peck stormed the visitors through their meals and out of doors to "explore the wonders of the coast." He stormed the staff upstairs. We washed and watched and helped and waited. By the time March made its sure demand, Chick could not choose a hairpin for herself, she'd grown so pampered. But frail she was not. I heard her screams. I know how many oaths she swore and the blood she lost, how she bore down until the foetus had to come out of her womb, ready or not, she'd had enough.

Three days later, Chick commandeered the house, the guests, the kitchen, and her infant son, putting the "fragile female" lie to rest. How any man could utter the words "frail" or "weak" or "helpless" as a preface to my sex no longer registered. Men were oafs when it came to women. They had missed the boat entirely. They did not know there was a boat, they were so fond of treading! Indeed, the patterns men and women cut in Dixie differed little from those out West. Catholics and Baptists needed the men to rule and the women to defer just as surely as Mormons did. But here in Dixie, a man had only the one wife to dominate. And his God had none, no Mother in Heaven at all. I chewed on that. Poor William Godbe would have more than the Mormons to fight if he wanted equality of the sexes and happiness for both—his crusade would take him coast to coast and all the way up to Heaven! It is true, a sort of seesaw happiness did pass from Peck to Chick and back. I watched their marriage for five years. It never did seem equal. They tussled. I wove. T hunted. We all of us behaved—masters, servants, and the paying clientele—until a man came who was none of these three, and fit in by sheer difference.

More a guest than a boarder, the tall surveyor arrived late in the winter of 1877. Reece Moon stayed in the servant's quarters, helping Peck mark land for a barracks for bachelors and soldiers on leave. Reece knew a bit of soldiering as well as surveying, and he tried to convince Peck that a bowling alley, built beside the barracks and open for public entertainment, would pay for itself in one season. Chick, spirited and keen, egged Reece on with his dreams about the bowling hall until Peck smacked his backside—indicating severe pain in the pocketbook—and the conversation turned to other things.

Those evenings, I served them brandy and iced cakes and was asked to stay. The front porch had an airborne feel. All the view was of oak limbs draped with moss and the darkening waters of the Gulf out to Deer Island. I wasn't asked to join or comment, only to share the approach of evening with them. Listening to Reece's travels, I felt enormous ease. Like me, he had no real home. He had sited railroads, mapped new towns, divided up estates all across the continent—as at ease in a mayor's office as a miners' canteen. He'd traveled north into Canada and south as far as Mexico.

"And no doubt left a grief-stricken woman in every town," Chick said, smoothing her hair up off her neck. She clucked her tongue. Anyone who didn't know her would have thought she fancied Reece.

His slow laugh penetrated the darkness.

Chick rose to plump her dress, smooth a seam, and then excused herself to tuck the baby in. Peck went to get cigars. The easy banter vanished with them.

I counted to fifteen and glanced at Reece.

"Cold?" he asked. His hands dangled on his trousers, as he spoke, the size and drape of wisteria clusters.

He rose to put a lap robe in my hands.

"Thank you." I gripped it. "Thank you," I said.

He returned to his seat and all talk ended. Silence like the grave. I had no graces, social or otherwise. I couldn't meet his eyes. I couldn't rise to leave. The man was so handsome my eyelids hurt. Blond and tall and ridiculously assured. That dreadful baby, those cursed cigars!

"Come walk with me," he said.

I looked up, stricken.

"Tomorrow," he said.

Peck pushed the door aside.

Reece rolled a brown baton between his fingers.

He lit it.

CHAPTER 17

I took him to the nearest bayou. I chose the narrow footpath among reeds, walking in front to hide my confusion. Reece stopped to watch an egret stalk the muddy shallows with sure elegance. "Poor fish!" He said, smiling. "They haven't any chance." Which struck just like that egret's bill and made me blush. At path's end, when Reece climbed a live oak tree whose branches overspread the water, I stood below in the shade, greatly relieved to be left to myself.

Out where the bayou met the Gulf, a string of pelicans cut a rippling line above the surf. One peeled up, stalled, and dove—not the clean quick strike of a tern, but a great walloping plunge. Count of twenty, the pelican bobbed to the surface and flung a fish down its thick throat. I laughed.

Reece dropped to the ground, beside me. "We can go, now, whenever you like." His tone annoyed me, so self-satisfied, so sunny.

"I never wanted to come in the first place," I said.

"We'll have to stay, then." He set his jaw, looking out across the water, as if he had all day for gazing.

"What?" I asked, completely baffled. But he ignored me. His profile reminded me of a book we'd studied at school—a book of Roman gods. Reece's stature, his charmed bearing, irritated me. It seemed an affront, all that manly surety. It certainly belonged to another world, not mine. "Why are we here?" I asked him. "Charity? Is this some extra little task Chick tacked onto your stay?"

"Nothing so serious, nothing so dire," Reece said.

"Well, then?" I wanted it out in the open, not left for their evening's amusement later.

"Well, Miss Martin, to tell you truly, I thought you'd like some fun," he said.

"Fun?"

"But I was mistaken. It's hopeless. The strain could be too great, on you and me and the pelicans." His shoulders slumped. "No," he said, "I am not man enough."

I giggled. He straightened, and offered me his arm.

We walked to town for cakes and coffee. I cringed at sight of myself in a shop window. A bayou walk requires only work clothes, and panic at our first walk together had led me to choose my most colorless attire. Reece did not seem to mind. He talked of architectural details, pointing to arched windows and leaded glass doors, and then a small verdant courtyard set back from the street. I saw the buildings and businesses of Ocean Springs as if for the first time. Apparently charm existed for all of us, at least all who took the time to stop and see.

We passed a marvelous hat in the milliner's window. Reece would not pause to let me admire it. He banged inside. "See if it fits," he said, over my whispered objections. "Just see if—" He placed the white straw hat on my head. "God Almighty."

I flushed with shame, saying, "What?"

He stared at me with such intensity. His eyes pure blue. "A pelican, Clair—it's roosted on your head."

Stung with humiliation, I turned to leave, but Reece intercepted me with a hand mirror. And there it was. The most beautiful straw hat with beaded netting, on a lovely, flustered woman.

"I'll take it," I said. Reece looked startled. "I've put money away! I know how to have fun!" I said in my defense. He nodded at the clerk, laughing, as she wrapped my hat in paper and chose another for the window, to take my pelican's place.

Reece and I spent many afternoons together. But only after he'd sat knee-to-knee with Tierre, telling him all he knew of the West and big black horses and railroad lines. T insisted he would have a corral full of strawberry roans, all saddle-broke and ready to ride around his ranch. We had to peel dear Tierre off and send him on errands in order to go out walking.

A short quarter mile from the hotel lay my favorite refuge, Bayou Beauzage. Its bright waters opened a pathway through the jungle. I focused on the small, slow vastness of the river, not the dark tangled trees. Reece pointed to an old raccoon scumping up a longleaf pine at water's edge. It stopped on a branch forty feet above us.

"I envy its lookout," I said.

"Oh?"

"Open sky! I prefer an open range to all this green shade, trees carving up light until even my thoughts are not my own—"

"You're not a Southerner."

"Yes, not." Language could pose a challenge when Reece's eyes fastened on mine. "Not to say that I don't love trees."

"Ah. Tell me more." Then talk flowed freely. My life seemed suddenly to matter, because for a few hours someone actually attended to it. Reece had seen more of the world than anyone I'd ever known, and his curiosity extended to me. It made me long for a life of interest. It made me long for a great deal more. I suppose I did show off a little, out of desperation to be heard or noticed or loved, or all three.

"Well, Southern trees are gluttons. Gluttons of light. You know the live oak on the Hotel Garriques' front lawn? That giant tree at least dignifies its gluttony—like an old cathedral."

"A sanctuary of green," he said.

"Shot through with sky. It claims the earth and the heavens, both, taking up plenty of space to do it. A Catholic tree."

He laughed and nodded. I went on. "Tierre's Baptists—they are the native cedars, scruffy little tufts when young, but let them find the light, just once, and watch out for their girth."

"Praise Jesus!"

"Lord, be praised! Now, Episcopalians, they are magnolias—gracious, but a never-ending mess."

"Aren't our hosts the Fontenots Episcopalians?" Reece asked.

I only smiled.

"And what of apostates? Disbelievers? Do we have a tree?"

I wondered if I could tell him, if I could even find the words. "I think I found our tree on a rutted road near the harbor, once. Peck drove us in the wagon through the woods. T smacked back branches, the trees were that thick. We topped a rise and started down, rounding a bend to where the sun burned down on felled trees. A whole stand of magnolia and sweet gum, gone. The leveled cover, that sudden absence of green, sent my eyes up into the only tree left standing. A tulip poplar. Tall and unkempt with paws for leaves, its flowers striped a garish green. Green and orange tulips eighty feet up. Green and orange tulips on a gawky tree—heart kin. Pure utility. The perfect expression of every force, inner and outer, brought to bear on it."

He nodded gravely. I sighed and said, "And I doubted I could ever be so true."

"You have a wonderful mind," Reece said, looking at me without distance. He may as well have hit me with a love club.

I huffed a little and finished my tale, which felt almost like testimony. "I knew from that one tulip poplar why men fell trees without regard, why they cut clearings. Not because the forest is endless. Not out of any pressing need. Human order pleases them above all else. In life, as in religion, they cut the many down to see the one."

Call it lust. Call it desire. Call it a heart pulse beating *Moon, Moon, Moon, Moon* all night long, begging for Reece to smile at me, that lazy smile that felt so wicked, like weeds on fire, so burning and so lush.

That night, when I joined them on the porch for the sunset watch, I had to keep my eyes averted. Chick's incessant talk of beaus and kisses made me feel faint. She gaily catalogued the many lovers who had brought her to the present, to Peck and motherhood, the end of all coquettish affection. Mothers kissed cheeks, she sighed, husbands kissed foreheads. Why had no one warned her of the impending doom of the romantic kiss?

"When I was fourteen, I thought a woman's lips would taste of strawberries," Reece said.

Chick laughed aloud. "What a disappointment for you!"

"Oh, but what they taste of—" he countered. And both of them laughed into their brandies. Peck had no idea what a maze of longing Reece Moon could lay inside a woman. I saw the honeyed eyes Chick used with Reece. I asked to be excused, citing a headache. She leaned in to me to say good night, dazzling as the floral scent rising from her silk dress. "There's a letter for you, Clair, on the desk in the front hall."

The gas lamps burned steadily in the hallway. I leaned against the wall, faint with her womanly charms. *If attracting a man requires feminine wiles, I may as well have been born a plough horse, I thought.* And to prove it, there was Ada's envelope plopped on the glossy wooden tray. Ada Nuttall and my sway-backed plough horse past.

I climbed in bed, fully dressed, and opened the letter. The same yellow stationery. The same careless hand. Yet again, Ada wanted me to come home. But she never said "home," and she never called me "honey." This letter was business, end to end.

27 February, 1877

Dear Clair,

You remember my son Stephen. He bought a ranch. A sheep ranch in southern Idaho that needs civilizing by a woman with guts and strength. That sound like anyone we know? Him and his partner also requires a young man to help them run the sheep to pasture. At the end of lambing season, one year hence, one fifth of the profits from the herd will be paid to said woman. The one with all the strength and daring. She can then pay her friend Tierre.

One fifth, Clair. And nary a soul to tell you what to do. It's new broke country. Don't think the work ain't hard.

Yours, Ada

I cried so hard my neck hurt. I could not calm myself. Right there in my hand lay the means to have it all—a true free life and access to Stephen, a future for Tierre with horses and pay, and best of all my beloved desert—and all I wanted was to feel the big paws of Reece Moon undulate every curved surface that I contained or could be made to contain. I wondered how long it would take him. My body harbored a guess. Twenty-nine hundred years or so. Lush had more pull than desert. Lush was here and lush was now.

"How do I look?" I asked Cecilia, flinging caution over my shoulder. The laundress had a knack for dressing. She raised her eyebrow a little higher than its usual fine arch and didn't say a thing. I took this as praise. She'd found nothing to criticize.

I left her to strip all of the beds without me and took the morning off. Cecilia was strong enough to do this by herself, and smart enough to do as I asked without questions. She might tell Chick and she might not. I decided I would give her the morning off tomorrow, and a fistful of pennies for the bakery. She loved their bourbon pumpkin pie.

Reece had only two days more at the Hotel Garriques before he left for survey work in California. I had no idea how to proceed, no plan, only the urgency of time and my anxious body. I wondered just how a woman let her desires be known, as we walked the beach down and back, and then out to the end of the hotel pier, stopping at the latticed bathing house.

"Ah, well," I began. After two weeks in his company, I didn't know where to look, his face so high above me, his long arms, his flat waist. I closed my eyes, the sun flashed, and the day became all lips and sighs, with our hands held at our backs, all tilting greed.

"Clair?"

I opened my eyes, the sighs and greed mine alone. Reece stood as he had before, a few paces off, but his brow was pinched. He gripped the lattice. "What are you doing here?"

Loving unholiness.

"Who packed you into that servant's apron? Why in

God's name don't you leave?" The criticism touched me, meant as it was to help not harm.

"And where would I go? Back to Utah?"

"Utah? The women are puppets there."

"Don't tell my friend Ada Nuttall that!"

"She is an exception?"

"Ada is more given to rule, if you knew her."

"Well, everyone has a past they wish they hadn't. You could go anywhere. Any state in the Union."

"I have eighty-two dollars, a marked face and a fifteen-year-old charge who thinks he's wrapped in God's own swaddling here. Tierre loves this place. And I love T. If we are born to things, I was born for him. And Tierre was born for Baptist shouts and hunting in the piney woods."

Reece shook the rail, dissatisfied. "You know he could do better. You both could."

"I am not free as you are, Reece!" I said. "You have no ties, no children. You aren't a married man, which makes you free as the birds above us—"

"I thank God every day for it."

His vehemence stopped me. It turned my thoughts around. "Are you so bitter? Against marriage?"

"Marriage is the perfect institution for taking on ballast. Look at Peck—thinks he is lord of his own castle and—and Christ, they load you up for the journey until sinking's the only thing."

I'd only ever heard the highest praise for marriage and its trappings. I asked him who "they" were.

"Every man who's knuckled under to every woman who wants his pay. Respectable society. The married masses."

"You believe women marry for money?"

"It is a largely unadmitted fact."

"And men marry for . . . "

"Lust, sanctified. Though the bargain struck is the devil's own."

"Your parents must have loved each other—"

"They endured each other. And grew rich and tight as ticks. Mother never saw anything of value outside of her own parlor. She tried to keep me in it, God help her, with no luck at all!"

"There are good marriages, Reece."

"There are good prisons, Clair." He looked into my eyes directly. "You and I can find a better fate."

If entrails could laugh, mine laughed for joy. Reece said we shared a fate, he and I, which meant our futures were intertwined. I floated through the chores that day stoking our future into blazing dreams. Late that night, I awoke from a vision of Reece in a patch of moonlight stroking my hair, touching my waist, just as an otherworldly threshing started up between my legs—a ponderous happy swallowing, like a hog in a tray of applesauce. Smoldering sweet corpulent wetness.

"Oh, Stephen," I said in wonder, facing his photograph, too happy to correct myself until after the gulping swallowing stopped.

CHAPTER 18

S heets flapped on the line, over and up, over and up, like the pedals of a soft pump organ. I was late. I didn't care. After my night of pleasure dreaming about Reece, I'd let the morning go to drowsing.

Cecilia waited tight-lipped in the doorway to the laundry. She had every right to fume about my taking another morning off. Sharp and comely, she looked like she had lately won some battle.

"Mrs. Fontenot wants to see you." She said it so curtly I changed my plan, and hugged the coins in my pocket so they wouldn't jingle. She didn't deserve bourbon pie. Not if she had to stick her bony, pretty face into my happiness. "I'll go see Chick and get the orders for the day," I said, without acknowledging her message.

On the rose path to the dining room, I lost my ire. Cecilia's show of mettle actually amused me. She would need it when I left with Reece, she'd be Chick's only laundress. Amazement struck—what lightness! I could put those years behind me now, everything made sense. Reece could see I was more than a serving maid. At last, a man who saw me truly, me and my "wonderful mind." But if we wouldn't marry . . . well, we would work the details out together.

The dining room basked in February light. No patrons. Breakfast had been cleared. I hadn't realized it was so late, Cecilia's peevishness so well-earned. I went to the parlor, which was also empty, then up to Chick's sitting room. The door to her bedroom stood ajar. Inside, reclining as she had the long months of her confinement, Chick lay in the half-dark. I asked if I could pull the curtains.

"Whore." She said it quietly, as if the word cost her.

I looked at her, amazed.

"The little whore." Chick hit the coverlet with her fist. "Reece is a bounder! A beautiful cad, he'd never marry her, the stupid thing."

I stood absolutely still.

She looked at me with fury in her eyes. "You didn't help her, did you? Did you help Cecilia to sneak out last night?"

Tears of cold judgment fell. Chick looked away. "Forgive me, Clair. I cannot yet see straight. I can't imagine and I won't imagine those two—the gardener found them on the lawn behind the azalea hedge. Cecilia's undone! She'll have to leave before nightfall. I will not have a whore in this house. And as for Reece, that lecherous—"

My body had gone steely cold. A dim pain reached me across twenty years. My mother had hated lechers. She'd fled them, risking unknown peril. Mother, too, might have hated Reece.

"He has ruined her. *Quel brute!* But a woman has her say. It is all her fault, that ridiculous girl. Rolling in the bushes like a snake. And was it worth it, was he?" Chick's voice grew shrill. Her foiled femininity could barely be contained. My own femininity lay chained at the bottom of a cold dry well. I started to consider Reece's betrayal, or if there had been anything between us to betray, when Chick rose from her bed.

"She is fired. I'll have Peck do it. The silly mongrel, the loose bitch!" Then she asked, as if we were in sympathy, "Whatever could a whore say in her own defense?"

This woman, with her magnificent home, devoted husband and bevy of servants fulfilling her every need, wanted Reece Moon as well.

I pulled the curtains back. Color took the room. "You tell me. You're surrounded with Peck's money."

I left her stunned silent. By the time I reached the woodshed, where T crouched in the sunlight with a beetle on his sleeve, I had decided our Mississippi sojourn was over. Hypocrisy makes the heavens reel. It tears away earthly shrouds. As bad as I felt about Reece's sneaking thievery of Cecilia's naked body on the lawn, as much as I had dreamed that would be me, I found the Fontenots' false superiority unbearable.

I could have Idaho and clear open skies for Tierre.

"Do you know what?" I said to him, turning the shock and sorrow I felt into good cheer, "we have an invitation from Ada, to go West." I took T to our cabin. I gave him Ada's letter and helped him read each word. This made slow going, so I reread it to him after. Tierre grew solemn and asked me if I wanted to go.

"I believe we've gained all we can here." And then, gripped with homelessness, knowing how uprooted we were in this place that would house us and place demands on us but never be our own, I said, "I want to go home, T." The longing overtook me just as the words left my mouth.

Tierre sensed my desperation and asked for time. He stacked a few pieces of cut wood against the cabin while I sent waves of unconsidered certainty to him on the February breeze. I didn't want to spend another night at the Garriques, a night when I might see Reece Moon. A night when, failing in nerve, I might apologize to Chick and resume our servitude. I watched T stand quite still, looking south to where the Gulf sparkled in the dense fragrant air. He tossed some pinecones at the woodpile. Then he came inside and said, "Where you goes, I goes, Clara."

I asked him to go tell Peck that we were leaving. He walked off with his head down. I started to pack our things.

Peck knocked on our door an hour later, face red from sun and female trouble. He could not fathom my defection on Cecilia's behalf, nor his own wife's bitter tears. He asked for an explanation, some way to make sense of things.

Tierre looked on, full of love for the man.

No sense could be made of the bonfire in my heart. Whatever had happened, for good or ill, I belonged to the ancient sage plains west of the Wasatch. I said, "We're leaving, Peck. Today."

"Without notice?"

"This is our notice."

I expected a cascade of words, some cajoling or kind regrets, but being cruel as he was kind, Peck only said, "Where will you go, a freak and a darkie?"

Tierre stepped to my side, on instinct to defend. I felt his surprise and guessed at his sorrow, but I didn't console him. I wanted Tierre to remember this view of Peck. "Do you see how deep his affection runs? How much he really honors you?"

Peck held out a five dollar bill.

I took a deep breath. It pained me, but I snatched the money from his hand.

We slept at the depot lodgings, compliments of Peck's five-dollar farewell. Reece found us there the next morning. I sent Tierre off to buy candy, and then stormed out the station doors. Reece caught my arm and I shouted, "Don't! Do not touch me."

Two passengers entering the station stopped to see if he meant harm.

Reece's eyes came into focus, then. He looked at his own hand. He let me go as tears riddled my face. I sobbed a good deal out by the tracks, and shook and glared at him, sickened by his nearness and the loss of my romantic dreams. Reece folded his arms and said with gravity, "I had no idea."

I looked off west. "And that hurts even more."

"Well, let me mend the rift I caused—" He believed that with a few apologetic words to Chick, he could win my job back. Though his train was leaving for California at noon, he had time enough to get things back to square.

I stared at the crown of his hard gold head. "You would have me go back, to the Garriques?"

"Hell, yes."

"But I'm free to go wherever I like. You said it."

He nodded. "Yes, you are."

"Chick called Cecilia a whore." It hurt, saying her name. It brought up the reality of them laying together. And the kisses. And the sperm liquid placed inside.

Reece's little smile cut spirals in my heart. "Envy. Pure and simple. Women thrive on it, married women in particular."

"I won't go back."

"What if I tell them to give you a raise? God knows you deserve it. I've caused this difficulty, and I should—"

"You should be talking to Cecilia! Maybe she could use your tender loving care."

"What if—"

"What if I am through living off of other people's dreams like they are more than bones sucked dry!" I rose to my whole five foot and four inches, and raised my voice higher still. "I can go anywhere. Any state in the Union! You said it yourself."

"Yes, I did."

"So I am going home."

"To Utah? Where's the sense in that?"

"What do you care? You have no right to an opinion. Especially when you treat those you love by leaving them. You are a scourge on all women!"

Reece nodded. "That may be. But I'll come out all right. You—well, you can be a mule's ass in Utah, or a mule's ass here with food and regular employment."

I slapped his face. Those gleaming eyes that only saw me as a servant. Not a woman. I walked straight back into the depot and ate all of the pralines that T bought. It felt like I'd been shot through a cannon, and Reece Moon was the fuse.

Ranch

Curlew Valley: 1877-1879

We waited for Stephen Nuttall at Kelton Station. Two dozen tents, the railroad tracks, and salt flats stretching away to the horizon. Salt and heat and little more at this northernmost outpost of the Utah Territory. It took a prophetic imagination to conjure a future here at the whited edge of an ancient lake. I felt prophetic. And strangely giddy. While Tierre looked north at a flank of sage-green mountains, hoping that way lay the Nuttall ranch, I gazed southeast at the faint blue line of the Wasatch Range. Zion didn't raise a sparkle, wasn't even a speck. Joy struck me like a stray arrow: *the Mormons have tamed what they can of this desert.* Smiling in the glare of the northern Salt Lake Valley, I realized just how little that was.

I was indeed a prophet if I could have my own work with pay in this austere Heaven, and a glance at Stephen Nuttall on a daily basis, along with freedom from the patronizing yoke of Mormon rule. Hadn't I told Audwin as much when we dreamed our own religions on the levee that day?

My little *hallelujah* stayed inside my chest. Nothing in Mississippi had prepared T for such emptiness. His black face glistened like a starling's back. "They ain't a tree in sight," he said.

I shaded my eyes and smiled. "No paths to rake."

"Where the folk here catch they fish?" he said, disgusted, and scuffed the answer in the dirt. Tierre was fifteen and too old for mothering. I doubted he would tolerate sistering, soon. I brushed my skirts of traveling dust and left T to find his own good humor, or not.

He'd been in such high spirits at Ogden Station, our first Utah stop. T had jumped off the engine car, gawking at the passersby and barely started to tuck his shirttail in when Ada Nuttall snapped him up. She did not balk at the color of T's skin. Ada held onto him like she'd never let him go, smiling up at the train windows, wind tossing the blue-black feathers of her hat. I stepped to the door of the coach. Sun caught my dress. Morning sun and a smoky breeze and Ada's eyes found mine. She whooped, wrangling T into laughter beside her. As long as I looked in Ada's face, that stout intelligent hard-browed face, the step seemed easy enough to take. One step, then a second and a third. But all the station swarmed with them, young and old, *white and delightsome*, and I knew how they lived—squared streets, Wardhouses, and rigid rows of poplars. I knew who ruled their thoughts. No force, not Ada, not even six years' absence from the Utah Territory, could loose me from that door. I would step off at Corinne and then again at Kelton Station, among the free, my grudge was still that fresh. So it was Ada who came to me, and stepped into the coach, and held me tight.

She spoke with zeal about Stephen's Idaho ranch until the porter hitched his way along the aisle, calling out points north and west. Ada patted my hand. Then she gripped it. "I'd best go find that T of yours, and give him a bushel of advice. Maybe two."

"Ada!" I said, as she gained the door. I buried my hands in

her thick brown hair. "We'll make you proud."

And right there Ada had bawled—two, three hard shakes, and she was gone.

Ogden fell away behind, and twenty miles later, when we skirted Brigham City, I pointed out the little hill above the cemetery where my cabin stood, though at such a distance T could not pick it out. We traveled on to Corinne, then west into the desert. The closer we got to Kelton Station, the more I felt release.

I'd only ever had two heroes in my life, Poker Jim and Ada's Stephen. Both lived the lives they wanted to, Mormons be damned. The fact that I would live side by side with Stephen didn't really grip until Ada gave me his letter in Ogden, saying where and when he'd fetch us. I'd drawn a hundred mental pictures of the twenty-seven-year-old Jack Mormon cowboy bachelor. The plain hand and deep blue ink of his letter made my pulse race. I knew that I deserved this new life—*desert, a dog, good work and sunsets*—but something in that blue script said I might deserve him, too. I chastened myself for womanly foolishness. I'd misjudged Reece Moon. In truth, I only knew Ada's version of Stephen, only a mother's view of the man. Stephen Nuttall could be intolerant. He could be haughty or mean. He could laugh out loud at sight of us—

I beat my skirts down again, to soften the first impression. I was bent to the hems when a man picked up my trunk.

His hair hung in waves, yellow streaked red with sweat under his hat. He swung through introductions as easily as he loaded our things. And though I'd heard all of Ada's glowing tales about her son, I couldn't help but think how unremarkable he was. Squat and freckled. Small features and a ragged brown beard.

Stephen didn't apologize, not for the tent-town of Kelton

or the wobble-wheeled wagon he fetched us in. I sat beside him with my hands in my lap. Tierre leaned up between us, all curiosity and nerve. "Who graded them railbeds? Who done died? Where these folk could buy a rifle or a hoe?"

Stephen answered T's questions. Then they talked about the ranch.

"How big a herd you gots, how many sheeps?"

"How many?" Stephen paused to make count. "Four hundred head."

"Lord a' mercy." Tierre slumped a little. Crossing the continent, he had imagined thousands. He'd scrutinized the layout of every ranch from the Green River onward, and forced me to choose: stripped pole or stone or picket. "You gots the fences all built?"

"No fences."

He leaned into my shoulder. "They ain't none?"

"Built a moveable holding pen, for the lambing."

"Oh, my Lord." Tierre closed his eyes. The sky paled behind him, the whole white midday expanse of it. He was the only bit of color in sight. After gazing awhile at his inner West, T opened his eyes and grinned. I guessed the next question before Tierre even asked it.

"How many horses you gots?"

"Shep, here. She's old, but she's sure-footed. Keeps to a trail."

T looked at the tired creature pulling us along, and slapped the seat in bold dismay. "Lordy, Clara!"

Stephen asked, "He a religious boy?" And then a smile that would teach infants and choirboys a lesson in bona fide radiance broke over his face. That instant change from unremarkable to stunning registered in my womb. I swallowed, swallowed and grinned, my lips pinched tight as the seams on a fifty-pound bag of barley. "Stephen is a boy of few words," Ada had said, and been wrong on both counts. Here was no boy, but a man, compact and knowing, who had surely and regularly hefted such loads. *Oh, my lord.*

We traveled north, away from the Great Salt Lake. Sage dotted the bare, dry buttes which never quite came to mountains, just shrugs of the earth, shrugs and dips and little ravines hoarding bright green stands of rabbit brush. At dusk, at the base of that sage green mountain range Tierre had admired from Kelton, we made camp. Stephen showed T how to lay a fire—this boy who had stoked engines across a continent—and Tierre's fire took, the first time. With his burlap coat pulled up around his ears, T said, "Clara never would say what about mountains." He sat, all knees, folded up as near the fire as he could get. His eyes followed the line of peaks. "Now I sees why."

"Raft River Range," Stephen said.

"They smells of Heaven."

Tierre and Stephen ate boiled potatoes while I took in the stars. In Mississippi, stars were fuzzy with distance, a puzzlework for sailors, fine slow-moving guides. Here, they were a palmful of brilliance, cast like dice just overhead. I'd forgotten to even miss them, the sevens and elevens rolling off the rim of the mountain, never bothering to mark out anything, with no use for gods or bears or pots and pans—

"You better eat, ma'am. Long time till breakfast."

T had fallen asleep in his coat. Stephen covered him with blankets. Then he stretched himself out on his pallet near the fire, slowly, as if his joints needed a little extra time to unkink. Stephen's thighs, wider than his hips even in repose, locked my star-filled eyes to earth. We were alone. Just Stephen, just me. I kept hard watch on the butt end of the wagon and waited for him to speak.

Wind scoured the face of the mountain.

"I expect you were surprised," I said, "disappointed like."

"Ma'am?"

"Sight of Tierre and me at the station." It seemed best, seemed imperative to get this out. Some people cringed at sight of my cheek, or stared and looked away pretending they hadn't seen the red blotch. A few turned mean. I preferred to preempt their cruelty.

"No, ma'am," Stephen said, "but I ain't seen the boy work yet. And I ain't tried your cooking. So I'll keep the gate open on that one."

I looked to see if he was making fun, and saw instead the dead-level eyes of Ada looking back, that good sense in her son.

I glanced up at the stars and said good night to Ada's darling. As I climbed into the wagon, I heard, "You got three blankets. Spread the hay over top. Hard dew, maybe a frost tonight."

I'd have missed it. I would have driven right on by.

We'd left the Raft River Range behind us long since. The low ridge we'd been climbing swung east, then curved north-west, forming a small valley before the prairie stretched on, flat and featureless, again. We descended. The ranch house lay in sight right from our rounding of the butte, but the wood and daub walls and the gray sod roof so resembled the desert around them, it was only with a loss in elevation that the building came up different from the land.

A squat rectangle with a bright blue door.

Stephen played a hand down over his beard. "Mother shipped the paint up, special."

It was the first and last of Ada's touches.

Bits of ceiling brushed onto his hat when we ducked in. "There's the kitchen, that's the bunk." The kitchen was a camp stove, a half-empty sack and a fry pan in the dirt. A dog slunk in, licked the pan for leavings, and slunk back out at the easy swing of Stephen's hat.

"Ow!" Tierre howled.

Stephen stepped out. "They ain't pets, son." Then he leaned back in, "Ma'am," and nodded and left me to it.

I bent toward the cast iron pan and stopped, letting a few tears fall. *Nine days' travel. That's all this aching is.* I took it by the handle and surveyed the dark remainder of the house. A crate with playing cards scattered on top. No windows, no chairs, no furniture at all. The bunk in the corner was of Stephen's design—a blanket folded the long way and laid right on the dirt.

I stepped outside and scanned the rise of sage behind me, the sage plain stretching away in front. Not a sound in the little valley. Even the dogs had gone.

"I'll be go to hell," I said. Then I asked my good friend Ada. *Where's the homestead? Where's the outhouse? Where's the cellar, the garden, the shade?*

I hiked uphill, between two small, rock-strewn springs. The dry heat was familiar, the tasks ahead all too well-known. They stripped the six years I'd been South right off, and I was alone, a girl again, dumb caretaker, dutiful maid, a sexless thing climbing for freedom from Erastus Pratt and the bonnets in the Big Field, climbing to find wildflowers in the hills, leaving the faithful to work their rows and cook their gains, and store and worry on them.

I cursed myself, and cursed my pride, thinking anything could be different. Born a servant, I'd die a servant. Curses marked every step of my climb until I reached the ridge and the hard blue ranges in the distance stopped me. Stopped my thoughts.

South and east, north and west—Stephen's ranch was ringed by mountains. Embraced on every side. Their long blue arms skinned years back off me, more years, even, than I had. Empty, and still, I walked the ridge to a clump of splayed cedars. There, I found shade. There the blatting of sheep drifted up from below, where three men moved like flotsam on a pale, slow sea.

We do not choose where prophecy takes us. I wondered, staring out at the unbounded ranch, if I had courage enough to live what I'd foreseen.

CHAPTER 20

"Don't thank God, thank the sheep," Stephen said, and winked. A band of white flesh ran from ear to ear—he'd pushed his hat back for the meal. It was as near as he'd ever come to removing it.

We sat with our legs dangling down, the width of the wagon between us. T sat cross-legged in the hay. He cut his usual Baptist blessing short, and made like he was plenty thankful. A sheep with a doleful expression poked me in the skirt and then leaned against my legs, daydreaming. I appreciated the warmth if not the aroma.

"Good biscuits." Stephen helped himself to three. He grinned at his plate, then out at the greening prairie where the herd munched without distraction.

I had cooked one meal. I had heard the ewes approaching before they arrived and surrounded the hut. I had sat on my trunk in the darkness alone with the door open—sheep staring in—wondering where along the trail of my years I had lost all sanity. I tried to keep the complaint out of my voice. "We'll need a table, Stephen, and a water barrel. And we'll have to have an outhouse and a cellar, both." I tasted the mutton. It fell into thick, sweet strands. "The house needs windows. I have money, and I'd be willing to buy for the house."

"House is yours to do with as you like." Stephen didn't look up from the plate he held butted to his chest.

"And Tierre has to work at his schooling. So we'll need books, and he'll require time for study each day."

Stephen's eyes narrowed in a shadow grin. "Sheep herder's a rich man if time gets counted for wealth." Behind the humor, I saw that he believed this. He had not lied to Ada, increased his fold, fudged a house and a creek and a few outbuildings to try to get us here. No, four hundred sheep and a one-room hut just left of nowhere—the man believed that he was blessed.

"I can get books from Harlan," Stephen said. Harlan was Stephen's partner, co-owner of the ranch, another unknown, unexplored feature of our new life. Stephen tossed his plate onto the hay and turned to T. "Well, son, what do you think?"

"Think I could use me more of that mutton," T said.

I touched Tierre's arm. "Stephen means about the ranch, about our staying."

"Shah," T said.

I firmed my grip. "Something is bothering you, now. I know it." We had no alternate plan, but I would make one if Tierre did not want to stay.

A deer fly cut past. Stephen snugged his hat back down till all the face that showed was ruddy.

T ducked his chin. "Well, I is afraid of them sheeps, Clara. They is so many and they ain't smart like dogs."

I cut the smile off Stephen's face with a look said *swallow bones*. "Well, don't watch them, T. You watch Stephen. See how he does. You watch Harlan. That's the way to learn it, how to handle those sheep, don't you think?"

T looked in my eyes. "What about that big ol' ranch house and them fine corrals, and the shady green pond with kindly breezes?" We'd read the Wild West dime novel I bought him for the journey till the pages fell out. We had indeed lost a few pages, coming here. And yet all T could worry about was my happiness.

"I am willing," I said. "You?"

Tierre looked at me with a dignity I admired. "They's work to do."

"All right, then. We will stay."

Stephen took Tierre's plate and hurled it into the brush. Then he poked T in the ribs and gripped the wrist that flashed out in self-defense. "Monkey trap—" he said, his thumb and middle finger joined like a steel bracelet around T's wrist. Tierre yanked and slapped and tried to wrench free, till both their bodies rolled off the back of the wagon. Panting and laughing in the dirt, Stephen said, "There's a secret, to get free—"

Tierre laughed and smacked at him, getting a knee into his stomach. "A secret from you, old man?" They reversed positions, dirt scunneling down Stephen's collar. "Nah, I rather be a monkey, any day."

Stephen dragged up onto his knees, his hand still locked on T's wrist. "Bet I can get to that plate before you can."

Tierre didn't even answer. He burst from the dirt like steam from a stack and broke Stephen's grasp in the going.

They raced out and fell onto the plate.

They scuffled in the sage.

Stephen came back empty-handed. "The boy likes mutton. That's a start."

The little hut held nothing but the cold out and the darkness in. T and I used old horse blankets on the floor. Stephen slept with the herd. The arrangements were tolerable, but for a single fear—Harlan Lawes, Stephen's partner. Harlan lived in

a cave out east of the ranch. I dreaded the thought of ever sharing the abysmally small hut with him or anyone else. I asked if
Harlan didn't lack for company.

"Harlan? Hell, ma'am—excuse my French—Harlan lives
like a coyote and thinks like a sheep. Or is it maybe the other
way round?" Tierre snickered. He'd spent a week of evenings
discussing ranching with Harlan after dinner out in that cave.
"Harlan don't much care for the comforts of hearth or the
company of women. He prefers his books and his dogs."

"He ugly as a bottom fish," T said.

Stephen smiled. "The herd don't seem to mind."

Like a spring runoff, lambing can be channeled but it
can't be contained. Stephen spent two days and nights out on
the range with Harlan, gathering the herd and separating the
drop bunch. T strung lanterns over the little lean-tos he'd built
from brush and sticks. I cooked morning to night, in prepara-
tion for the siege. When Stephen took T out to set up the
lambing pens, I walked east to introduce myself to Harlan.

I saw him over the backs of a hundred gray sheep. A dog
barked. His bowler hat turned toward me. A black bowler
pillowed on gray hair. Harlan's poncho caught the wind. He
raised a hand and the dog stopped barking. His hand dropped,
and the dog trotted right to his side, its blue eyes still on me.

My smile of greeting failed me, as I drew close. I even
forgot my own ability to shock at first sight. Here was the bulk
of a john boat, on stilts. Big chest, wild hair, huge nose, his
bottom lip unnaturally yellow, the top lip lost in fleece. Harlan
only looked at me slantingly, keeping his enormous eyes on
the herd.

"It's Clair Martin. From the ranch. I came to bring you
these." I drew two warm jars from my coat pockets.

Harlan frowned, his eyebrows forming a hedge. He took one jar and turned it. "Stew?" he said, looking doubtful. His gruff English accent rebuffed my gift.

"No! No, sir, it is mash. Peelings and corn meal and meat scraps I boiled to pulp for the dogs."

Harlan's hand traveled down his beard. "For the dogs it is intended—and they will all of them enjoy it."

I laughed. "Will you dare to try my biscuits?" I held out a half dozen, bundled against the weather.

His lips pursed. "Dog biscuits?"

"Never you dare!"

His eyes tilted to look at me. "Fresh, are they?"

I opened the cloth, and Harlan Lawes smiled.

Listening to Harlan's measured description of the herder's job and the wrangler's job, Stephen just laughed. "Lambing is a month-long hell of blood and death and losses. Only reasonable thing about it—it ends." He rubbed his hands together. "Eventually."

At first, it seemed a holiday to me. The ewes paraded through a rail chute, one by one. Harlan sent them right or left: the mothers with bags full of milk into a pen, the late lambers wrangling off with T to crop at the promise of new grass. Stephen never stopped moving, from the herd to the penned mothers and back, signaling the dogs, close and far. The spotted dogs were stand-in men, moving with foxes' feet among the herd. I leaned on the rail marveling at their skill until Stephen shouted, "Clair, jail time!"

I joined him in the pen. A newborn lamb lay there, still as the earth beneath it. Stephen held its mother with a hook. "Peel the skin off the snout."

I stared. The infant never moved. I reached down, touching the wet orange film. The ewe *maa*-ed in protest. "Be quick about it. Don't be dainty. They ain't."

I pulled the transparent cover off the snout.

"Now thump it. Thump it good."

Confused, I thought he meant the skin in my hands.

Stephen kicked the newborn, scooting it over the ground. "Damnation. Lost the firstborn. You'll have to pick it up, now, toss it out over the fence."

I knelt in the dirt in cast-off overalls and slid my arms under the limp body. It clung, but when I stood the lamb sank through my grasp, hit ground, and a shuddering bawl started up, the lamb raising hell with its first breath. Stephen let the ewe in close to lick the newborn clean.

"Jail time, after all." He winked at me and led them off, and I knew a moment of relief.

But relief never really had a chance, after that. The first lamb came at nature's hands, only needed a good hard thump to claim a breath. But many came out tangled or hind-first. Harlan played midwife, and a patient, steady one he was, through all the gore and cold and losses. When twins came, the second lamb was often refused by its mother. He would skin a dead newborn from a different ewe, and fit its wool on the second-born lamb like a coat. Harlan called this orphan a "bummer." He gave the bummer lamb with eight legs and two tails to the dead lamb's mother. Then the job became mine, to pen the couples in tight quarters in a lean-to, so they could cinch their bond. I hand-fed lambs who were too weak, started reluctant teats, forced stubborn ewes to feed their young with the help of Harlan's dog, Ginnie. Ginnie had no love for stinginess. She crouched at the margin of a pen, staring an old ewe down. Her airy growl, never sounding, never ceasing, sparked interest in the most indifferent of mothers.

Meanwhile, I baked and cleaned and kept a pot of soup on the stove night and day. When I slept, the sounds of the lambing never left me, nor the smoking lanterns, the man's shadow I cast. One night, I was dragged awake by Stephen's voice: *I need you.* He stood over me, heaving from exertion, holding a ewe in his arms, a head projecting from its vulva, swollen twice its normal size.

In the stove light, it glowed purple.

He almost toppled when he set her down. "Scrub your hands. And oil them."

I did as I was told, but I wouldn't step close, fearful of the deadly mother-child knot.

"You got to birth this one."

"I can't."

"You can and will."

Fury gripped me. The air in my lungs swarmed like boiled water. "Get Harlan—"

"Harlan's hands are too big." Stephen held out his own hands. They looked immense. "Close your hand and enter her."

At my touch, the ewe slammed forward. "Impossible!"

"Gentle, now. Ease your fingers in. Your fingers are the light they need. It is dark in there." His gaze was steady. His will strong. I knew he had entered the unknown like this a hundred times.

I eased two fingers in the wet lip. Slick, and warm. Though the ewe resisted, there was room. Fear evaporated as my hand slid in. The whole cold world dissolved around it, clasped in such warmth to the wrist.

"Can you find the front feet?"

My hand swam in dark comfort. "No."

"Or the shoulder? Something must be doubled up—"

A contraction clasped my arm. I swam in deeper, intoxicated by the heat, the swollen head of that lamb against my chest smelling of autumn and drenched grasses. "One!"

"You found it? Shoulder or hoof?"

"A hoof."

"Now, bring it toward you, slowly. Can you find the other?"

I rotated my whole arm and a small hoof filled my palm—recognition without words.

"Bring them forward, now. Don't rush it. Your release'll do the work."

The ewe's whole body shook, a revelation to me. I had forgotten the mother existed.

"Do you have them?" Stephen seemed anxious. I couldn't imagine why. Time and care had fallen by.

"What?"

"The front feet?"

"Yes—"

"Then pull, girl, pull as she pushes!"

I leaned back on my heels and the vulva opened wide, passing a rust-colored lamb onto my lap. It writhed, legs stroking outward like the swimmer it was. Stephen knelt at its side. We stroked the face free of its birth gravy and the mother licked its limbs. Stephen sighed, pale and wet-handed. My legs were slick. My heart pounded. He laughed—whiskey and onions on his breath—shaking his head. "Bear's ass! I'll tell Harlan. Looks like we got us a new midwife." I felt his voice, his approval, in my ribs. I wobbled to my feet.

"Go on to bed, Clair," he said. "You've earned it."

I fell into that safe, dark place, again, as the new lamb sucked first milk. Not all births lead to suffering. Some give warmth and joy.

Lambing season gave way to leave-taking, too soon for my taste. The men were off to summer pasture. As Tierre and I had never been apart since we'd met at Baruch Place, I spent the whole morning watching him stow the wagon with provisions for his first herding trip, all fifteen years of him. The jaunty walk, that sweet point his chin took when he was glad, his eyes like sun in trees. I might not see him till September. It was April. I wondered how I'd live without his light. T stopped whistling and looked at me. "You 'fraid, Clara?" he asked. His summer work lay ahead, a welcome mystery. Mine lay here: no outhouse, no garden, no ditch for irrigating it.

"Afraid of what," I said, affecting courage, "so much nothing? I am amenable, if the desert has lessons to teach."

"*Amen*-able?"

"Don't start that Bible thump with me!"

T laughed, and the fear went out of my face.

Stephen glanced over, gauging the length of our close good-byes. Harlan had gone ahead to scout a first night's camp. Stephen and T would meet him with the herd. Stephen led Shep into the traces, his body as stocky as T's was lean, with a tight grip to his gait, not a gesture to spare. The patches on the butt of his trousers were short and flappy.

Tierre eased into my line of sight, that is right between me and Stephen. "Who all you gonna miss, Clara gal?"

"Don't ask or I'll start crying," I said. "You will be alright without me?"

Tierre leaned into my shoulder and said, "Now, they is a trick, Clara. To that monkey trap a his."

"What trick?" I asked, as if I had no interest.

"They's two." He laid his long open fingers in my hand then crimped them tight. "You gots to let go what you is ahold on. Loose the fist. Don't grip at nothing, to slip free."

Stephen climbed up onto the seat. He snugged the reins, and I felt Tierre's body tense. T was halfway to Harlan's camp already. Men and their desperate callings.

"What's the second one?"

"Hunh?"

I encircled T's wrist and tugged a bit. "The second trick, to getting free of Stephen?"

"Ain't no trick a'tall, gal. Like when he flang my dinner plate in the brush. Force a craving! The strength'll come. You just gots to crave some other thing more."

That night I built a fire near the closest spring. I fed the flames with billets of sage so dry they seemed to breathe and then explode, no smouldering to them. I hummed one of Tierre's songs, *Oh, the long road home.*

Dark of night, wrapped in a blanket, I clung to earlier hymns and traveled down snatches of melody until, just before sleep, my mind gathered like smoke over a valley and settled on Brigham City.

Ada assured me not one tree had stood in that valley before the Saints came, only sage and wild grasses, the white of the sego in spring. The faithful loved repeating this, to trumpet all they had accomplished in a decade: the desert tamed, their yield of fruit and grains, our fields and yards huddled like bee-boxes around the Tabernacle lot. But what I felt, as a girl, was the pull of that prior landscape, barren of things. Not one tree. I couldn't imagine it, which made the unsacred pull to know even stronger.

Now, the unimaginable was mine.

CHAPTER 21

The bare patch where Stephen had quarried sod for the roof became the site for my new garden. It lay twenty feet from the hut and thirty or so from the near spring. I forced myself to forget the luxuriance of the kitchen garden at Hotel Garriques. Who needed thick beds of strawberries and towering rows of pole beans? I had rocks, cracked earth and bigger rocks, which I knocked loose with an old axe handle—the only tool at the cabin—and pitched one by one off to the side. I worked with my skirts hiked to my waist. I could have worked buck naked. I could have danced a quadrille on the lumpy sod roof, it felt so good to be lonely.

Not lonely, but in charge. In charge and underway. I'd made a contract with the land, not that land speaks or signs its name to anything, but it assures us all the same. I'd spent a warm night up on the ridge. I saw an unbroken field of stars, and the morning reveal every stump and weed without exception, and I knew that such uncontained beauty would sustain me.

When a plume of dust and the creak of wood and metal drew my gaze north to an approaching wagon, I felt possessive of my garden. My work, my land. Then an indescribable sweetness drove me from my knees, as two weeks' solitude magnified to ten. Stephen's hat and Stephen's shoulders wobbled out of the heat. *He has come for me.* I stood in my ghost of a garden fearing I looked as eager as I felt.

Stephen gave me no greeting, his face caked with dust. He showed no curiosity about my work and gave no praise, either. I would not ask for praise. Half the garden was cleared. Any fool could see the progress. I asked after T.

Nod of the chin, Stephen indicated the wagon bed behind him.

"What is it? What—what is wrong?"

"Boy's feeling poorly."

Tierre moaned as I climbed in. He wailed at my touch, then wept a little as I lifted the blanket off him. Giant blood blisters girdled his left ankle, his lower leg and foot swollen an angry dark red. T squinted at me, reeking of liquor. He could not get his eyes to focus.

"He's drunk!" I said.

"That was Harlan's doing. A quart of whiskey and a gunpowder plaster, best cure for snakebite—"

"Snakebite?" I wanted to slap the grin off Stephen's face. "It's a wonder he hasn't died!"

"Nah, it was just a warning bite. Just a little hello from a startled rattler."

"Has he had any water?" I shouted, though Stephen leaned close.

"Did you want a drink, son?"

"He isn't your son, you ape-faced devil! Heaven help any child who is."

They had cut Tierre's pants off at the knee to accommodate the swelling. Amidst the blisters and bruised flesh and crusted gunpowder tracks, I found the strikes, two neat little holes just below Tierre's ankle. I touched his leg at the knee, to see where the swelling stopped, and T cried, "Clara, don't be mean!"

"I am so sorry. I need to see how serious it is."

Stephen said, with disdain, "It's ugly, but it ain't serious."

I ignored Stephen Nuttall's log-headedness, for the time. "Does your right foot hurt, Tierre?"

"Everything hurt!"

"Can we get you to the spring, get some mud on those blisters? Give you a nice cool drink?"

Panting and lightheaded, T sat up. I jumped down to help him. He screeched a little scooting out of the wagon, and hopped a slow path to the water with his right arm slung over my shoulders. With tenderest care, I did what I'd heard to do—encase the horrible blistered skin in mud. T shook with agony, but he endured it. He took a small sip from my canteen and lay back to let the mud plaster harden. I put my hat over his face for shade and kissed him lightly on the shoulder. So lightly only I knew.

Back in the garden, I sank to my knees and started digging. I pounded the earth, sick at heart I might have lost him. Tears threatened, but Stephen came over. He said, with an impatience that spiked my ire, "Clair—"

"I am too busy for talk," I said, piling stones in my apron.

The dry weeds cracked under Stephen's heel.

"I have a garden to clear and irrigate and plant."

"That boy, Tierre, he don't have a lick of sense."

I looked up and marveled in cold wonder. "You've worked the range since you were six. Who is the real fool, Stephen? Tierre has been here short of two months! What on earth was he doing without boots on?"

"Ain't my fault he ran down to the river barefooted one

morning—I'm the one's lost three days' herding fetching him back here."

I folded my arms across my chest in disbelief. "Well, I will be sure to thank you for your extravagant kindness once Tierre suffers through unbearable pain and the swelling goes down and the blisters all heal and he can walk again. Now, fetch him home in the wagon before he gets heat stroke," I said, back down on my hands. "And if you are not gentle loading him in, you can eat sod for dinner."

They drove away, both relieved to be shut of me. The she-bitch in the garden howled out her grief alone. Love seemed all ditches and trap doors, snakebites and blinding dust.

I never did apologize for calling Stephen an ape-faced devil. He apologized, though not with words. Stephen apologized with staples. From the small stage station twenty miles northwest, he managed to bring us home a bounty. Beans and barley, flour and eggs and lard. He lowered a used rocker off the back of the wagon and a wheelbarrow loaded with old tools. Then he took a kitten from his shirt and handed it to me.

I never have cared for cats—they feel like snakes in fur.

"Don't spoil her. She'll rat the garden and the barn when we build it after the rut this fall."

Tierre intercepted the scrawny kitten, cradled it on his chest and hobbled inside to give it a drink.

Stephen didn't leave. He stood in the midday sun like he was cooling in the shade of a split willow bower. He said, "You got room for turnips?"

It was the first interest he had shown in my plans. The first interest he'd shown in anything other than sheep. "Room in my garden?"

"Yes, ma'am."

"I suppose I do. Are you partial to turnips?"

"Winter feed, for the sheep."

I wiped my ire into my handkerchief.

Stephen took up a shovel. He poked the ground a bit. At every thrust, the shovel hit ground with a clank. "Poor excuse for soil," he said. "You think sheep dung would improve it any?" I gritted my teeth to keep from criticizing. "Sheep herder's a rich man, if dung gets counted for wealth. Yes indeed, the king of all he surveys." He swept his hat outward at the scrub. "A fool for stool!"

It struck me, Stephen's humor. It tunneled in.

He slapped his hat across his knees and grinned, his hair slicked down from sweat like a barber's boy's. "You ought to smile more often, Clair. God in Heaven knows it's true."

"Sheep and God are two subjects I find resistible. If you'll be bearing your testimony, I will just go inside and blanch the cat. It's the only way to cook them proper—blanched, not boiled."

Stephen rocked back on his heels. "Heck, it's no wonder you was friends with my mother," he said, laughing.

"I love your mother!" I said, and instantly regretted something so personal, so private as love was added to the mix.

He tucked his hands into his armpits. He stood with one leg locked, the other bowed at the knee. Body like a hand wrench and a smile that would melt glacial ice. It melted, and pooled. If there ever was a man I wanted, I was looking at him.

Stephen said, "Mother is a wonder." He kicked the dirt, scuffed it up into a powder with his toe. He put his hat back on. "Sheep dung," he said in earnest. Then he nodded. "It couldn't hurt."

—⸻—

Stephen made Tierre stay and heal up, help me to get the irrigation ditch dug and the rows planted. Said that was man's work and he'd be back to fetch him in two weeks. Then he loaded some salt lick for the sheep, and struck out to find new pasture. As he was leaving, he said to me, "Smart choice, putting the garden there."

And he made no mention of sheep.

Tierre could walk after a few days, and once the swelling in his foot and ankle allowed for a boot, he worked outdoors every daylight hour. Within ten days, T's trench reached almost to the spring. I cleaned the hut, or tried to—greasy webs and soot, the dirt floor ground to a maddening powder. I told him at lunch I could not live another day without light, that I'd rather sleep under the stars than in that hovel.

He elbowed me to listen. I heard horse hooves pounding down the track. We gained the front yard just as a horse and rider pulled up.

"Opal White," the stranger barked. Her skirts were split up the middle and she rode like a man. Talked like a man. Spit like one, too.

I took T's hand, hoping she didn't have a gun.

"Hell, if you ain't a peculiar crew."

No gun was visible, but her boot had lumpy possibilities.

"You talk? Either one a you?"

Tierre took a step. "We lives here!"

"Good!" The woman laughed, swinging down. "Hell, it's a start." Her front teeth matched the yellow of her hair. "I live there," she said, jabbing an arm west, back the way she'd come. Her tongue ran around inside her wrinkled cheek, a live, burrowing thing, while she waited for one or the other of us to speak.

Tierre gaped at the silver bit and tooled straps of her horse's bridle.

I stood with my hands stuck out, like they'd been fastened in stocks. "You live in the Raft Mountains?"

A short stream of tobacco juice cut a snake in the dirt. "I am the nearest you have to a neighbor. And them are my tools you're digging with."

"Oh, you've come for your tools, your shovels and such! Stephen never said—" Relief became regret. "Have you come to fetch them already?"

Opal's wrinkles fell from wry grin to gruffness. "You think ten days ain't long enough to keep a neighbor's working tools?"

"No, ma'am, of course. T, go and gather up all the tools from the garden." I marched off after him, then realized I'd left our visitor standing in the sun. "Would you care to sit inside, Mrs. White, have a drink of water in the shade?"

The woman scratched her crotch.

"Or, we have biscuits, biscuits and beans."

Opal studied the back of her hand, and the reins where they dangled. "I might just."

I spread a blanket near the door and served up beans, poured a cup of water, privately cursing the house that was no house, just a heap of dirt and boards. Opal White hadn't appeared to notice. She stretched her legs out and cocked an arm behind her. Worked her spoon into the bowl sunk in her lap.

"Where's Stephen?" she asked.

"Off with the herd."

"Must have taken them north to the Black Pine Range. He grazes my land, he knows the price." Opal looked up, her eyes like steel in milk. "How long you been here?"

"I—" I couldn't calculate to save my life. One day had

been so like the next, I hadn't kept count. "We arrived at Kelton Station, March twentieth."

Opal's pale eyebrows flicked up. "Eight weeks—"

"We had nothing to work with but an old axe handle till Stephen brought your tools."

A biscuit circled the inside of her bowl. Opal looked at me as she chewed. "You done good." I flushed with gratitude. "Though, the house could use a window, to my thinking."

"Oh, if I could lay my hand on a saw there would be light in every—"

"Yours, for the loan of these beans. I'll send a saw over with one of my men."

"Thank you. Thank you, Mrs. White. I am sorry if we struck you as unfriendly. It's just that Stephen hadn't warned us."

"Stephen sees a need and fills it. No harm done." She held her empty bowl out with a sigh, so I refilled it, with a biscuit on top. Opal ate like she talked, without fuss. "Most women would be half dead from lonely out here," she said.

"If I hike a few miles, I can watch the stage line drive by. No one's found us yet, except you, not even the Indians." It struck me then, how unseen neighbors might show up some-day, and I ought to know a bit about them in advance. "We had Indians where I grew up, Bannocks and Shoshone. Which Indians live up here?"

"The same."

"I have never seen one."

"Thank the U.S. Army for that. Bunch of horse thieves and no-accounts. They ain't burning coaches or stealing food from the good folks of Southern Idaho any more."

"Where have they gone?"

"Fort Hall Reservation. Up north."

"With the Brigham City Indians. And it's a good place?"

Opal spat on the dirt floor. "You are a curious girl. They're nomads. Hell, to nomads, one place is as good as the next."

I doubted it, heating up at her trim disposal of an entire people. "So now they own the reservation?"

She laughed, an ugly short burst. "Truer to say the reservation owns them. The brutes have a homestead, guaranteed, and good old Father Washington pays their bills. Luckiest lazy bastards I never met." Opal hitched herself upright in two strokes, butt first, shoulders after. "Keep the shovels for the while. Can't see a neighbor starve for want of implements."

We found T stroking her handsome roan. Opal took the reins from him. She gave him a hard look and a sniff. "Ain't any niggers live in Idaho."

I saw it strike him. Saw it stamp his mood down hard. I said, hoping Opal White would notice my choice of wording, "In Mississippi, colored folk make nearly half the population."

Opal chuckled. "Give the railroad time. Nah. Niggers from the railroad'll be thick as flies." She rode off.

"That ain't no woman," T said, several times, "No, ma'am, that a rat in pants."

"She could be ignorant, T. Opal might have meant no harm."

He cut me a look. "You just wants that bukra's tools." T walked to the ditch, kicked Opal's shovel aside and took up the old axe handle.

I didn't contradict him. Best to let his anger peg itself out, best to wait, let him know I loved him later, when sun and sweat had raised up a kingdom all their own, and Tierre had moved freely in it. I knew from long experience T would come right. Mean words never stopped him. Of greater concern was that price Opal mentioned, the price for grazing her land. I hoped Stephen knew to keep clear of it. If I prayed, I'd have prayed for that.

CHAPTER 22

S tephen pulled in at dusk two weeks after he'd left us, and Tierre dashed outside to greet him. They would never be mistaken for a father and son, but it was a reunion nonetheless. In all that lavender dust, I felt at sea.

"He is a lively one," Stephen said, ducking inside, bringing the dust in with him. My garden was not worth Stephen's notice. He'd driven right past it—tilled and irrigated, the first rows planted—and didn't say nil.

"Tierre is glad you're back. Thought he might have to garden the rest of his days."

"Smells good." He stepped to the stove.

I moved to the bucket to dip up water. "You can thank T for that. I stewed up a rabbit he caught with some barley he saved from scorching."

Stephen tilted the lid. "Dumplings." He smiled.

I waited till he backed off to taste the stew for salt. I could smell him, the sweat on his clothes. "Wash up and find Tierre. We'll eat shortly." He left, and for an instant I was washing Stephen Nuttall myself with my two hands, the wash cloth and the soap. I slammed a lid on my imaginings. I dished up stew.

T and Stephen talked all through the meal, mostly *Ocean Springs* this and *in Ocean Springs* that—things and people I did not care to remember. I scooted the little bouquet of wild vetch and bighead clover to my side of the table. That bouquet, my sorry attempt at civilizing things.

"Maybe Stephen doesn't want to hear about Ocean Springs."

T's face fell.

"Nah, I don't mind hearing."

But T wouldn't budge.

"You caught this rabbit with a sling, son?" Stephen asked.

"Up on the ridge, out from them trees in the gully." T clanked his spoon on his plate. "In Ocean Springs, we caught us rabbits fat as house cats. You know, them spoiled kind, and smoked 'em until they was glassy brown. Possums and wild turkeys, too! Them summering gentlemens ain't had a thing on they minds but the kill. Some even ask me to 'company them on account a I *knowed* the place. I knowed more than chop the weed and rake the path."

"Huh," Stephen said.

"And Clara wasn't just no launderess. She kep' a loom right in our own cabin, and she weaved rugs—"

"I wove them—"

"Just like I say, she weaved them fancy bed rugs for the guests. She work that thing sun to moon, I swear. Gnats the only thing would ever stop her."

"Gnats?"

"Gnats that pinch until you wished the bowels of hell swallow you up!"

"Do *not* talk of bowels at mealtime, T."

Stephen said, "That's Bible talk, isn't it? It's been a long while . . . swallowed up into the bowels, swallowed down into the bowels of hell—" Stephen looked at me for confirmation.

I would not answer a Bible question if I knew it.

"Aunt Ada said you had you bowels of leather," Tierre said, with admiration.

Stephen choked on a biscuit. He laughed out bits. "That what Aunt Ada said?"

"In her letter."

Stephen cleared his throat with a cough.

T took the letter from my sewing box and handed it to Stephen.

May 18, 1877

Dear Ones,

The sight of you two still sticks in my eyeballs. It made an old lady feel a girl again, seeing you both at Ogden Station. I trust you are well settled and not dead of starvation. I only hope, cause Stephen never died yet though I think his bowels are made of leather. Tell Stephen to feed you good. His momma says so.

Grace and gravy, Ada

"Well, it looks like it was you and Clair that fed me good tonight. And I thank you kindly."

T batted his eyelashes, first at Stephen, then at me.

The trickle of irritation I'd felt since Stephen came back grew fangs. This was to be our nightly fare, chit and chat and *thank you, kindly?* I wondered if a wholesome game of checkers wasn't next. I snatched their plates for the washing up. "It is 'the bowels of compassion.' That's what the Bible says! And supper is no time to talk of such." I turned my back on them.

"She ever take a thank you?" Stephen asked Tierre. They stood outside the kitchen window in the dark of evening, looking west.

"Clara take and give. I don't know why she be so wrung upon, these days."

My dreams that night would have told them. I touched Ada's shoulder, and Stephen turned to answer. He bent to kiss me, and his eyes were Daniel Dees'. Three in one, they grinned and laid me down. Then Ada whispered in my ear, *Honey, gold is where you find it.* I struggled to free my arms from the coarse blanket. I sat up believing Stephen Nuttall was a meal, Ada the cook, Daniel a serving spoon, and I was close to starving.

I rose and pulled a dress around me. Seeking any kind of freedom, I walked uphill toward the ridge. It followed like a fever pulse, how I'd burned for Daniel Dees, twice married! More the shame, I'd burned for Ada. What would Stephen Nuttall say to that? It was just the one kiss, that once. Ada's kiss that left me split open like a peach, fresh-made as a baby. Maybe Ada had forgotten.

I wandered on, gazing at stars, knowing in my bones that Ada hadn't.

"Our clothes are filthy. We have no soap. I need seed potatoes and onions for the garden. And the windows need cloth for stretching, to keep the dust out. I need better scissors to cut T a coat, and heavy gauge thread and—" I was grateful Stephen stopped me. My voice had taken on tones of pure complaint.

"Let's go." He snugged his hat down, his fingernails rimmed with dirt.

I frowned.

"Let's go," he said again, as if I hadn't quite heard.

"Now?"

"Yes, ma'am."

"Right now—?"

"Well, ain't that what you was asking? To go shop at the stage station?" He looked around for T, like he could use some help translating.

"I might like to have a warning. I might like to change my dress or get my seedlings watered or such." I stared off out at the brush, furious at the stinging in my eyes.

"I will put Shep in the traces and go find Tierre. We can leave anytime. Just shout." And he walked off, not a hitch in his voice or in his gait.

Inside the house, it was all I could do to keep from howling—the dry stink of an animal's den. I put on my yellow dress and looked for a long time at the fine straw hat at the bottom of my trunk, its brim curved like the tucked wing of a pelican. White netting and tiny beads and a label inside said *New York City*. Reece Moon was a cad.

I closed the lid.

I shook my hair out, clasped and pinned it.

I climbed into the wagon bare-headed and called for T.

The long trip eased things, some. After the first few barren miles, the prairie greened to meadow. Grass clicked against the hubs. We followed the Raft River Range, travelling due west. In time, two valleys opened away to the north, the prettiest valleys I had ever seen. Small and untamed. The Black Pine Range divided them, with shoulders the color of dark smoke.

T took his hat off and placed it on my head. "You has the shade awhile."

I nodded my thanks.

"Found you any wildflowers, yet?"

"No."

"That dress so pretty they be ashamed." I kissed Tierre's cheek.

Stephen pointed out Opal White's ranch, where Clear

Creek ambled down from the Raft Range through a covey of hills. Juniper groves outlined her pastures. Plenty of wood for hearth and fencing, plenty of water in that creek. I was lathering up a fine envy, when a continuous field of blue a quarter mile distant dashed it. I jumped off the seat and ran.

"It isn't camas!" I shouted back at them. I'd never seen this bloom in Brigham. The stalks were three feet tall, the globes of papery flowers much too large, too subtle a blue for camas. The petals were tubular, like wild onion, but twenty times larger.

Tierre caught up with me. He picked a blue ball and swung it on its stalk, watching the flowers toss. "This big as a baby's head! This big as old Delia's cheeks. You remember how Delia stuck herself on you, that night you come while we was reading?"

"You had a broken leg."

"I did."

I laughed. "Mina, mina, mina, min."

"Old Delia." T said, slashing the air with his flower stalk for daring to cross him. "You was strange, Clara gal. But nah. You wasn't a stranger long."

When we returned, Shep stood grazing in the meadow, with Stephen nowhere in sight. Not until we walked around the wagon and saw his scuffed boots hanging off the bed.

"He sleeping, you think?" T whispered.

He had rolled his sleeves up and made a bed in the hay.

T touched the sole of Stephen's boot. Then wiggled it. "Aw, we ain't been gone that long."

I put the hat back on T's head. "Must be our turn to wait."

We turned around.

A lizard shot over the rutted road. The clouds, high and still, looked like they'd never seen rain.

T shook with laughter, then stopped himself.

"What?" I asked in a whisper.

His face sobered, but he burst out laughing again.

Clapping a hand on his neck, I lowered his head to his knees. I whispered in his ear, "What, T?"

"You seen them hairs, them hairs up Stephen's nose?"

"Tierre!"

"Look like them nostrils was sewed together. Big old stitches."

"Looked to me," I said, "like a porcupine had crawled right up—"

T wept tears. "Two porky-pines."

I sheaved my skirts up and dropped to the dirt laughing.

T fell on his butt. "The man needs to trim them things."

"You bring the machete? Maybe a cane knife, or maybe—"

"Don't, Clara, my sides is breaking." He groaned, half hiccough, half sneeze.

We sat, stupid and empty, looking out on the verdant plain.

T sniffed. "We still got Opal's saw?"

I fell into his arms and laughed until my ribs threatened to crack. I smacked Tierre's arm. "Why are we sitting in the dirt, the middle of nowhere?" I said, gripping the dear boy's shirt.

"'Cause we too weak to stand up?"

"Stephen said Shep keeps to a trail."

Tierre cleared his eyes with a fist.

"T."

"You old she-devil—"

"Are you going to drive it, or am I?"

We mowed a trail through the grass, trying to get Shep back on track. T held one rein and I the other. As the wagon jangled into the ruts, I looked behind us. Stephen hadn't wakened. He'd only wedged down deeper in the hay.

The farm woman's eyes bugged in alarm as her hand gripped a dung shovel. Once again, I saw myself through a stranger's eyes: outside the chicken pen, a girl stood waiting. She had ash brown hair and a yellow party dress and half her face on fire.

Kicking a chicken aside, the woman stepped to the fence, to get a better look.

"Good day, ma'am," I began. "I am Clair Martin. I'm new at the Nuttall's place, the Nuttall ranch."

The woman wore round buns over her ears, had round cheeks, round bosoms, big round hands. "Stephen Nuttall's? Out at the twin springs?"

"Yes. He said you might have eggs to sell."

"I might?" She unlatched the door, but stayed firmly the other side of it. "I always have eggs, fresh laid, best layers in the valley." She intercepted a hen edging toward freedom, and knocked it soundly backwards with her boot.

"They sound healthy." I offered her my sack. "I'd like to buy two dozen. If you can spare them."

The woman drove her shovel into the ground. "Have you been scalded?" It was a demand, not a question.

"No, if you mean my face. I have had the marking since birth. I'll just do without those—"

The pen door slapped and the woman took my sack. She looked at the network of reds on my face, looked hard, and could not keep from wincing. "I never saw a birth rose so big." She shook the sack. "You think you're taking my eggs away in this? You'll have a burlap omelet." She started for the house. "Agnes Smart. Aggie to my friends and customers. Come on in. We'll see what we can find."

The frame house, one story with an attic, seemed pure

luxury after months of living with dirt on all sides. I said
so. Aggie turned from the pantry. She might have been fifty,
yet her oval face didn't have a wrinkle, even when it showed
concern.

"Are you the only woman at his place?"

"I am."

"Well you'll just have to come to town more, when you
get lonely for talk." She washed her hands and set a plate of
raisin cakes on the table. Round cakes with white sugar icing.
"Milk or tea?"

"Milk, please." The cakes made my teeth ache, just looking at them.

Aggie laughed when I took a bite. "Are they as good as all
that?" I glanced up, jaws sunk in Heaven. "You've been too long
without the company of women and kitchens."

"When my crops come up, we'll do better than dried
beans and biscuits."

"You plan to try a garden?"

"I have one."

"Up in the scrub?"

"My squash have just poked up."

"You have squash seedlings, already?"

I dabbed at my mouth with one of Aggie's cloth napkins—the feel of it was fine. "Yes, ma'am."

Aggie said, ice quick, "You wouldn't be a Mormon, would
you?"

I felt it chill my veins. "I am not."

Agnes Smart smiled a cat-like smile, not elated, not
happy even, just a sign that all was right with her—for the
time. "The spiritual pride of those people? I cannot tolerate it.
First and foremost, Mormons are materialists. And the worst
sort of materialists, in my view—" She tapped my plate. "Smug

ones. No, I go to Marsh Basin only when and if it can't be helped. More often, I send a list along with Duff."

"Marsh Basin?"

"Nearest town, the next valley over."

I took a sip of milk, as sweet as the pastry to me. "I didn't know the Mormons lived in Idaho."

"Mormons and sheep herders are your only neighbors! And the Mormons own all of the towns."

"But Brigham City is the northernmost Mormon settlement."

"You been gone from the area awhile?"

I nodded.

"Well, Duff and me keep things simple here at the station. I say a prayer on Sundays. He sells a Bible or two at his store. But the real towns, Marsh Basin and Elba and Albion, up toward the Snake River? They are all Mormon. Blink twice and the Mormons will own your feet. They will not stop their northward march until Canada's been claimed. You mark it."

I did not want to.

"Busy as a hive of inebriated bees, those people, only I won't buy from their shopkeepers. It's all the same goods we can get here, just another day older. It is a tired peach and a failing pea that rides in a crate from Utah. No, the Mormon households have the only goods worth purchasing, so I grit my gums and buy from them." Aggie bit into her second cake. "I don't suppose Stephen would have taken you there, to Marsh Basin. No, I don't suppose he would." She grinned around the mouthful. Then swallowed and sighed. "A man is young but once." Aggie leaned over the tablecloth. "He has his fancy girl there, you know, a sweetheart."

Her news and her cake in my empty stomach raised my temperature some. I wiped my lips. "Stephen?"

"She's a trifle severe, to my thought. Suzanna Peake fills her time with books and ideas, legalities and such, did some schooling of late, in Boise. Well, principles are a fine thing, a very fine thing, I say, but will they stock the cellar?" Aggie patted her brown hair buns in place, one then the other. "And she is daughter to a known polygamist!" She looked at me with the same bugged eyes as when we met, and once again I felt penned out, alone and empty handed. Aggie didn't notice. She stared out the kitchen window. She ate another cake. "Nothing can talk a bit of sense into a man in love."

I found them in the smithy, behind the post office dry goods store. The stage station amounted to three buildings: the smithy, the dry goods and Aggie's house. Four, if you counted Aggie's coop. I leaned against the outer wall. Forge and bellows, smell of smoke, the clanking metal—it calmed me, like Lars' livery on a Saturday afternoon.

I listened to the twitting of a bird. So much sky, and just one bird to fill it. Life was like that. My life.

The scene inside the barn struck me as right, correct, just fine: Tierre leaning his skinny back into Shep's hide, grinning at a story as he told it. T loved his animals and an audience, any kind. The man with the blackened face and blackened arms, he loved to lose himself in sparks and heat. Sitting on a tipped stool, Stephen loved Suzanna. And the woman in the doorway? The one who stood alone? She had two dozen eggs, and the promise of four chickens.

T saw me, end of a tale of Robert's bravery in the War. He clapped his hands. "Clara, they gots cloth at the dry goods. Mr. Duff, he gots one whole bolt and Stephen said for him to write your name on it."

Stephen tipped upright, as if he'd been caught out. The

aggravated woman who'd delivered all the morning's sharpness had found his hideaway. "I knew that you was wanting cloth," he said. I noticed for the first time how slight his forearms were, how his bottom lip fussed with the fringe of his moustache.

I nodded hello to the blacksmith, then said to Stephen, "Thank you. I do."

He flinched. Then he smiled.

"You brung money?" T asked.

"I thought I'd open an account. Will Mr. Duff take gold, you think?"

"Shah, gal, you crazy?"

T shadowed me into the store and up to the counter. Stephen waited a few steps behind. Duff, who looked even drier than his goods, stared at my left cheek until the first coin exited my purse. Thirteen gold coins followed. Duff Abrams wiped the counter clean and slid each one across, from dust to dustless, my side to his. His hands trembled, whether from age or anticipation, I couldn't say. "Ma'am," he said at number fourteen, with what sounded like religious fervor.

He looked at Stephen. "Pay on your bill?"

"Miss Martin's account is separate, Duff."

He entered the total in a ledger while T breathed into my hair. Then the fabric was lifted from under the counter. T chuckled. Stephen's boots made a scuffing sound, side to side, as I stood before the ugliest calico cloth ever printed—mud green with pale irregular dots, misprints that looked like chickens, chickens in every pose, young and old, cocks and headless hens and little lines of chicks pecking their orange way home.

An eternal family, I thought. No doubt, the cloth had been there since time's dawning.

I inhaled. "I'd hate for you to have to part with all of this." I swallowed. "So we'll take fifteen yards."

From Duff's parched face bloomed the straightest set of teeth, white as pickets and as sharp. "Yes, ma'am."

Duff measured as I mused on my choices. Stout candy jars lined the wooden counter, and I had used the word "we." In three months' time, I had scotched together a family, a temporal family, one without blood ties, belongings, or conjugal love. I picked two sticks of licorice—one for Stephen and one for T—and a horehound for myself. Duff Abrams tore the fabric, past to present.

CHAPTER 23

B lack bird. Dull shine. All lean curves to the watcher, black on blue. Black on blue till the bent neck and trailing legs become backdrop, and the bird is sky.

Two fly over. One gliding, one pumping its wings, like black emaciated turkeys, but for the bills. The down-curved bills—as long as their necks—form perfect opposing curves in flight. Slack horizontal S-es.

For pleasure I walked, being all alone. I ranged a little, to see things I'd never seen. Like those black birds. And this salt bed. I tipped my head to the cattails, empty of wind, then looked over my shoulder: white salt blistered to the banks of the distant creek. If I lay still enough, long enough, the two birds might land, might wade the marsh nearby prodding the water with their strange beaks. Too strange for the Salt Lake Valley. Stranger than the heron's sharp business.

The evening train blew by, toward Kelton. The birds veered off, taking my serenity with them. In spite of the grandeur of the indifferent world, I thought of Stephen. How, like the visitor birds, he could draw sustenance from so little. His pleasure in the ranch, his relaxation in time. On the day he left, he said, "Opal will stop by to check on you in September, before she trails her rams up for breeding." He'd said it and winked, as if September was the day after tomorrow.

The glare of the June sun wet my lashes. His indifference made me ache. I tried to follow his example, take time as it came, tame the ranch, tame my restlessness, this lone summer. Do my work and let it be, use the slack times in between for pleasure. Twenty miles from home, I could make it half way back by dark, sleep on the banks of Deep Creek and climb the Wild Cat Hills tomorrow. The garden would go a day without water. My food would last. Good and reasonable, it all seemed, while I lay on my back and the vastness of the desert soothed me. Then I stood up—upright, human—and once again meaning mattered. *Home, bird, scrub* pulled my heart through a wire mesh of meaning. It snared, like Stephen's monkey trap, only this was a trap of my own making: this longing for home when I already had one, the dark desire for freedom when everything around was free.

29 June, 1877

Dear Ada,

I had forgot how empty this land is. It is an old man, it's like his thoughts, where Ocean Springs was the warm lap of a woman. Well hot, steamy hot and insects, and undergrowth you had to stay to the paths or hack a way through or lose your way completely. And isn't that like a woman? That's what men say.

Stephen and Tierre are off with the herd till September. I mailed this letter in Kelton. I walk a bit, no men to cook for.

Do not forget to write me.

Clair

12 July, 1877

Honey Dear,

We are as devils possessed, getting the Salt Lake house out-fitted and men hired for the new mine. I leave the house affairs to Florence—you know how she loves nesting. Nest a person right onto the streets! I work more than is wise and the good earth heaves up its wonders in recompense. Salt Lake ain't as provincial as I feared. Florence misses Brigham and Henry and such but I tell her one is dead and the other dying, she owes her heart to the living. She brung her children, all but Florrie who is with child a third time in Logan, and still determined to make her marriage come right. Cut and run, I'd tell her if she ever asked me. She don't. And I have a plenty lively household with all the other little Gradons here. A need for company seems to of roosted in me, now I got relations in house. Greetings to T and Stephen, when they grace your life again.

Yours, ever, Ada

28 July, 1877

My dearest Robert,

You would not know me to see me. It is Clair Martin writing from the Idaho desert. I feared my hands had turned to rock and would not hold this pen. I fear worse for my mind, but I leave you to judge of that.

Tierre is herding sheep up in the mountains all the summer long, so you can guess he is died and gone to heaven. I keep the house and garden, though we live so uncivilized I feel like I just move dirt here and move dirt there. Dust to dust. I shepherd dust.

I have dug my own garden, which you would shake your head to see. There is not one tree to use its leaves for heat jackets around the vegetables. My hot pepper plants are up to my knees. I had the seeds from Ocean Springs. I bet they are the only such in Idaho.

Both our springs bloomed out in little white flowers. A heron has come to drink there. A great blue. I hear it call even when I have missed seeing it, I hate to miss that.

Tierre is much improved at reading. I sent Shakespeare and Sidney up to summer pasture with him. Mr. Tennyson and I share the evenings here. He finds the parlor rough and to his liking.

Give my regards to all who knew us. I send my fondest wishes.

Yours truly, Miss Clair Martin

It rained, early in August. From darkened sunup to dusk, the sky a fragrant gray. Lightning touched down in the distance, from out of thunderstorms purple as nightshade. They dragged their hems along the prairie and vanished into the surrounding darkness: breath on glass. The house smelled of damp sod, freshened earth, and a jar of flowers from the spring. Nothing to do, nothing to do but watch and listen. Rain striking and sinking, endlessly. Time measured in the vibrations of the kitten on my lap.

I decided to burn sage as Ada did, to clear the sorrow.

Land sweet. People scarce. Till they returned.

CHAPTER 24

Tstood taller than me, when they returned in late September, nearly as tall as Stephen. He walked more like Stephen, with a thrust in the legs I hadn't seen before. He talked of dogs and flocking traits, mountain trails, the palate of the white-tailed deer, then told me how the sheep would forecast rain. The adults overate, as they would not graze or travel in a storm, while the lambs frisked about shaking their coats as if already drenched to the skins. "You think that crazy? You should hear them sheeps talk." Then he had me aching with laughter—his snorts and gargles, strangled sneezes, wheezes and bleating. "And you should see them rams, Clara."

"I should?"

He leaned against the wagon. The length of his legs confounded me, legs of a stranger whose pants need mending.

"Lord a'mighty, they could rut till it drop off."

Stephen coughed and said, "Tierre—"

"They did those females night to day, and hard? Oh, gal, they never stop, even to eat, and them rams be skinnied to death if Harlan didn't of penned them up and fed them after a week—*make* them to stop."

I blinked and stopped laughing.

"It's the loneliness talking," Stephen said.

"You were lonely?" I asked.

T looked at me, wild-eyed, jutting his chin.

"Not everyone's cut out for herding," Stephen said. "Tierre here, he's a city boy who needs a big human herd."

T stared at the house, shaking his head. "You should of seen them rams. You should see 'em! Damn fool things."

The herd raised dust and drew flies. Harlan and Stephen ate four meals a day, to make up for time lost. Tierre followed me around talking until my ears wished for lids, and I longed for the dead even quiet of my summer days. Until T said something in the garden that stood my selfishness on end. When I suggested Stephen might buy him a rifle, to give him a pastime hunting for us during the coming winter, Tierre slapped his pants and dragged his bucket down the row. "He ain't never gonna buy no rifle."

"You won't know until you ask," I said.

"I ask—maybe fifty times." He ran his hand over an onion. "I ask, till Harlan told me he ain't got no money. Stephen gots nothing but sheeps."

"Well, that's silly. Stephen buys things. Look what he's brought us from the stage station."

"Them things is on account."

"But he pays on his accounts."

"Not yet, he ain't. It was Ada bought this land off of Opal White. Stephen and Harlan work for Opal three odd years and Stephen, he took all his pay in sheeps. Took payment last winter, didn't have no place even to lay. Slept with Harlan in that old cave. He built the house hisself, fetched logs from the hills, cut the sod when he heared that we was coming—"Tierre stopped to watch the carrots tumble out of my apron into the bucket. His anger faded, as if the facts were too big for that.

"Stephen didn't have no money to pay for the shearers to come last spring, Clara, and never had no lambs to spare for market—had to build up the herd. He ain't earned a penny or spent one."

"Then we are living off his future."

"We is, yes. And it don't look like we's ever gonna get paid. One fifth! Lord in Heaven, one fifth of nothing."

I sat in the dirt, then scooted over to take T's hand. "It's so soft."

"Wool fat. From the sheeps."

I thought awhile. "I don't suppose he'd take my money, to help to pay for things."

"You'd hurt him good."

"And the money would soon run out. No, T. We have to think. We have to think on how to make this ranch pay cash money."

He looked around, disgusted. "We gots no tools, and nothing to work from."

My first thought, exactly. And my second. But memory, unlike reason, requires no practical supports. As I bent back down over the row, thoughts flashed: I sold flower cards by the dozens, Ada had slaked Gentile thirsts, and Audwin—Audwin Fife had sent himself to medical school by carving wooden trinkets for the rich.

I spent the next day inside with my pressed flowers. Mississippi flowers, paper, scissors and glue. I placed roses in a flat wreath of goldenrod. Pansies with sprays of yellow honeysuckle. Violets dotting azalea blooms. After supper, when Stephen was leaving to bed down, I asked if he would mind my going to Aggie's in the morning. Hair clung to his neck from the evening's chores—chopping sage and leveling land where the barn would soon be raised. His eyes were brown and focused as he gripped the bedroll under his arm. "I won't be needing Shep till Thursday, to haul in the lumber from Opal's."

It galled me, his answer which was no answer. I never asked for much. "So, I can go on my own, then." He laughed at my bluntness. His good looks were so uncalculated, so suddenly and freely given—and for me so unerringly deadly. I turned to gather up the dishes.

"I don't know if that'd be a good idea, Clair, a woman such as yourself, out on her own—"

"I can drive the wagon!"

"I ain't talking about the wagon."

"I know the route."

"I ain't talking about the route—"

"Well, fine then."

"I am talking plain damn prettiness."

I could only wheeze.

"You got a neck like a alabaster vase, Clair Martin." He said it right behind me. I felt it in the roots of my hair. "Course, what would a boy with two porky-pines stuffed up his nose know about that?"

"You—" is all I could say, "you, you—"

He leaned in and kissed me, soft and furry on the bone of my left cheek. And then he was off.

I chased him out the door, yelling, "Tierre, Tierre Durham, come help me thrash this boy!" both of us laughing and tearing through the scrub like fire.

Aggie all but swallowed the first card down, then the second and the third. She demanded I keep them, they were so pretty, but I told her I could make a hundred more. We agreed to have Duff Abrams take them to Marsh Basin with Aggie's eggs each week. He knew the Mormon shop owners and could talk prices. A quarter per half dozen, just like in Corinne.

I knew the cards would sell as fast as I could make them.

Women loved to couch their words in flowers. The greater problem remained—how to use the money they brought in. Stephen never would have seen my logic that the proceeds should be his, so I chose a form of secret contribution. I paid on his bill, in increments. Though Duff had long relied on faith in Stephen's paying him, I saw Duff Abrams' faith increase seven-fold with a sign.

My own faith wavered over Stephen. I could not grasp his heart's intent. I feared no man could ever want me. But when he shared his tenderness, life shone—the sweet words, the little kisses. Whole days would pass when all I saw of him was the sweat that came in with him for supper. Then he'd sneak inside middle of the day and touch my neck or stroke along my side. We would kiss and say more silly things, and I'd be happy for awhile. Shame and doubt dogged me. I felt shame for the ugly face I had. And doubt that I would ever outdo Suzanna. I spent so much time veering between the two, I didn't even notice when the weather took a sharp turn toward cold.

Stephen moved back and forth like a man possessed, from the range with Harlan to the woods near Opal's ranch, to saw down trees for the barn. T went with him to Opal's for the ripping and planing. The first brief flurry of snow accompanied their ride back home.

Aggie came that afternoon to help cook meals for the barn raising. She brought two dozen chickens and a letter from Ada. I took it up to the ridge.

8 October, 1877

Dearest,
You must have felt the chill. The trees here dropped their color overnight. Never been a prettier autumn. Now Alfred is raking up

piles big as hillocks in back, and Una despite her eighteen years is helping him knock them down. They fly at the piles like hawks, like little children plumb bewitched. I guess they still are children. I am glad for their company, still I hope you will come with Stephen to visit me at Christmas like he always does.

Ever and always, Ada

I shifted my feet in the crotch of the old cedar, looked off at the Wasatch, then down into the gully, and cried for missing Ada—Ada's snorted laugh and Ada's long stories, Ada's greasy amber tea. I wouldn't go at Christmas, I knew I never would. The Mormons had killed my father and my mother both. Not with knives or poison, but just as surely with the pull of their words, their history and their ruling laws. The Mormon Church had left two people in its wake, two dead among the thousands who gave their lives in building Zion, as dead to me as the leaves piled up below my feet. Old cedar leaves, needle thin, with frost-blue berries on the red husks of sloughed branches—year on year they fell and gathered there, fell and gathered, crushing the underlayers to naught.

Underlayers.

What is in your heart, that's all you've got.

CHAPTER 25

The barn crew drove past us with a clatter, three freight wagons loaded, and all the men on foot calling advice to the dogged drivers: Stephen and Opal and a burly man who wore a beret. I spotted T and came alongside. A cut on his cheek hadn't been cleaned or tended. I knew enough, in that company, not to mention it.

"Hey Clara," he said, keeping his eyes on Stephen's wagon, wheels and hubs, the listing of the beams inside. "You gots thirteen hungry folk to feed. God in Heaven, they eats like hogs. And Opal, she the worst."

I broke pace and ran back to the cabin to see how Aggie was faring with the meal.

"It'll be thirteen, plus us plus Harlan," I said.

"We could feed a multitude, darling."

"Your strudel is a sight."

"Feed men like kings and they work like oxen. You had best check on our chickens."

I galloped out back to the fire. Twelve fat chickens browned with a vinegar, molasses, pepper sauce. The skins had just started to crisp.

We judged the progress at the barn by sound, kept at

the fire and the dish tub till dusk. Then Aggie walked to the barn to fetch the wagon so we could load the meal: bean salad, boiled potatoes, oat muffins and sourdough rolls, chicken and strudel and sweet turnip custard. I had tested for taste so many times, I'd already eaten a meal.

I dried and hung the last of the pans and walked out with the dish tub to empty it, when a horse and rider came sloping down the track. I watched awhile, then thought to pack another plate for the help, when something in his size or in his coloring, something in the jaw or the bearing of the rider made me stop.

Light of dusk, it could have been anyone, but I knew it was Reece Moon.

He smiled as his horse bent its neck to snuffle at the tub. He took his hat off, pale hair plastered at the temples.

His eyes were blue in any light.

"My God," I said.

"No, it's your old friend Reece Moon," he answered, easy as breathing.

"Friend?" I could not juggle my reactions, they came so fast. My loins were delighted Reece stood before me—but all my other instincts did battle. I plunged my hands in the water, spooking his horse. It danced a slow circle, then came back.

He cocked a leg wide of the bedroll and swung down. I gaped at the size of him, the smell and size and substance of this man standing by my wash tub, come from the Great Nowhere.

"Can you spare me a drink?" Reece asked.

"No!" I wiped my hands across the streaked turnip on my apron.

He stepped back, smacking his hat against his thigh. "I am not welcome?"

"The last we talked, I was the backside of a mule."

"And I have come to apologize." Now both his hands rested on his hips, and the smile on his mouth was broad and kind.

"Well, friend or foe, I can't have you drinking from the dish tub!"

I led him toward the house. I could not think what to do next, till I saw Aggie coming. I fetched him a drink and left him at the door, ran out to her and scrambled up onto the wagon.

"You'll lose a leg, Clair, mind your skirts next—" Aggie's eyes hit the ranch house door. "Who is that? There's a man at your door."

I was still breathing hard from the run.

"You know this man!"

"I do. I know him, from Mississippi."

"By the blush on your face, I would say he's come for more than water and a how-do-you-do."

"I have no idea what he's come for, but can he stay for dinner?"

It sounded so silly, we both laughed.

"Smooth your hair and settle yourself," she said. "You leave the dinnering to me."

Aggie shook Reece's hand and loaded him into the front seat, then helped me ferry hot dishes into the wagon bed. He looked on a little stunned. Perplexed, perhaps, at his situation—a long lonely ride to the riches of ranch women.

Work at the barn site stopped as we rolled up in the wagon. The crew had raised a dozen posts. They straggled over as Aggie called out, "This is Reece Moon. A friend of Clair's from Mississippi, come to call."

Stephen pushed his hat back revealing the moon-white line. "Stephen Nuttall," he said. "I own the ranch."

Reece said, "It looks like you have a fine plan, here."
Plan, not *ranch*. No one could see the wealth of the place but
Stephen. I hoped he hadn't noted the slight.

"Mr. Moon?" Tierre jumped down from a stack of lumber.
"Well, if it ain't Mr. Moon, Lord have mercy."

"Tierre!"

"Gracious Lord. Clara, you she-dog devil, why you ain't
told me Mr. Moon been coming?" He shook the wagon, then
grabbed my ankle. "A blonde egret catched between two canaries! Well, come on down so the man could get out and say a
proper hey."

T helped me down as Opal shouted, "You brung us dinner, Clair, or just your fancy man?"

Everyone laughed and the meal began.

Aggie filled plates from the back of the bed while I carved
the barbecue chickens. Kneeling in the straw with a knife sunk
in one bird, I said, "Give him seconds first, Aggie. Reece has
come a long way." He grinned, handing up a plate.

Reece told us the Utah and Northern Rail had hired
him to survey track north to Montana. Said the route had
changed from Soda Springs to the Fort Hall Reservation,
and a new route meant new maps. He had arrived in the Salt
Lake Valley last week, and remembered that his old friend
Clair had a friend in Salt Lake City, so he'd looked up Ada.
Said she was every bit as fearsome as I'd painted her and as
smart as three men, to which Stephen replied, "She is my
mother."

Reece focused his gaze on Stephen, made an easy nod and
said, "My admiration, friend, and my condolences. I believed
myself a well-traveled man, an expert judge of the female
character—" he shot a glance at me, "that is, until I met your
mother. I've known women who tamed their households and

women who tamed their men. Mrs. Nuttall could spook the hair off a razorback."

"Ada didn't make you feel welcome?" I asked, curious about the ways she might have offended him.

"As welcome as the pox! It does a man good to have the dust knocked off him. It never hurts to lose a little male glitter. Mrs. Nuttall kept her whiskey and her hospitality to herself, though she eventually told me where you were." Then Reece, to let the subject rest, asked Stephen about his herd.

Stephen tallied the losses and gains of the year, told the pricing for lambs and ewes, extolled the features of his new barn and his plans for next year's rut. Then he spilled out news I'd never heard: he aimed to build a proper house when our spring lambs were shipped to slaughter. A two story house, with pillars and a porch just like his father owned in Ogden. It seemed fantastical to me, knowing he had no money. But Stephen assured Reece, "It will rise behind Clair's garden, there, east of the near spring, with the windows looking out over her rows. They'll catch the sunset, the front windows—" He pointed west, to the darkening horizon rimmed brown. Then he removed Reece from the gathering, heading off with him to talk surveying and walk the home site. Aggie and I rounded up the plates and silver. We loaded the wagon and made for home.

Aggie said, "Nice knowing you, Clair. You make a handsome couple!"

"That is ridiculous," I answered.

"False modesty does not suit you or any woman. I saw Mr. Moon's admiration. Do not scoff at a man who'll keep you warm nights, and provide for your old age. You'll end up alone like me."

"Oh, Aggie," I said, and let the conversation fall to silence.

Reece's strange matrimonial attitudes were too hard to explain.

Once the beans for breakfast soaked in the kettle, Aggie turned in, bone tired. A thread of music drifted into the cabin, a mouth harp and singing. I scooped the cat up from my ankles, set it in the crook of my arm and walked in darkness to the garden.

The barn frame stood against the hill above the spring. Men and music underneath, a guttering fire. Stephen claimed that a two-story house would rise below it, looking out on the foursquare of my garden. He was strong-willed enough to raise a house with nothing, from nothing. Half of what he planned already stood in place. I sat down, smelling earth and raw timber. I stroked the cat and listened to them sing.

> *My ceiling the sky, my carpet the grass,*
> *My music the bleating of herds as they pass.*
> *My books are the brooks, my sermons the stones,*
> *My parson's a wolf on a pulpit of bones.*

I didn't hear Stephen walking toward me through the brush, but I saw him come, a dark shape against the skeletal outlines of the barn. He stopped a pace off, and, turning his head, sang the end of their verse,

> *. . . that small things I should not despise,*
> *And my parson remarks from his pulpit of bone*
> *That the Lord favors those who look out for their own.*

A surprisingly sweet tenor voice, Stephen had.

"You could join us, did you like to, Clair."

"Oh, no. Thank you. It's pleasing from here." I needed the time and distance from Reece. His arrival and Aggie's thoughts about us coupling still unsettled me.

Stephen squatted, setting a knee in the dirt. "That was fine cooking."

"Aggie's chickens, bless her heart, and her apples for the strudel—"

"You won't take credit, will you?" The force in Stephen's words startled me. His brow was furrowed and his lip pushed out.

"Yes, where credit is due," I said, sharper than I would have liked.

He scuffed forward on one knee. "Hellfire, you are a bright spark." I marveled how a face could change so suddenly from ire to joy. He flung joy like a wet sack of sand. It struck me, and I laughed.

"Bright as the evening star, Clair. You've made this place. This ranch, I mean. It never had a heart until you came."

"The queen of all she surveys—" I said, quoting Stephen, "a fool for stool."

"It ain't much!" he said. He leaned in, putting his face near mine, planting both his fists on the ground. "It ain't much, yet. But just you see if I don't change that."

"For Suzanna?" He'd grown so sober, I couldn't resist the little plunge. "Your Mormon friend, your sweetheart? She may be glad for my garden. Though what she'll think of Tierre and me. And you and I will have to stop kissing."

"I aim to tell her. I do. Soon as I can get to Marsh Basin."

"That you've built a barn for her?"

"That I need to be free. For you, Clair. I seen that long before now."

My heart contracted with a strange fierce weight. "I don't know much about you, Stephen. I only know I'll never understand how a man who has slipped the Mormon Church could ever court a Mormon girl."

"It ain't all sanctimony!" He sat back. "They got arms and legs and breath."

"Was it her arms or her breath that won out, over the

sanctimony?" I watched him closely.

He only said, "You belong here, Clair. You belong here with me."

"Says who?" I asked, to beg time for a smarter response.

"Says every bone I got in my body. Every one of them says it is true."

I turned away and marked the stars just rising. Orion! He was the man I needed, whose shoulders never failed. But all he did was twinkle, and Stephen breathed right here by my side.

"I'll tell Suzanna. Will you tell Reece he's got to move on?"

"And it's as easy as that?"

"It ain't easy, no. But needful. These things got to be said."

I tightened my shawl. "I will tell him in the morning. And you and I cannot touch, no kissing, not anything until you've told Suzanna." I tugged my sleeves down at the cuffs, then started for the house, vexed and satisfied, sentenced to love him.

Sleep never came that night. I lay awake, buzzing with newness, enduring the heat and the cold and the close stink of supper on the cast iron pans. Every meal you ever cooked joins the present night's meal, which joins with the rank smell of iron. It seemed to me like coupling. Reece called marriage a prison, and aimed himself to be free. As if, because he did not pledge himself, because he roamed the continent at will, he was not part of creation. *But what if we are rivers*, I kept thinking. What if, like the cast iron pans and every watercourse I'd known, we carry with us the taint and disaster and the waylaid intentions of what came before, and like any oxbow river or well-seasoned skillet, good comes through all the same?

You have to claim your place. The earth is holy. It gave me Stephen, amen.

Dawn was still a few hours off when I closed the door behind me and listened for stirrings at the barn. Sage and moonlight conspired in the darkness, the prairie stretching away, vast and still and unpeopled. Stephen and T and I were less than the stones we'd pushed aside to cut the garden, less than the sod on the roof. A hill of ants broken open—rushing to check the damage, count their losses, hide the eggs, and claim and reorder their own—would have more claim to this land than we did. Still, I loved the place. I was rooted here. And there was no room for Reece.

"Clair."

"Yes," I answered, not a moment's pause.

"I cannot put a hand to his barn."

I saw where he knelt in the yard. "Reece—"

"Goddamnit, I won't." A bitter laugh escaped him. "I feared for your health, your survival. Now, I fear for your mortal soul. He'll marry you."

"Oh—no, that is unlikely."

"Unlikely? It is done. Mrs. Nuttall plays to win. She had a fledgling ranch and a single son, both in sore need of civilizing. Your friend has cut a deal, she's offered you up. She brokered your bondage here."

I didn't know how to tell Reece about Ada's stubborn brand of love. I couldn't see where to start. "You're mistaken."

"You're deaf and blind." Such fury in a man who did not dare to care. "Stephen is ignorant, an ignorant do-gooder with a prairie dog's zeal. You think he'll turn this godforsaken place into a homestead of any value? He couldn't find his own way out of his pants."

"Well that's perfect, then," I said quietly, "for this deaf blind mule's ass."

"Hobble your own life! I will not put a hand to his barn or your bondage."

"Is this what you came to do? Deliver judgment yet again, on everyone who falls short of you, and ride off on your own? You have not changed."

His horse grazed near the track. He strode to it and mounted up. Hating to part from him a second time in anger, I said, "Reece, wait. May I write to you? Where are you going?"

"Fort Hall, Blackfoot, Shelley—" Every town an accusation.

"Reece. Please—" I gripped the stirrup. He kicked free, knocking me back. Then he leaned down briefly to grip my shoulder.

"No man will ever please you the way I can."

He rode north at a gallop, leaving only that curse, as bitter in my mouth as cast iron.

Envy, pure and simple, I told myself.

Stephen would prove him all ways wrong.

"You ain't sick, Clara?"

"No, T."

"You on your monthly time?"

"No." I punched the bread down. The rhythm of the kneading calmed me. "We'll be ready to eat when the muffin crowns cool. Are you hungry?"

"I is."

"And cold, I'll bet."

"Thanks to your coat you made, I ain't all froze."

I covered my loaves with a cloth, dusted my hands off, stretched my back. "Is Stephen still at it?"

"We built us fifteen lamb pens already. Stephen, he gots notions breed faster than—" T looked at me, light of alarm in his eyes. "Mr. Moon say where he been off to so sudden?"

"Fort Hall, I believe."

"That man left a'most soon as he come."

I had nothing to say on the subject.

T swallowed and said, "You certain you ain't poorly?"

I cuffed his chin. "I am healthy, wealthy and wise."

"Not much," he laughed. "Not hardly one of them three."

I slipped a knife around the muffins, shook them out of the pan. "Give a shout to the barn—I'm ready to serve."

"What you fixed?"

"Red beans and rice."

"Aw, Clara, don't pull that leg."

"Duff had smoked pig hocks, Aggie had rice."

"Red beans?"

"Yes, sir."

"With peppery gravy?"

"The peppers I brought from Ocean Springs." I took the string of dried peppers from a wall hook and slung it around T's neck. "King of the Mardi Gras!" I said.

T put his arm around me. He raised the lid with the sleeve of his coat and inhaled. "Let's us leave Stephen to his sheeps, and eat it up ourself," he said at the same moment a still small voice inside me said, *Here is your man worth loving.*

CHAPTER 26

Stephen worked like a mule with its eyes on Heaven. Tierre met him, step for step. It was all I could do to keep them fed. They spent three days raising a plank outhouse and then a side shed on the barn, banging and sweating in the snow. Tierre burst in for dinner, announcing the shed was to be his—he'd have his own room. They roofed and sided it with cast off shingles.

The next day Stephen built a bed, a double bed frame, and hauled the parts inside. Just before he left for Marsh Basin, to talk with Suzanna, he boarded up the windows of the house against cold, so the sorry walls were all my sights. But his handiwork gleamed in the lamplight—this was no ordinary frame knocked together in haste. Two roughly carved lambs knelt in peace on the headboard. It was my turn, to fit our bedroom out and make it right.

I sewed and stuffed a mattress tick the following day, singing. I glared at it all that night, wrapped in my blanket on the floor, wondering where Stephen slept. Snow must have slowed him. Of course—and Shep was old.

The glint of sun on snow the next morning, the flagrant blue sky lifted my spirits. I declared myself a holiday. I took an old oilcloth of Aggie's out to the barn. It was a cast-off, stained with mildew and chickens. I swept it clean and laid it across the pens, waiting for a design to firm itself in my mind. Then I folded the cloth in fours and traced the pattern on.

I worked with Ada's blue door paint and straws pinched to a point for a brush. No flowers, no vines, just blocks of color with a zigzag border. In the center of the canvas rug, if my will held, I would paint an oval full of flowers. It would take a day to paint what I'd drawn, and one day more for the paint to cure.

I painted till nightfall.

Stephen didn't come.

Tierre didn't either, but I knew he'd been out herding. T slept with Harlan in the cave. Where Stephen slept that second night, I could not bear to think on.

Painting flowers, my heart in ashes, I finished the rug the next day. I brought it in the house to dry. More than once, as I painted, stabs of regret made me see Stephen as a coward and a traitor. Suzanna in his arms. Reece Moon gloating over my choice to stay. I stoked the stove and sewed two pillows from Duff's mud-green calico. That night, I did not sleep.

Stephen pushed the door open around noon, the next day. Shook his hat and laughed out loud. "Ain't you a sight. I would not dare to touch you. I'd turn blue."

I felt scorched at his return, a little shy. The rug lay in place and our bed upon it. Mattress and linens and all. He breathed easily, full of health. Snow from his coat collar melted down his chest.

"How are things?" I asked.

"I brung eggs from Aggie, and a chicken she slaughtered for Thanksgiving."

"Is it so soon?"

"Six days. She says to hang it in the barn, it'll keep."

"You stayed at Aggie's for three nights?"

"Slept on Duff's floor."

"You did."

"The snow and all—" He brushed off a sleeve. "And I got the things you wanted."

There was only one thing I wanted. "So you made it, to Marsh Basin?"

"The road in ain't as bad as all that."

"Ah." That meant Suzanna. The way was cleared for us. Three days' worry collapsed into joy. I glanced at our new bed, expecting smiles and kisses and a long introduction into the pleasure of things.

"You seen Tierre?" Stephen asked, startling me out of my reverie.

"He fetched dinner at noon. He's out with Harlan."

"Well, I'd best roust him," Stephen said, pulling his coat together. "We got a new stove coming."

T and Stephen hefted our old pot stove, clamped between two poles, and hauled it out the door toward the barn. The heat of the house went with them into the darkness. Wind made a scouring path in through the stove pipe hole, brushing my cheeks. Chafing them. Our first night together, our first night ever to be alone, I hadn't reckoned on wagons and company, but company was what I got.

One of Opal's hired men, the burly one with the dark beret, backed a wagon up to the house. He and Stephen lowered a packing crate on a rope down two planks, but the crate lodged in the doorway, too wide by inches to slide through. The man swore quietly.

Stephen shinnied inside with a crowbar to wrench nails from the green wood. Loose slats littered the floor. Leaning into a black iron stove, he said, "It's from Mother. She shipped it up to Duff's. Merry Christmas, Clair." Opal's man stepped in. Strained and serious, they humped the huge stove inside and brushed off the packing, checking parts.

"You got something warmed for him, Clair, before Wesley heads back?"

I resisted the impulse to smack Stephen, hard. Wesley must have thought me the maid or the hired girl. "I can't well warm a thing. We have no stove."

"Oh, that's aw'right, ma'am," Wesley said. "I ain't cold."

"Too hard-working to be cold?" I asked.

Stephen banged the lengths of pipe into a stack.

He guffawed. "Yes, ma'am. That's right."

"Well, maybe you could take a raisin twist or two with you, keep you company on the ride back to Opal's."

He nodded, standing to the ankles in straw and busted crate.

"My name is Clair Martin."

"Yes, ma'am," he said. He never looked at me straight. "You cook a fine chicken. Bar-bee-cue." As the stove cut furrows across the swept dirt floor, I tied four rolls in a cloth and handed him a fifth for tasting. I said, over Stephen's clanking, "Pleased to make your acquaintance, Wesley. And thank you for delivering the stove. I hope your trip home is uneventful."

With his dark beard dripping onto his boots, he said, "Is that all, Stephen, all you was needing?"

Stephen's legs stuck out from behind the black belly of the stove. The clanking stopped. "Where'd I leave that stack? Clair? You seen the heat stack?"

Wesley thanked me for the pastries as he ducked out, lifting the two board planks.

I waded to the stack and kicked it across the room to Stephen. Then I went to my rocker, saying nothing, staring at nothing until the room's fierce cold drove me to the bed. It occupied a corner with the oilcloth under it, turned a little, to intersect the room. My trunk had offered up its bounty: two lace pillowcases just showed under the blue wool spread.

Hat on, his coat still buttoned, Stephen said, with all the tenderness of a command, "Lay in a fire, will you? I'll check on T."

I said to the wall, "Where is Tierre?"

"He's got his own room, now. Can't have the barn burnt down for lack of pipe—" Stephen shut the door on the end of his sentence.

I raked through the kindling in the box, shoved the hair out of my eyes, and layered bits of bark on straw. Fire sped along the twigs and flared. I fed in wood, slammed the door and stepped back. It was a handsome stove. Grape vines and grape clusters. Stephen had turned the dent in the stack to the wall so that it barely showed.

I was a pine knot in the silver stack. I was a child, all cheeks and eyes.

The door behind me clicked shut. At the pull of cloth on buttons, I turned to face the bed. The cold wool blankets only made me shake as Stephen crossed the room.

"Stop," I said, turning. "Your boots."

The edge of the painted canvas divided us.

He held his jacket by the throat. "Yes, ma'am." He slung it over the rocker and untied his laces.

No kindness now could make up for the bleak efficiency of his return. Stephen had the instincts of a stone when it came to love. Bales of politeness wouldn't alter that. I started to tell him but he rose and took my hand. His eyes moved over my face, my hair. And when at last he'd seen enough, he smiled, stepping in, and laid us down.

Fear swam up through the kisses. "I do not want to bear children, Stephen."

He only said, "Oh, honey, there's ways, and I know 'em." When he lifted my skirt, with his eyes on mine, my body went cold. Desire fled. For all his tenderness, sharing the bed with him felt as serious as death. The Elders said a woman's entire worth lay in her womb, the repercussions were eternal. Here I was skin to skin with love, at last, and deeply at their mercy.

"I am afraid," I said. "I am not cut for marriage, not cut out right!"

He smiled. "We aren't at the altar, Clair, we're in a bed in Idaho." Then he told me to relax, just relax, and open, and it wouldn't hurt.

"Show me!" I would see in advance what I was to give myself up to. I took his penis-bone in my hand. I turned it this way and that.

"Damnation, woman!"

It was like a little shovel, a shovel made of flesh.

For all of Stephen's enthusiasm, it took him three weeks to enter me, my womb tight as a fist. The Elders had done their best to lock my thighs against invasion. That's how I learned Inger Olsen had not rent me with his wrenching midnight how-do-you-do! Stephen did. With great care, a little whiskey, and laughter.

Once I too entered the field of desire, I shared Stephen's hunger and his ease. We relished the nights and roamed the days, side by side, insatiable as bears, and the dreariest tasks were honey. Hard work, hard love. I guessed it was a type of harmony. I never had heard bears sing.

Tierre, too, had had his own first night—the first night in his life sleeping in his own room. I went to visit him that next morning. The shot of smoke rising from his new stack hung heavy in the frosted world. The barn had paled with frost. My throat had frosted, my skirts gone crisp with cold. The sound of T's singing was the liveliest thing for miles. I knocked. The singing stopped. T held his door open a crack, wearing long johns that bunched at his ankles.

"May I come in, see your new room?"

He narrowed the gap. All I could see of him was one eye, one eye and T's firm lips. "I was fixin' to wash."

"But—"

"Wash and dress. Sheeps ain't run off to Kansas by theyselves, I don't guess."

"No, they haven't."

"Well," he said and closed the door on me.

Tears sprang to my eyes. Tierre couldn't be moved to share our joy. Not yet, but I hoped that he would. "Don't you want breakfast? T?"

The throaty stove pipe, the music of a barn owl were all my answer. Then, his singing resumed, a happy taunt:

> Oh! the way to Heaven is a good ol' way;
> Oh! the way to Heaven is a good ol' way;
> Oh! the good ol' way is the right ol' way;
> Oh! I wants to go to Heaven in the good ol' way.

Tierre grew impossible to please. By day, by night, meals, gifts, whatever I did brought scorn or indifference. You'd have thought I'd joined the anti-Baptist league. With Stephen, T listened only long enough to get the gist of the day's instructions, and he was off. More often, he shared his time with Harlan. I suffered T's judgment, keeping the hurt to myself, thinking *He'll understand when he loves a woman someday.*

Meanwhile, winter was truly upon us. The snow piled up

but only briefly as the range winds held more sway. Christmas bore down like a blight. Ada expected both Stephen and me to join her. In what capacity, I could not say—as friends, business partners, bethrothed, or next of kin. I doubted her welcome once Ada laid eyes on us together, unmarried. And, truth be told, Zion's capitol was the last place on earth I ever cared to see. But she'd already paid for our tickets by wire: two tickets awaited us at Kelton Station. If Reece was right, and Ada had put Stephen and me together with intent, well only then could I see joining her at Christmas as joyous.

I let Stephen rattle on about the holiday and even let the boys sing a line or two of "Silent Night." But when Harlan asked what I was wearing for the long cold ride to Kelton, I let them know I was not going. I sounded so stern, so final, Stephen didn't tease and Harlan didn't laugh it off. Tierre looked at me directly, for the first time in a week.

"I will send my gifts for Ada and the Gradons with you, Stephen."

"I might be gone three weeks. Two in good weather." Stephen looked like he'd only ever felt sorrow, only ever known how to grieve. "You'd be alone, the whole holiday."

"I don't much care for this holiday."

"But alone, three weeks, in winter—"

"I'll have Harlan and Tierre."

"You'll miss the lights and the merriment of Salt Lake City," Harlan said. "As well as Mrs. Nuttall's good cheer. We'll be fine without you."

I replied, very slowly, "I will not go."

T watched me, calculating and subdued.

Stephen took my arm. He spoke as if we were alone in the room. "Why, honey? Tell me why, so I can tell Mother—she'll be hurt."

I said, "I will not stay among murderers."

Stephen looked at me, blankly. Harlan's eyes went wide. A clear, cold trickle of malice linked Ada to my kin. Whatever my love for her, she sided with the Saints and always would.

"Your momma and daddy," T said.

Stephen balled his napkin in his fist. "You got a grudge."

"A grudge? I suppose I do. And I am staying here with my friends," I said.

But Tierre, well, T had other plans. He tilted his chin. "That ticket need a rider, I could go—"

We all looked at him. He'd been nine months with only our company. "You'd like to see a larger world," I said. Going could ease the gulf that had risen between us, give him new sights, new sounds, a look at Salt Lake City and a taste of Ada's world. "Harlan, how about the sheep? Do you need more help than I could give?" I asked.

Harlan considered this.

"I'll cook for you. And keep the dogs well fed. I could do a little herding."

He smiled. T nodded. Stephen crossed his arms in silence. We never spoke of traveling to Utah again.

Stephen was up and dressed and fed before I realized he had even risen. I heard T greet Opal and start to load their bags. Gloves in hand, Stephen bent down, lifted me in the dark and held me till our bodies lit. He rolled my lip between his, hungry and tender.

Opal called, "Shake it, Nuttall. 'Less you got my breakfast hot."

He called, "Coming!" and stroked my hair. He put his gloves on. "If there's trouble, you got Harlan." He leaned down and licked my lip, lapped it like milk.

"Good trip," I said.

"All right then. I'll be back."

Opal snorted and spat as Stephen stepped out. "Hallelujah!"

T rushed inside to say good-bye.

"Have a good trip, Tierre. Give Ada my regards."

"Yes, ma'am."

"You be safe. And have a grand time. You come back to me—"

"Yes, ma'am."

CHAPTER 27

I visited Harlan midday, when the sheep lay folded so close that the dogs stood sentry on their backs. I drank tea laced with whiskey as he tended his small fire. If the wind was right, the sky calm, and no coyotes dwelt on the margins of his thought, Harlan told tales. "And then there was the time . . ." may as well have been *Once upon a time*, for he talked not of the West, not of sheep and snow and desert, but of great English ships with beautiful names—the Forest Monarch, the Claddagh Lass—sailing in and out of storms, in and out of ports laden with cargo, sometimes lost, sometimes sold for astonishing gains, Harlan the hungry, bony boy who heard everything and marked it, and was called on by the captain more than once to repeat the terms of a transaction. Harlan recited them, just as surely as if the pages of a ledger had been laid open and read.

I asked how he'd come by such a memory. He ventured a guess. It was the books he'd devoured as a boy. Harlan slurped hot whiskey from his cup. "We ate lobsters in the Carib, dove down and speared in water blue as indigo. The royal family never ate better than we sailors in the Carib."

"Did you ever sail to New Orleans?"

"Once. A foul place."

"Or the Mississippi Coast?"

"No. Boston and New York, New Orleans, San Francisco. None rival the cities of Europe."

"Did you ever get home to England, then?"

Harlan's eyes cut to the flock. He doused the fire, tipping the kettle onto the coals. With two quick swipes, the embers scattered. He called to the dogs and shouldered his pack, leaving me to my half-drained cup.

Some questions are best left unanswered. Better yet, unasked. Aggies' question hung like a noose, midair, and I stuck my neck in it, unprepared. She and I had been discussing chicken houses, the dimensions of nesting boxes and the size and length of runs, when I looked around her coop and said, "T's room off the barn is just about this size, course our coop will be smaller than yours."

"T's on his own now?"

"Yes! Stephen's fixed him up a room."

That was when Aggie's sweet bun eyes bulged, and she asked, "And where does Stephen sleep?"

"He—" was all I managed, when Aggie's eyes hardened and her chin rose. "We—" How a face so round could look so sere, so judgment-lean. "Stephen and I, we—"

The coop door banged and a chicken flew into my face. Aggie paused at her back step. "You should be ashamed!"

I walked to the side yard.

"Clair Martin, you ought to be ashamed of yourself— sharing your flesh with him. Shame or no, the Lord repays us! You are muddying the holy name of marriage!"

"Whose marriage is so holy? Yours?" Aggie had lost her husband to the silver mines—lust for silver had meant more to him than a life with her. I threw this hard, to stop her, and she gave a little yelp as I pushed open the gate and snow tumbled through.

The eaves of the smithy offered me shelter from the snowflakes drifting down. I watched as Aggie forged a path to Duff's and back. Oh, the laces of life—they were too long, and most of them tangled. Just as one loosened and gave a little ease from suffering—pain in the instep, pinch at the toebox, and the ankles never did come free.

Duff didn't refuse my money or my business. But he stood wide-eyed across the counter as I passed him the cards I'd bundled for Marsh Basin. He bounced on his feet when I asked after Stephen's bill, but turned the ledger so that I could see. I thanked him, wanting to beg his pardon for the anxiousness I caused. I could not understand it, how Aggie and Duff and Tierre—people who cared for me—how anger and sorrow were all they felt now I resided in Stephen's love.

Dumplings bubbled in the dark lamb broth. Harlan filled our cups with whiskey. We cradled bowls of soup in new mudgreen napkins. He smiled, drawing the bowl up to his chin.

Full of soup and pudding, my tremulous voice led Harlan's baritone through a few carols. Sacred infants, holy nights and hoards of angels kept me poking at the fire and rinsing dishes. Then I feigned a sore throat and contentment, and we gave our gifts.

In the even gray of dusk, Harlan walked home and Christmas ended. Nothing in my manger. The night ahead empty as unsewn sacking. *Oh, Stephen.* The fire of his hands.

They returned from Salt Lake City soon after the New Year, Stephen as ardent as T was cool. In fact, between T and Stephen an icy river might as well have been in flood. I busied myself with housekeeping, letting Tierre navigate his own foul mood. The trip to Salt Lake, it seemed, had only soured him more.

When I walked their dinner out to them, Stephen and Harlan stood together, talking hay and spring lambs. T stood a quarter mile off, face to the wind. I went to his side.

He squinted, though the day wasn't bright.

"Dinner," I said. "Dinnertime."

He did not show a sign that I had spoken.

"Tierre?"

He blinked.

"T, look at me when I speak to you—"

"You ain't my mother!"

The words cut in, as they were meant to. I reached for his arm. He arched it away and cocked it at his hip. "I is sick to death of looking at white faces. Throw a tarp over the whole white world, cinch it down, it wouldn't be enough—"

"Tierre!"

He hadn't raised his voice, or his eyes from the flat of the horizon. He just kept squinting, leaning on the wind. I could have reprimanded him, but I knew anguish when I saw it. Anguish subdued. I knew it, inside out.

"What happened at Ada's? Did someone do you harm?"

He shrugged. "I met me a few More Man biddies."

"You did."

"Come to give Ada holiday regards. Friends a hers clutchin' they babies to theyselves callin' me 'Cain's seed' and 'Son of Perdition.' Man come up from the sidewalk to help, say, 'It just a loathsome darkie. Don't take fright. I gots a gun.'"

"He threatened you with a gun?"

T looked me in the eyes. "I'd a tore him in pieces, Clara. Some dandy in a top hat and smooth shoes."

"So only words passed between you—"

"Yeah, words. I ask that gentleman a question. On Aunt Ada's doorstep. With a bogeyman pistol in his pocket on Christmas day. 'Your religion, the More Man-ism, it say my black skin been Cain's curse, I knows it. But does you know what my religion say? Baptists say the curse a Cain been white skin,'" Tierre said. "*More Man.* They almost name it right. *More-White-Man* be more like it. And God help us if the world get more a that."

"It was the only religion, T," I said. "When I was growing up, it was the only everything—"

"Well, no wonder you hates religion, Clara, all the trash them folk laid at God's feet!'"

I took his hand, and he let me. "It is a wonder this nonsense rules the world, Tierre. I am glad you're back."

"For the while," he said, and then started to sing:

> *I've been in the storm so long.*
> *You know I've been in the storm so long,*
> *Oh, Lord, give me more time to pray,*
> *I've been in the storm so long.*
>
> *This is a needy time,*
> *This is a needy time,*
> *Singing Oh Lord, give me more time to pray,*
> *I've been in the storm so long.*
>
> *I am a motherless child,*
> *Singing I am a motherless child,*
> *Singing Oh Lord, give me more time to pray,*
> *I've been in the storm so long.*

In bed that night, restless and troubled, I asked Stephen what had happened to T at Ada's house. He slipped his arm under the blanket. He stroked my armpit with his thumb.

"Stephen—"

"He'll get over it."

"I sincerely hope that's so, but did anything happen, beyond the words exchanged on Ada's doorstep?"

"He's sixteen and a man—or ought to be." His hand moved down my side.

I gripped it. "Stephen—"

"Hell, I'd left home and broke a dozen horses by sixteen. Nah, by fifteen—"

"Don't compare yourself to him. You have no idea, not a bit, of what he's endured. I know they cast aspersions—"

Stephen grimaced. "Mother spoiled him like the King of Siam." Then he nuzzled down, kissing my neck.

I felt gratitude for Ada's kindness, gratitude pinched by guilt. "And your mother, what did you tell her about us?" He sighed, seeing conversation was what I wanted. "About you and me," I said.

"Mother was curious, but she didn't ask outright."

"She waited for you to tell her—"

"And I didn't."

"So she thinks we're . . ."

"Due for a better house. She's sending up a crew late spring, after the lambing. Bunch of laborers and a load of bricks."

Startled, I said as sweetly as I could, "We have debts, Stephen. We owe Duff and Opal, and we owe Aggie, yet you'll take more of your mother's money and men to build a new house?"

He didn't even flinch. I swear the words *My woman deserves a better house* just flowed out of his smiling lips as he bent to kiss mine. I kissed him back and thanked him for his discretion with Ada. An ignorant Ada seemed better than an angry Ada, or a deeply disappointed one.

"So no one struck Tierre, or threatened him or—"

"Shut up, can't you, Clair?" Stephen had both his hands on my waist and a look in his eyes that did not welcome interruptions.

I shocked us both. I began to cry. Stephen tried to wipe my tears but in the darkness and the pull of bedding, his aim was off.

"Bear's ass!" I yowled.

"Are you all right? Honey?" He turned my face to the firelight. "I didn't mean to blind you, Clair—" When he saw my wet eye shake open, he grinned and tucked in behind me, locked in, tight.

"What if you had?" I asked, weak with laughter and worry and strain. "What if I was blinded?"

Stephen pressed in close. "It would be like I'd lost my own sight. I would myself be blinded."

27 December, 1877

Clair,

I do not doubt you find Tierre changed. Honey, you can blame it on me. I asked him to answer the door, my door, and none the wiser there'd be harm till I heard it slam to with the force of a quake. I ran, saw T fomenting, and looked out the glass—two Ward Sisters and an Elder and their broods fleeing down the walk like hens afire. T said they had shrieked and hid their babies' faces from sight of him, clutching each other and crying, "Seed of Cain!" Well, honey, it was awful hearing him tell it, seeing the startled faces of Una and Florence, and Alfred with his fists bunched at my side. I tried to make amends. I fought with Stephen for three days, said Tierre's a man, and he deserves a man's wages. We can't keep him for mush

and a bed. *"Harlan don't make a wage, and I don't either."* But that
was their choice, I said. *Stephen would not budge. So I wrapped
up one of my Henry rifles, for Christmas. To give Tierre a sense
of his worth. Now he has his own gun for the hunt, well, I feel I
have tried to make things right. As for his longing to see his own
kind—what can we do? He is a spiritual boy, Clair, and a social
one. No church for him, and no girls to charm. Oh, mercy, robbed of
delight. I don't doubt you can do better than me, find that boy's fire
again. Light it.*

Yours, can you forgive me, Ada

I slipped into T's new room on the second week of the
new year. Rifle over the door, blankets near the stove, and a little can in which he boiled his water to make mush. He needed
everything, lacked nothing. I remembered the Sisters' astonish-
ment, looking in at my cabin on the Bench. The Ward Sisters
had hiked up to check on me, early on, and been appalled and
made a list. They'd brought everything I needed. None of them
knew freedom when they saw it.

I inched my collar up against the snow and closed Tierre's
door behind me. He was home, "for the while." Out of that
storm. Or so I thought, being me.

CHAPTER 2 8

Aletter arrived late in February. The envelope said "Tierre Durham, Nuttall's Ranch, Abram's Stage Station, Idaho" with the initials R. M. where the return address should be. I worked around the letter all day, telling myself I must be wrong, it was some other R. M. we knew. I hauled water from the spring, broke the ice and topped the barrel, then came inside, dried my hands and picked it up, touched the ink. I went to the wood stove and opened the stoking door, but couldn't bring myself to throw it in. Whatever Reece might have to say, about me or anything, he had a right to say it. It was already written and done.

Stephen banged in early, the first one home. He hauled me up against him, hay and snow and all. "Clair, let's garden."

"But supper—"

"Is on its way. Is cooking up fine. Ain't I right?" He brushed his beard across my face.

"You smell like an old camp fire."

"Oh, honey—" He pulled his hands out of his gloves. "Clair." He grappled with his coat.

"And you're sure Tierre won't come?"

Stephen knelt on the floor at my feet. "Harlan and, unh,

they was—"Then all the talk was his hands and my hands. We had a good deal to say. The happiness dropped down through me like singing, like water on a plunge. By the time Tierre came in for supper, I had the floor under my heels again, but my senses still trickled, cool and sweet.

Stephen rocked in the rocker.

"Smell like cinnamons," Tierre said. "You fix dessert for supper?"

"No, that's for after," I said.

He hung up his coat.

"Harlan got his reading glasses from Cincinnati," Stephen said to T. "And a letter came for you."

Tierre moved to the table. He looked at the envelope, didn't pick it up. "Lord in Heaven. Oh, my Lord."

I said, "You could take the package out to Harlan, T. There's time before supper."

"Yes, ma'am," he said. He snatched up the letter and the package, and ran out, dodging back in to get his coat and a lantern. Snow heaved in the open door, and fluttered at its closing.

We heard him shout and shout again.

"He'll spook the sheep," Stephen said.

"Good news, I hope."

We waited the meal three quarters of an hour, then ate without him. Tierre came back in time for cake.

"You'll be wanting supper first—" I said.

"Nah, I could eat backward this once, Clara. Celebrate." He took a square of spice cake and pushed it in his mouth.

"Don't let a fork stop you," Stephen said.

For all my apprehension, I loved seeing T glad hearted. He chewed and swallowed the dinner cake down.

"What are we celebrating?" I asked.

He slapped the table. The pan jumped. "My freedom."

"Your what?" Stephen stopped rocking.

"My freedom. My chariot done come." Tierre danced a few steps. "I got me a job with the railroad."

My mind couldn't catch up with his words.

"You got you a job here," Stephen said, pointing at his feet.

"This a new job, a real job."

I felt as wide as a penny, but I smiled. "With Reece?"

"Yes, praise the sweet Lord Jesus, yes, ma'am!" He flashed his jaw at me and pushed a second piece of cake in.

Stephen sat up. "You can't."

T winked at me and chewed.

Stephen stood, emptying the rocker. "You can't leave."

Tierre wiped his mouth with his sleeve, still grinning. "Who say I cain't?"

Stephen frowned. "I say it."

T cut him a glance. "T's a free man."

"Stephen," I said, hoping to soften things.

"A man, are you?" Stephen stiffened, then shook his head. "No man leaves with his work undone. We have a contract—"

"A half a one fifth, and debts on the ledger? Y'all keeps my share." T leaned down to me with confidential humor. "He gone crazy, Clara? You feed him some of that loco bush?" But humor was a sacrilege to Stephen just then.

"I ain't crazy," he shouted, "I'm a damn fool, boy. I knew it all along—you ain't worth dung with the herd, but I kept you on, I kept you on for Clair's sake, and I let my mother throw good money and a first rate rifle after you. A rat in a bag would have been more help on this ranch—"

"Stephen!"

"You're good for nothing," he said, "you ain't good for one damn thing, so just take your black ass off to that railroad see how hard they make you work. I'd like to see the sweat pour off your back, just once—"

I pushed my hands over his mouth but Stephen tore them off, pulled me into his side and held me there.

Tierre blinked back fury. "Who a man? He some hayseed makes his woman a whore?"

Stephen raised an arm, to shield me from the hearing.

"Look at you, Clara," T bellowed.

"If Clair didn't love you and I didn't know it, I'd tear your godforsaken heart out here and now."

"Stephen." I whispered it.

"Get the hell out."

Stephen. I had no voice.

When the door closed I stood clasped to his side, staring at nothing. He released me. He turned the rocker so his back was to the room and sat there, shoulders hunched like a child's.

I cleared the table and washed our dishes.

Once the lamp was out, I lay next to him, but not right next. Stephen said one thing to explain himself. "We got three hundred and fifty lambs dropping in March, maybe more."

I tugged the blanket over to cover my knees. Stephen did not comfort me, or feel a need to apologize for maligning T. He lay rigid as a post. Sheep were all that mattered.

Somewhere in the dark lay the peace that I was seeking. My mind just never caught it up.

I knocked. Tierre opened the door with soap on his jaw and embraced me, drawing me inside. He set his razor down and held my cheek on his chest. A young heart pounded there. I could feel bone. "My hair, it's dripping on your undershirt."

"Pretty hair," he said, stroking it. "I never meant to hurt you, Clara."

I closed my eyes. "It's Stephen who's hurt."

"What can I do?" he asked, anger flaring.

"Nothing. Not now. You could have stayed to help with the lambing. Stayed on through spring." I stopped. I shook him. "I can't believe you're leaving me—"

"Who left who, first?" T's sharpness only lasted for an instant. "You think you's home, Clara. God help you—you cain't see a snake in the dirt until it rattle."

Stephen's eyes had glittered like a snake's, last night—he hated not getting his way. And he covered this fury with stealth, with stillness, with remove. He hadn't spoken a word to me, not one word or a glance. He left for the range early. Like the king of creation. Like a willful crossed child. I began to wonder if staying put to keep your territory was the same as having real courage.

Tierre patted my shoulder. "Long as Stephen be right, everything go fine."

"How can I even think of life here without you?" I said wistfully.

He batted his lashes. Then he said in earnest, "I gots to go."

"I know it. And you're sure that you'll be provided for—with work and all."

"Mr. Moon, his letter say *come on*."

"Did you write and ask him to hire you?"

"Yes, ma'am."

I tugged the wet wool off his skin, flapped it a little. "Who'd have thought it would be you going off with Reece?"

"He tried for your stubborn self, already."

"Perhaps."

"But you rather took a short, ignorant hickabilly."

I nodded.

"That hayseed."

"Mhmm."

"Sheeps farmer."

"Yes, T."

"You loves him?"

I sighed.

"Then make his sorry self marry you, gal."

"It isn't as simple as that."

Tierre dragged his toe across the dirt. "There it is," he said. "Right there."

"There's what?"

"There it is!" T pushed me over. "Easy as a jump across a broomstick."

I spanked him and jumped back to his side.

"'This yo' wife,'" he said.

"'That yo' husband.'"

"'I's yo' master.'"

"'She yo' mistress—'"

T took my hand and we jumped.

"'Y'all married,'" he said, and brushed his hands together like a satisfied, sanctified preacher-man.

Tierre left two days later, with all his belongings folded in a blanket and the Henry rifle lashed on top. He knocked at the ranch house door. I stepped out into blinding sunshine. I kissed him and touched the brim of his hat, longing to stand awhile, share the morning with him, but Tierre's whole body was ready to spring. He hadn't been so fidgety since Baruch Place, the day his cast came off. I leaned in close, while I had time. "T, I want you to know—I don't hate God."

He twisted me up and off my feet. Then, whistling like a mockingbird, as ardent and as arrogant, Tierre marched off down the track.

Stephen stepped out. The sun warmed us, standing there together. "Yep," he said, ending three days' silence. It would be bearable now, maybe even fine, as Stephen's resentment had no target. T hiked away from us, and I asked myself if it was people or the land that filled our deepest need. I watched Tierre's figure until it merged with land.

I didn't hate God. I didn't believe in one.

CHAPTER 29

We readied the barn, strung lanterns, and packed food into Tierre's old room, which now served as camp kitchen. A dozen lean-tos, covered with blankets and brush, stood between the barn and the hill. I took T's part, tending the range ewes. Three times a day I trailed a new batch of droppers into the barn for Harlan. Most of my patients reached him in time, though a pair of twin lambs came out in the scrub. I tied their legs together as I'd been told so they would feed together, each to a teat, and both grow strong. They wrenched laughter out of me, the twins, bumping their way like a French Quarter drunk behind their mother, all the way to the barn.

I slept on the range those nights, as well. March is a hard month in the Idaho desert. I slept as hard as March. My third night out, I was lifted awake by Stephen, literally lifted onto my feet before sleep let me go.

"It isn't even day," I hissed. "I need a few hours' sleep."

"Move the herd in."

"I will not—"

"Clair!" He shook me and my mind took focus: the clouds had vanished. Wind cut tears from my eyes.

"I'm freezing," I said, astonished.

"Move the sheep in close." He mounted Shep and rode off at a canter. The dogs were up, circling my feet. As soon as I hefted my stick they shot off, barking to rouse the herd.

My teeth knocked together in the darkness. I gave all my attention to closing the gaps in my blanket where the wind tore in. The dogs never faltered. I let them lead. At the banks of a gully, I tossed myself and my exhaustion down right along with the sheep, all of us undulating in and up and over like a mindless serpent, twenty feet wide. The frigid night gave us one purpose, endowed us with one need. And the thought rose in my mind, *The Endowment House*, where Mormon couples went to bind their troth for time and all eternity. *I've finally reached the Endowment House.* I laughed aloud.

Then I smelled smoke.

A campfire raged in the lee of the barn. A signal fire, lit for me. Smoke hurled across the prairie. Sheep and fire—something told me not to mix the two, so I started west toward the dark house, and the dogs, exultant, shaped the herd.

Harlan intercepted us at the garden. "Good girl," he called. "Any droppers?"

And the cold night's union was rent. "I don't know—" I turned around. "Harlan, I don't know." I ached to scour the long trail back for missing lambs.

"Never you mind. Bed them in the lee and mark the droppers." He kicked his way through the herd to the door.

They had bedded themselves without me, huddling against the house. The most encumbered ewes had lost the fight for shelter. Easy to mark at the perimeter, with my scarf, my blanket, my hat.

Inside, Harlan knelt at the tail of a laboring mother. She lay beside the oilcloth rug. He had penned the rest in the corners with tipped chairs. "We'll need more wood."

I filled the box for him and went outside for a second load. A glowing stream of smoke still marked the signal fire at the barn. I remembered how angrily I'd awakened. I ran to Stephen to make apology, but he wasn't at the pens, wasn't in the barn or out with the couples in the lean-to village. I found him in the shed kitchen, cooking a newborn in a pan.

"Stephen! Have you lost your senses?"

He cut a tired smile, folding the dripping lamb in burlap. "Chilled down," he said.

"So you baste them?"

He leaned his face into my hair. "No, give them a good warm bath." He offered me the lamb and I sat down to dry it.

"Your herd all right?"

"They are wearing my clothes and sleeping in our bed!"

"Well, ain't you the charming hostess."

"I am sorry I woke so cross."

He smiled and yawned, stretching. "Here, I'll take it to its mother." I appreciated Stephen's ready forgiveness. It felt so natural, working with him, easy as breathing to be what he wanted. Like we were two arms of one strong body caring for the ranch. But our give and take was all that came easy. When I stopped to use the outhouse on my way back to the cabin, a ewe and lamb huddled there—no room at the inn.

"We are insane!" I told Harlan, once inside. "But if I know that we are crazy, how can we be?"

The house had warmed a few degrees. He slumped over his unlaced boots, rubbing both feet. At his age, this was no game.

"Are you hungry?"

"I'll get to the kitchen, directly," he said, making no move to rise.

I touched his shoulder. He didn't resist, so I kneaded his

thick neck. A scarf encircled it, old silk stained brown from use.

"Where did you get your fancy neckerchief?"

He stiffened, and his reluctance passed into me. "My sister," he said. I knew to ask no more. I let my hands do the talking. Harlan rocked under their pressure. Silence reigned in the beleaguered room, as the new mother hunched against the wood box, her lamb asleep at her side. This was no matronly show of affection. Harlan had lashed them together with a strap.

"Why are the sheep so blessed helpless, Harlan?" I asked, trying for humor. "They need our help for every last thing."

"That is what they've traded. For the shepherd's love and care."

"Their common sense?"

"It little serves, when all of their thinking is done for them."

"Well, it makes hard work for us, all of this mothering!"

He laughed. "I know people that helpless."

"So stupid they can't even recognize their own kin?"

"When the kin go against prevailing wisdom, yes." A jolt of empathy passed between us. Harlan's shoulders lowered with a breath. "Who is the most famous shepherd you know, Clair?" His question tripped me up. I wasn't sure of anyone who'd made a fortune running sheep.

"'Be not forgetful to entertain strangers: for thereby some have entertained angels unawares . . .'"

"Angels?" I said. "I thought that we were talking famous sheepherders, Harlan."

"And farther down in Hebrews—"

"Hebrews?"

"'Now the God of peace, that brought again from the dead our Lord Jesus, that great shepherd of the sheep...'" Harlan wrenched forward. He turned his massive head. "You've been without a herd how many years? A human herd."

"Six, nearly seven."

"You left the Mormons for good—" I nodded. "And you take Stephen to your bosom without thought of marriage."

"Wait—"

"With no regard for public or religious opinion." Harlan blushed here, though his tone stayed steady.

"How is it anyone's business but our own?"

"What if you have a child?"

I blushed, this time. I pulled a chair up and sat backwards on it, facing him. "We won't."

"Said the straying and possibly very black sheep—"

"I mothered Tierre! And he's a fine boy, a fine young man."

"Who also lives outside the reach of any herd or tribe. How do you hope to survive?" he asked with complete honesty. With purpose, as if he needed to know.

"I—" I started, "I know I can figure it out as I go."

He smiled and looked so sad.

"You're alone, too, Harlan. You have no tribe—"

He nodded.

"Your sister belonged in that herd?"

His eyes said *yes*.

"Then you and I," I said, mussing his hair, hoping to sweep him into a fresher track, "we are *wild* woolly sheep. Emphasis on wild." Harlan looked tired enough to fall asleep on that chair. He moved to his pallet, but stopped to ask, "Do you know what a mother does, in the wild, Clair?"

"Give warmth, and love—"

"Protect! Defend!"

I stood straighter. Harlan's vigorous views on mothering

seemed right. Lambs and mothers tied tight. Their keepers watchful, brave, adamant and wise. "Thank you, Harlan," I said, "for leaving out the part about marriage and 'the undefiled bed'—in Hebrews."

He wrapped himself in a blanket, closing his eyes. "Only God can judge," he said.

The next day, I found Harlan asleep in a lambing pen with the cat curled at his side. I stood awhile, watching. Some sights require that. He was old enough to be my grandfather. I wished he were. There was something sacred in him. Not showy sacred—simple as dirt. A hurt hard decency. I shut my ewes in their pen quietly, and left Harlan in peace. I headed back out to my herd of late droppers.

A hazy sun warmed the prairie. Three birds stitched their way east. My boots in the scrub, my heart—all good and empty. The swing of heel and toe—huge, silent, empty. Tears were empty, the sky empty, the blisters on my feet. My overalls, stiff with afterbirth, channeling winds—empty. Empty roots and stalks, furred, milk-white leaves congregating as an empty shrub. *Sabbath! The Holy Day!*

I turned my ankle on a rock and swore.
The Holy Moment, then.

When lambing slowed to a few births a day, Harlan took charge of the herd of new couples. He moved gladly with them onto the rangelands east of the barn.

"He loves his solitude," I said, watching him go.

"He's a little sweet on you," Stephen said, distracted, working his moustache.

"The admiration is mutual," I said.

The tremor in Stephen's eyelid never stilled. It had started at T's leaving. Short-handed and short on rangeland, he never stopped considering our survival. Looking up at the barn rafters, then out over the pens, finally settling on my face, Stephen said, "Think you could take the able-bodied, run them west for fifteen miles to graze, then circle back and find Harlan? You'd be gone four, five days. You could take Shep and the wagon. You could ride the whole time, sleep inside at night. I'd rig the canvas cover on. I got supplies saved for the week. I need to stay and birth the last thirty ewes, and—"

"Stephen?" His eyes searched the near air in frustration. Five days away, five whole days by myself. I pulled his beard till his jaw dropped. "Just you try and stop me."

Stephen came in while I was packing my books and lapwork. Except for trips to Aggie's, I had not left the ranch since I'd arrived. Even with sheep for company, it was an outing. I'd taken the white straw hat out of my trunk, and plaited my hair. Dirty plaited hair under a New York hat—it was impossible to tell its effect in the chip of Stephen's shaving mirror. But he came in and said what a mirror could not. "Now, there's a pretty sight."

"You think the hat sets off the bloody overalls?"

"I think you're trying to make me abandon my duties."

I laughed. "No, I just—"

"I think you're trying to make me change my ways."

"No, Stephen—"

"I'm a shepherd." He took my wrist. "I ain't a farmer."

"I know!"

He took my other wrist, too. "But I got tools. And I can garden with the best of them—" He leaned in. "Leave your hat on, we won't muss your hair."

The ewes ran wild with desire on the lush plain, fanning out to tempt fate and coyotes, no matter what the dogs and I intended. All day, I searched them out in little bunches and herded them back to the flock. Where was the wealth of time Stephen had once called a shepherd's treasure? I'd righted a dozen sheep the first two days, stuck on their backs with their legs toward Heaven and no hope for salvation. Day three, a ewe bogged down in a gulch that the rest of the herd just walked around. She soaked up water and sank. Shep pulled and I pushed, but it was the dogs' frenzied messages of death that finally hauled her out. Ginnie—Harlan's best dog—trotted in proud circles around me begging for the next challenge.

Covered in mud, my own coat dripping, I laughed at her. She loved this work. We herded hard all day and slept like the dead every night, after feeding on mush and Rossetti—

> *I shall not see the shadows,*
> *I shall not feel the rain;*
> *I shall not hear the nightingale*
> *Sing on, as if in pain:*
> *And dreaming through the twilight*
> *That doth not rise nor set,*
> *Haply I may remember,*
> *And haply may forget.*

I met Harlan at dusk on the fifth day. The herds blended together and I collapsed.

"Would you like supper?" he asked. "A little coffee?"

"I want to sleep till the century turns."

He stroked his beard. "A difficult drive?"

"They invented trouble when there was none! But your dogs. Such workers, such friends."

We ate fresh lamb, roasted with apples that Harlan had soaked in whiskey. I drank the whiskey apple water down until my knees had their own pulse. We took shelter from the evening wind inside the wagon, and I read him "Goblin Market," stumbling only a little on the lines, as I had already read the poem twice before. Harlan gaped when the goblins flew at Lizzie, kissed and embraced her, offering up their evil dishes. Growling, he listened as they clawed and jostled her, though she stood "like a lily in a flood." He sighed when Lizzie would not drink the poison fruit, and then he stopped me, asking to hear again how her sister Laura's hair "streamed like the torch Borne by a racer at full speed" in her grief, tasting the juices on Lizzie's battered face, whose bitterness would save her from obsession. At the closing lines, "For there is no friend like a sister," Harlan caught his face in his hands.

I finished reading and touched his arm. "Harlan, your sister?"

He turned, staring at the book, trembling, unwell.

"I am so sorry. How did you lose her?"

"To 'wicked quaint fruit-merchant men'!"

I looked out the break in the canvas, into darkness, then back down at the book. Such power in a page—the power to chasten, if not to heal. I said, "She does not deserve you."

"You are an angel, for saying it. Albeit the earthliest angel I've ever known."

"You needn't tell me till you're ready," I said.

Harlan shifted his weight, to face me. He leaned back against the hard-used canvas and said, "The spirit of God moved in me, once. God the healer, God the trickster, God the liar. At mass murder, I had to stop." The pulse at his neck moved the old knotted scarf.

"I was a missionary," he said, as if telling some other man's life. "First in England, but I learned my family had moved back to Sweden at my father's death, so I asked to go on. The Brethren were only too happy to have me 'open a new field.' And the spirit of the Lord preceded me in dream. Before I had reached Gefle by ship, my sister Erika foresaw my coming. Sitting in church one Sabbath Day, doubting the truth of the Lutheran sermon, she asked for inner guidance and a visitation struck her, as the minister spoke: a man stood before her holding three books, in which, he said, were contained the everlasting gospel.

"Imagine her joy a week later, when her oldest brother— twenty years gone on the seas—stood on the threshold of her door with the Bible, the *Book of Mormon* and the *Doctrine and Covenants* in his hands. It took no time to convince her and her neighbors of their truths."

I crossed my legs up under me, leaning a knee on Harlan's leg.

"Three weeks later, July of 1850, I was arrested and taken to court for preaching heresy, and for all of my public healings. The magistrate, a man my own age, asked for a picture of 'this wonderful prophet.' He took the Prophet Joseph Smith from me and held his image over a lamp. As it smoldered and burned, I saw the city of Gefle burn to ashes. When the judge pronounced my banishment, I cursed him and his progeny to the flames.

"Erika trembled when she heard of the conflagration, but I assured her we would all be safe, safely settled here in Zion. And come to Zion, we did.

"She was quick to take a husband in Salt Lake City and to embrace the life of a Saint." Harlan grimaced. "Being older and less comely, I married a good deal later. And I bore the glories and the stains of life among the chosen as best I could."

I could not keep myself from asking. "Did you know the Prophet Joseph Smith?"

"Yes, I met him, and heard him speak many times."

A bubble the size of a seed rose in my chest. "Ada told me when Joseph spoke, his face shone as radiant as an angel's."

"Yes," Harlan said, "and the more young ladies there were in attendance, the whiter his countenance grew."

I smiled in wonder as the hard little bubble popped.

"He was human, Clair, an inspired boy—more the sorrow to the faithful who've forgotten it. And they have all forgotten, under Brigham's shadow." His brow creased. "I would have marched to my death for that boy, ten years my elder. Joseph was a natural leader, but he was not divine—no, an exuberant boy in a grown man's guise. It wasn't his perfection but his humanness that I loved."

"So it is just a pile of words, what they have made of him?"

"Never trust the words from any preacher's lips!"

"But they testify! I heard Brigham Young promise a thousand people salvation and Joseph at the gates to welcome them, a holy picnic with the prophet, all for laying railroad track. He conjured it so plainly I could smell the meal myself."

"That is the root source of Brigham's power—mimicry, performance. He would have made a good actor. A good one, mind you, but not a great one."

"An actor?" I barked out. "Hoo!" It echoed in the valley. "Well, I didn't care for that play, not much!"

"It is a play, Clair. In the early Church, we all spoke with and for God. Brigham broke that covenant. He claimed sole right to divine authority here in Zion. He and he alone had God's ear. 'What did we know and suffer in England? Why did we come away from Sweden?' I asked Erika, but she could not or would not see it. My sister faulted nothing but my vision and my faith."

Harlan sighed, his massive head all knob and pore and bristle. "I tried to regain the early spirit of my conversion. I even founded my own church, the Lawes of Love. All our study was the Gospels and the love in Christ's teachings. The Prophet Brigham tolerated it. He even seemed to find my little flock amusing, but my sister shunned me utterly. When my wife died, Erika sent only a formal note of condolence. It ran that way for several years: she would not see, I would not hold my tongue.

"Then, July of 1869, Erika came into my house and held me in her arms and cried for joy. I could not fathom her return, but I rejoiced in it. 'Good news, brother!' she said, clapping her hands. 'The city of Gefle, just as you prophesied, has burned.'" Harlan wrenched upright. "The Lawes of Love! Humans don't want love any more than they want peace. I saw this in the mark of institutional brotherly love upon my sister's face."

"The city burned?"

"Gefle was nearly destroyed. The blaze began in the very house where the prophet's picture went to the flame, and on the selfsame day."

"Oh, Harlan—"

"They could have fed me to the dogs on Main Street all those years and Erika would not have intervened, until word came from Gefle. Then, I was a prophet."

I'd had no access to this side of Mormon faith, to priesthood power and dreams fulfilled and God's sure intervention. How strange that such a position could be rife with conflicts, too. "Do you miss it, Harlan?"

He closed his eyes. "No."

"You can't go back—"

"No!"

"And yet you can't look away."

"I cannot."

And there was the gist of his melancholy.

I took Harlan's hand. I firmed my grip, forging a muggy pact between us, the apostates. "Well, your whiskey-soaked lamb is all the proof I need of your divinity," I said. He actually touched my cheek, the one stained red. Then Harlan took his walking stick and heaved himself up. I heard him whistling to the night sky. Hymns and a reel or two. Harlan Lawes loved night watch, much like his nights at sea—a man alone who wasn't really alone, steering the quiet vessel for himself.

CHAPTER 30

Stephen and Harlan had chosen the twin springs as their ranch site to keep clear of human troubles. It lay beyond reach of towns, trails, fences, stage lines and such. It held no attractive features at all, too high on the ridge for meadow grass, no trees to shade or cut. We had two year-round springs and that was that. Stephen and Harlan had reckoned that with no neighbors, they'd have no neighborly disputes—like the man who marries an ugly woman to save himself the struggle of keeping his wife to himself. Men and their best-laid plans.

While our herd had swelled to nine hundred sheep—a genuine cause for pride—homesteaders dotted the unclaimed valleys around us. The rich bottomlands. A few ranchers moved in with their own dreams, and those dreams brought Hereford cattle. Which meant, in that mild sunny April of 1878, we had a strong whiff of prosperity and nearly nowhere to feed our herd.

Stephen pounded stakes at the corners for the new house. Then he and Harlan left to thread the flock between homesteaded claims in the Black Pine Valley. My great lone summer lasted one week—I had a building crew for company. Ada's men brought six windows and a load of timber with them. The bricks came later, with crew and cook.

They made their own camp near the second spring and kept out of my business. The foreman, a short knobby Italian, said "bella, bella" all day long. *Beautiful* was his answer to everything. I gave off suggesting or asking or trying to get my way, and in the end the house was beautiful. Like it rose out of a creek bed into sky. They mortared a rock foundation, singing as they scavenged the ridge for stone, easily tripling the dimensions of our old hut. Then came walls of brick, straight and true, until the bricks ran out, whereupon the one-story, four-room structure went crossbreed, the crew hauling river rock all the way up from the Raft River. Our house had meandering fox-red, gray-wolf walls, with wooden window ledges.

The strong *V*'s of the roof struts reminded me of a shorebird's wings.

Clara, I aint fownd Reece yet, grade croo got me, no black men, greeks and chineses, stinky from heat all of us is and working working T

Clara, what you gona do in a house wit a floor gal, spred som dirt aroun just to feel at home, I sent word on to Blackfoot like you sed after Reece, we see Tierre

Clara, you must be lonsom the herd gon to pascher, we busted sevn mile of bed north of Malad yesterday, we all looks foward to Fort Hall wher beds music and such is, I hopes Reece Moon be ther T

I seen my first indjuns, Clara, they aint so ferce and som of the wimens pretty, got a telgram from Reece ses he meet me at Fort Hall Never thout Id be ichy to see a whit man face but I is his, Fort Hall! fort Hall! T

Clara you aint writing to a pick man no mor, you is writing to a survay or and I rides the survay wagon helps Reece with things You sure you keeping them chickens or is the chicks keeping you? We got the song of the Snake river nites Pretty song, Clara gal Tierre

2 September, 1878

Honey Dear, Peach Pie, Pickle Lily, we hear your cry!

Florence has written her best thoughts on chicken rearing and I send along my favorite recipes. Do you know how many yields we lost, them early days, from ignorance and weather and muddling through? Don't be downhearted—we ain't all of us good at every thing, and thank heavens. Tell Stephen not to send me payment from the profits this fall, just to put all his earnings into your new house. Capital improvements. I don't suppose a dirt roof ever harmed a woman, but I sleep easier knowing you got plaster and beams over your head. Una and Albert send their best and hope you'll come for Christmas. I don't suppose you'd break my old heart twice.

Love, Ada

How could it make a difference, autumn in a land where there were no trees with leaves to turn? No bared branches. No piles to rake and smell and burn. And yet it was a time of ripening: the sage muted from months of dust, the hills gone copper brown, the mountains to the north blue as larkspur in the heat, and the sky, evening after evening, collapsing with its weight of colors into an amber sea. The reeds at the dry spring rustled. The few brown cattails left looked foolish and prim amid the creamy tangles of seed-gone-everywhere. I felt as mild and calm as autumn by the time the men came back. The ewes were serviced. The herd had managed to scavenge its way through much of south-central Idaho.

Ginnie's runt male pup whined, watching the sheep trail in, sniffing the air at my heels. The pup had stayed with me through the long summer, helped to fill the lonely hours, watched me build a small lap loom, and trembled with excitement as I plucked every scrawny chicken in a tight-lipped rage. However much the roil of incoming sheep and the quick dogs coming home roused his interest, I had Digger's heart.

"Digger," I said, "go say hello. Go on." His head lowered onto his brindled paws, but his tail was up and wagging. "Get!"

Digger flew off and lost himself in the ruction.

Harlan, bronze from the nose down, tipped his bowler back to kiss my forehead.

"I have a bath drawn, Harlan, cool and full, and all that water's waiting on you."

"I may drink it. I may drown," he said, limping inside.

Stephen stopped to appraise the house. Then he sauntered up, trying to snap his shirt clean, but the dust wouldn't stop flying. He pulled me off the front porch into the sunshine with his free hand and kissed me. Dirt and salt and deep laughter.

"Do you like it?" I asked.

He squinted like I was crazy. He took my waist between his hands.

"The house, I mean, not the kissing—"

"It is one of a kind," Stephen said, and went back to our fond hellos.

That night I served them supper, Stephen and Harlan and Wes, lined up like a barefoot jury on the new front porch. Wesley had joined them that summer. Thought my cooking and Stephen's bossing outdid Opal's any day. His beret sat like a soft pancake on his head. After supper, he carried his boots off to bed down in the barn. Harlan hobbled off barefoot, too, but stopped to pull his boots back on. Stephen sighed. "We must have walked three hundred miles."

"No trouble, though?" I asked.

"Sheep are nothing but." Then, unlike the man I used to know, Stephen forgot all about the sheep. He placed the dirt brown soles of his feet on my shoes. "Bedtime," Stephen said.

Even with a house so grand, Stephen saw only flaws and what remained to be done. "My woman deserves better" became his constant refrain. The house was just one story, it had only one fireplace, the rooms, except for the kitchen, were all undersized. I pointed out the height of the windows, the view up to the ridge from our bedroom, how Ada's fancy stove fit perfectly between the hand-hewn work table and the storage bins the crew had built from scrap wood. I'd painted the handles blue with the last of Ada's paint. The carefully mortared river rock fireplace, Stephen admired, but all else fell short of his dreams. When his fretting grew too tiresome, I walked him outside and pointed him toward the sod hut, left him standing there to ponder the improvement. Even Opal spat and said, "Sweet Jesus!" when she saw our house. She scraped her boots in tribute, before entering the door.

In November, I came down with fever. It vexed me, making the cooking and laundry difficult, my head weaving from exertion. I would stop to rest until my mind settled and my jaws relaxed, and then resume working. But the cold sweats alerted Stephen to my troubles. He mopped my brow through a night of chills. Then he brought Harlan in to tie on the apron while he rode to Kelton for a doctor. I took to bed not by choice or persuasion—I could not keep my head up, couldn't see. I vomited so often Harlan pulled a washtub alongside the bed.

The doctor did not say what it was, he only said it wasn't mountain fever. "You see spots, you call me out here fast." Someone brought water and made me drink. My forehead blazed, my eyes wouldn't clear—calling for Robert, calling for Audwin, calling for T. I heard the name of Jesus, but I didn't want him, and the slow whispered words *She's so frail* papered over with *Nah, Clair's a tough old bird.*

Time lost its hold on me. The fever erased days from nights, pulling the threadbare cover of survival over me. There weren't covers enough in the world to warm my body—the cold came from within. At some point, in a dim cloud of knowing, I felt my mother, all her warmth. How long I floated against her I can't say. *It ain't fair* came in ragged strains. Ada's strong arms pounded dough against a table. I begged her to stay. But no one could, as draining silences tore the patchwork of memory, and my body rode the fever without guides.

I believe I heard the blast of cannon fire. I crossed a parched desert with bare feet. Then, at long last, I rose into a warm cove flooded with sunlight. I stroked the dry soft strands, felt the ribs, the neck, the puppy teeth gnawing my fingers. One piercing bite on a cuticle and I was awake, sitting up sweaty and light as a reed, in my own bed. In Idaho. Fresh snow lined the sills of our windows.

Against such currents I had been swimming!

I lay back down among the covers, pulling Digger in.

It was the first sight I had had of him in perhaps a dozen days. Bent to stir the fire, Stephen was all pants.

"We can't graze Marsh Creek this spring," he said to Harlan. "Sweetser claims his cattle got to have that land."

Harlan grunted, pawing his shirt open at the neck.

"And that stream this side of the California Trail? The

one at Circle Creek? The one you said had waist high grass and the City of Rocks for shade?"

"Ah," Harlan said, like he'd found a pocket of cool air.

"Well, Shirley's moved in, built him a stone foundation and penned the cove."

"What part of the creek does he claim?"

"All of it—"

"He has no right."

"He's got four thousand head of cattle. Says they're the future and sheep are shit. Got himself an army of hands, even more men than Opal, and you can bet they've got guns."

"But the emigrant wagons, and the Kelton stage, how will they get through?"

"Oh, Jack allows for passage, on the Trail and all points south. We could try to single-file them by the City of Rocks and on to Junction Valley. Keep on south to Dove Creek Pass—"

"After lambing, we'll have fourteen hundred sheep." Harlan mopped his forehead. "And every stream in Utah will be dust by June."

I made a sort of squeak, part sneeze, part smack of dry lips.

"Clair, honey?" Stephen jumped to my side.

"You trying to dry me like jerked meat? Eat me for Christmas?"

"Praise God, Harlan, she's alive." He felt my forehead. "The fever's broke!"

"I'm alive," I laughed, "and dry as tinder. Couldn't someone open a window?"

Harlan held a cup to my lips.

"It is God's work," Stephen said. "The Holy Ghost." He pressed my hands. "The Holy Ghost has borne you witness."

"The Holy Ghost . . ." My thoughts skipped lightly backward. "No, never in my life. It never has."

"But right here! In our house, you was healed." Stephen glared at Harlan for affirmation. Harlan kept still. "I anointed you and laid my hands on you, and—"

"Did you? Did you hold my hand?"

"I laid them on you, Clair, and prayed, and God answered. God has healed you through my hands."

I looked in Stephen's face and saw a stranger, his eyes lit with a flame. A flame too smooth for lust, fire smooth as a ripened cherry. Taut, and almost irresistible. What lay beneath such glossy skin?

I blinked. "I don't know anything about that."

Stephen kneed the bed, moving the mattress under me. "But you are healed." He dared me, dared me with his eyes to say different.

I patted the bed frame. Digger hopped up. I buried a hand in his ruff. "Digger here did more to heal me than any ghost ever did—the laying on of hands! He slept with me. He must have, he was under my hand when I first came conscious."

Harlan took Stephen's shoulder, seeing the fury rise. "Rest, Stephen. That is what Clair needs after two weeks' fever. We should go start on the new fencing."

But I reached for Stephen's hand. "I am glad to see you," I said, smiling.

He shivered though the room was hot. "You can deny God, Clair. You can deny Him, but I know. You can deny Him all the way up to the gates of Heaven—"

"Oh, stop." My voice cracked from disuse. "This is Heaven! Right here." I turned to the wall and brought Digger in close. "My Heaven has no gates."

The grace of waking to new health seemed to me, above all, an earthly pleasure. God could have done the healing, but it seemed lump-headed to say he had. Harlan told me that the strain on Stephen had been too great. He'd had an unshaken belief in my recovery until the delirium grew terrible. Then he paced, tormented, through one whole night. He kicked in a water barrel, shot the rails off the porch. Then he called Harlan in to anoint my head and pray with him. Harlan refused. Wesley, being Protestant, would not do. Stephen shouted, "If she dies while I'm off getting the Elders, Harlan, it's on your head!" Then he rode to Opal's to bring priesthood holders back with him. They'd formed a healer's quorum of three.

"He left me alone, with the fever at its worst?"

"He thought he was losing you, Clair. All that saved him was faith. The faith of his childhood answered him in time of need. That is a deep fount. And you revived. Do you know how convincing the answered prayer can be?"

"Well, you didn't rely on faith!" I said, and Harlan looked pained. "You stayed here by my side. Even a dog knew better than to leave me here all alone."

Though Stephen held fast to his claim of faith healing, he warmed soon enough to my body and our bed. We had ample time, as the snows came heavy and fast. There was no argument, this year, over my going to visit Ada for Christmas. I was too weak to travel. Harlan dropped Stephen off at Tenmile Creek, early in December, and the stage took him south to Kelton Station.

The ranch and the snow and every lovely thing in either looked to me like accusations—where we'd been happy, where I'd first known home—all because I couldn't surrender this one thing: God could have done the healing, but I wouldn't say he had. It didn't help that Stephen used the miracle like a cudgel for the Almighty. It only deepened my resolve.

Harlan lightened the chores while Stephen was gone. He stayed in the house, sleeping on a pallet in the parlor. "The so-called parlor," Stephen always called it, grousing over our lack of furniture, but I loved the place empty. Light moved through the rooms unobstructed, swung the whole house behind it like a box on a string. We had a bed. The kitchen table seated eight. "You only ever occupy those places anyway," I said once, teasing him.

"My woman deserves better," he'd said, yet again. And something shifted in my heart, subtle as ice the moment before it cracks. *Oh, little fox, don't let your tail get wet in that cold water. Not to mention your eyes, your heart, your belly, your stealthy paws.*

At Christmas, we gathered at the kitchen table, lit a candle, wasted no time. Wes said he never could be cold out herding with his new felted cap on, that it gave hotheaded a new meaning. I nearly wept over the beaded moccasins he'd bought me. Harlan gave Wes whiskey. Wes gave Harlan a new knife.

I passed my package to Harlan, a small rug I'd woven on my homemade lap loom to brighten his cave. His eyes flared, opening it. When he smiled, I knew I hadn't given a gift too personal. I hadn't wanted to invade, only to warm his home.

Harlan's gift to me froze my blood. I managed a "thank you," holding the framed cross-stitch in my lap. I packed up a warm meal for his night watch with the herd. But Harlan didn't leave, he lingered at the table. I tidied the sideboard and hung the pots.

When there was nothing more to do, I turned, strangling my apron. "'God bless this house'?"

Harlan convulsed in a deafening sneeze.

"God bless you!" I said.

He sawed emphatically back and forth under his nose. "Begging your pardon?" he said, to make his point.

I looked at the cross-stitch and laughed in anger. *God bless this house.* "Well, what do you expect me to do with it?"

"I thought you might hang it over the front door."

"Where everyone can see it?"

"Where Stephen can."

I walked out. I sat on Harlan's pallet, staring at the doorway, hating the thought of it. In my house—

"You have only to think of a sneeze when you walk past it," Harlan said, joining me. "Won't it make someone happy, Clair? Won't it make for peace?"

Wes' beautiful handmade moccasins were unsigned, but I knew who'd stitched the ditty. The old cross-stitch said "Erika Lawes"—a fabric sermon from Harlan's faith-bound sister.

I decided not to wear the beaded moccasins, after that. I hung them side-by-side in the parlor, to ornament the room. Let God Almighty bless the entry to my house. Beauty blessed its core.

CHAPTER 31

Stephen burst in ahead of his mother's Christmas crate, calling my name. "I love you. I love you, honey," he said, and I couldn't tell if he'd seen the cross-stitch sampler, and did not care.

We toted the loom posts, large and small, the cane roller and raddle, the weights and a dozen spools of warping yarn into the empty guest room.

"You sure this ain't the elbow piece? This here?" Stephen said, waggling a hinged slat. "Now, why'd Mother send us a hog trough, or is it maybe a window box? And where'd she ever find this big old ogre mother's rolling pin?"

"I don't know!" I laughed, begging him to stop.

"You don't know?"

"I don't know! I only worked a loom, I never built one."

"Well, let's pray for inner guidance, then," he said, kneeling in the chaos, shifting his weight and crooning, "Our Father, make this machine come clear unto us, make the crooked straight and the complex plain and the sheep give milk and Harlan's head sprout a bounteous crop of wavy grain—"

"Or we could write to your mother for instructions."

"—and make us write unto Mother for the dad-blamed instructions. In Jesus' name, Amen."

And so it sat, my scattered industry. By the time the instructions for the large English floor loom arrived, ranching had claimed our lives again, every minute and more. I put up food for the lambing in March, knitted and mended, foraged wood, chopped ice from the spring twice daily—both springs, so the sheep could drink their fill.

The Christmas trip seemed to have done Stephen good. He was kinder, more relaxed in his own skin. I said as much. He said he'd gone to see his father in Ogden, on his trip home. William Nuttall had welcomed him. They'd broken bread together for the first time in twenty years. Stephen met his sixteen children. Sang carols with them and his father's three wives. To hear him tell it, a kinder, wiser man did not dwell in all of Zion.

Stephen had asked his father for a blessing. Blessing received, man to man.

That night, I awakened to an empty bed. The barn doors showed no light. Cold though it was, I dressed to take Stephen a lantern, thinking he'd gone to check on the sheep. In the dark of the parlor, I heard whispering. Stephen knelt with his hands clasped at the windowsill and his head bowed.

I waited till his prayer ended. "Stephen?"

"Yes—"

"Come to bed."

He looked out the window, dark as dark could be.

"Oh, come," I said, and it wasn't the cold that made me shake.

The next day, on our trip to the Raft River station, Stephen only rode along as far as Opal's ranch. A dry snow coated the foothills behind her house. Stands of juniper etched the natural boundaries for her broad pastures. Clear Creek ambled toward us, among pines and a trickle of aspens. Stephen walked up the road to the ranch in what looked like a home in a vision. Iin spite of myself, I saw a parable. Watching him, I thought *Prodigal son.*

Stephen didn't say why he was going to Opal's, but the small leather book in his coat pocket told me why. Half a dozen straws garnished his *Book of Mormon,* and a bookmark with a gold inscription: *Where the spirit of the Lord is, there is freedom.*

This troubled me more than all the rest. What kind of freedom did Stephen seek?

On my return trip, I knocked at Opal's bunkhouse door and found a half dozen hands mending tack and oiling saddles to strains from an untuned piano, played by a man who appeared to be drunk. Stephen came in from a back room, slapped a friendly hand on the piano player's shoulder, and we were off. I told myself Stephen just wanted an afternoon of company—of course he longed for the company of men. But when I tried to join him in the barn that evening to help knock together the lambing pens, he shooed me off with: "A woman ain't got no babies is a woman with time to spare, right, Wes?" It sent me from the barn in an instant.

I shouted back, "I found a few potatoes, is all, they aren't mealy. I wondered if you felt like having a pudding, tonight."

"I'd like to set my mouth on such," Wes said.

"Stephen?"

"Yes, ma'am," he said, "pudding sounds agreeable, just fine."

Stephen's hunger for the gospel did not ease with outer observances, it only grew. I didn't comment on the nightly prayers, the weekly scripture study group at Opal's, or the grace that Stephen said at every one of our meals. He could preside, and I could pretend to listen. But he wasn't satisfied with his own devotions. He felt God on his shoulder, in his conscience, at his heels. Man was called to increase the faithful in Zion. I could feel it when he touched me, the conflict in his soul.

One night, when the sheets sank over our bodies, brittle with cold, sealing us in like a letter, I wished that I had dimmed the lamp, wished I could not see the deep trouble creasing Stephen's brow.

I reached for the light, but he stopped me.

"I have thought about it, Clair. And you won't like to hear this, but I prayed about it. And I know there's only one thing for it." He held my wrist. "We got to marry."

I drew myself up, breaking the seal, and knelt over him with my arm still in his grasp. He trembled. "It's cold, honey. Come on back down."

"I am not afraid of cold."

He linked his fingers in mine. He gazed at my hand. "Don't you love me?"

I burned, even as I shook.

"Clair? Don't you want my children?"

I pulled the blankets in to his chest. "There is one reason, and one reason only why we have intimate relations—and it isn't children."

"But a man and a woman, well, they was made—"

"To multiply and replenish?" Even in the immensity of the quiet outside our window, I felt the rush of expansion, the restive new settlers all eager to demand their own—greedy and willing, nomads without love. I wondered would it ever be enough. "We *have* multiplied on this earth, Stephen! It is past time to replenish."

"Have we? Honey, are you with child?"

I pressed my pillow to my chest to stop the shaking.

"Nothing could make me a happier man. I'd make it legal and blessed, I'd give that child my name—"

"There is no child, and you know it! I don't want a child. I can't! I never knew my father, Stephen. My mother abandoned me, I have no kin—"

"I'd be your kin. And Mother—hell, I think she loves you more than me—she'd bless the stars if you became my wife."

Then I saw stars, their seed—the seed of the Brethren scattered like stars over the cosmos by their invisible hand-maid helpmeet no-name wives. "You want to be a god at my expense!"

Stephen wrenched me down to him.

"Don't you! A Mormon god with a see-through wife, your own mute Mother in Heaven—"

"Clair, don't."

"You would not marry me, not for my self. You'd marry me for a principle, and for a child or two or twelve to claim, and for a thousand chances to win me over to your religion, to try and beat me down with it. But you won't—I will lie with you, Stephen, and I will care for you," I took his hair in my fists, "with all my strength I care, but I will not marry!"

Flat on his back, staring up at nothing, he said, "Then God forgive you."

My hands went to my cheeks.

"You are lost in a darkness so great you cannot see His plan."

I left our bed and the cold simply became me.

"All you got is death. Death in life."

I stopped at the door. "Your faith, your deepest belief, isn't even your own. It isn't about you. It's about him, and them." Then my jaws and my arms and my belly relaxed. "I am not afraid of darkness, inner or outer. I have held it in my arms—I am not afraid of death."

Card wool. Draw the spiked boards over and over the soft fleece, the cleaned body of my labor, labor of lambs, of grass and rain and love doomed for a lurching boxcar. Clap the carders together, rake the fibers and tap the leveled curls loose, let them fall around my feet. Steel and fleece, two more unlikely partners couldn't be found in nature. But nature hasn't brought them into contact—this is a coupling of human invention. To make the crooked straight.

Harlan climbed the front porch steps, dragging his left leg up. Age had sprung upon him suddenly, though it was slow enough bringing him down. He came into the guest room where I carded and spun. The spring shearing was over, the Mexican crew had come and gone in two days. He glanced at the piles of wool, the parts of Ada's floor loom pushed to the corners. I let the drifts of fleece speak for me—what I'd done rather than boil another meal for him—but he didn't ask for lunch. He asked if he could bring me anything.

"Stephen?" I could not hold it back. "I want nothing else."

"He has gone to town, for news of the rangelands."

"He has gone to town for Suzanna!" I raked the carder across my bosom, tearing a button, then hurled it across the room. Stephen had bedded in the barn all through lambing season. We lived in separate worlds.

"Suzanna . . . " Harlan said. "Suzanna Peake? Stephen's old sweetheart?"

The pain in my face answered.

"She has moved to Boise City. She doesn't live in Marsh Basin anymore."

"You're certain of it?"

Harlan shifted his weight onto his good leg. "That I am, Clair."

I laughed, hard. "Then God bless Boise City!"

I caught Stephen drying his socks at our kitchen stove, late one April afternoon. I intended to get a conversation from it. Though I blamed his stubbornness for our distance, my own mulish heart met his step for step. He scooted the rocker closer to the heat, when I asked why he couldn't make room for my beliefs as well as his own.

"Truth is truth," he said, shrugging.

"But I could not go to your Heaven. I wouldn't. None of my friends would be there—"

"God ain't a politician, Clair. His decrees ain't of the people, by the people or for the people. Well, 'for'—but not by popular vote. They are truth by reason of His wisdom, as the Creator of all." He spoke so like a Brother, I could no longer find the free-living Jack Mormon cowboy I'd met two years before. He had vanished. His disappearance seemed worth a fight.

"Will Tierre be in your Mormon Heaven?"

"No. He ain't baptized and never will be—"

"So God says that colored skin is inferior, and you believe it?"

"How could I doubt it if He said it?"

"I have colored skin—"

"You got a blotch. Some kind of a birth blotch on your face. It ain't a sign of evil."

"I don't believe evil has such signs!"

Stephen sighed.

I kept on. "Look at all the evil's been done and gotten away with—by white folks, Stephen, whites and colored alike.

If you'd ever spent a day in New Orleans! I washed for the poorest. I nursed them through the plague. I slept where the rats wouldn't stay. Every thief isn't marked, nor every killer. And every white man is not fine."

He only shifted his feet to the fire.

"Tell me how a baby's whole body can be marked as evil in advance, before it's even taken a breath, much less done any acting for good or ill?"

"God knew us in the former life," he said. "He knows who's noble and who ain't."

"He knew before I was born, did he, that I'd be able to think for myself?"

Stephen kicked the stove and regretted it. "Niggers are Cain's seed, and marked to stay separate. The Prophet Brigham Young said that God didn't curse them forever, it's just that the niggers'll be the last to share the joys of the Kingdom. The Prophet Brigham said—"

I slapped my palms on the table.

Stephen cinched his eyes. "The Prophet Brigham said—"

"And what does Stephen Nuttall say? What do you know about your God, yourself?"

He didn't respond.

"Nothing?" I shouted.

He weighed my words like poisoned bait.

"Well, I've done some thinking on it, Stephen. And I think you've turned your God into an idol. Your God is an object, just one more thing to fear and serve."

"I fear Him! And I'll serve Him. The glory of God is worth our fear. The Prophet Brigham said—"

"The prophet of property? The prophet, seer, and revelator of cash! Has that glutted buzzard found any new ways to turn the desert into roses?"

Stephen closed his eyes. "God forgive you. The Prophet Brigham Young is dead."

"What did you just say?"

"The Prophet died. From the cholera. A sore loss to the Kingdom of Zion."

My heart leapt. *They're free. They are all of them free.*

But Stephen's enthrallment hadn't waned. "The Prophet said it clear as day, Clair. Nothing we do now, and nothing that Civil War done, makes a bit of difference until God's curses are removed."

"So it's all right to go on persecuting them?"

"It ain't. Brigham said whites who abused niggers would be cursed as well."

I patted my apron. "Well, Brigham hands out curses like a dealer deals cards."

"You don't understand—look at history! We're the ones been persecuted, good God-loving Mormons are the ones been driven out and put upon, time and again, under the Gentiles' hands. Do you think it's over, now we're out West? You think we're safe? You don't know how many U.S. marshals raided Marsh Basin this winter, hunting after innocent men and their wives—do you?"

"I don't know much of anything goes on outside this ranch."

"Seven marshals, armed with guns. Chasing men, women and children who done nothing but followed our Heavenly Father's word. And you mark my own word on it— now they got a Idaho law says non-Mormon juries can sit for polygamy trials, every man caught is a man who'll rot in jail, his wives are widows and his children'll starve. There's your justice, that's your democratic rule." He stepped away from the stove, away from me. "I told them they should go north, they should all move up to Canada, pack up and leave, let the U.S. marshals drown in their own spit."

"All I wondered," I said quietly, numbed by his distancing of himself from me, "all I thought is, if you and yours have been persecuted, how can you persecute others?"

"Jesus in Heaven!" He yanked his boots on. "Though they listen they do not hear." Stephen circled to the door, keeping the table between us. Tears streaming down in anger, he said, "I can't believe—it makes me sick you love a bunch of niggers more than you love me."

CHAPTER 32

L *eave them alone, and they'll come home . . .* Terrible with him, terrible without him, and three or four months of unknowing in between. Uncertain as I was of Stephen's return, the summer gaped before me like a decade.

Wes and Stephen had decided to take the herd the westerly route, grazing along the Raft River and then up toward the City of Rocks, though none of them was happy with their prospects after that: fourteen hundred sheep in June, no water and precious little grass. Harlan stayed behind for several days, sorting provisions. When he went into Kelton for supplies, he took Digger with him in the wagon. New to the wonders of travel, my dear friend Digger wagged his tail and barked unceasingly, standing up on his hind legs to swallow the breeze.

Where the spirit of the Lord is, there is freedom. Digger found the Lord in a hot May wind.

Ten days later, a banging in the barn yanked me upright in bed. I went to the window. The intruder was not shy. Light streamed over a wagon pulled half into the barn. A shadow knocked from here to there. The herd was gone. What was left to steal—harnesses? lumber? the old camp stove?

I loaded the house pistol. Digger followed me outside.

"I would stop," I yelled, holding my nightgown in one hand to navigate the ruts barefooted. "I would stop it right now, if I was you!" I stared into the brightness, leaning against the wagon wheel to take aim. "Come on out, damn it."

The crooked wheel rose to my notice as the man stepped into view. Our wagon, our own, and Stephen with a load of horse blankets, squinting into the dark. He looked more desperate than a thief, his hair in his face, breathing heavily. He caught the blankets up with his wrist and flung them into the buckboard, spooking my grip. "I got to, Clair." He took a pitchfork and heaved straw into the bed, closer and closer to the wheel until I backed off, watching the tines, watching his callused hands.

He threw the fork in and backed the wagon.

I ran after it to the house.

He had loaded the cast iron pans in the washtub and dumped them in the doorway. I called to him as he hurried into our room. "Stephen—"

Trunks opened and closed. He came back out with a terrible bundle of shirts and winter clothes slung in a sheet, bearing down on me with the answer to a question I had never asked. "Don't you think I know you need release?" The bundle grazed me, knocking me sideways.

Stephen took the tub and banged out the front door.

He loaded the wagon and then stared at me, unblinking. "You got the house and barn, everything. You got everything—"

Digger barked from the wagon as they rolled forward under a dim slice of moon. It took a quarter of an hour for the barking to fade, point source of an unbending river of dust.

—◦◦◦—

Harlan's letter arrived three days after Stephen's departure, releasing me from hellish uncertainty. Good of him. Formal, complete. "My Dear Clair" it began, and I trembled at his kindness.

The grass is used up here and we must press on. Wes will stay behind in Marsh Basin until he receives word from you, that you are well. We will have made our circuit of the Raft Range by late June, and will come to you directly, then.

The next paragraph was what allowed me to leave the locus of my grief—our house, our barn, our life together.

I regret to say Stephen has taken himself and two Mormon girls to homestead in Canada. He felt they would find safety there. When he heard their father had been apprehended for cohabitation, their livelihood gone and their mothers despondent, Stephen took himself to Marsh Basin, vowed to assist, and thence to the ranch for what supplies he could gather. That you will know. What you may not—they are married, Clair, by the Bishop's word. An uncle gave his horse and rig.

Do be strong, Clair. Be wise, above all, wise. Harlan

I sent word back to Wes, as Harlan asked me to: *I will not use the knives!*

And I didn't. Not the knives or the needles or the rake or hoe. I moved my things into Tierre's old room in the barn— just a few clothes—and piled all Wes' belongings in the loft. It made alone feel that much better, being closer to T in spirit. Each day as the sun rose, the ranch became intolerable. So I walked. First, to Kelton Pass, to watch the stage drive by. Then to Clear Creek, up above the pastures of Opal's ranch. I followed the honeyed stream up canyon, climbing into the foothills of the Raft River Range. Doves called from the red bark willows. Wild roses and geraniums dragged at my dress. At creekside, I ate a meal, listened to the waters, stared at the gold-orange stones and pale dry sand. Everything came into my senses like the kick of a mule. Pines above, green ribbings of aspen. All of the wildflowers I had so loved.

I hiked home, my heart a hot bit of coal. The mountains and homesteads and lush river valleys—that green, that bounty, could wait.

I needed bare earth.

I needed overalls.

I needed cauterizing.

Flat feet, flat belly, flat back. Give me a cave, I'll sleep in it. Give me sunrise, I will level it in a squint. Give me three ideas—I can slap them flat, flat, flat. With only sand lizards as my witness, I ate a raw potato—the jerky, the preserves in the larder were gone—and, naked but for my hat, I lay back down and chewed. *Chewing separated me from the rock.* When I stopped chewing, everything stopped. *Juice trickles down, mouth full of pulp, and the strings of my jaws in their just-open posture. The blossoms of blazing star, the upright sage, even the ground squirrel chirring—all stop and wait for the needle of day to pierce down through, pierce through and snap off so that bones are rock, air is water, sun land and—the squirrel felt it first: sand, gravel, boulders, mountain . . . all are single, all continuous, the continuous body of earth.*

I endured a wild uplifted sinking.

Because the bowls of my nipples burned, I turned on my belly. Rock met bone.

Bigger than love. Bigger than love, this emptiness. And death is a comfort: excess of emptiness, with company. I have seen it—the joy, like nausea, of maggots tumbling in a carcass. Stephen and his silly You-niverse. Death holds me unconditionally, as does the stone brown unbroken body of the living earth.

Must have been the end of June. Must have meant two
hungry men were waiting on a meal. I kicked my way through
the throng of bleating sheep, after a week-long roundabout
in the Black Pine Range. I'd climbed Black Peak not by any
real ambition. My body just rose and rose until the air was
cool and I could see in all directions. I sat in a tiny snow
patch. The snow-topped mountains of central Idaho knuckled up the desert, due north. South of our ranch, a squat blue
mountain floated in the Great Salt Lake. Height and distance soothed my heart like Doctor Psalter's Bunion Cream.
Where was Audwin, when I needed a good laugh? Height
and distance. Nothing else helped. And even then I played
whole days out in my head, of Stephen setting up with his
two girls in Canada. *A little tyrant needs willing servants*—I'd
been a whole village of them. *Acquire and acquire and acquire
for the Lord!* Stephen couldn't acquire me so he found two
tenderhearts to mold to his bidding. My mind howled and
ran in circles like these.

Nighttimes were silent, but for the coyote clan.

I hiked home when hunger or deer flies or a powerful thirst took hold. Just now, I was so thirsty I decided the
boys could wait. I closed the shed door, breathed in shade and
reached for the water jug. Sitting cross-legged, I sneezed and
took a long drink. A rat watched from the empty larder. It
flashed out of sight at the knock on the door.

I didn't answer. I had that right.

The knock repeated.

"I'm fine, Harlan. I need to sleep." I stretched out, butting
a foot against the door.

"The herd has raided the garden, Clair. Devoured it, I
should say."

"All they got was turnip greens, and welcome to them."

He paused. I dozed into my arms.

"Will you join us, for supper?"

I was not ready for sympathy. My foot flexed into the door. "There's only flour and peas."

"Tierre has made a split pea soup, and it actually smells edible," he said.

I scratched my cheek.

"Clara? You gots a real house, why is you sleepin' in my old room?"

I laughed, a strange sensation. I stood, opened the door and threw my arms around Tierre, marveling at his strength, his height, his being right there in my arms.

"T and Sugar!"

"Clara gal!"

I appraised the sinew of his neck, the hard line of his jaw. He was tall as Harlan. He'd become a man. I patted his dusty black mane. "Your hair, T—it looks like an eagle nested and died up there."

"You ride a hundred mile in the June heat—Lordy, Clara, you is golden as the range."

I could not speak, staring at the three missing fingers on his left hand.

He looked down at my overalls. "And I sees you has taken to wearing the britches, now Stephen done gone."

"I do when I like."

"He gone for good?"

Harlan stepped back and stared at his boots.

"Took the cast iron pans and the pitchfork and my dog," I said, a bit shaky, but grateful for the change in perspective on my doom.

T led us inside to the kitchen, where the sweet smell of

pea soup and the sight of this larger, grander version of my boy
made me tipsy. He pushed aside a ragged deck of playing cards
and served four steaming bowls.

Harlan and Wes made short work of the meal and their
month gone herding, the gist being that they had nowhere left
to graze, and it was only June. Harlan asked Tierre, with his
usual wistfulness, about life in the greater world. Perhaps he
sought perspective on his own doom. "Is the railroad carving a
bright path through the wilds of Idaho?"

Tierre didn't answer him.

"Tell us a story of progress, of history in the making."

Tierre said, "Progress I seen, sure enough, cut from the
sweat of mens you won't never hear about. History? Ain't no
such thing but half-lies and make believe."

Wes laughed. "Tierre's pounded too many rail ties, Harlan.
Something's got jiggled loose upstairs. You saying there's no
such thing—as history?"

"What I knows, what I seen, ain't no such thing."

"As *history*—"

"What y'all calls history gets built with a pat a this and a
daub a that, mud and daub like. Big old walls. Most all the mud
goes down on the side of them gots the money."

Harlan's eyes flared in recognition.

"The rest of us gets buried inside. Painted over good."

"Whitewash!" Harlan said.

"What I seen, most of it been white," T replied.

"My granddaddy fought Jim Bridger for a wife," Wes
said. "You telling me that ain't history?"

Tierre plonked his spoon into his empty bowl and looked
Wes right in the eye. "I ain't heared of it."

"Maybe you ain't, but it happened."

"What year?"

"Well, I don't know—"

"Where'd he fight?"

"Let's see, I think—"

"Who won out?"

"Bridger did! He fought dirty."

"You ever heared of that, Harlan? Old Jim Bridger been a dirty fighter?"

Harlan frowned.

Wes screwed up his shoulders in a huff. "You mean, it ain't history if you're the one gets beat? Or it ain't history because you ain't heard of it? You may not of heard, but it happened all the same."

Tierre said, in a dead-level voice, "Bridger had hisself three Indian wives. A Flathead, a Ute, and a Shoshone. Which was your granddaddy fightin' to win exactly?"

Wes flushed and refused to answer. T flexed his lips, case closed. I cleared the table to insert a cooling influence, but Wes wouldn't let it rest. "So we," he said, loud enough for the sheep to hear, "we got no past? No stories even?"

Tierre said, quiet as anything, "We got stories. Stories is *all* we got."

Harlan took up Tierre's deck of cards and shuffled awkwardly with his big hands. "If there is only one story, Wes, one history, and that history is written by the victors, then we have been pushed handily off the rim of it."

T placed an Indian head penny on the table. "If you all's in, ante up."

The bond between Tierre and Jim Bridger came clear later that night. We sat with our backs against the old hut, sunset lighting the carrotleaf tangled in sage. Tierre's bedroll was laid out inside. His dappled horse drank at the spring. His clothes and his hair and even his woven canteen were filthy. Beaten with use. I took his hand. Only the thumb and index finger rose past the first joint.

"You didn't say if you were here to visit or to stay—"

"I ain't said 'cause I don't knows. And you ain't said why Stephen done left."

I didn't even sob, telling Tierre, because I saw the beauty in it. "I would not bow to Stephen's gospel. I couldn't be Mormon, T." I nudged his sweaty shoulder. I firmed my grip. "You can stay now Stephen's gone. We could use another herder. Harlan's getting old. You could live right here in the hut. You don't have to ask permission—"

"Well, Clara, maybe I does," he said. "You lost you a mate, but meanwhiles, I has gained one. I got me a wife and two childrens."

"Two!"

"Yes, ma'am." Tierre dried his forehead on his sleeve. His wife Kay had a seven-year-old daughter named Mincy. Tierre's own son, Frank, was three months old.

"A family man?" I hugged him tight, laughing when he told me he and Kay had jumped the stick.

"Clara!" He shook me off. "It ain't no joke, I got four hungry mouths to feed. I come to see could I maybe do that, here."

Four mouths. Four more. My hands sank into my pockets.

"And that ain't the whole of it." Tierre took a drink from his water bag. I asked what tribe had made it, the geometric pattern so tight it did not sweat a drop. "Kashess, she weave it. Them is quills from a porky-pine."

"Kay is Indian?"

T said with force, "Shoshone full-blood. Mincy, she gots Bannock blood, a Bannock daddy—"

"What a long time ago!"

T tipped his chin. "Since what?"

"The first man I ever worshipped was a Bannock grazing his horse up in the hills. His face still gives me shivers."

T said, "Well, I married me the handsomest woman I ever seen."

"You always were smarter."

"Yes, ma'am."

T settled into his story, said the loss of three fingers had gained him a wife. "Wasn't my fault a big load of rail ties fall on my hand, and when the boss, he haul me into the trading post at Fort Hall, some pretty, brown healer woman help to steady me as the doc cut my bones." He waggled his finger stumps. "Them Shoshone think mighty highly of a man gots nerve."

I slapped his hip when he told me this. "Kay fell in love with you right then!"

T pressed his lips together. "Cain't say. I been too busy sweating and spilling my blood."

"To fine effect, you old devil dog."

He'd stayed on at Fort Hall with the Indians, waiting on Reece. There wasn't much there but Indians. A government agent. A trading post. A small military post with enough soldiers to keep tempers tense and the Indian women living in fear. Hangings and shootings and tit for tat wove a tight band around the Indians and their white caretakers. Isolated together at Fort Hall, the Shoshone waged peace and the Bannock waged war. The Shoshone tried to take up farming, while the Bannock ranged off the reservation for game and pinyon and camas root. Late last spring, Buffalo Horn and his men had found settlers' hogs eating the camas root on the vast central Idaho prairie. The prairie that had sustained the tribes for centuries. And been safeguarded to them in their treaty. Seeing his sacred garden churned to waste and mud, Buffalo

Horn led two hundred Bannock brothers to Oregon to incite the Paiutes against the whites in all-out war. The Bannock War failed, of course. And the Shoshone, when their hundreds of acres of cultivated crops fell to the grasshoppers, they roasted and ate hoppers for two years instead of potatoes and wheat.

Tierre welcomed Reece and the survey work when it came. He was only too glad to strike out north with three horses, their saddlebags and Reece's instruments. T had all the income and freedom a man could ask. But the farther they travelled from Fort Hall, the more he felt the weight of injustice he had left behind. He'd passed the pipe with Kay's father. He had broken wild horses with her kin. He had helped hide Tambiago, a Bannock brave enough and fool enough to kill a thieving white man in front of the trading post. And T and Kashess were lovers. Tierre didn't feel right leaving her alone for so long.

"So you never made it to Montana."

"What I need Montana for when I gots Kay? I loves her, Clara. I swear on all my bones to get her and our babies off that damn reserve before she cripple, waiting and watching on the government like it was kin. No ma'am! I knows what the Indian Agent gots to keep them all alive with." He panted here, straining to keep the emotion in. "Danilson, he ain't a bad man. He beg and beg. But the government? It send him three and a half cent. Three and one half cent per day—man, woman or child. They is all of them hungry as mongrel dogs. It hurts my heart. Shoshone give they lives to the U. S. government and get a flat boot in they bellies in return."

This was the whole of it—a black man, his Shoshone wife, her daughter and their mixed breed newborn son might not be so welcome, even in our lonely patch of paradise. Hard enough to get Harlan to consider it. Harder by a hundredfold to get Wes to sign on. The Utah and Idaho Territories were not renowned for sharing either land or resources with Indians. They'd tipped the balance in their own favor, and I wondered how we could tip it back. At least enough to make the ranch support us all.

I asked Tierre the only question that mattered to me. "Do you think Kay would be happy here? Without her people and only us to know? The land is parched, Tierre, there are no trees, it hasn't much appeal."

"Clara, where you think Kashess spend her childhood? Where you think her people been till now? She know Twin Springs. Yeah, right here. She know Tenmile and the Curlew Valley and the big old Bear River. She tan antelope hides in the shadow of the Black Pine Range—just where I rode down—thirteen summers. Don't you mind about Kashess. Don't you worry. This here is home."

CHAPTER 33

An ace lay face up on the kitchen table. All the talking was over and done. That morning, Harlan had agreed Tierre was the strong arms and legs he needed to keep the ranch going, and he knew T's hunting skills would help to feed us all. But Harlan's measured welcome of Tierre and his new brood just turned loose all of Wes' fury. "I work long hours without pay to help a squaw and her spawn I'd rather shoot than shit with?" Wes refused. At which point T said, without an ounce of emotion, "Cut you for it." He set the cards down and let Wes shuffle.

"Harlan?" Wes said, looking for support.

Harlan looked on, impassive. Nobody spoke. Then Wes set his jaw and shuffled the deck. He held a hand over it. "High card takes it," Wes said, folding his arms as Tierre slid his two fingers down one side and lifted off his cut. Ace of hearts. Wes pulled a five of clubs and said, "Jesus in hell!" When Harlan clapped a hand on Wes' shoulder to offer conciliatory words, Wes rose and took the table with him. Cards scattered and the cat, who'd just put her head in the door, leapt out of sight.

"You know how long and hard I worked. You hand me my life back like it was dirt or worse?"

"You have a fine future awaiting you, Wesley," Harlan said. "It isn't here. We'll pay you and gladly in sheep now, or in money at summer's end. You have our word."

"I don't want your word. I'll take the sheep."

"And we'd appreciate a hand with things for the next few days," I said. "Then I will bake you a large vinegar pie with extra sugar. It travels well." Wes tipped the table up with one hand and set it in place, looking flushed and clumsy after his violent outburst. He was, after all, a bachelor. And I was a woman, who knew the straight and narrow way to a man's heart.

I didn't ask T later if the cards were marked. It did not matter one whit. The way was opened for Tierre and Kay and Mincy and Frank. In my wildest, loosest longings I could never have hoped for it.

I fastened all of my thoughts on Tierre's family's bright coming. T rode off that night to fetch them home. He said traveling at night was safest for a black man. Night riding and keeping to untraveled paths. Kay and the children tarried thirty miles east at a farm set up by Mormons who hoped the barren plains at the Utah and Idaho borders were far enough removed from settlers to host a permanent Indian farm. Tierre admired the Mormons' foresight and dedication to this band of Chief Washakie's people who refused to live at Fort Hall. The Mormons apparently did not admire T. A minor scuffle with a Bishop over how to plant seed corn—that and Tierre's darker than Lamanite complexion—meant the Durhams could not stay. For which I felt deep gratitude.

Wes helped us haul Harlan's things from the cave into the guest room in the big house. The long walk to the cave tired Harlan's hip. His days of lone living were over. We shifted a few things around, drank a toast and called it home. Then Wes moved Stephen's carved bed and the old pot stove into the sod roof hut, Tierre and Kay's new home. The place was modest, but a grace note above the brush tepees the Indians used at Fort Hall. T said their hide coverings were torn and gone. No buffalo to hunt and no freedom to go hunt them. Well, Kay would have four walls and a roof. I spent two days scrubbing and airing the old place and replanting my garden. Wes built a wire fence around the garden plot to keep the herd out. On the fourth day, expecting Tierre back, we paid Wes for his labors. He lit out for Boise City with eighty sheep and a square set to his shoulders.

Of course, Harlan and I had to settle up. There were debts to consider, and who owned what of the ranch. That conversation didn't come easily for either Harlan or me. He agreed that we had both labored equally the last two years in sweat and care. Stephen had left me "everything," which meant Harlan and I were partners, in full. The bleak state of my inheritance made for the harder talk. We owed Opal for the barn lumber and last year's rut. We owed Aggie for eggs and Duff for all of Stephen's provisions. Harlan had seen I was the only one who ever paid on Stephen's bill. I told him being in arrears raised a knot in my stomach. Those store debts were my debts, too.

I asked how much we had earned at this year's shearing—our only income, and I hoped it was enough.

Harlan blew on his coffee and licked the wet off his moustache. "Eight hundred head at a dollar a fleece, after we paid the Mexicans."

"So we have eight hundred dollars in cash—"

"Four hundred." He looked at me. His bottom lip sagged. "Stephen took half."

"And you've never taken a thing—you only spend a pittance on newspapers and whiskey!"

"Any sensible man would fear a winter in Canada," Harlan

said. "A winter with two wives and no money would be suicide."

I swallowed hard at the mention of wives. I had almost stopped imagining Stephen's new life. With the word "suicide" hanging in the air, I said, "Harlan, how old are the Riblett sisters?"

He ground the soles of his boots on the wood floor. "Thirteen and fifteen."

I gave Stephen a moment of my undiluted disgust, then said, "I would rather swim in a cactus sea than love a man again."

Harlan laughed and spiked our coffee. We took up the harder things.

He had no written understanding of how much or how little Ada's share was in the ranch. I knew Stephen had never paid her a cent. She'd set him up to start, then let her darling boy invest every penny of gain to build up the herd. Well, he'd abandoned his share in this hardscrabble ranch, which meant Ada had gambled and Ada had lost. As for the house, neither Harlan nor I had asked anyone to build us a fine abode. He did feel some compunction, as Stephen's former partner, to tell her about her lost son and lost investments. I said, "Harlan, you let me deal with Ada," having no intention of dealing with her anytime soon. Heaven help our friendship when Ada learned I had driven off her one and only son.

I heard the sheep relishing a cooler than usual day outside, chewing the desert to dirt. Harlan set the last of Tierre's pea soup down for our lunch. I was staring down into my bowl as Harlan suggested we sell the majority of our flock at Kelton Station, keep a few hundred sheep and start all over again next spring. Negotiate range land with the neighboring settlers. This year, there was no grass.

I asked how much a ewe would bring at Kelton Station in July.

"Fifty cents."

"And we'd get four times that price per head if we held out until fall?" I knew it was a sore point for Harlan. His dream of retirement far from the pulse of human woes had pretty much fallen to ashes. He felt a fool watching the open range convert to grazing lots. He felt penned out. Meanwhile, my pea soup spoke of verdant valleys. "There's grass," I said. "There's grass up past my knees in the Raft River Range."

"We grazed it east to west and back," Harlan said tersely, like I had laid one too many straws on his tired back.

"Not around it. In it. There's a creek above Opal's, and the canyon isn't steep."

Harlan knew it well, Onemile Canyon, Opal's late summer range for her rams. It could feed a thousand sheep happily through summer, Harlan said. Fine grass. Pure, flowing water. "When were you there last, Clair?"

"Three, four weeks ago. The valley was so lush I believed I was the first human ever to enter that canyon." I gave my aimless grief-filled journeys a little nod of thanks. They had actually come to something, after all.

"Onemile." Harlan breathed a few gratified gulps of air. "It connects up top through a pass to George Creek. We would have access to all of the high slopes of the Raft Range, north and south." Then he frowned and set down his spoon. "Do you aim to wheedle and beg Opal for the rights? She'll ask a frightful fee in sheep and labor. Labor we cannot afford to give without Wes—"

"Harlan!" I cut him off. "Opal White can't claim an entire mountain range just because she's Opal. We owe her two hundred dollars for lumber and fifty ewes for the fall rut?"

He nodded.

"Let's pay her, now. Four hundred ewes at a dollar a noggin.

Let's make Opal happy, settling up our debt, and have a nice advance payment on next year's rut. Plus four hundred fewer bellies to feed."

"And Opal plays a ditty on her hornpipe while we march a thousand ewes in to devour her prize pasture land?"

"You can skirt her ranch. If you and Tierre came in from the south, a few miles before Opal's, and quick-grazed up to George Creek Pass—"

"She might never know." Harlan finished my thought for me.

I smiled. As if the infidels between us and happiness had been routed. We couldn't sell off the herd. I had to keep tight hold on our one chance at prosperity, determined as I was to swap my hardships for T's release. Harlan bowed his big head and thought a moment, an overlong moment.

Then he sighed his appreciation. "My compliments, Miss Martin."

I laughed. "Don't thank me, Harlan. Thank Tierre's green split peas.

I believe in history. Because I'd been abandoned into it, history had always seemed to be the river of other men's woes. A very real river, indeed, now I stood soaked to the skin and shivering. Here I was in a house of Stephen's making, with a herd grown vast by the sweat of Stephen's brow, and I did not have the man. Which magnified my sense of being simply no one. Yet again. Drenched with losses.

I found working in our bedroom to be tolerable, though I could not sleep there. I used my lap loom in the bold light. I dragged in all of the pieces of the English loom—plenty of room to build it, with the double bedstead gone. I hung the four small rugs I'd managed to weave on the walls for company. The patterns seemed rough and cloying. All I had ever attained, it wasn't much.

I slept at the spring to fight off the heat and trapped flies and failure. Once the sun had set and I'd let go the business of the day, there I was: insignificant, useless, loveless. I tried each night to imagine my mother's face, singing or speaking, scolding or giving comfort. I needed her love. But I could see nothing, not even the sweep of her red hair.

On the fifth night out, under clouds as thin and texture-less as muslin, lit by a low half moon, I heard Ginnie bark and Tierre's quick answering call. Figures in the yard, talk like a slow-moving river. The sound of poles in brush. T's voice, not his words, and the horse and travois coming very near.

They crossed below the garden. I could see Kashess' hair, the bundles on the stretched skin, maybe children bedded. The horse stopped a hundred yards off, at the second spring. A splash: drinking, perhaps cleaning. T's laugh. Then silence, the bending of reeds under the dim heathery sky.

The sounds of their lovemaking were sweet.

I could not bring the word *pretty* to bear on Kashess' face, which in the blank light of day held so much suffering. Her face seemed given over to it, as her body was given over to making camp, stopping a moment to be introduced, wait-ing as T talked to me, then cinching the ropes tighter on the many long poles so they could raise their tepee near the sod roof hut.

I told them no, the hut was theirs to have. I'd placed one of my hand-loomed rugs inside the entry. I'd scrubbed the oil-cloth rug and filled the kindling box. The mattress was nearly new.

T said Kay preferred to do it her way.

It kicked me in the heart.

Tierre showed off the baby, a dark bit of hair and wrinkles. Only Frank's head was visible within the cradleboard, which was tall and beautifully beaded. The tanned leather of the pouch looked so soft I had to touch it. I almost dared to touch Frank's plump cheek. "Clara, meet Frank Tootabba Robear Durham. 'Frank,' since I hope he speak true. 'Tootabba' mean black sun. When he come out, Kay says he been shiny like a sun. 'Robear Durham,' well, you knows—"T shook his head. "He a wonder, Clara. Pure Shoshone, with a splash of me."

Then T roused Mincy, who squinted her seven years almost upright, smiled and fell back to sleep on the blankets on the ground, her black hair crossed on her chest.

"She all confuse, sleeping daytimes and walking the nights."

"Good trip?" I asked, hoping Kay could hear kindness in my voice.

"Mincy gots a cold, I think. But we done good."

"You didn't tell me what Mincy's name means."

"Mincy? It mean Mincy. She just her ownself, you'll see."

Kay paused a moment at the passing of birds overhead. Some flock heading off somewhere. She listened with her whole body. She looked at me as if this were significant, and, not knowing what on earth to do, I smiled, said, "Birds."

"Them is ibis," T said, "you see them bent necks?"

I looked at the dark bodies heading south, their necks and bills like crooked *s*-es. The visitor birds. A whole flock of them. It warmed me, rooted me right there to the spot.

"Gone to wade in the Bear," T said.

I laughed. "A bird expert, are you now?"

"Mr. Moon, he know every kind a thing everywhere we been to."

I lowered my voice. "Where is Reece now?"

"Old blondy? He run off to Wyoming. Been a ranger at some park there . . . Greenstone, Yellowstone, some such a place."

Kay cut brush in her plaid blanket skirt with a worn blanket shawl over her shoulders. I asked Tierre if I could help her. He said breakfast would be the biggest help, so we walked off to the house to get it.

Before we'd gone fifty steps I said, "Kay isn't happy."

T kept walking.

"She never once smiled."

"What you think she gots to smile about, acre miles away from her folk? Nothing, but me."

I asked Tierre if she knew we were both orphans and knew what it was like to live without kin. T put a hand on my arm to stop me. He tapped the toe of my boot with his. The gentlest smile broke on his face. "The Shoshone ain't got even the notion of a orphan child from what I seen. They babies and they chiles, no ma'am! They gots so many mommas—their ma and her sisters and even their own sisters been called mam. Same with the menfolk being pa, and then they's aunties and grandfolks like a big old live oak tree down home, wider than it be tall, ain't gonna let no child fall outside from its protecting."

We stood together in the summer sun without a tree for fifty miles.

T laughed out loud. "You should of seed that Fort Hall census taker, Clara. Pity the man try to untangle them two tribes. Wouldn't none of the names stay in place. Got him a ledger, got pages of little itty cramped-up family trees—two lines in, you'd a thought the page shat bees."

I felt them crawl, felt them swarm right over the lineage that I had always been told I lacked. "No orphans," I said. This bee swarm never had lived in rows, in tidied boxes—it hung on a free limb called the soul.

T's eyes held mine.

"Would it bring Kay comfort, knowing we've survived it? Knowing we are separate, and someways wise?"

"It ain't no comfort, we ain't got a parent to claim between us, Clara! Kay gots dozens. Now she done left, how happy you think they is?"

I could not say.

T softened. "Her name—Kashess—mean 'wait awhile.' If you does, Clara, you'll see, her smile been worth the wait."

CHAPTER 34

We shared one day together before Tierre rode west with four hundred sheep to mollify Opal. On that shared day I discovered Kashess knew a few words of English, and her hands could talk a blue streak when Tierre moved too slowly or lacked an understanding of the import of her needs. White people would call this henpecking. Kay signed like some women pout. She talked with T as his equal. They haggled. Which made me awed and puzzled and hopeful. Her loose hair fell to her waist.

Kay could also be silent as a newel post. It proved hard to include her in our conversations and undertakings. Her demeanor loomed mightily over us, though she only stood as tall as me. Mainly Kashess, with her broad, down-curved mouth and penetrating eyes, looked on. Harlan was only too happy to be among children. I hadn't known it, but Harlan's charms expanded with the young. Frank eyed him with fascination as Harlan waggled his head of unruly hair. Mincy pounced on Harlan's large midriff. She patted his belly and giggled. Slender as a reed herself, she could not get over the size of it. She leaned her whole weight into him, bouncing on that kettledrum, as Harlan whistled a tune for her, in waltz time. After that, wherever Harlan went, Mincy followed at his heels step for step. The girl child was all legs and arms. She carried a hammer Harlan gave her tucked down in her beaded sash and tried to help him with his chores in earnest, though the sound of giggling marked their progress through the day.

When Harlan left with the herd the next morning, Shep pulling the old wagon, dogs prancing in anticipation, Mincy sobbed with her head buried in her little poncho. She loved fun, and fun was riding off into the dusty morning to find her father and feed their sheep.

It was July the third, 1879, and I, Clair Martin, was finally in a "family" way.

Kay moved like a small cat through the chaparral, her hands plucking weeds and wild grasses. She worked for hours afield with Frank strapped on her back, harvesting the hill behind the brush tepee. It was an imposing bit of work, that tepee. Easily twelve feet tall, Kay had interwoven cattail reeds with rabbitbrush to clothe the poles. Her house was fragrant, even from a distance. Like sleeping on a stream bank, I thought. Noisy on a windy night. I wondered if the stars shone through.

Although Kay took the turnips I brought her and listened to my advice on how to cook them, I saw no more of them. Suffering pinched her wide eyes and haunted her mouth, tender as if swollen, as if bruised. Kay boiled meat at their campfire and baked unleavened bread in the ashes. I ate alone in the house.

T and Harlan had assumed they were the herders and I the homebody, but when it came to children, give me sheep. I had no skills with children. I couldn't imagine a way to engage them. I tried to interest Mincy in my lap loom. When I showed her how simple it was turning the shed stick and passing the bobbin, beating the warp down tight, she fingered the straps on my overalls, and then fell asleep on the floor. It seemed weeding and cleaning house and building a complex English floor loom were enough to make a bat snore, so Mincy wandered off to play in the barn or chase the cat or hang on her mother for company. She did come for a fleet hello each morning, to join me when I watered the garden. She'd crouch at my side as the creek water rushed in, spin in a circle and then race the water to the end rows. I didn't mind losing a few carrots or the random disarrangement of my new potato mounds by her flashing bare feet. Those shared mornings were my whole contact with Tierre's family.

I watched them from a distance, the long slow work and simple meals. I supposed it might be a better life than the one they'd had at Fort Hall, but I wasn't convinced. And what of the Washakie Farm? Any morning I could wake up to find the tepee empty, and Kay and the children gone. It swelled my tight heart like a biscuit—how easily I could fail Tierre. That fear hampered an easy exchange of help and the forging of new bonds.

My only comfort lay in work, so I built myself a loom.

The instructions were terse, the posts were heavy, and the final measurements exacting. If the hulking loom didn't stand plumb, the warp would lie at an angle and every web be ruined. I held my temper with the mortise joints, with all the pegs and screws. When the huge frame stood together at last—nearly seven feet tall and wide—I nailed four small blocks to the floor to fix the posts, preventing any and all shifting of the frame.

It stood right where our bed had been. I slammed against the frame to test it. That loom would never budge.

We kept a bucket lodged under a boulder to collect our mail. It lay four miles southwest of the house on the stage line that ran between Kelton and Boise City. Pro Walgamott stopped his coach there to let any passengers he might have locate their brains in the shade of a tormented juniper before they faced the next ten mile stretch. Pro was kind enough to bring me stamps and paper from Kelton, at double the price. He brought news and the occasional magazine for Harlan. He left a red handkerchief flapping from the juniper if we had mail. Saved me a half mile of walking, on days the bucket was empty. This day, the red flag waved.

22 July, 1879

My Dear Clair,

We inhabit the high crooked valley where the Raft River Range and the Bally Mountains meet. As you said, the grass is lush. The days stay almost cool, and the nights require blankets.

Opal White did not like our offer of four hundred sheep. She did not like it, but Tierre trailed our ewes in all the same and she counted each and every one. At three hundred and fifty Opal spat and said, I'll be damned if this ain't the smartest thing Stephen ever done. When Tierre said Stephen was in Canada, Opal replied, Well, that's even smarter. I admit I laughed so hard at this my hat fell in the dirt.

We will graze the herd down to the salt flats next month and then turn east, toward home and the fall rut. Tierre brings this letter to Marsh Basin and hence to the mail coach and to you. He has gone for flour and chocolate.

In five to six weeks we will scrape our boots on the front porch.

Give a fond hello to the family from me and from Tierre. He works as if born to it.

Yours sincerely, Harlan Lawes

I had brought a letter, as well, to post.

26 July, 1879

Dear Robert,

It is Clair, here, writing from the Idaho wilds. You are in my thoughts and wishes. I thought you would welcome word of Tierre. He is grown into a man. He did survey work for the railroad, and found himself a wife. They have a baby. Tierre knows his what and where and he never lets anything stop him.

I have built a loom here, as big as half a wagon, only I can't turn on a warp with all the men gone herding. It's just a hulk, my English loom. I use a small lap loom I built. Nothing fancy, but I sometimes wind on a striped warp and sometimes weave in a striped weft. It's a sorry bit of plaid in white, gray and brown.

This is a lonely time. I look at what's past and think how did we do it, it seems like mixing beans in a little bowl. Most of the nourishment ends up on the sideboard.

How are you, Robert? How are Delia and Mr. Dill? No plague I hope.

Your friend, Clair Martin

When I saw the snail track of horses coming toward me out past Tenmile, I put Harlan's letter in my pocket and put Robert Durham's letter in the bucket. I took out a pencil. In sheer loneliness, I wrote:

26 July, 1879

Dear Ada,

I hoe and weave and hoe, look at the bare hills, weave, make soap, ply my needle. What word from you? Send word,

Clair

No confession and no admission, either. No plea for understanding. I just opened the door to a conversation, and let Ada furnish the house if she so chose.

Turns out Kay wasn't only harvesting those hills for herself. I came home from the mail bucket to find a big pile of rabbitbrush on the front porch and a basket full of paintbrush. The heart red flowers were already wilting in the sunlight, so I put them in a ceramic crock. The bouquet enlivened my room. It seemed so kind of her. Of course, that was all wrong. Kashess came inside the house, entered my room and stood transfixed for a moment before the loom. Then she took the flowers in hand and, lacking words, smacked them against my rugs with a frown, my little rugs hanging on the wall. I knew she objected to something. I knew she aimed to make it right. I just had no idea what or why.

With shoulders erect, she went to the kitchen, tore the red flowers to pieces and crushed them in the bottom of a small pot. She poured in water and said, "Kuttento'i." She repeated herself. Then she banged on the stove. That cue I took. We boiled the paintbrush for an hour. The rabbitbrush, too, chopped to pieces in a larger metal tub. About this time I realized that we were making dyes, so I took out the vinegar and made a hot fixing bath. I glanced up for Kay's approval before lowering four skeins of my yarn into it.

Kashess said, "Women work."

I stopped. I said, "They certainly do."

My stews cooled naturally overnight, the paintbrush, the rabbitbrush and my yarn. Once dyed, those yarns sang pale orange and desert yellow. That's how I learned things speak without uttering a word. Sage speaks tender brown to wool. Juniper root speaks dark brown. I stirred fine stove ashes into the juniper bath, and that brown spoke darker still.

Kashess and I wound a warp onto the English loom together. This was not a process without problems. I'd built a set of shelves to hold my spools of yarn. I'd chosen a design and measured the long warp. I had filled and capped the raddle with great care—several hundred strands of warp yarns in their order—and lashed the raddle to the loom in back to ensure a smooth turning on. My mouth actually watered doing this work, I had waited so long to weave again.

I found Kashess in the tepee. I asked with gestures if she had time to help.

Turning a warp onto a loom is an art best accomplished by two people, one in front to hold tension on the yarns and one to crank the round warp beam in back. I positioned Kay at the back of the loom, showing her how the apron rod slid through the warp yarns just so. I removed the warp stick—my insurance against tangles—smiling at the uniformity. I jumped to the front of the loom to put tension on the warp just as Frank reached around his mother's back and grabbed the raddle. Being lashed down tight, the raddle didn't move, but its cap sprang off, startling Kashess. She rose from a crouch, Frank yowling for the object of his stubby hands' affection, as half the warp strands slumped onto the floor along with the tipped apron rod. I yowled even louder than Frank at sight of my spoiled warp.

Neither Frank nor Kay liked swearing, so they left the room.

In a white heat, I too left the room, knowing nothing but a tangled ruin would come from so much longing coupled with so much anger. Twenty minutes later, I sat on the floor between my loom and the wall, tying on the fallen warp, strand by strand, to the apron stick. At just the right moment, Kashess rejoined me. She leaned Frank's cradleboard upright against the doorframe, out of reach of the loom. Nimble and quick, she took her place at the back beam as I pulled the warp taut in front. She gave the crank one slow turn and then another. Without a word, we wound on the warp. Then Kay left me to it, threading the heddles and the reed, tying the warp onto the cloth beam. Oh, hours of pleasure without distraction or haste.

"I've been waiting, waiting all summer long to use my loom!" I told Kashess later, to apologize for my fury. Smiling, I shot both hands toward the ceiling and jumped for joy. Kay brushed her palms together. She made no comment, but it looked like a cracker had lodged in her throat. I took it to mean happy, her almost-tears. Women work, don't you try and stop them.

The pounding of the treadles recalled those frightful Sundays I had played organ in Daniel Dees' church—but with my loom, the end results were lovely. I finished one basketweave rug, and, longing for different colors than my desert palette, I tore my summer dresses up for rag strips. I spared the blue wool plaid. I had too much respect for Evelyn Dees' handiwork to dismantle it for my own.

I ripped widths of cotton. I used three different colors and ran them up against a bulky, two-ply wool. I felt the color in my fingers as I wove, in my arms, my legs, my chest. The shuttle kept busy of its own accord. Time—time ceased to exist.

The collaborations with Kashess had strict limits. I tried teaching Kay to spin, but her glum, stooped body and fierce scowl put an end to that. I tried to help her winnow ricegrain. A day spent gathering and winnowing and grinding in the August sun for a cup of flour when I could buy it at Duff's in a fifty-pound bag? We divided our labors. Hers were Indian, mine were white. I did ease her day some by taking Frank. Kay could cover more ground without the cradleboard on her back.

I leaned him up against the bedroom wall in his handsome home. I sang to entertain him while I wove. It can't be said my singing is pleasing, and Frank just hung there like a lump, all bound up in what looked to me like a beaded prison. Little fuzzy black head and curdy eyes, lost without their mother. When I unlaced the top, to give some freedom, Frank Tootabba flailed his arms, flailed and flailed them following some internal rhythm. What dread urgency possessed the boy? I could not tell. Happy or sad? I had no idea, but the waving arms put me off my rhythm. So I took young Frank from the cradleboard and set him up his own little kingdom. Penned him in the corner with two tipped chairs, just like we'd penned the ewes. Gave him a rug to wiggle on and as many of the items from the kitchen as had no blades or points. Old Black Sun liked their shine. I tolerated his crying and he tolerated my singing. Each of us got what we wanted for the while, and a new order ensued.

When Kay returned to our arrangement, a cry escaped her lips. The empty cradleboard, the tipped chairs, no Frank. I regretted causing her alarm. But Frank shrieked a war whoop and Kay leapt to him, picked him up and swung him in an arc side to side with her whole body. Side to side. Instant relation, instant calm. Every baby in the world deserves a mother like Kashess. Even when she stood in the doorway of her shaggy tepee barking out orders, it sounded like love.

CHAPTER 35

Two things upended August. Ada wrote, and Tierre came home. Ada's letter said only to meet her on the Boise stagecoach line, she was headed north to Canada on 20 August. I wrote her back.

> *11 August, 1879*
>
> Ada,
> *I built your loom. I spun and died fourteen fleeces. Yes, I will meet you at the stage stop past Tenmile, 20 August in the afternoon. Pro Walgamott knows the place.*
>
> *Clair*

As for Tierre, I stepped out to get water one sunup and his mare stood in the yard, striped with sweat, Shep tied to the saddle on a lead. Two of Harlan's dogs jumped up and licked my hands. All was quiet at the tepee. I gave them time. I walked both horses to the barn. I worked slowly, combing them out, throwing blankets on, filling the trough with hay. Beautiful, strong smell of horse, and hot breath on my neck as I checked their hooves for stones.

Tierre found me weaving. He smiled and said, "Well,

alright." He said he and Harlan thought we could use a horse and a few provisions, so T elected himself the delivery man. He looked so at ease in his body, like his skin and bones and spirit fit just right. He asked after Kay's and my progress. I told him she seemed perfectly content, as long as she kept an acre or ten between us. "She doesn't like my work, and she doesn't much like me."

"Clara. When I ask Kay to come, come an' live on this ranch, she heared all about you and she listen and you know what Kay ask? She ask what kind of woman is it own her own home, own the work of her hands, and no man to tie her up, she Blackfeet? I say, 'No. Clara her own tribe. She a white woman, but.'"

"But what?" I asked.

T settled the straw he'd been chewing deeper in his mouth and smiled. "Shoshone and Blackfeet is bound enemies."

"So then she hates me!"

"Clara Worry Martin, y'all miss my point. A good enemy been the measure of the tribe."

I rode with Tierre halfway to the mail bucket, on his way to meet the herd. Riding through the great untrammeled cloudless August evening, I almost sang. Joy in numbers. Space to operate. The old Mormon hymn, "Love at Home" rang in my veins. T and Harlan had two more weeks out on the range south of the Raft River Mountains. He insisted I keep his dappled horse, said Shep was meant to pull a wagon.

We did a little prancing, that horse and I, riding home. I teased a canter out of him and didn't even lose my seat. By the time we made it back, the front porch lay in darkness. Sunset had razed the plain of its few features. Everything earthbound sat humbled and dim next to the ascendant sky, evenings as comely here as they had been in Brigham from my cabin on the Bench. And as solitary. I had one of Harlan's dogs for company. Hadn't I claimed all I needed was desert, a dog and sunsets?

I slept on the front porch under herds of stars that night.

The next morning, I rode to meet Ada.

I worked the creases out of my new overalls, sitting on a boulder in the shade of the old juniper. The saddle bags below me held a gallon jug of water, jerky, and biscuits in case Ada needed a meal.

I had washed my hair and tucked it in my hat. I'd sewn a new blouse, a white smithy blouse, and starched and ironed it for the occasion. Even my stockings were clean.

I scuffed at them, as the thread of dust drew closer.

My knees twitched like a mail order suitor's.

Pro Walgamott didn't budge from his box, just grinned, or maybe it only looked like grinning as the chunk tobacco slid around under his lip. Ada helped herself out of the narrow coach door, in a sensible gray and brown dress. Her hair was gray, covered with alkali dust.

"Bear's ass, Ada," I said, taking our meeting by the throat, "it's been awhile." My heartstrings trembled. She said not a word. She nodded to herself, staring at me. Then she brushed off her dress. Ada looked shorter and blunter than when we'd met, like her nail had been pounded down a few notches by one determined hammer. When she shook the dust from her bonnet, her duckbill bonnet, her Mormon calico bonnet with the cotton gathered in around the brim, I coughed out a laugh without meaning to. A holy busy bee—one of God's hand-maidens had come to call.

Ada held her bonnet by the strings and said, "Somebody's broke your heart."

I wrenched out a laugh, and whatever longing had survived my months alone in the desert tore my throat. "Well," was all I could manage to say in return.

"My good-for-nothing son."

I said, "Oh, he was good for a thing or two—"

"Don't you say it, not to me!" Ada chewed her cheeks. "You never wrote one word."

"He visited you at Christmastime—"

"You know damn well Stephen never told a thing."

I felt a stab of conscience, but it changed that fast to blame. If it hadn't been for Ada, I'd never have fallen for Stephen at all.

"It's treachery!" she said. "Best thing in my life, and now he's gone. Off north, to the wilds. I will never get to live near my only son."

"Not unless he hankers after prison."

"Not unless you got his baby in your womb."

It gripped, as it was meant to, like spoiled meat in the belly. "There is no baby."

"No," Ada said. "No. Lean as a rail. Angry and smart. You got nothing left of him."

"I got everything—that's what he said the night he stole away!"

Ada paled, looking off at Tierre's horse, his sure legs and strong back. "You loved my son? Did you love him, Clair, heart as well as flesh? How long you been at this non-conjugal understanding?"

"A year and some."

"And he wouldn't marry you. Then Stephen is an idiot—"

"Oh, he asked me to be his wife, his Mormon wife."

Ada looked so tired. "Oh, Clair."

"It was God who drove him off, Ada. Or rather my lack of God," I said, just as Pro Walgamott twitched the reins, making the horses jump and the stagecoach lurch to fine effect.

"You call this service, Pro?" I shouted.

He spat. "I got times to keep."

"What you got," I said, "is a paying customer and a law-suit, if you break our necks. I can hold those horses, if they're too much for you."

He grinned and chewed. Cinching the reins, he looked away, east.

I took Ada's arm and walked her out of harm's way. I said, "I hear your William has taken a third wife to his bosom," to put a fine point on things.

"Another man thinks he's grabbed God's lapels."

"Intolerable," I said.

She nodded.

"Well, Harlan and I have grabbed up the pitiful state of our ranch, and hired Tierre to help us. There's no range and precious hope of gaining any. If you want to stake a claim in it, say so now."

Two tears tracked down her cheeks. "It's a fine thing, lov-ing you, Clair. You won't have me, and you won't have my son. But you'll take all the love we give you in things."

"I don't," I said, "I don't believe I am so hard as that, Ada. Goodness, all I ever wanted was to be myself."

She reached into the coach. She put a crate of peaches on the ground. "For pies," Ada said. "Tierre likes pie." She climbed inside, and the coach sprang forward before I had even thanked her. I stood in the flurry, pressing a handkerchief to my mouth.

Goodness, I thought. Well, that was one word for it. I put her peaches into the saddlebags and jogged the horse forward, to test the distribution of weight. I did not want to crush them. I felt a chasm of sadness, to be sure. I loved Ada Nuttall in the only way I knew how, by finding my own line to follow through life. That is how she lived every day of her life. That is how I hoped to live mine.

By the time I shut T's horse in the barn an hour later, I had a smile on my face. I walked toward the house marveling at change—how quickly the old briny puddle of life freshened. Like it or not, life freshened. An eight-mile ride and a fifteen-minute talk, and Harlan and T and I owned the ranch outright. Ada would find some new lives to manage in Stephen's two wives. That or run them ragged in trying. I was rehearsing a hacked-up sign language version of "Kashess, we own the ranch" when I saw Mincy standing on the porch, tears streaming down her cheeks.

"What is it?" I asked her. Kay stepped outside clutching Frank. She pointed past the porch. Harlan's brindled dog lay snarled up in a pile of blood by the woodpile. Unmoving. Mincy tried to go to him, but Kashess took hold of her. "Ka!"

I scanned the ranch. The tepee had been leveled. I pushed them inside the house. Glass from the window lay shattered on the floor. Frank screamed and Mincy cried and Kay said, as best she could, that she had had a visitor. A visitor with a gun.

I raised a fist. "Has anyone laid a hand on you?"

Shaking, she frowned and drew a hand down her dress, meaning she was fine. What wasn't fine was her terrified children, her tepee, the window and the dog, and halfway blown to pieces, my cat lay in a patch of red sun beside the kitchen. Mincy cried for both her friends. I took my pistol from the kitchen drawer. "Who was it? Who did it?" I asked, knowing he hadn't left long since. He couldn't have. The tears were too fresh. The shock too deep. "Which direction did he go?"

Kay pointed west. She said with urgency, "Opal man."

"On horseback?" I was out the door with Kay's *yes*. I crouched over the body of Harlan's dog, past all human help, then ran to the barn. T's mare took the bit. I mounted up, no time for a blanket or saddle. A few smart blows in the crotch taught me to lean in, grip with my knees. Kelton Pass. Kelton Pass, he couldn't have ridden farther. Opal knew we had grazed her canyon, and she'd sent a hand to say *Go to hell.*

The dry wind cut tears from my eyes. The pistol banged in my pocket. When I saw them against the foothills, a rider and horse, I eased up, trotted onward, cooled my thoughts and hardened my nerve.

The rider was in no hurry. He slopped from side to side, his horse's walk exaggerated in the heat. He didn't even turn until I rode up beside him, and only looked concerned when he recognized the marking on my face.

I kicked his leg, kicked his horse's flank and fired my pistol in the air. That quick, the herder lay in the sage. T's horse threw its head and spun around, but I clung on, keeping the violent little gun pointed roughly at the man. When he looked up, my pistol followed his chin. "Do I shoot or do we talk?"

He laughed, spread-eagled in the dirt, dirt caked in the creases of his hands. For an instant, I saw Tierre's hand there, and the payback for his suffering. The ground exploded and the herder scrambled back.

His pants were soaked with urine, his fingers intact. I felt a moment's gratitude for that. "I want to make myself clear— what is your name?"

A whoosh came from his throat.

"Speak up, friend, I couldn't hear you."

"Clive."

"Well, it is cowardice, Clyde, pure undiluted cowardice, waving a gun at a woman and shooting animals at an empty ranch, and if you don't tell Opal White and every goddamned herder from here to Texas what I think of cowards, I will be sorely disappointed. I may have to trade this pistol for a rifle and disacquaint your ribs from your windpipe." I inhaled. "Is that clear?"

"Yeah."

I stared him down.

"Yes, ma'am."

"You leave my home and my people in peace. If Opal has a grievance, let her lay it out over peach cobbler and whiskey at my place. That's an invitation. Now throw your pistol in the brush."

He hesitated.

"I have three more bullets. You decide."

His weapon sailed off into the scrub, the way his horse had gone.

"Thank you."

Tierre's horse turned and broke into a gallop. I had never ridden bareback. I'd never fired a gun. I laughed aloud, vaunting home with the wind in my teeth, thinking about Jim Bridger.

I asked Kashess to leave the tepee down until Harlan and Tierre came back. No need to announce to any riders passing by that Indians lived in the vicinity. She helped me clean the parlor of glass. We all buried the animals on the ridge. Kay blessed them with a sprinkle of tobacco from her small medicine pouch. She tore the wind in six directions with a wand from an eagle's wing. Mincy laid a big squash flower on their grave. Then it was time to forget. I doubted Opal would come running to hear my apology, so it seemed best to put the ranch behind us for a couple of days. Get a fresh perspective. Get Kay and the kids out of that mess.

We walked to the Black Pine Range for firewood. I packed peaches and hardtack. Kay rigged the travois on Tierre's horse, and we carried the children into the night. The next morning, we dawdled at my favorite creek. We played the Shoshone hand game, a sort of *Button, button, who's got the button?* with a stick in the button's place. I chopped wood all day while Kay and Mincy gathered a mountain of kindling. That night, Kay prayed over our meal and then over our blankets laid around a campfire in the scrub. She seemed always to be praying, singing a tuneless tune like Poker Jim's, only without the slanting humor.

I slept hard after all that work with the axe. I dreamed hard, too. Tierre came walking straight toward me with his entrails held in his hand, gut-shot and too in love to die in the desert with sheep. He fell in a tangle like Harlan's dog just as he reached their tepee. It was hung with skins, beautifully painted. Looking fresh, as if just tanned. I woke up sweaty with sorrow. A low hum filled my ears. I would never have believed this but for seeing it—Kay stood singing at our small fire, eyes closed, and the sky was erased. I don't mean clouds had moved in. The sky was black in all directions, but for the earthbound sparks, no light. I watched her without moving. I saw the sparks were not just fire. They danced around her, in and out, like a servant fans a king. Like a pulse. A breathing. I could not think of any other way to account for them—the hundreds of dragonflies that had come to witness Kay's prayer.

My mind cleaved open, just in time for the fire to flicker out. Smoke made a hazy barrier between us. I couldn't see Kashess. I couldn't see the breathing sparks. The sky over me, still black, might just be high cloud cover. But who could turn clouds black? And who erase the stars?

Who was this woman with her own quorum of dragonflies attending her? My life and all I knew became a mystery, a new and utterly unfamiliar world.

CHAPTER 36

I plied Opal White with cobbler and whiskey. Neither of us was in a laughing mood, but I will credit her with this: she laughed off our trespass at Onemile Canyon as an innocent's mistake. Opal loved being superior. And sarcastic. I let her be, I had plans. She seemed more intent on figuring out just who on earth I was than why I'd stolen her rams' sweet feed. Her eyes had gone goggly at the English loom and the rug I had nearly finished. She leaned down and sniffed it. Put a leathery hand on the yellow stripes with a starflower border. Not that I believed she cared a whit for female household furnishings, she just could not make the finery square with me. My sagging overalls. My willingness to live in the heart of nowhere. My staying on even after Stephen left. My cohabiting with riffraff. Opal took to the whiskey when she couldn't make sense of it. She did enjoy her cobbler. I gave her a third slice.

I averted my eyes from the peach mash in her yellow teeth and said that since we were neighbors, I had a neighborly offer to make her. I hadn't talked it out with Harlan or T in advance, but I saw we had to keep our enemy close. We wouldn't last another season against her men and her guns.

I said, "We own a hundred-twenty acres here, as you know."

"I sold it to Stephen so, yeah, I know."

"Well, I sorely hate to see good land go to waste."

Opal snorted and swallowed.

"We will never have a big outfit like you do, Opal. Our desires are modest, where yours are grand. So I would consider—since you and I have cleared our grievances, and have an even clearer understanding as ranch women—well, I would sell you back forty acres at less per acre than what Stephen paid you for it."

A chunk of cobbler hit my plate. Pointing the tines of her fork at me, squinting her milk-blue eyes, Opal said, "I owned this godforsaken bit of Utah once. What makes you think I'd want it back?"

It was my turn to spit peaches. "Utah?"

Opal glanced at me for signs of a double-cross.

"You mean Idaho—" I said.

"I meant just what I said, and I don't want it."

I felt like I'd been hit.

Opal said, "You got nothing, and plenty of it. How much you asking for that rug?"

I went into the bedroom to cool my fury. I bounced both hands on the tight trim rug. I said, "Twenty-five dollars," my heart pounding, asking a king's ransom for my work. But fifteen dollars for the weaving and five dollars each for the murdered dog and cat would put me almost even with my fallen land deal. Opal could take it or leave it.

"You don't say." She stood in the doorway, eyeing my rug.

"Best rug in the territory, Opal."

That tensed her up. "I'd give you fifteen dollars for it—"

"I can't let it go for less than twenty."

With a barely perceptible grin Opal said, "I'll have it."

Once we finished our business, I hiked straight out the kitchen door and all the way up to the ridge. The Black Pine, the Raft Range, the Promontory Mountains lay still in the midday haze, just like the first time I laid eyes on them. *Utah.* Ada's punch took awhile to land—a jab sent to a girl in Mississippi in a letter two years back. Well, now I certainly owed Ada nothing. She drew me West on a lie.

My eyes looked north toward Idaho while a lizard in the cedars scratched its workaday music. Then I looked south to Utah and the gray rainbow of the Wasatch Mountains, heaved up from the Salt Lake Valley eons since.

I sat down in the shade of the splayed cedars with twenty dollars in my pocket. I had only appeased Opal for the while. Like Ada, Opal White couldn't be trusted. They were mountainous women with mountainous appetites. A turkey vulture descended on a draft over the Wildcat Hills, slight as a bit of dark straw, its wings canted upward. It drew on the draft a long while, teetering up and down without flapping. That vulture and I had a pretty good deal. We would search and glide, search and glide until our bellies were full. How to keep the children safe and happy—that might take more wings.

The boys came back. They had a few good tales and nearly all the ewes they'd left with, and I was relieved to see Tierre's insides were all inside of him. I took Harlan aside and asked about the Utah and Idaho swindle. Harlan wiped his forehead on his handkerchief, then tucked it up his sleeve. It stank of sheep. He said, "Ada didn't think you would come to Utah."

"Ada was right. How far is it? The state line?"

"Three and three-quarter miles north."

"Damn, I almost made it."

"Does it matter so much?"

"You left Utah, Harlan, yet you can't take your eyes away from it."

He agreed. "I cannot."

"I can and have. I left that flock. In Utah, I'm just a bummer lamb—I wore their false skin for years and was mothered indifferently."

"They kept you alive, Clair—"

"I am grateful for it. And even more grateful to be shut of them, them and their pyramid families, their eternal families with the man on top."

Harlan shook his head and said, "Pernicious, and peccable—"

"What's that?" I asked.

"Liable to sin."

"But not to find the source of sin among them. Not when God's spirit is always saying, 'It's them! It's the Gentiles, the Indians, the Christians, the Negroes. You are the chosen, they are worse than dirt.' Well, I tell you what, Harlan Lawes—we have founded the church of mavericks, right here. No violence allowed. No greedy sinners."

"Perhaps Tierre should be with us for this discourse."

"Oh, T and Kay and the babies, too."

T and Harlan heard about Opal's cruel intrusion when we had all gathered to feast on lamb stew that night. Tierre almost left right then with his rifle, but Kay stopped him with a straight arm as I told them about how I had given chase and turned the tide of that cowboy's day. About Opal's cobbler visit and the rug I sold. It calmed T some, but the list of those who would not be included in our little church grew as T told us why crazy, white men with guns made Kashess—his fearless bride—shake.

Two things. Her grandfather, Tindup, had had a dream two days before a Shoshone massacre in 1863. A nasty business, T said, middle of winter when Colonel Connor and his troops, out of sheer meanness and boredom, slaughtered an entire village of Washakie's people on the Bear River. The Shoshone were far from white settlements, camped up north, gathered to spend their winter in peace. Tindup saw the pony soldiers in his dream come to kill them all without mercy, burn the tepees, scatter the berries and grain. "Time to leave!" he told his tribe. "Do it now, tonight!" Camped four miles south, Tindup and Kay and her parents listened to the massacre from dawn until dusk. Kay clung to her grandmother through it all. She was eight years old. They fed and warmed and dried the tears of a dozen people who followed their campfire to safety that night. They found six more alive in the heaps of dead the next day. Kashess saw it. She walked the ground between burned homes and butchered children. The soldiers had cleaved the heads of the women with axes to end their misery, after raping them on the snowy ground. "Kay *listen* when dreams talk."

The second run-in with a white man's gun sent T and Kashess to us. They'd had to leave Fort Hall without a farewell or a plan. For two days, Kay had sat out front at the Indian Agent's office after a U. S. soldier had raped her niece. She didn't speak, she didn't fuss, she wrapped herself in a blanket and waited for justice. Danilson, a reasonable man, noticed this glum sentry at his front step and stopped to ask what Kay could want. Food or liquor or tobacco? She said she wanted the soldier who violated her niece posted back to Salt Lake City. Which Danilson ignored. A small crowd gathered out front as that same soldier came the third morning to give Kashess her due. He couldn't kill her with witnesses, so he shot his rifle right and left of her, trying to get her to move on. Tierre stepped up and called out, "You miss her twice!" which raised some hoots from the white onlookers. The Indians looked grim. He said, "Got me a Henry rifle take her with one shot. I cut you for it. High card wins."

The soldier said, "For the squaw?"

"For the rifle. Yo' rifle for mine." T's weapon put the soldier's sorry gun to shame. With a tide of humiliation rising up at his back, the soldier turned from Kashess and took T's bait. Of course he lost, to the crowd's delight, so T said, "Double or nothing? You may needs a rifle, being a soldier and all."

The second cut, T took everything the soldier had on him—eight dollars and his ridiculous pride. Then Tierre took himself to Kay's tepee, packed his two guns and all she owned and left with the family that night. During his telling, Kay had backed herself into a corner. T brought his wife to the bench and sat her down next to him. Put an arm around her. Mincy crawled up in my lap to make room, a sweet bony child smelling of sage and gravy. "Kay faced them bullets," T said with pride. "But she ain't gonna face no more."

This led to a fiery discussion. Opinions rose fast and furious as sparks from a bonfire. Do this, try this, insist on that so our sheep could graze next summer. Bar the doors, buy another rifle, hire on a hand, sign contracts with the neighboring ranches.

I only had one thing to say. "Sell them."

"Sell the sheep?" Both Harlan and Tierre stopped, too stunned to laugh.

"We could sell a few, sell a couple three hundred," T said.

"All of them, and good riddance." The idea had come to me the previous night, a sleepless night and productive of good. I confess I prayed, in the manner of Kashess or how I thought she prayed. Not so much asking or pleading but singing up a fervent willingness, a readiness to see and hear. Then the evil that had been done to us showed its face, and the way through the thicket came clear.

I looked from T to Harlan. "What in hell do we need sheep for?"

Tierre flung a palm down and made the table jump. "You the boss. We be gone in the morning."

"Tierre—"

"Ain't nothing for us here, ain't no kind of living to be made."

"I've thought this out, and—"

"You thought? I gots to work, I don't want no charities."

I held Mincy closer. "I am not offering charity. I am saying let the cattlemen and the herders do the butting up and grabbing for justice with their guns, and let's get everything the livestock buyers will give us down in Kelton—what, Harlan, two dollars per head?"

"A dollar and fifty for yearling lambs. Two and twenty for well-fed ewes."

"Times a thousand!" But my enthusiasm was not catching. "That's some peace and prosperity there, T. And if we have no sheep, they have no cause to kill us."

"Or a thousand fewer reasons to kill us," Harlan said.

"And here's what we do have. Kay can gather food where we see nothing but desert. You can work the ranch, T, cut hay in the bottoms for the horses. And you'll hunt, Tierre, hunt the Raft River Range and the Black Pine Range, bring us game to eat. That's what you're good at. Isn't that what you love?"

"I don't gives a damn for what I is or ain't good at. I wants my chiles to eat."

"They will eat, and live safer here and happier than if you were gone to summer pasture five months of every year—and us forever having to guard our doors with guns."

"She paints a picture," Harlan said. I could see in Kay's eyes she understood a change was coming. Frank did a little bounce in his cradleboard.

"Harlan, you could go to Corinne, maybe look into barnyard animals, bring back an assortment and settle in here."

His brows bunched. "As a gentleman rancher?"

"Yes. We all love your cooking. And your hip's no good."

He rocked in the old rocker we'd pulled up to the table for the meal. Tierre fiddled with his lip. He wanted to believe, but the burden of life in the last two years made that difficult. "Only one thing she ain't said. How we gone do it, how we gonna survive? Cash rules, Clara." Kindness entered T's voice. "Sheepherders is dung on the lowest rung. How you think to get us cash, next year and the next, if we ain't even gots sheeps?"

I set Mincy off my lap and stood up. An impromptu orator, I said if Opal could be bamboozled into paying twenty dollars for one of my simplest rugs, we'd have fools falling all over themselves to make us rich once I got going. Which was an overstatement, but from long association with T I knew overstatement made the most convincing story. "I have wool enough to last the winter, and Opal can pay us back her rutting fee in fleeces. Mincy here," I gripped her little hand, "she can help with the carding and dying. I couldn't do it all myself."

Tierre's eyes narrowed, the way they used to when he gave sass. "You done thought on everything, didn't you, Missy?" But he didn't toss an insult. He just smiled.

"Pure selfishness. I am sick to death of sheep and dust and flies."

And so we sank into obscurity. A fine place to be when the world's in a roil.

CHAPTER 37

I sewed a doll for Mincy. Black button eyes and long black hair. She wore a soft leather dress with seeds tacked on the hem. I whittled two tiny hammers. One for her belt, and the other I sewed to that doll's right hand. Women work, after all.

After T delivered the herd to Kelton, I joined him out back to slaughter and dress the sheep we'd kept. I found him sharpening his knives at the stone behind the barn. Three ewes and a yearling lamb stood in the shade. All that was left of our empire.

I examined the hammer. I tested its weight on my shoulder, trying several grips.

T turned. He took the sledge from me.

"I want to help," I said.

"No you doesn't."

"How can I eat what I cannot kill?"

T straightened the strap on my overalls. He said, "I does the killing for you, Clara."

I fell knee-deep into Tierre's love.

"You go an' work your loom, I could teach you how to tend to the smoking after."

And though I'd thought myself impervious to tears, I

wept hard at the sounds of the slaughtering. I sat on the loom bench through two deaths, then went to the garden, pulled the planks to water the rows I'd watered that morning, let the cold spring water run and run.

We built a smoker that afternoon, a rickety-looking sheet iron hut, and put the mutton in to cook. Then, with kidney pie and some day-old biscuits, we walked to the brush tepee. It may have looked inferior to the sod roof hut, but the tepee was almost cool inside as breezes moved right through it. Kay had placed my little rug inside their doorway.

"Your new homestead," I said.

T squatted on his heels. "We have y'all to dinner tonight, once Harlan get home."

It seemed Harlan Lawes had been to Paris, France, not the frontier town of Corinne. He looked like a man who had stolen some other man's party, showing us his new possessions guardedly. A bay horse, a new wagon, and two dozen hens, red and amber and scrappy as pugilists. They led Harlan in a raucous dance. When they pecked at his feet, he hurled the grain right at their heads. "We can always boil them," he said. Money hadn't changed him—still the same lugubrious smile.

Then Harlan cinched up his nerve a notch and showed off our new milking sheep, so wedge-headed and linen-eyed it looked like it needed a bonnet to stop squinting. We named her Sister. Harlan promised Mincy a ride. He'd bought two gray Rambalains for wool, a very pregnant pig, a meat grinder and sausage stuffer, curlicue cheese molds, a butter churn and eight bottles of wine "for sauces." Our gentleman farmer spent the afternoon with Mincy and a cookbook cradled in his lap. She called him "Grumpy Harlan." For the first time in two years, Grandpa Harlan took his ease.

That night, we ate cross-legged on blankets in the tepee.

Or tried to. Harlan sat on a bucket. I tasted the bread and meat that had no taste. T relished every bite, saying he was glad his babies' mouths hadn't been killed by salt or sugar. With enough shots of whiskey, I too liked Kay's cooking. Then it was story time. Shoshone children never go to bed without stories from their elders. We reclined on our blankets as Grumpy Harlan, being the eldest, gave it a try.

"There once was a fearless little leaf who all her life had longed to see the ocean. The ocean is the very biggest sea. So she fell off her tree into the sagebrush. Wind picked her up and pushed her along. She stuck for awhile in a horse's mane and flew off into a young warrior's leggings. The warrior rode her to a village full of shining tepees. And among those tepees the leaf settled gladly down. But a bird picked her up, bound for its nest, a nest high up in a tree. A falcon swooped in, the bird chattered 'Oh!' and the leaf fell from his talons into a tiny creek. The creek led to a tributary. The tributary widened as it met the river. The little leaf said, 'Will you take me to the ocean?' And the river, who loved God, said, 'Even the smallest tributary ends up in the great sea.'"

To which T said, "Amen."

Mincy, who hadn't understood a word Harlan said, slept smiling in her father's broad lap.

Kashess held up my beaded moccasins, the ones I'd hung on the parlor wall. She had Frank on her back and was dressed for a journey. "Women work," she said, handing the moccasins to me. I asked if I should pack for more than a few days, a pinyon harvest at the City of Rocks being new to me. She nodded *yes*.

"Is Tierre coming?" I knew he loved eating the little pine nuts, ground or toasted.

She shook her head *no*. Frank called out his impatience, as a pampered male will do.

I put on the beaded moccasins and helped T load the wagon. Kay and Frank and I said our farewells. Harlan handed in a sack of smoked lamb and boiled eggs and butter. Mincy clung to the wheel, whimpering for her mother, but Tierre peeled her off, tickled her belly and swung her over his shoulder. "Next time, girl daughter."

I had my crusty reputation, my pistol and my wits to protect us. On such a fair morning, they seemed enough. We set off on the ninth day of September to recapture a part of Kay's thousand-mile round.

We forded the Raft River—a shallow, glassy crossing that early in fall—and headed northwest. These were mountains I had never seen before, substantial peaks of pine and juniper and jagged rock, with patchy snow in the high hollows. Kay said nothing. I could feel her happiness in the return. Our new wagon was fleet. In four hours we reached the Almo Valley, which opened up onto the town of Marsh Basin. Miles of yellow grasses lay before us, trees in rows in the distance marking off fields, triggering *Mormon* and *poplars* and *home* inside my breast. I could have driven straight on, parked in their spiked shade and dropped my head back, watching the leaves spin down yellow and gold around, but Kashess said, "There, now," at a cattle trail a few miles south of the city.

Our trail wound west through a grazing herd, then up a canyon studded with boulders. We passed a new homestead, as pretty as Opal's place. Kay loosened her dress to nurse the baby. That quick, I stopped the wagon and jumped down to stretch my legs. Mothering made me jumpy. I filled our water bags at the creek, then looked upstream. I may as well have been an insect in a bowl. The boulders, tall and tipped and gouged out where the canyon widened, became unreasonable, even threatening—like men, like giants with their heads knocked off. I hurried back to Kay and the ripe, plump lips of Frank Tootabba fresh from his mother's bounty.

Kay was readying his cradleboard. She said, "You have no child."

"No," I answered, "I didn't want children."

Clutching Frank's body end to end, Kay laughed, hard. "Children want us!" Her eyes challenged mine, and I saw Tierre had been right. Kay's blazing smile was worth the wait, even if it vanished as soon as it appeared.

We drove between gigantic loaves of stone. Stone so tall I actually held the wagon in the shade of one to read the carved signatures there: *Moore, 1846. Slate, 1851. McGregor, 10.4.67.* Then I looked up, tracing the double ruts west. The California Trail. One hundred and fifty thousand people had passed this way, before the railroad linked the country, Harlan said. Two deep ruts and a few carved names were all that greeted us.

Trails and emptiness. Stone men and milk.

Kay pointed up a dry arroyo.

The rocks and pillars of rock grew more fantastic as we climbed. Mountains rose before us. The world below tumbled away in disorder—a City of Rocks, indeed, abandoned to bird flight, mad with its own mysterious logic and the sun's hardening heat. At Kay's bidding, I parked the wagon in the shade of a pinyon pine. The old tree flexed in the strong wind, casting a trembling shadow over us.

I squatted behind it to pee. A yellow-breasted bird sang there in the branches. *Chee-chee-chee, t-t-t-t-t-t.* Black body. Yellow-striped cheeks. I leaned back. Two birds, darting out and away through the blasted larkspur. Cactus long past bloom draped its dried purple at my feet. I felt like royalty, as near as I would ever get. No men. No sheep. Not a trace of society, high or low, to trouble us. I thanked whatever listens, said "thank you" out loud.

Kashess hummed and prayed over the empty gathering sacks, "coyote talk" to bless the harvest. I went for wood and dragged a dead stump back. It chopped up easily, splintering into billets for the cook fire. We ate in blissful silence. I cleaned the dishes and laid our beds out in the wagon at sunset. Kay's deerskin had a smooth, sweet grain. I threw my wool blanket alongside Frank's cradleboard in the hay.

Legs dangling in the cool night air, I listened to Kay work by firelight. It bore no resemblance to the work that I had known. She played a whistle and danced softly in a circle. She sang to the sticks we would use for knocking the high cones down, she burned herbs from her medicine pouch and sang to the laden trees. My skin pricked in amazement at how rich her song could be without her tribe. I fitted my hands one inside the other, rolled them together, callused and empty. Dry as the old stump, vacant as its twisted root.

I lay back, wondering if Kay would pull her black curtain to erase the stars. I cried without sound, the emptiness of my own life too immense to hate or fear or even fight. I did not feel Kashess' coming, only realized it with her singing softly to her son. "Taboshe, Tootabba, taboshe . . . " Oh, the voice was certain, no arrogance to it, making no claim but plain singing. One voice and the baby's even breathing. My sweat, my lone body in the hay, arms hooked around the bristling blanket. I was not meant to hear, not made for it, could not—

Kashess stopped singing.

I drew my knees in as Kay said, "Ghost trail."

I looked up past her long black hair and her lifted face to lights streaming over the sky. My knees relaxed. "The Milky

Way—" that old mountain stream caught in an instant, flashing.

"Your mother goes that way," Kay said.

"My mother is dead."

"She is the arrow, unseen."

I looked away. "What arrow?"

Kay touched my cheek. It pierced me, her tenderness. I said into the blanket, "Don't."

"Let it fly. Let her, then see."

Eyes closed, I knew what I would see.

Kay kneaded my hand. It felt like mercy.

"Then see," she said, "then see," as grave and rhythmical as a lullaby moving over the fear and inflections of fear, light as skippers skating the mirror surface of Box Elder Creek. I leaned in, I could only lean in to her touch, watching cold meltwater from the mountain pour down, and gravel stained with water where Swede's prints lay, willow sap and scrub oak budding out into the sure, if late, arising of leaf and green. Yellow, green, gray-purple—then a vibrant fall of water in a sourceless breeze as Kashess took my wrist, my arm. The height and heft, the pull of her voice—*sacred, mother,* it said. Her hands reiterating everything.

My legs took root, both legs alive with the memory of mud and water, mud and drowning. I saw my mother's enemies, the rancor of their hearts, their teachings, cudgels, tapers, taper, one tail of light . . . gone out.

Full darkness, Kay held on. Suspended in dark, awaiting a sign, she hovered with a hand over my heart until the black scrim collapsed and I had no more eyes than those within me. *They are everywhere!* The mother-fathers in their alcoves of light, broad as trees in air, blue of their sky, single, blended, hundreds, a thousand, all one, strip, pair, separated color and—*bliss.*

Kay held on.

Color, bliss!

She rested a hand on my cheek.

Sky, color, bliss—

Both of us drifting there.

And I could hear the baby's breathing.

"She gots a name for you, Clara." T laughed with a hand at his hip, leaning his broad shoulder against the pen we'd just built for the hens.

"She does? Kay chose a name for me?"

Tierre grinned. "Neesumbat."

"I'm a bat?"

"Nah, girl." He nudged me. "What you done up in them pinyon groves?"

"Gathered enough seeds to feed your belly through the winter," I shot back.

"Old Neesumbat—old 'Knows It Herself' Clara Martin."

"That's what Kay said? That's what she chose for me?"

"M'hmm," he said, with more than a shadow of doubt.

"Well, they were everywhere!" I said. "Vision, not flesh."

Tierre shrugged, as if to say *you gots me, there.*

That is the simple truth of it. In the hard abundance of this mysterious world, I had let one mother go and gained a thousand. Not just the sky clan who resides in my breast. I have Tierre. I have Harlan and Kashess, and her two growing children. I have Audwin Fife and Robear Durham. Just like Kay, Robert sees beyond.

What I couldn't know till Kashess laid her hands on
me—history is a slow spiral, so broad we can't be pushed off
by the victors.

God has no edges.

And we know how to wait.

AFTERWORD

Kashess gave me a whistle, her old elderberry whistle with just two holes. She showed me how it trills to call the spirits. I have no medicine pouch, as yet, so I wrapped it in the last of the mud-green calico. And that was that.

What good are a thousand parents if you don't commune with them?

ACKNOWLEDGEMENTS

My ancestors inform much of my life, and *Tributary* is filled with their stories. I asked myself, growing up in the Salt Lake Valley, *whatever happened to the ones who got away? Tributary* was born from this question.

Thanks go to my early readers and editors Wendy Street, Mary Bothwell and Risa Rank. I owe deep gratitude, too, to Carolyn Uhle, Diana West and Jeff Fuller for resurrecting my interest in the manuscript. Jeff provided expert editing, insights into my characters and dashing red kneebands. Thanks to Anne Richardson for help late in the game. Lastly, Kirsten Allen, my editor at Torrey House Press, helped raise Clair into full focus. It took twenty years. A late bloom beats no bloom by a mile.

Loving assistance came from Julie Kramer, who opened a shamanic perspective, and Rose Soaring White Eagle, my Shoshone friend, healer and guide, who took me to the Washakie graveyard. *Aishenda'ga.* I will never forget the land or the people buried there. Gaylene Garlitz contributed expert weaving advice and let me wind a warp onto her loom. Personal support came from artist Jeanne Rogers, who always has the right story to tell.

I grew to love Ocean Springs, Mississippi, the hellishly hot little oasis of liberalism in the South where I wrote much of this manuscript. Time spent researching Clair's world was a multi-faceted pleasure. The Special Collections Libraries at Idaho State University, the University of Utah, and the New Orleans Public Library held invaluable resources.

Many articles opened doors on local histories, including *Tullidge's Quarterly Magazine* (October, 1880) and Edith Carlson's, "To Albion—With Love" (1988). I found the following books particularly helpful: Leon Litwack, *Been in the Storm So Long: The Aftermath of Slavery* (1979); Charles Wayland Towne and Edward Norris Wentworth, *Shepherd's Empire* (1945); Louis Irigaray, *A Shepherd Watches, A Shepherd Sings* (1977); Austin and Alta Fife, *Heaven on Horseback: Revivalist Songs and Verse in the Cowboy Idiom* (1970); Charles E. Rosenberg, *Care of Strangers: The Rise of America's Hospital System* (1995); Otto H. Olsen, *Reconstruction and Redemption in the South* (1980); Wallace Stegner, *Mormon Country* (1942); Jessie L. Embry, *Mormon Polygamous Families: Life in the Principle* (1987); Vaughan J. Nielsen, *The History of Box Elder Stake* (1977); Anne L. Macdonald, *No Idle Hands: The Social History of American Knitting* (1988); Glenda Riley, *Women and Indians on the Frontier, 1825-1915* (1984); Brigham D. Madsen, *Shoshoni Frontier & the Bear River Massacre* (1985) and *The Bannock of Idaho* (1958); Beverly Crum and Jon P. Dayley, *Shoshoni Texts* (1997); Stan Steiner, *The Ranchers: A Book of Generations* (1980); M. C. Green, *Yesteryears*; Bessie M. Shrontz Roberts-Wright, *Oakley Idaho: Pioneer Town,* (1987); Virginia Estes/Daughters of the Utah Pioneers, *A Pause for Reflection* (1977); and Donald Worster, *Under Western Skies: Nature and History in the American West* (1992). Gratitude, too, to the Online Etymology Dictionary for keeping my language honest.

I owe so much to my brilliant teacher Jamgon Kongtrul Rinpoche. And to Tierre Covington—who stole my heart when he was in first grade—thank you for accompanying Clair on her journey.

Women's histories have the power to change everything.

BARBARA K. RICHARDSON

Barbara K. Richardson's debut novel, *Guest House*, a rousing road tale, launched the first literary Truck Stop Tour in the nation. In *Tributary*, Richardson revisits the history of the northern Salt Lake Valley, land of the Shoshone Indians and the home of her Mormon ancestors.

Richardson earned an MFA in poetry from Eastern Washington University. Her work has appeared in *Northwest Review, Cimarron Review,* and *Dialogue —A Journal of Mormon Thought. Guest House* was an Eric Hoffer fiction finalist. She lives and writes in the foothills of the Colorado Rockies.

Visit her website at www.barbarakrichardson.com.

ABOUT TORREY HOUSE PRESS

The economy is a wholly owned subsidiary of the environment, not the other way around.

– Senator Gaylord Nelson, founder of Earth Day

Headquartered in Torrey, Utah, Torrey House Press is an independent book publisher of literary fiction and creative nonfiction about the environment, people, cultures, and resource management issues of the Colorado Plateau and the American West. Our mission is to increase awareness of and appreciation for the transcendent possibilities of Western land, particularly land in its natural state, through the power of pen and story.

2% for the West is a trademark of Torrey House Press designating that two percent of Torrey House Press sales are donated to a select group of not-for-profit environmental organizations in the West and used to create a scholarship available to upcoming writers at colleges throughout the West.

Torrey House Press
http://torreyhouse.com

See http://torreyhouse.com/catalog for our thought-provoking Tributary Discussion Guide.

——— *Also available from Torrey House Press* ———

Crooked Creek by Maximilian Werner
  Sara and Preston, along with Sara's little brother Jasper, must flee Arizona when Sara's family runs afoul of American Indian artifact hunters. Sara, Preston, and Jasper ride into the Heber Valley of Utah seeking shelter and support from Sara's uncle, but they soon learn that life in the valley is not as it appears and that they cannot escape the burden of memory or the crimes of the past. Resonating with the work of such authors as Cormac McCarthy and Wallace Stegner, *Crooked Creek* is a warning to us all that we will live or die by virtue of the stories we tell about ourselves, the Earth, and our true place within the web of life.

———⊗⊗⊗———

The Scholar of Moab by Steven L. Peck
  A mysterious redactor finds the journals of Hyrum Thayne, a high-school dropout and wannabe scholar, who manages to wreak havoc among townspeople who are convinced he can save them from a band of mythic Book of Mormon thugs and Communists. Though he never admits it, the married Hyrum charms a sensitive poet claiming that aliens abducted her baby (is it Hyrum's?) and philosophizes with Oxford-trained conjoined twins who appear to us as a two-headed cowboy. Peck's hilarious novel considers questions of consciousness and contingency, and the very way humans structure meaning.

Also available from Torrey House Press

The Plume Hunter by Renée Thompson

A moving story of conflict, friendship, and love, *The Plume Hunter* follows the life of Fin McFaddin, a late-nineteenth century Oregon outdoorsman who takes to plume hunting—killing birds to collect feathers for women's hats—to support his widowed mother. In 1885, more than five million birds were killed in the United States for the millinery industry, prompting the formation of the Audubon Society. The novel brings to life an era of American natural history seldom explored in fiction, and explores Fin's relationships with his lifelong friends as they struggle to adapt to society's changing mores.